The Boys of Summer

It seemed only natural to nickname them the 'Onslow Boys'. Every time they swaggered in the front door of the Onslow Hotel after a hard week's work, their laughter was loud and genuine as they settled onto their bar stools. I peeked through the restaurant partition, a flimsy divider between my world and theirs. I couldn't help but smile whenever I saw them, saw him ... Toby Morrison.

Quiet seventeen-year-old Tess doesn't relish the thought of a summertime job. She wants nothing more than to forget the past haunts of high school and have fun with her best friends before the dreaded Year Twelve begins.

To Tess, summer is when everything happens: riding bikes down to the lake, watching the fireworks at the Onslow Show and water bomb fights at the sweltering Sunday markets.

How did she let her friends talk her into *working*?

After first-shift disasters, rude, wealthy tourists and a taunting ex-boyfriend, Tess is convinced nothing good can come of working her summer away. However, Tess finds unlikely allies in a group of locals dubbed 'The Onslow Boys', who are old enough to drive cars, drink beer and not worry about curfews. Tess's summer of working expands her world with a series of first times with new friends, forbidden love and heartbreaking chaos.

All with the one boy she has never been able to forget.

It will be a summer she will always remember.

Warning: sexual references, and occasional coarse language.

The Boys of Summer

C.J. Duggan

Dedicated to my best friend, Sascha.
For the drama, humor, tears, support, loyalty and most of all love!
Bringing sanity to me each and every day.
I love you more than is measurable.

*"Love is not necessary to life,
but it is what makes life worth living."*

— Anon

Chapter One

I shouldn't have opened it.

But I did. I mean, it's what you do when a wad of paper hits you in the back of the head, right? You unfold it in the hopes that maybe, just maybe, it might be a note confessing undying love from a green-eyed, dreamy, Italian exchange student. If there *was* such an exchange student at Onslow High. A girl could dream. There wasn't a boy in sight that you could even hope to admire, and there certainly wasn't anyone else you would even remotely want to attract.

My best friend, Ellie, plucked the scrunched-up wad of paper from where it had settled in my hoodie, which, to the boys behind me, served as a makeshift basketball ring. She was fast, real fast — even more so with her lightning-speed dagger eyes that she cast to those snickering in the back row.

"Just ignore them, Tess, they're not worth it."

I barely heard Ellie's words as I took in the crude drawing of me. I knew it was me, thanks mostly to the giant arrow that pointed to a box-shaped figure with the words 'TESS' highlighted. A stick figure would probably be flattering for most high school girls with image problems, but this wasn't stick form; it wasn't even a box. It was a drawing of an ... ironing board? Was that what it was? A speech bubble protruded from the pencil-thin smile. To their credit, the smile was drawn in red pen. My guess, it was to offer the ironing board more feminine authenticity.

"Hi, I'm Tic-Tac-Tess," the speech bubble said. "I'm flatter than two Tic Tacs on an ironing bored." *Ironing board was spelled wrong, idiots!*

I stared at the image for the longest time, muffled laughter and the unmistakable sound of high-fives being slapped from behind me, but it was only the sound of an unexpected voice that finally broke my attention.

"Do you care to share, Miss McGee?"

Ellie's elbow in my rib cage snapped me out of my trance to find Mr Burke overshadowing our desk. His thick, bushy eyebrows drew together into an impressive, yet frightening, frown.

Frozen, I made no effort to hide the note that was all too quickly plucked from my hands. Mr Burke re-adjusted his glasses and cleared his throat as he slowly examined the crumpled paper that had held me so entranced.

I could feel it; all eyes were on me, and I tried not to cringe as heat rushed to my cheeks. My heart slammed against my rib cage; a new tension filled the air as the class fell silent. We waited, bracing ourselves for the outburst that Mr Burke was so famous for.

I flicked a miserable look to Ellie who offered her best 'don't worry' smile.

Along with the rest of the class, I held my breath and silently counted down. *In 5, 4, 3, 2, 1… cue the screaming.*

"WHAT IS THIS?" Mr Burke bellowed. His red face surpassed my flushed cheeks, a vein pulsing in his neck. Before I could form a sentence, he did the worst thing possible, the very thing I feared the most: he read out the note.

"TIC-TAC-TESS?" He held the drawing out to display to the class.

Oh God!

"Flatter than an ironing board, hmm?"

Oh no-no-no-no-no.

I slid down in my seat. *This couldn't be happening.*

I cursed the boys in the back row with their stupid red pencil, crappy illustration and subpar spelling. (It was Dusty Anderson.

Had to be. Or Peter Bricknell – no one else in school spells as badly as him.) I fantasised about them being dragged out by their ears to the principal's office, systematically getting booted in the behind like in a bad slapstick movie. There was also lots of crying and apologising in my fantasy. I quite enjoyed watching Peter cry. Instead I was to be punished, as was the rest of the class. Punished by a whole lot of shouting, I mean. Mr Burke's irate, verbal onslaught ranted and raved about idiotic time wasting, short attention spans and even the evils of paper wastage. Never was bullying (or the fact they had spelled ironing board wrong) mentioned. I mean, seriously, how does anyone get to Year Ten and not know how to spell board?

No, the bad guys wouldn't be punished. Instead, what had begun as a private joke, generated from my evil ex-boyfriend and his lackeys, was now shared with the entire class. It would soon spread to the rest of Year Ten and then, inevitably, the entire school. Brilliant job, Mr Burke.

That was how it began. Pretty much one year ago today, I had become stupid Tic-Tac-Tess. Even when the more supportive teachers overheard the taunts and duly gave stern looks and warnings, it did little to appease the situation. Even though the hype had moved on to some other unfortunate soul, the latest being Matthew Caine's drunken, school social scandal that had him vomiting over Mr Hood's Italian leather loafers. The effects of that infamous day in Mr Burke's Biology class still haunted me.

There was no rhyme or reason to high school. What made you team captain one day could make you a social outcast the next. I was neither popular nor a freak-a-zoid; I was no one, a real Jane Doe, and that's the way I liked it. I avoided the spotlight, which ironically followed my best friend, Ellie, everywhere she went. Boys were like moths and Ellie was the flame, which in my eyes was not a great thing. I'm not a prude or anything, I've had boyfriends and done stuff with them, but she's my best friend and I'm just worried about her. And I had reason to worry: I had overheard canteen-line mutterings of Ellie being a 'slut', but I would never tell her that.

So I chose the comfort of remaining in my friend's shadow; beautiful, bubbly Ellie with her perky, honey-blonde ponytail, a light dusting of freckles on her perfect ski-jump-curved nose. Ellie always looked like she had stepped out of a 'Sportsgirl' catalogue. And there was Adam, our other bestie, who's full of charisma and charm, and he's really funny, too. Everyone loved Adam, particularly the teachers. He was late for everything, but when he *did* arrive, it was always with lesson-disrupting flair. With his bed-tousled hair and his beaming smile, he could charm the knickers off a nun. His words – not mine. Ew!

The three of us made unlikely allies, but we'd been friends all our lives. Sure, Adam would disappear at recess over the years for some male bonding, from the sandpit in primary school to the footy field at Onslow High. He would always return and plonk himself next to Ellie and me, leaning over to steal a chip from one of our packets, earning him a well-deserved punch in the arm that had him screaming in dramatic agony.

He was such a drama queen. Ellie and I always predicted he'd be an actor one day. "Destined to be a thespian," we told him.

Adam would do a double take, his eyebrows rising.

"A lesbian?"

Ellie and I would groan in unison. "No idiot, a thespian!"

"Oh, riiiiight." He would nod, a wry smile fighting to break out. He'd known exactly what we'd said. Yeah, that was Adam.

The two shining lights of my two best friends' personalities seemed to be a good buffer for me. Ellie said I was really intelligent and had the biggest brain out of anyone at school, but I didn't know about that. We all balanced each other out in some way and watched out for one another, and it was never more evident than in times of peril.

As Ellie and I turned into our Year Eleven locker room to gather our books for English, our smiles faded and I froze. Dread seeped into me just like it had in Biology twelve months earlier. Except this time, it was a thousand times worse.

I will not cry. I will not cry! I repeated to myself over and over again as my nails dug into my palms with such ferocity that they threatened to break the skin. Laughter, loud and low, surrounded me from all angles in the room. A mixture of faces represented shock, horror and disgust, but the general mood was hilarity. And relief that it was happening to someone else. My gaze shifted directly to where I assumed Scott would be, laughing the loudest, but he was noticeably absent. Only a few of his friends loitered, their beady eyes trying not to flick from me to each other. It wasn't working. They were obviously waiting for a reaction, one I would never give them. I never did.

I just stood silently looking at my locker. The door had been smeared with something brown and sticky. My breath hitched in a tight vice of absolute fear and loathing. I noticed what I suspected was a string of caramel drool that dribbled diagonally to a mashed, chewed, chocolatey nugget that appeared to have been regurgitated onto my lock. It was a bizarre moment of bittersweet relief. It was only chocolate … and spit. Yeah, my relief was short lived.

"Looks like someone had a nasty reaction to a Twirly Whirl."

Dusty Anderson deliberately bumped my shoulder as he walked by me. Laughter following him out.

"More like a Twirly Hurl," added Peter Bricknell. More laughter erupted, but strangely no high fives. I would have thought this was definitely a high-five occasion.

"Oh, fuck off!" Ellie yelled after them.

I think her outburst shocked me more than my defecated locker did. If steam could physically pour from someone's ears like in the cartoons, it would have been pouring out of Ellie right then. Instead, a death-like stare and flared nostrils had to do.

"Ellie, don't," I implored. "It'll just make it worse."

"Worse? Worse than this?" She pointed.

The few loiterers that had remained in the locker room slowly exited as Ellie continued her tirade.

"You know who's behind this, don't you? That low-life ex of yours, that's who."

I didn't need to agree; I knew it was Scott. It always was. Not to mention I was well aware of his particular fondness for Twirly Whirls. First there was the note in Biology that had sealed my fate as "that flat-chested girl" and the rumours he spread shortly after that claimed I was frigid.

But *this* was by far the worst thing he had ever done. Before this, it was the odd, empty Tic Tac packet in front of my locker. That hadn't happened in months, though. He had lulled me into a false sense of security. I was such an idiot.

I sighed and straightened myself to fake indifference.

"Well, I better get it off," I said as I walked over to the wheelie bin, dragging it over from the corner of the room to my locker and assessing the damage.

Ellie calmed down a bit as she came closer. I could feel her body tense, and she quickly looked away. "I'll, um, go and find something to wipe it off with." She started to back away.

"OK, but don't go and tell anyone – promise?"

Ellie sighed and looked at me, sympathy pouring past the anger. "I won't promise forever, Tess. If he pulls any more crap like this, not just this, but anything, I will not be silent." She left, to hopefully find some hospital-grade disinfectant and a blowtorch to open up my combination lock.

Ellie returned with some paper towels, and Spray and Wipe detergent she procured from the school cleaner under the strict promise it was not to be used as an ingredient for anything explosive and returned ASAP. I made some leeway by finding a stick and slowly peeled off the regurgitated, slimy mucus blob that sat directly on my combination lock. It was then I heard Ellie dry retching into her hand, turning away. Such help. I chucked the chocolatey stick in the bin and went to console Ellie, her colour drained from her face.

"You alright?" I couldn't help but laugh as I patted her on the back. She couldn't form words as the chunks threatened to rise.

Animated whistling closed in at a brisk pace (a sound I would recognise anywhere) and Adam waltzed in. His relaxed, calm demeanour didn't say, "I'm hightailing it to class because I am fifteen minutes late"; instead, his surprise registered as he rounded the corner of the locker room to see me and Ellie kneeling on the linoleum by my locker, Ellie's face hovering over the wheelie bin.

His eyes narrowed from Ellie's sweat-beaded face to mine. "What's wrong?"

Before I could answer, Adam's gaze moved beyond us and paused on the splatterfest that was my locker. The steely look of fury that had surfaced in Ellie earlier now travelled through Adam. He looked back at me and with a deep, calm breath he came to stand beside us to survey the damage.

"One guess," he bit out.

"Yep!" I turned to re-evaluate the situation. The sight hadn't improved much, even with the gooey blob on the lock gone.

Without another word, Adam dropped his backpack to the floor, wrenched the zip open and delved into the contents.

"You don't happen to have a pressure washer on you, by any chance?" I mused.

He ignored me; Adam was on a mission. I could tell by the crinkle in his brow that all too quickly vanished as he found what he was looking for.

He pulled out ...

"A banana? Seriously?" He was an odd boy.

"Urgh. Adam, how can you eat at a time like this?" Ellie cringed.

Adam peeled back the yellow folds, biting a big chunk out, and chewed vigorously, raising his brows in a 'hubba-hubba' motion. He then walked over towards ... oh no.

"Adam?"

He fell short just before Scott's locker and offered us his best winning smile as he swallowed his mouthful. He held the banana in the air like it was some talisman, some holy grail.

"Ladies, I give you the banana." With that, Adam smashed it against Scott's locker, smearing it in a vast sweeping motion. The mushy, granulated chunks were thoroughly mashed into the crevices of his combination lock. And Adam did this all while humming a joyous tune. He then hooked the banana peel through the lock loop; it dangled like a motley alien form.

Ellie laughed, sat back on her heels away from the bin and clapped her hands, colour finally returning to her face just as it drained from mine.

"Adam, what are you doing?" I was part horrified, and part in awe of his heroic gesture.

Adam stood back, hand on chin in deep thought as he admired his handiwork. "It will have to do! I'm really regretting not grabbing that chocolate Yo-Go this morning. That would have gone on real nice."

"Please, no more chocolate," Ellie begged.

Adam dusted off his hands, "Well, best get crack-a-lackin. Wouldn't want anyone to think this was some sort of act of revenge or anything."

"You know who they are going to blame, right?" I pointed to myself with double fingers. "Ah, hello."

"Don't worry about Snotty," Adam reassured.

"Besides, we can be your bodyguards," Ellie added.

"Well, either I'm going to need to sleep with one eye open, or you two will have to take shifts in watching over me so that I'm not murdered in my bed."

"Not a problem. I already climb into your room every night and watch you sleep, anyway," Adam winked.

"Pfft, dream on!"

Adam's wicked smile broadened. "Oh, but I do."

"Urrgh. If I wasn't going to spew before, I am now." Ellie rubbed her stomach.

I playfully sprayed Ellie with disinfectant, causing her to scream and leap to her feet, dodging behind Adam. She grabbed his shoulders and held him for ransom. He faked fear. "No, please, anything but that!"

I did a fake-out squeeze and they both winced, which had me giggling with evil pleasure. This went on for a few more minutes, dodging and screaming until Adam spotted the chocolate-covered stick protruding from the wheelie bin. I could see the cogs turning in his mind and they weren't just any cogs; they were evil cogs.

"Don't you dare!"

His smile was wicked; he deliberately watched my reaction as he picked it up.

"*Adam!*"

"Bwahahahaha!" He chased me around the locker room with the vile mucus-choco stick. It was a good thing that the locker room was set far away from the main school building; there was no fear our shouts would unveil our lateness to class. There was no controlling the fact that we were laughing so hard we could barely breathe.

Adam and I spent the next ten minutes spraying and scrubbing my locker while Ellie watched with a horrified expression from across the room. Adam worked on my lock as I wiped down my door.

"What's your combo, McGee?"

I raised my eyebrows. "As if I would tell you."

He sighed. "Relax, I'm not going to send you love poetry, I'm just going to see if it works."

I finished the last wipe and gave him a pointed look. "You are totally going to send me love poetry."

"Pfft, dream on!"

I slapped his shoulder and clenched my chest in mockery. "Oh, but I do."

Chapter Two

Third period and I was a prisoner in double English.

I prayed that Scott didn't need to go to his locker between classes. My heart pounded against my rib cage, and my hands were clammy as I watched the agonisingly slow tick of the clock above Mrs Romano's desk. Would Adam's actions start an all-out war? I already thanked the timetable Gods that Scott was not in my English class.

My plan was simple: hightail it to the locker room, grab my stuff and be gone before Scott even noticed his redecorated locker. Then I would just avoid him for the rest of the year. Which sounds totally hard, but wouldn't be considering there were only three days left of school. By then we would all be cheering 'School's out for Summer', Alice Cooper style.

Three days; three … more … days.

A wad of paper landed next to my hand, and I flinched, for more than one reason. Luckily, English was pretty safe, no horsemen of the apocalypse in this class, which made it a welcome refuge. I secretly unfolded the crinkled paper under my desk.

You smell like Spray and Wipe.

My mouth twitched as I glanced sideways to where Adam sat, two people across. I met his devilish eyes, and he grimaced dramatically.

I discreetly eyed Mrs Romano, sitting on her desk at the front of the class, eyes downcast, animatedly reading aloud from her text. I scribbled my reply and did the tap down the line to pass it along. Like a lady would. I focused intently on the book I was meant to be following along with, knowing that I wouldn't be able to contain myself as I envisioned the raise of Adam's brows as he read my reply.

What's that, banana man?

It went back and forth for the remainder of the class, which I was grateful for as it made the time fly. Once the bell rang, I was jolted into the cold, harsh reality that awaited me.

Lunchtime.

I didn't even think to wait for Adam or Ellie; I was too focused on running to the locker room and praying that the combination of detergent and boy cooties hadn't jammed up my lock. Adam had tested and opened it easily enough; surely it would be okay? I dodged and weaved through the thickening flow of bodies down the hall, cursing the distance between my locker and the English room as I got stuck behind a group of giggling Year Seven girls. I burst through the doors and quickstepped down the stairs. I heard the distant yell of "No running!" from Mr Hood, but I had to risk it. Detention would seem like a holiday camp compared to facing off with my ex.

After tripping over my foot and dropping a textbook, I inelegantly made an entrance into the locker room. There were not many people in there, but the few who were there were laughing, crowded around Scott's locker which had been marinating in banana for the past sixty minutes.

I ignored them and made a beeline for my locker with enough time to unload my books, grab my bag, and hide in a bush for the rest of the day. I froze, my sparkling padlock in my hand. What the hell was my combination? My mind had gone completely blank. Panic set in as more students flooded the room and saw Scott's locker. I bit my lip. No, no, no ... I looked up, finding the eyes of Kim Munzel, the resident grunge girl of our year, on me. Her green, scary eyes were caked with heavy make-up that was partly covered by a gel-sleeked jagged fringe – the longest part of her crudely short haircut. She seldom spoke and when she did, it was with a bad attitude. So why was she smiling at me?

She grabbed her bag and walked up to me, her dog chain clinking on her low-rise baggy jeans. I turned my attention back to my lock, pretending that it was the most interesting thing in the world. At that point in time it really was.

What was the bloody number?

Out of the corner of my eye, I could see Kim had stopped next to me.

"Hey."

I glanced around. Was she talking to me? Oh God. Yes, she was looking right at me.

"Hey," I said in a small voice.

"Did you do that?" Her head nodded towards Scott's locker, which was now semi-circled by a crowd.

Before I could get my thoughts together enough to form a coherent sentence, her smile tilted to form an evil grin.

"Nice job." Her scary eyes looked me over as if giving me a seal of approval, and then she left. So. Weird. The crowd peeled back to allow her through. She had that kind of effect. The locker room was now full of students; a mad hub of activity for the lunchtime rush.

Oh God! I fumbled madly with my lock, guessing combinations in a frenzied effort. Scott would be here any moment. I turned the dial and tugged in desperation as if I was MacGyver and this was the last chance to crack the code before the bomb went off. Some people asked themselves: 'What would Jesus do?', but I always asked myself: 'What would MacGyver do?' MacGyver would probably be able to pick the lock with a crusty, chocolate-covered stick. I'm sure he could.

TUG! TUG! TUG!

I thudded my head against the locker; it smelt like disinfectant and was probably cleaner now than it had been in the past decade of use by past students.

I felt hot breath blow into my ear as a voice whispered, "4-3-2-5-9-6." I jumped, spinning around to see a laughing Adam.

"Geez, McGee, jumpy much?"

"432596! My combination! Oh, praise sweet baby Jesus." I turned the dial and heard the magical click of freedom; it was the most beautiful sound I had ever heard. Which was ironic considering it was counterbalanced with the most horrible sound I could have heard right then: Scott's angry voice. Oh crap!

"What the ...?" his voice trailed off as he closed the distance towards his locker. The crowd parted eagerly. They'd been waiting for this moment; their eyes darted from him to me and back again. Just as I feared, you wouldn't have to be a rocket scientist to figure out they would assume it was me. I swallowed hard, fighting the urge to throw up.

Adam stood stock-still beside me, silently taking in the scene. I felt the press of someone on my left. Ellie had appeared from thin air and was at my side. If it weren't for my bookend buddies, I feared my legs would give out. I slowly turned to my open locker; best not to stare. While I pretended indifference, I heard him yell out to me.

"Oh yeah. Nice one, Tess," he sneered.

I did my best 'I'm bored' look from my locker. Scott stood next to his. Wow, if looks could kill. He was flanked by nervous-looking buddies, who were slowly opening their own lockers. Some friends they were, none of them even offering to get him a paper towel.

Scott hurled the banana peel across the room and opened his locker as if it wasn't covered in mush. He threw in his books and slammed his door shut, casting me a filthy look before storming out. His entourage looked at each other and appeared to be as surprised as I was. Like the mindless zombies they were, they quickly scurried after Scott, throwing uncertain glares my way.

I was just about to let my shoulders sag in relief when I heard it, right next to my ear. The solitary sound of a slow clap.

Adam.

"Way to go, Tess, way to go!"

It was as if I had just been carried out of a factory by Richard Gere or something.

This was not how I expected the day to go. Although things had taken an unexpected turn that had me smiling into my opened locker, Scott's voice echoed in my mind.

"You may have won the battle, Tess, but you haven't won the war."

Lunch and the rest of the day passed with surprisingly little drama. Scott's banana-rised locker stayed like that for the rest of the day; I think he was trying to prove a point or something. The typical boy mentality of not caring, though the look he had thrown me had been chilling. If I knew Scott, it would be eating him alive.

Ellie and I walked in mirror image, our thumbs hooked into our backpack straps as we pushed our bodies forward to balance the weight of our textbooks on our backs. I had made sure I had packed up all my valuables from my locker in case there was a mysterious attack overnight.

Adam circled us on his bike.

"Sooo, have you thought about my business proposition?"

He wasn't addressing Ellie, he was addressing me. I knew he was, because I automatically cringed every time he asked the question, which had been every damn day for the past semester. I also knew it was directed at me because Ellie, from the very get-go, had squealed and said, "Count me in!" Traitor!

Adam must have read the look on my face.

"Aw come on, McGee! It's gonna be awesome!" His circling was making me dizzy.

"I just don't think I would be any good."

He rolled his eyes at Ellie. "I thought you promised to talk some sense in to her?"

"Hey! I've been on operation 'get a rocket under Tess' for weeks. I even got her parents involved."

"Yes, about that." I stopped walking abruptly to confront Ellie, nearly causing Adam to fall off his bike.

Ellie gave me her fluttery-eye blink of innocence, the very one that probably fooled all the boys. Well, it didn't fool me.

"Mum has been giving me hell, saying, 'It will be good for your confidence, Tess' and, 'It will give you some extra pocket money for the holidays' and 'You might meet some new people'." I repeated every Mum-saying with enough exaggerated whining to sound almost authentic. Even to my ears.

Ellie folded her arms. "And all that is so bad because?"

I paused. Because it was out of my comfort zone. I was not good in foreign environments. I wanted to spend the summer with Ellie and Adam riding down to the lake, watching the fireworks at the show and eating ice cream at the Sunday markets. I wanted to regain that same essence of past summers and how wonderfully lazy it had all been. Not slaving away at the Onslow Hotel.

"It's not rocket science, Tess," Adam said. "Come on, it'll be the three amigos. No parentals. We can play pool all summer long and get paid for it."

"It will be so fun," Ellie said, "serving drinks to hot guys." Boys were never far from her thoughts.

"Yeah – and cleaning up sticky messes and dirty dishes; sounds like a riot," I said. "Can't we just hang out at the lake?"

"We ALWAYS do that."

"Not last year."

"Correction – YOU didn't do it last year; you were attached to Snotty's face the whole holidays. WE went to the lake and the market and stuff, and this year we want to do something different, don't we, Adam?"

"Yes, yes we do, and we want to do it with YOU."

The Onslow Hotel was almost like a tiara of Onslow in that it was positioned at the very peak of a hill overlooking the entire town. Ellie and I painfully walked up there a few times, agreeing that 'Coronary Hill' was an appropriate name dubbed by the locals. We had learned our lesson and chose for future reference to trek the long way around the back roads on bike, swinging around the imposing hotel structure to the quick trail home. Our bikes had blazed a path downhill as we screamed, our feet on our handlebars. So Adam was predicting awesome times ahead at the Onslow Hotel? I seriously doubted anything with the word 'Onslow' in it could ever be connected to awesome.

It was obvious that the fore-founders of our grand community severely lacked in the imagination department. Onslow was a small town, population of less than three thousand, nestled in the valley of the Perry Ranges. It would be more in line with being a retirement village if the rolling hills weren't the backdrop to Lake Onslow, a sprawling mass of man-made lakes that swept as far as the eye could see. Local legend claimed that it was bottomless, and Lord knows we had tested the theory. So far, it checked out: we could never touch the bottom.

As students of Onslow High finished up from school, we

would cut through Onslow Park, walk past Lake Onslow where the Onslow Hotel overlooked the town of … oh, what is it called? Oh yeah, *Onslow*!

They looked at me with their pathetic, pleading doe-like eyes.

Even after a full three weeks of having to endure 'that' look, I still felt my heart race in anxiety at the thought. I had never had a job before, even though my parents had nagged and nagged me to get one.

I knew all the answers to the questions I was about to ask, but I tentatively asked again, anyway.

"So how many hours?"

"Weekend lunch, twelve to two, and dinner, six to nine."

I didn't need to calculate, I had done it a thousand times. Adam was good, he didn't smile or even show an ounce of excitement. He was serious and business-like, knowing that if he was any other way it would scare me off.

"Ten dollars an hour?"

He nodded. "Cash in hand."

I definitely didn't need to calculate that either. I'd had all of my hypothetical money spent for the past three weeks.

Ellie wasn't as diplomatic as Adam, and started to bounce on the balls of her feet.

Adam inched closer, maneuvering his bike right up to me. "Come on, Tess. My uncle wants me to be dish pig for the holidays, doing it without you guys would make it what it is, a pretty shitty way to spend my weekends. But I don't know, I thought if you guys were with me it would be a blast. We always make our own fun, and just think of it. We can go and blow all our money together on Big Ms and dirty deep-fried chicken wings at the Caltex afterwards."

That had me frowning in disgust more than anything. He'd been doing so well until now, but suddenly it seemed like he'd totally forgotten who he was talking to. But I now saw something new in Adam's pleading eyes. He had made it sound like an awesome adventure because his uncle and dad had given him little choice for the weekends but to slug it out in dirty dishwater for a good chunk of his holidays. He had sold it to us on the angle of money, free soft drinks and an array of cute boys. Admittedly, it did definitely have its perks.

But the bigger reason my icy facade had started to thaw was because if I didn't do it, I would barely get to see my best friends on the weekends, and I wouldn't be able to join in on all the 'in-jokes' they would share from all that time together over the summer without me. Plus, Ellie would no doubt snag a cute, new, Onslow-Hotel-visiting boyfriend for the summer, and Adam would be buying everyone chicken wings at the Caltex and where would I be? At home, doing chores because my parents wanted to drill some sort of work ethic into me, in some other torturous way as a form of revenge for not getting a summer job with my work-savvy friends. There would be no ten dollars an hour for the displeasure either. I thought of one of my mental purchases, a cute little summer dress I had spotted in the window of Carters' clothes shop, and smiled.

I re-adjusted the weight of my backpack as I looked down at my foot, tracing a circle in the dirt. I squinted back up at Adam who was waiting intently.

"Does the restaurant have air conditioning?"

Adam broke into a broad smile, like a cat that got the mouse.

"Like a freakin' igloo."

Smug bastard, he didn't need to look so satisfied with himself. I fought not to smile and looked from him to Ellie, who was acting as if she had a brigade of ants in her pants.

I sighed in defeat. It wasn't the summer I wanted, but it was the summer I was stuck with. "Alright."

"Sorry?" Adam questioned.

"Alright, I'll do it."

"Sorry, I didn't hear you. Can you repeat that?"

"I'll do it!" All air was knocked from me when a squealing Ellie body slammed me into a bear hug.

Bloody hell.

"Okay. Well, hopefully Uncle Eric will think it's okay. He is pretty desperate, but I can't promise anything. If you're lucky, I guess …" Ellie and I set in on him, giving him a dual beating in the rib cage, but he preempted the attack and sped off on his bike, our textbook-filled packs preventing us from giving chase.

Adam called back, flashing a winning smile.

"You won't regret it! We are going to have the *best* summer!"

Chapter Three

The arrangement had been to meet at the Onslow Hotel for orientation in our spare school period, so we could get the feel of our surroundings.

Little did we know it was actually an ambush and we were about to be thrown into the deep end. A billowing cloud of steam blew up into Uncle Eric's face, threatening to melt it off entirely. This was just as disturbing as the loud hissing sound he was creating in an attempt to froth up milk on the coffee machine. I looked on in horror; how was I expected to be able to master this beast of an apparatus? I had never made a cappuccino in my life! Ash teetered on the edge of Uncle Eric's cigarette as it wavered every time he spoke.

He was a big, bearded, gruff, biker-looking kind of fellow, who cared little for his health if the caffeine consumption and chain-smoking was anything to go by. As far as I knew, the reason Adam had roped us in to help out was largely due to Uncle Eric's wavering health. No doubt it was a bonus that we were still in school so he could pay us minimum wage off the books. Kind of like a sweatshop for child labour.

He gave us an assessing look.

"We could do with some fresh blood around here. Tess and Ellie will be front-of-house in the restaurant."

There was a not-too-subtle agenda: Uncle Eric tended to work in a way of capitalising on people's strong points so as to attract the right clientele. Little did he know that I was silently freaking out over a coffee machine, let alone what else this job might entail. *Just breathe*, I told myself.

Just. Breathe.

As if sensing my unease, Adam elbowed me and threw me a friendly, reassuring smile. Ellie, who was as giddy as a schoolgirl, flashed me her pearly whites as if what Uncle Eric was saying was truly magical. I felt nauseous with information overload. I had only been inside the Onslow a few times for the odd dinner gathering, but Mum and Dad were not regular pub goers. They were more accustomed to wine and home-based dinners with close friends than pub hopping.

Now the beast of a coffee machine lay silent, the noise replaced by yet another scary sound: Uncle Eric wheezed out an uncomfortable series of chest-rattling coughs. I folded my arms and fought not to wince as the sound and smoke blew my way.

"Thought you quit that nasty habit, Unc."

An older version of Adam appeared through the divider that sectioned the main bar from the restaurant – Chris. He brushed past us in the small space, ensuring he slammed Adam hard in the arm as he made his way towards a lower cupboard, crouching to search for something. They never used to look alike. Adam went through a phase where he thought he was adopted because Chris looked so much like his parents, but nowadays there was no mistaking the resemblance. Lean, with clear alabaster skin, big deep, dark eyes, and dark unruly hair. The main differences were that Chris kept his hair cropped shorter, he was taller, and he held himself differently. Adam was a lot more outgoing whereas Chris was the far more serious sibling; he tended to go about in life as if the weight of the whole world rested on his shoulders.

Chris found an exercise book and flicked through it, a crinkle forming between his brows as he concentrated.

"What habit? Coffee or smoking?" Eric mused.

"Both," Chris muttered. His brow furrowed further as he thumbed each page.

When we arrived to begin our trial at the hotel, Adam had

looked forlorn. Not a good sign. Not much seemed to worry Adam, but when I saw Chris behind the bar taking stock of inventory, I automatically knew the reason behind Adam's sullen mood without even having to ask. Uncle Eric had chosen Chris to manage the bar.

Smart move, Uncle Eric.

Knowing what Chris was like, we knew he'd run a tight ship and not give us an inch, especially Adam. Suddenly goofing off and free pool seemed like an impossible dream. This was strike one against the 'dream job' I had envisioned. Strike two quickly followed.

Uncle Eric moved aside.

"Tess, why don't you make Chris a coffee? Show us what you got."

Oh God! Why didn't I pay attention to how he did it?

I moved closer to the machine, fearing it would come alive and burn me with its evil steam spout. I was just about to fake the 'I totally know what I'm doing' routine when – saved by the bell! The bell being the distant jingle of jewelry and a gay, breezy voice that could not be mistaken for anyone other than Claire Henderson. Eric's younger, oddly glam, attractive wife. Well, glam and attractive for Onslow standards, anyway. I had heard Mum and Dad say on more than one occasion that it was an 'odd' marriage, and not just for the obvious aesthetic reasons. Claire had a tall slender frame dripped in Gucci and smothered in French perfume. Her silky, ash blonde hair was never out of place. I know opposites attract, but seriously? Claire Henderson leant over the bar, reaching for the keys to her Audi convertible.

"Hello, poppets! What do we have here?"

"Orientation," Chris said. He flipped through the mysterious exercise book but with less interest now.

"Of course. Adam these are your friends, the ones you always talk about? You must be Tess and Ellie."

We offered pleasant smiles; wait a minute, I'm wrong. *I* offered that smile. Ellie was beaming in such a way I feared we all may have been blinded by it. She stepped forward with an animated hair flick.

"I'm Ellie Parker, Mrs Henderson." She took Claire's hand to shake. "I love your shawl. Wherever did you get it?"

Claire Henderson honed in on Ellie with interest.

"Why, thank you. It was a gift, to me from me." She winked, and she and Ellie beamed at each other, instant friends. It was so clear, Claire Henderson could see herself in young Ellie Parker. It was a like magnetic pull towards each other, like for like.

Ellie beamed, Claire beamed. They didn't just enter into a room, they filled it with their vibrant energy and just when I was about to ask my own question about the shawl, Claire's bright, friendly eyes cut from Ellie to me and dimmed. A crinkle pinched between her perfectly manicured eyebrows, a crinkle that looked as though it really shouldn't be there considering I'd heard she had her plastic surgeon on speed dial.

"Ah, Tess, sweetie. Tut tut tut." She waggled her finger. "Uncross your arms and stand straight. Body language is everything."

I quickly unfolded my arms and stood straight like a soldier. All of a sudden I was very aware of every body movement I was going to make. What else did I do unconsciously that might be offensive? I blushed and felt like a naughty five year old.

Without further thought, Claire jingled her keys.

"I'm off now, poppets, don't work too hard."

Oh, we weren't allowed to work too hard or have bad body language, I thought bitterly. And on the same breeze Claire Henderson blew in on, she blew away. Probably to her townhouse in the city that Uncle Eric purchased for her. Another conversation overheard from my mum to one of her friends.

"They don't even live together! He has his pub; she lives in the city all week. What kind of marriage is that?" my mum would ask in dismay.

One that obviously skipped the 'in sickness and in health' vows, I thought, as I studied Uncle Eric's grey complexion. No doubt made worse by years of working indoors in a dark bar surrounded by cigarette smoke and a lifetime of pub meals. Was this what he meant by fresh blood? My heart sank. I knew it was only weekend work, but it was a weekend with minimal sunlight, no fresh air and no lake.

This was going to hurt.

The remainder of the trial went on in a string of awkward

chaos, even when Uncle Eric retired himself to his residence upstairs. Crusty old Melba, the kitchen hand, took over some of the orientation. She whipped us into polishing silverware and glasses, folding napkins and various other jobs that we all apparently did 'wrong'.

"Hearts like a split pea, this generation, honestly." Melba snatched a napkin out of Ellie's hand and showed her how to fold it the 'right' way. It was nice to see not everyone succumbed to Ellie's charms. Not even Adam's good nature could steer Melba in a less moody direction. And he had known her all his life.

"Did she really babysit you when you were young?" I whispered to Adam who was helping me frantically to polish cutlery.

"She sure did," he sighed.

"That is the scariest thing I have ever heard," I said. "I didn't know your parents hated you."

"I guess when you have three boys you need the Terminator for the job."

We snickered, and her beady eyes settled on us from across the dining room. We quickly looked back down and polished like we were demons possessed.

I went to get a cloth from behind the restaurant bar when I noticed that the book Chris had been so focused on earlier was, in fact, a reservations book. I skimmed a couple of pages, working out just how busy to expect my days to get. I found today's page and saw a reservation circled in pink fluro texta. It highlighted something sinister. A lunchtime group booking for fifteen … today!

My breath hitched. *They knew about it all along?* I wondered if Adam knew? Was this some kind of test? My heart pounded as the double doors swung open and a congregation of permed, blue-dyed hair poured slowly into the restaurant bringing with them a mass of high-pitched chatter.

Chris appeared beside me and reached for the book; he took in my ghost-white complexion with mock interest.

"I know, a pokies tour bus," Chris said as we watched elderly people flood into the restaurant. "It's as frightening as it looks."

What were they doing here? We didn't even have pokies, did we? Maybe they were just travelling through for lunch and then off to wreak five-cent havoc elsewhere. I swallowed my fear as a group assembled in front of me.

"Try not to stress, Tess. They can smell fear," Chris whispered into my ear. I barely registered his laughter as he returned to the main bar.

I would be fine, old people were nice. They would be easy, surely? Where on earth was Ellie? And Adam? They'd been at the table folding napkins a second ago, but the table stood abandoned now. All of a sudden the glint of spectacles shone my way in a domino effect. The old people shuffled towards me.

I fumbled for a notebook and pen, ready for action. Poised and standing straight behind the counter, I flashed what I hoped was a winning smile and not a scary one.

I can do this. No sweat, this I can do. Just take down the order and handball it to the kitchen. Piece of cake.

Just when I was about to write my very first order as a confident, gathered, working woman, the leader of the group merged forward. She smiled at me sweetly, putting me instantly at ease. Then she sucker punched me in the guts.

"We'll have twelve cappuccinos, please."

Shit.

After what could only be described as a hellish first shift, I sat in the main bar, deflated with an ice pack on my steam-burned arm. My eyes were watery from the pain of clumsily branding myself in my haste, but the watery eyes were mostly due to humiliation. To my utter relief, Melba had taken over the making of the cappuccinos. I worked the floor with Ellie to conquer the more straightforward aspect of taking lunch orders.

I mean, what could possibly go wrong? Apart from not knowing the lunch specials. Or whether we catered for the lactose intolerant. Or if our menu was diabetic friendly. Or if it was offensive to someone with coeliac disease. Was our menu *offensive*? Christ! Old people have a lot of problems. Of course, I knew none of the answers and my table of eight stared at me as if I was some idiot they wanted to squish with their walking sticks. I tried to take solace in the fact that Ellie knew equally as little as I did, but I heard a chorus of laughter at one point and saw Ellie charming her table and writing profusely. Her table was looking up at her with adoring smiles. I had looked back at my bored death stares.

It took all my strength not to get upset the fourth time I had to trail back to the kitchen to ask the short-tempered cook another question. I didn't know what I feared more – my table, who I had diagnosed with chronic evil, or the psychotic and feisty cook, who would throw pots and pans and swear profusely when things didn't go her way. There was not much of her, but geez she could swear like a sailor and throw a heavy-duty saucepan with force. The only thing that literally pushed me through the kitchen door and back into the restaurant was Adam and his infectious attitude, though a greater part of me wanted to punch him in the face when I thought back to the very reason I was there. I had been abused by Melba, a busload of geriatric gamblers and a psychotic red-headed cook.

And then a third-degree steam burn. Okay, probably not third degree, but it stung. I drowned my sorrows in a glass of Coke that Chris had placed in front of me without a word. The door burst open from the restaurant.

"THAT was the best shift ever!" Ellie beamed, followed in by Adam who still wore his dish apron.

"Seriously, how cool was that? It was so busy, but good. Made time go so fast, and I even got a tip." Ellie pulled out a five-dollar note with glee.

"Looks like you had a table of high rollers," I added glumly.

It was then that Ellie took it down a peg or two. "I saw you had to return a meal to the kitchen. What was with that?"

"Which time? When it was too hot? Or too cold? I actually contemplated blowing on her meal for her."

Adam winced; he didn't need to have the full account of my nightmare. He was painfully aware of every time I came through the kitchen door with a new complaint. Each time I did, a little piece of me died.

Adam slapped and rubbed his hands on his thighs.

"Well, the worst is over ladies, you survived your first shift initiation. It's all downhill from here."

Ellie clapped with joy.

"Yay." I glared at him.

Ellie smiled sadly at me. "How's the arm?"

I sighed. "I'm afraid I will never be an arm model."

"I'm so sorry, Tess. I know how much you were counting on that to get you through university," Adam said in mock sympathy.

"I was going to be a wrist-watch model. You know, travel the world, but, alas, it's not to be." I shook my head and tried not to smirk.

Ellie couldn't contain herself.

"You're such a dork, Tess."

"You are who you hang with," I threw back.

Adam squeezed in between us, threw his arms over our shoulders, and kissed us both on the head.

"Oh gross, boy cooties!" I squealed.

"Thank you for doing this. It'll get better, I promise. You, me, and McGee are going to have the best summer ever, you'll see."

Chapter Four

Last day of school was little more than a giant social event.
There were no classes of any substance; instead, students wandered aimlessly around the school grounds. We weren't privy to a 'muck up' day as we weren't Year Twelves and any mucking up from the senior students had been monitored so severely that we had half expected to see watchtowers constructed for teachers with binoculars and dart guns. Such limitations were largely due to an incident from two years ago that had Andy Maynard fused to a goal post with electrical duct tape by a group of hooded Year Twelve boys. The school frowned upon that and banned Muck-up Day all together. That didn't mean there wasn't any anarchy in the schoolyard.

Our theme for the year was Toga. All Year Elevens arrived draped in sheets that would have had all our mums going ballistic because we took them without asking. We all walked around, our shoulders exposed like we were in Roman bathhouses.

"It would be all so authentic if it wasn't for the gum leaf crowns everyone is wearing," Adam mused.

I re-adjusted my leafy headgear. "What choice was there? I think it looks good."

"Oh God, Tess, this is humiliating." Ellie's eyes darted around, hoping not to be recognised.

"Relax, Ellie, it's our last day of school, no one will even remember what we wore."

We weaved and maneuvered our awkward costumes through a group of Year Eight boys playing hacky sack.

"Yeah, well, if this makes it into the Yearbook, I will never forgive either of you," Ellie threatened.

"Oh, come on, Pretty Parker, just think of it as the multicultural aspect of the Miss Onslow Show Girl."

I cringed. There it was, the one thing that turned the usually beaming, bright, confident Ellie into a stone-faced Ice Queen.

Ellie had entered the Miss Onslow Show Girl Pageant in Year Nine (so she was old enough to know better), and it was something Adam had relentlessly mocked her about ever since. I recalled the glee in his mischievous eyes as we sat in the showground stands watching Ellie radiantly wave to the crowd. I thought Adam was going to pop a blood vessel as he fought not to lose himself to hysteria when the Mayor of Onslow, Hank Whittaker, started singing Stevie Wonder's 'Isn't She Lovely?' After a full afternoon of sitting in the sun and being forced to witness every age bracket of the Miss Onslow Show Girl, I couldn't help but lose it, too. Maybe it was Adam's infectious laugh, or perhaps I suffered a touch of sunstroke? I don't know. More likely, it was witnessing Mayor Whittaker, a gangly, balding, fake-tanned man with unnaturally white protruding teeth and a torturous falsetto, mime as he captured a butterfly to his heart and then released it into the air, as if he was a Backstreet Boy. From that day on, any time Mayor Whittaker ran into Ellie, he would blind her with his bleached veneers and refer to her with his pet name for her. Hence, 'Pretty Parker' was born. It was no Tic Tac Tess, but still, Ellie came second and never entered again.

"There is no such thing as a multicultural section in the Miss Onslow Pageant, idiot."

Adam placed his hands up in mock surrender.

"Sorry, Ellie. I guess I need to brush up on my beauty pageant trivia."

I could see this getting ugly. "So, the break-up party tonight. What time do we rock up?"

Ellie's head snapped around. "What are you wearing? Do you

want to come to my place first? We can pick something out."

"How come I never get invited to these pre-party fashion parades?" whined Adam.

We both ignored him.

"I haven't a clue, really," I said. "What time do you want to rendezvous?"

"Make it seven at my house. By the time we get ready, we will be fashionably late." Ellie flicked her hair over her exposed shoulder.

Adam rolled his eyes and mimicked Ellie behind her back. I threw him a discreet frown.

"Sounds like a plan," I said, as I lifted my awkward sheet to step over a wayward empty chip packet.

"So we're not wearing the Togas tonight, then?" Adam pressed.

"No," Ellie and I said in unison.

"Aww, come on."

"NO!"

Adam circled us, and chanted in his best imitation of a caveman voice while fist pumping the sky.

"Toga! Toga! Toga!"

We were about to pummel him in a joint beating when he tripped on the hem of his sheet and went flying in a very inelegant fashion that had him sprawled on the concrete, revealing his board shorts underneath.

I suppose we should have checked if he was okay, and not mortally wounded. We would have done so, too, if we weren't crippled by fits of laughter. Ellie even snorted. That made us laugh even harder, to the point that we all but forgot about Adam who lay there, possibly bleeding to death. But he wasn't. He leaned back, and squinted up at us with a wry smile spread across his face.

We bent down, offered him a hand to get up and helped him dust his once-white sheet off. His mum would not be happy.

"And that, my friend, is the perfect reason why we are not going in a Toga," I said.

According to Ellie, it was always important to make a grand entrance at a party, to have all eyes turned to us. In fact, she revelled in it. As soon as we arrived, Ellie was on the lookout for John Medding, who was hosting the break-up gala. He was your everyday sporty boy – popular, pretty cute. He would usually hook up with a girl when he had some Dutch courage from a few beers. He would then choose to never make eye contact or speak to her again. This was my forecast for tonight, given I had seen it a dozen times before, but Ellie didn't think that far ahead. For now her gaze circled the party.

I wanted to dance. I loved dancing. I wanted to move until my feet were blistered and every time a song I liked blared out of the speaker, my heart sank.

The makeshift dance floor was housed in an industrial-sized shed, filled with gritty machinery emitting the faint smell of oil. The large space was shrouded in flashing disco lights haphazardly hooked up to a twisted extension cord leading to God knows where. I had lost Ellie in the commute from the main house into the crowded shed. The party was massive! Obviously not an exclusive Year Eleven break-up party like originally planned, I couldn't even spot a familiar face. I busied myself with grabbing a Coke from one of the eskies when Ellie bounded excitedly up to me.

"I'm going for a walk with John," she whispered.

I didn't share her enthusiasm.

I watched Ellie walk hand in hand with John, until both were engulfed by the blackness of the night.

Instead of dancing like I wanted to, I found myself doing my usual best friend stakeout, perched on the bonnet of a car, legs crossed, staring anxiously towards the woods that surrounded the Medding property. Worse still, I was expected to be 'entertainment' for Zeke Walker, John's best mate. He caused the car to dip as he sat next to me on the bonnet.

Having realised that we were to be left alone together while Ellie and John went and 'admired nature', his presence caused me to slide to the furthest edge of the bonnet. I had played the friend part before, left with whatever prospective best friend belonged to the boy Ellie was crushing on. I had even kissed a couple to pass the time, but as Zeke skulled the remnants of his beer can, crushed it against his head and let out an almighty belch, I nearly fell off the bonnet in an effort to get away from him.

Ellie, you owe me big time!

Zeke, who was quite beefy and had a tendency to squeeze his pimples in class without apology, was one of those vile boys that had been put on this earth to make girls cringe.

"So, do you wanna fuck?"

This time I did fall off the bonnet, shocked at the out-of-nowhere question. He must have read the disgust in my look as he shrugged.

"You know that's what they're doing."

I ignored him. If I ignored him, maybe he would go away?

"That's what John said anyway, he said that ..."

"I don't give a shit what John said," I snapped. Here was another one. John had clearly heard that rumour. He assumed Ellie was a sure thing. They both did. I was angry at Zeke and John for believing that. And I was angry at Ellie for not caring what they thought.

"Whoa, touchy!" Zeke said.

I wanted to stomp off, to leave Zeke, the belching idiot, to himself. But I felt uneasy and wanted to be there for Ellie when she came back, make sure she was okay. I wouldn't just leave her.

Silence fell over us again, except for the occasional belch or spit. Finally, it seemed that Zeke got bored with my enthralling company.

"Screw this. I have better things to do. I'll find out later how he went."

He walked back to the party; I glared at his back and fought to contain my anger.

"PIG!"

He flipped me the finger without a backward glance. I hated him, I hated him and I hated John Medding and all his stupid friends that waited in the wings for all the details. That was the only reason Zeke had stuck around, not out of concern for anyone's wellbeing, but to be the one to get the goss hot off the press.

Jerk!

I wanted to march into the woods, and yell for Ellie, when I heard the distant snap of twigs. My first thought was that maybe Ellie was headed back to the party. But my eyes soon adjusted to that of a darkened silhouette. The long confident stride of the stranger momentarily paused as if they had noticed me. My own form was clearly lit by the disco lights that flashed behind me. The stranger's walk slowed, appeared more guarded. They continued towards me, the lights that flickered from the party gradually lighting his face with an array of pulsing hues of colour. My tension should have ebbed at the sight of just another late gate-crasher to the party; instead, I sat transfixed. My heart stopped. I knew that face; it was a face I had always known. A face I hadn't seen in a really long time.

My head spun at the sight and the memory of Toby Morrison. A boy I had never spoken a word to, a boy I had always admired from afar. He closed the distance between us. He looked at me for what was probably the first time, though I had looked at him constantly. I held my breath as he stopped by the car, our eyes locked in a long moment, his lips parted with what would be our first exchange. I breathed in deeply and braced myself for the moment, the moment I had waited for as he finally spoke ...

"Get off my car!"

I almost toppled over as I slid off the bonnet, mortified. He reached out to steady me as he laughed.

Was he laughing at me?

"Whoa! Easy there." He smiled wickedly. "Don't stress, I'm just messing with you. It's not really my car."

He steadied me with a gentle touch to my upper arm. A scorch mark burned into my flesh even after he removed his hand.

It was then that I realised I had a fist full of Toby Morrison's T-shirt gathered in my hand with a white-knuckled intensity. I must have grabbed a hold in an effort not to fall flat on my face and further disgrace myself.

Toby's eyes flicked down to his bunched T-shirt with an air of amusement. His brows lifted in a 'Do you mind?' gesture that caused me to let go as if I had been electrocuted. Being electrocuted surely couldn't have burnt more than my flushed cheeks at that moment. I prayed that the bad lighting masked them.

Toby half laughed as he plunged his hands back into his pockets and stepped to my side; he tilted a fraction closer as if he was about to reveal a secret.

"Relax ... I would never own a Holden." He winked and then turned his confident stride towards the party.

I watched his figure as he retreated, and took a deep breath as if I had forgotten to breathe 'til now. My head whirled.

What had just happened? Toby Morrison had just talked to me. And had we just shared a joke?

Or rather he had made a joke, and I all but fell over and stared all googly eyed at him like an idiot and not said a word.

NOT. ONE. WORD.

I watched as his figure became smaller, but still clear enough to see that he was stopped every few feet with people and hand grasps and pats on the back. Everyone knew Toby Morrison, and I seriously wanted to, too.

When Toby Morrison disappeared into the thick of the party crowd, I took a moment to firstly move far away from the car, whose ever car it was. I needed to analyse what just happened, play by play, detail for detail. His smile, his look, his laugh, and his hand on my upper arm that I swear had burned into my skin.

My back rested against the chill of the cement water tank. I cupped my cheeks and felt the scorching burn of my skin.

A distant rustle interrupted my thoughts, and I noticed two figures had emerged from the woods. John was doing up his belt and Ellie was three paces behind readjusting her skirt, her hair all in disarray. John walked straight passed me and headed for the party. I guess the silent treatment began now and extended to Ellie's friends. I waited for Ellie, who seemed surprised to see me still waiting for her. I plucked a twig out of her hair.

"Why aren't you dancing?" Her voiced sounded sleepy.

"Oh you know, I don't have a dancing partner."

Now was not a good time to do the responsible, chastising, best friend speech. I could see that she looked past my shoulder, wondering where John had gone.

My anger had grown more like a swirling furnace in the pit of my stomach. Ellie faked indifference, something she always did when boys treated her that way.

"Have you seen Adam?" she asked.

I wanted to be snide and ask *how could I?* I had been busy hanging out with foul Zeke.

Except for my run in with Toby Morrison!

All of a sudden I didn't feel so angry anymore.

"You know Adam. If we were fashionably late, he'd be later."

We headed towards the thudding of the music, and weaved our way through the mass of bodies. I was acutely aware of the snickers behind their hands as they looked Ellie up and down. Guess news spread fast at the hands of John Medding. If Ellie noticed, she didn't let on. Instead, her head bobbed to the music as her eyes searched for Adam. I looked as well, but my gaze also searched for Toby, who wasn't anywhere. I wondered what he was doing at a Year Eleven break-up party, he had graduated from high school years ago. And more importantly, where had he gone?

We made our way past the shed and headed towards the house, opening the back door to be flooded by the pounding of a stereo. We slid past the crush of bodies wandering into what looked like a dimly lit, stuffy rumpus room filled with sporting memorabilia.

"Ellie! Tess!"

We turned and saw Adam in the distance, his body higher than everyone else's as he was dancing on a billiard table with a bunch of tarty-looking Year Ten girls. They appeared to be wearing more make-up than they were wearing clothes, and he wasn't so much dancing with them as wedged between them. They all jumped up and down which was a mean feat for that many people on such an apparatus.

Ellie and I shook our heads at the sight. Adam owned the platform with his bad rhythm and beer in hand, decked out in his mangy Toga. The only one still dressed like that at the party. Ellie and I recognised it as exactly what it had been meant: a sign of rebellion.

"Can you believe it?" Ellie shook her head.

I laughed at the sight. I *could* believe it, actually.

"Hey, look, I'll be back in a minute. I'm just going to see where John got to."

I cringed. Sometimes Ellie only saw what she wanted to. "Ellie ..." but she cut me off.

"Back soon!" She kissed me on the cheek and disappeared through the crowd.

I hated watching her go, watching her move towards her impending doom. As I worried, I felt the distinct caress of alcohol-infused, hot breath on the back of my neck. A clammy pair of hands blocked my vision.

"Suuurpriiiseee," a voice slurred in my ear. I broke free and spun around to see the bloodshot eyes of Scott Miller.

I screamed inside my head and frantically looked for an exit.

"Hey, Tessh. You're looking mighty fine tonight." His eyes moved over me with a slow caress in a way that made me feel dirty.

"Now, I have a bone to pick with you," he swayed slightly as he waggled his finger at me, a dopey look of mock anger on his face.

Why on Earth did I ever go out with him?

"Wow, with me? That's fresh." I crossed my arms. I was doing the thing my mum said over and over again: 'Never try and reason with a drunk person'. But a part of me wanted to know more about this bone. Another of mum's sayings was 'A drunk man speaks a sober man's mind'.

Scott pursed his lips together and screwed his face up in an over-the-top action that made him look ugly.

"I have a confesshion to make, Tesh."

"That you're an asshole?" I said.

He dramatically waved my sentence away and stumbled into me so he could whisper into my ear, which came out as more of a drool.

"I love you. I alwaysh have, alwaysh will. *Hic!*"

Oh, vomit!

Maybe that saying was wrong; maybe a drunk person just spoke bullshit. That's what I counted on, but then I saw the raw look in his eyes.

Oh God, was he welling up?

"Why did you break up with me? Do you think I want to be mean to you? You jusht give me no choish."

Before I could retort, I saw his lips pout and they came in for the kill.

Oh no no no ...

I tried to maneuver away, but he had me literally backed into a wall, and past Scott's face that loomed towards mine, out of the corner of my eye I saw that we had caught a group of people's attention. We had caught Toby's attention.

I wanted to die a small death.

Oh, urgh, Scott Miller's tongue was in my mouth. How did this happen? I pushed into his chest with all the force I could muster.

"Get off me, you creep!"

"Aw, come on, Tesh."

He reached for me again but stopped short. He spun around as an almighty crack sounded from behind him, followed by screams and chaos. The music stopped, panic set in as everyone looked around and wondered what had happened.

That's when I heard it, the sound that made my blood run cold, a sound so loud it could be heard above all others. Adam's agonised scream.

Chapter Five

"Pool tables are not meant to be danced on"

My dad's disapproving frown pierced us in his rearview mirror, where Ellie and I sat slumped in the back seat. They had been woken in the middle of the night with a reluctant phone call to pick us up from the hospital. After the initial panic, relief soon followed in the knowledge that we were unscathed. Well, mostly unscathed.

"Poor Adam," said Mum, more to herself than anyone else. "He looked as white as a sheet."

I fought not to burst out in hysterical laughter as I thought to myself, *yeah, whiter than his filthy Toga sheet*. Thankfully, I managed to control myself.

I was exhausted. We dropped Ellie off at home, and I nodded off by the time we made it to our house. I was jolted awake by the slamming of a car door, and managed to stumble my way inside and crash into bed.

The only thing that had me escaping my parents' fury was that I hadn't actually done anything wrong. I had scared them half to death by calling them from the hospital, sure, but I needed them to look at the bigger picture: I wasn't drinking or smoking or acting irresponsibly (aside from Scott's tongue in my mouth but that was *not* my fault).

I must have looked troubled at breakfast the next morning,

because Mum gripped my shoulders and gave them a reassuring squeeze.

"Adam's going to be fine, honey."

Oh yeah, Adam.

Guilt seeped into me at the thought that Adam had not exactly been in the forefront of my mind. Poor Adam! He had been joyously rocking out when the pool table broke in half. He had done so well to balance and not fall over his Toga, which he'd ended up tucking into his shorts, offering partygoers a sight that could never be unseen. But no, it was not the Toga that had been responsible for breaking his arm in two places.

"I spoke to his mum this morning," Mum said as she topped up my juice glass.

I straightened in my seat for the update. "What did she say?"

"Adam was pretty drunk last night." Dad looked up from his newspaper, his eyes bored into me as if I was being interrogated.

"I hadn't seen Adam all night," I defended. "I was with Ellie."

A fact that would not comfort my parents. Over the past year, they had slowly started catching on that Ellie's taste wasn't for alcohol, her taste was for boys. Ellie wouldn't be the sweet, little, church-going, accountant's daughter forever. Even parents talked, and, all of a sudden, I felt uneasy.

Before the conversation could turn in a direction I didn't want it to, I excused myself from my parents' knowing gazes. "Speaking of Ellie, I might just give her a call," I said. "You know, to see if she's okay," and I scurried from the room.

One positive for Adam taking all the attention was that Ellie seemed unperturbed by the fact that John Medding was a giant douche bag.

Our telephone conversation was dominated by Adam and what had happened last night (minus my Toby encounter), but then it moved on to far less desirable topics.

"So what was with you and Scott? Seriously, Tess, what the fuck?" Ellie's angry voice pierced through the receiver.

"Ugh, I know!"

I threw myself back on my bed wanting to erase the entire memory of last night. Well, perhaps not the *entire* memory. I thought back to Toby appearing out of the dark – the blue, yellow and red flashing disco lights shining on his beautiful smile. Me stumbling rather inelegantly off the bonnet. I cringed. *So classy!* At least I hadn't burst into tears, that was something.

"Hey, did you notice some older people at the party?"

Ellie replied in a manner that had me imagining her shrug. "Older, younger, it wasn't just a Year Eleven break up, I think anyone was invited."

"But why would you want to go to a Year Eleven break up?"

"Tess, it's Onslow. People go to the opening of an envelope; seriously, what else is there to do in this town?"

"I suppose." I wrapped the cord around my fingers as I lay on the bed.

The thought had never even occurred to me that Adam wouldn't be okay to work the next night, which I guess it probably should have since he had a broken arm and everything. I called him after I spoke to Ellie; we chatted about how much trouble he was in and if he was in any pain. It all seemed so normal, so natural. So when "see you tomorrow night" was met with awkward silence from Adam, a newfound dread swept over me.

"You are going to work tomorrow night, right?"

More silence.

"Adam?"

"I'm sorry, Tess, I won't be able to."

I sat up straight on my bed, alarm settling in.

"Sunday?"

"Tess, how can I wash dishes with a plaster cast?"

"I don't know! Rubber gloves? Surely there must be something else you can do?"

Adam sighed. "It's not just that. Mum and Dad are pretty pissed at me. They think I broke my arm because I was drinking. They went on and on about it. Not to mention Mum's ruined sheets."

"Pfft, I told you," I groaned.

"Anyway, they don't have a great deal of trust in me; they say I have to earn it back. And they don't exactly want me surrounded by alcohol at the hotel."

My silence echoed down the phone. "So? When will you come back to work?"

"I'm not going to, Tess. I'm not allowed." I could hear the regret in his voice.

But that did little to appease me. "What?! What do you mean you're not working?"

"Mum and Dad are sending me to my nan's house in the city. They said that it will do me good to get out of Onslow, but I know that they just want me to be a slave to my nan."

"How long for?"

"Until my cast comes off – six weeks."

"Six weeks! Adam, that's the whole summer holidays!"

"I know, I know," he said, "believe me, I know."

I should have felt sorry for him, a whole hot summer imprisoned at his nan's house. Unable to go swimming in the lake, hanging out with friends, working at the Onslow Hotel that he had looked forward to all semester. All his summer plans gone, just like that. I *should* have felt sorry for him. But I didn't. I didn't feel any ounce of pity except for myself.

This was not what had been sold to me as a summer we would 'never forget'. "You, me and McGee," he had said. Now I was stuck in a job every weekend for the whole summer. Without Adam, it wouldn't be the same. Adam was like the buffer, always there to cling to when Ellie would wander off with some new boy. Adam was always there to make me laugh, or vandalise a locker for me in the name of revenge. He was my anchor, how could I do it without him?

Who would give me sympathetic looks every time I came into the kitchen with a complaint? Who would punch me in the arm after our shift and promise it would be better tomorrow, even if it was a total lie? I felt lost. My hands clenched the phone with a white-knuckled intensity. My heart sank with the thought of walking into the Onslow Hotel tomorrow without him.

And then the anger set in.

"Well, I am so glad I did you a favour. I really fancy whittling my summer weekends away in a pub infused with cigarette smoke and rude tourists."

"Tess, I'm sorry. This blows, I know. Believe me – I would give anything to be there. The thought of taking my nan grocery shopping while she counts out her change at the cash register in five-cent pieces does nothing for me."

Again, I had no pity. I would happily trade places, but my days of doing Adam Henderson any favours were over. Never again!

"Yeah, well, you have fun with that! I'll think of you with your sweet nan sipping cups of tea, while I get abused and have to dodge a frying pan from crazy Rosanna."

"Te…"

I slammed down the phone, cutting him off. "Not interested." I glared at the receiver.

"Poor Adam," Ellie puffed as we made our way slowly up Coronary Hill.

"Mmm," I replied.

"Come on, Tess, he didn't break his arm on purpose."

"Didn't he?" I gave her a pointed look. I knew I was sulking and being unreasonable, but Adam's words echoed in my memory: "The worst is over, it's all downhill from here".

How ironic, I thought, as I physically made my way *up* the hill to my impending doom.

My heart clenched as I looked over Lake Onslow. It was dotted with locals and tourists lapping up the remainder of the dimming sun. They would stay out for as long as the mozzie repellant lasted. It was a beautiful balmy evening, perfect for enjoying the breeze that flowed off the lake on a summer's night. Instead, I was about to enter the Onslow Hotel, which was like a giant tomb to me.

Ellie and I decided to mix it up. Instead of entering the restaurant via the beer garden out back we walked through the front bar entrance. It was five o'clock, so the place was deserted save for the odd widowed drunk that had been propped up at the bar surrounded by empty chip packets and pot glasses for what looked like a rather productive day. Chris gave us a curt nod as we made our way through the front bar to the restaurant.

"How's Adam?" Ellie asked.

"He'll live." Chris took the empty beer glass from his patron as a sign of being done – that, and the old fella had nodded off at the bar.

"Time for a taxi, Ned, before the riff raff get here," Chris yelled, jolting Ned from his slumber.

"Taxi!" the old guy shouted.

Ellie and I exchanged glances and couldn't help but giggle as we walked through to the restaurant.

Melba was wiping down tables. "You're late!"

I looked at the clock on the wall; it was two minutes past five.

"We were just …"

"Loitering in the bar, I know what you young 'uns are like, but I have news for you – there'll be no jumping on the bar or table top dancing or breaking bones on my watch, ya hear?"

Oh goody! Another reason to hate us even more.

Melba gave us directions to prep the dining room before meals started at six. We busied ourselves to further avoid her wrath and gave each other the odd smirk as we settled into our work. It was then that Chris walked through the partition, weaving his way through tables and chairs towards us.

"Melba, is it possible that you are looking younger every time I see you?"

Melba scoffed, "Oh, you, quit it." She waved him away and quickly gathered up the extra tablecloths to carry back to the kitchen, a ruby red blush creeping up her neck and cheeks. My incredulous stare turned from Melba's retreating figure to Chris, who looked at me.

And there it was, that Henderson charm.

"What?"

I shook my head. "Nothing."

His face melted back to stone. "We have a promotion going on this weekend, for the Irish Festival."

"Ooh, to be sure, to be sure," crooned Ellie as she sidled up next to Chris, who all of a sudden looked uneasy. He took a subtle step back.

"You're to wear these as the uniform tonight."

"A uniform?" pouted Ellie.

"It's only for the weekend." Chris chucked us both unnervingly small black tops, which I held up against my torso with a gulp. Before I could question the size, Chris was gone.

"Come on, let's get changed before Mad Melba returns."

I had thought I looked summery with my leggings, ballerina

flats and a long, flowy, dusty pink top.

That was before. I stood in front of the full-length mirror in the ladies' toilets, my mouth gaping open in horror. I had literally poured myself into what there was of the tight, black top with the Guinness logo on my chest.

"I can't go out there like this," I said. My voice shook.

Ellie stepped out from the cubicle tucking her top into her non-offensive skirt.

"What's the problem?" She froze when she caught sight of me.

"Wow!" Ellie's eyes widened.

I grimaced. "I look like I'm in a cat suit." Turning to the mirror, I tried to pull down the stretchy top but it infuriatingly drifted upwards.

"You look hot, Tess!"

I chewed on my lower lip, trying not to get upset.

"Can you please go ask Chris if there is another size? Something bigger?"

Ellie had to shake herself from her daze as her gaze looked over me. "Ah, Tess, I don't think–"

"Ellie, please!"

I paced the toilets, waiting for Ellie to return waving a XXXL top in her hand. Unfortunately, it was not to be.

"Tess, seriously, you look fine. In fact, you look smoking-hot fine!"

I didn't want to be 'smoking-hot fine'; I wanted to be blend-into-the-wall fine.

Ellie grabbed my hand. "Come on, we can't stay in here forever. Chris said we were going to be flat out tonight so we better get to it."

Perfect.

"Oh, wait." Ellie pulled me up, and all but yanked my arm out of my socket.

"What?"

Without a word Ellie yanked the elastic from my hair and ruffled it up.

"*Ellie!*"

"Just trust me," she said.

I took a deep breath and stood still. She ran her fingers

through my hair and folded up the top half with the band, for a messy half-up half-down look, before fixing my fringe to frame my face.

"Much better!" She smiled.

We came out just in time for a staff meeting. Chris's words were cut off abruptly when he saw us join the group. His eyebrows raised in surprise as he took in my apparel. Not in disgust or mockery, but the way a guy checks out a girl. The way boys usually looked over Ellie. He coughed, cleared his throat and refocused on his clipboard. I felt the heat flood my cheeks as I quickly sat down in an attempt to hide myself behind a table. I sat next to Melba who didn't give me the same look of appreciation. She was looking at me in more of a *'You look like a whore'* way.

We were given our battle stations speech; what our roles were to be, and what was expected of us for the night. The Irish band would be setting up in the beer garden, and the restaurant was fully booked. My heart beat faster as I recounted my disastrous first shift. It hadn't exactly boosted my confidence (especially now that I looked like a ninja). Ellie was jigging her leg like she always did when she was excited.

For what time remained before the expected arrival of our first booking, I took it upon myself to memorise the dinner specials, taking note of any vegetarian selections. I tested my pen for ink, dated the order pad accordingly and, before I knew it, the six o'clock rush had begun.

I fumbled and stuttered at my first table, but luckily they were a family of locals. Ken and Wendy Martin and their three adorable kids. They were patient and kind, and helped ease my nerves. I took their order without drama and spiked it proudly on the kitchen spike.

"Order up!"

"Well, look at you," crooned the usually foul-tempered cook, Rosanna. She smiled at me, her demeanour disturbingly friendly. But I knew this was the calm before the storm.

"Twirl for me." She circled her finger in the air in a spinning motion, giving a wolf whistle of appreciation.

"You'll be breaking all the boys' hearts, Tess."

I cringed. "I don't know about that," I said, and quickly

retreated from the kitchen, running straight into Ellie.

She pulled me into the alcove where the high chairs were kept.

"Oh my God, Tess! You should see who just came through the front door."

Before I could ask, she let out a squeal. "I'm going to take their order," she said, and disappeared.

Okey dokey, there was either a celebrity in the bar (in *Onslow?*), or a hot boy. My money was on the latter and my suspicions were confirmed by the distant hum of the jukebox, which meant that the poolroom was in use.

My friendly family table continued to be everything true and lovely, which almost made up for my next table … almost.

Chapter Six

My burden to bear for the night was to serve two posh tourists, who spoke in clipped sentences and looked at me as if they had stepped in something nasty.

The full-figured lady sported a grey bob that was immaculately kept in place. No, really, it didn't move; there must have been a full can of hairspray on there. She was clearly highly flammable. I clasped my notepad tightly, glancing around with unease; trust Claire Henderson to think candles would make for great ambience in the dining room. The place was a giant death trap for this woman.

She smiled at me but it didn't quite reach her eyes. Her husband complained about the lighting, the air conditioning, and the sound of the music filtering through the paper-thin walls of the poolroom. Their rudeness frazzled me, which was bad, as the last thing I needed was to make more mistakes as the night picked up in pace. More patrons poured through the restaurant's French doors, all sun-kissed and starving from their day in the sun. The restaurant was at full capacity, a buzzing cauldron of chaos, so when I brought out the wrong meal (because I had written down the table wrong), Rosanna started to lose it, and I quickly vacated the kitchen, slamming hard into Chris's chest.

"Whoa, Tess, slow down."

I bit my lower lip in an attempt to hide that I was upset.

"We're going to switch things up a bit, okay? Uncle Eric wants you to take over Adam's place in the kitchen for a bit. Thinks it might be for the best," he said.

Meaning I wasn't quite cutting it out front. A part of me was relieved, but another part of me was mortified that I had just been demoted, if only for the night. In other words, they thought I wasn't doing a good enough job. They would never have sent Ellie in to wash dishes, not in a million years.

"Ellie's going to take over your tables." Chris took the notepad and pen from me; another slap in the face. I nodded and solemnly turned back to the kitchen. My summer was now downgraded from hell to the pits of hell, with Melba and Rosanna.

Thanks, Adam!

I stood in front of the sink for what seemed like forever, overwhelmed by the huge pile of dirty pots and pans, and ever-increasing stack of plates. I didn't know where to begin. I tied the sodden dish apron around me, too afraid to ask if there were any rubber gloves. At least I wouldn't have to worry about being seen in my cat suit. As I waited for the sink to fill, I cast a look at my pride and joy, my meticulously French manicured nails. I had filed, shaped and coated them in preparation for my big working debut. I had always prided myself on having nice nails and thought I would put an extra-special effort into them, knowing I was to be serving customers. If I was to be incompetent, at least they could say, "Well, she had nice hands."

Nice hands that were now submerged in blisteringly hot, dirty, dishwater.

Ellie swung through the kitchen door, smiling like a Cheshire cat; she never said anything about my new position. She was too busy humming a joyful tune and spiking her docket.

"Order up!"

I unloaded a stack of dishes near the server, peeking at the docket and wondering if the little piece of paper had anything to do with her being in such fine form. A docket with several meals listed sported the heading 'The Onslow Boys' – (Poolroom). A little smiley face had been drawn into the O, and the penny dropped. Ha! Well, at least someone was having a good time.

There was much swearing and pot throwing at the peak of service. Through desperation, they had Melba take a few orders, and with Melba's people skills being what they were, it was a true sign that they were under the pump. At least I was friendly. For the most part, Melba was really a kitchenhand for Rosanna and they kind of complemented each other. What I mean by that is that Melba refused to take Rosanna's crap, so it worked.

I had created a clean space in my sodden little corner of the world; I even felt good about my achievement until I looked down at my destroyed nails, the once immaculate polish melted from the heat of the water. As I took a moment to survey the damage, the background was filled with more swearing and clattering, accompanied by the frantic dinging of the service bell, all of which I was sadly getting used to as the night wore on.

"Order up," Rosanna screamed.

Ellie was noticeably absent, which caused Rosanna to lose it big time. Before all hell broke loose, Chris burst through the kitchen door and spotted my nearly clear sink.

"You. Meals. Go. Now!" He held the door ajar, pointing to the restaurant.

"But Uncle Eric said I was to–"

"Uncle Eric is upstairs watching *Touched by an Angel*, so what I say goes; we need you to take the meals, now!"

I frantically untied my dish apron and smoothed down fly-away strands of hair that had curled from the steam. Before Rosanna hurled the meals across the kitchen, I grabbed them and headed through the door Chris still held open.

"Get them out of here! Get them out of here!" she screamed.

Happy to escape the mayhem and relieved I hadn't been knifed in the process, I looked at the docket that lay haphazardly on top of the chip pile on the dinner plate. It read the 'Onslow Boys'. With immense concentration, I walked two plates through the restaurant en route to the poolroom. The mystery of Ellie's disappearance was solved when I saw her taking orders for a table of twelve. She managed to glance at me as I walked by, and putting two and two together she pouted at the fact I was delivering 'her' meals.

I pressed my back against the swinging restaurant door and

pushed my way through to the front bar. I had never been in the bar in peak hour on a Saturday night. Actually, I had never been in here *at all* until I worked here, so I wasn't entirely sure what would greet me as I walked steadily through my final barrier, a flimsy concertina partition, and into the bar. The smell of cigarette smoke and stale beer hit me first, followed by the loud music that flooded from the poolroom. The front bar was dominated mainly by an older clientele, enjoying the blessed happy hour. The bar aligned with an array of men in attire ranging from flannelette-covered work overalls, to stubby shorts and Blundstone boots. Foreigner's 'Urgent' blared from the speakers as I made my way gingerly through the mass of bodies. Men parted for me with lingering gazes. I smiled politely, excusing myself as I brushed by strangers, dodging and weaving with great care, holding onto the dinner with a white-knuckled intensity. I headed to the poolroom to deliver the Chicken Parma's to the smiley-faced Onslow Boys. I paused under the archway, taking in the packed, smoky poolroom. The music was twice as loud in here. Just as I summoned enough courage to yell out my order, I was drowned out by a blast of laughter and shouts as someone missed a shot on the pool table.

"That's two shots to us!" yelled a tall, muscular boy. Sean Murphy. I knew him mainly by his all-star status as the ruck-man for the Onslow Tigers. He was now looking at me with piercing baby blue eyes, a colour I had never seen before.

He flashed a smile that made my stomach flip, and as if sensing my predicament, he shouted out for me, "Grub's up! Tobias, it's your shot."

A lone figure leaning over the jukebox flipped through the song archives; he pushed his final selection before turning to grab the pool cue from Sean. I threatened to drop my plates when I noticed Tobias was Toby. *The* Toby! *My* Toby!

Our eyes locked, his brows raised in surprise, and then I realised he wasn't the only one looking at me. All of the Onslow Boys were looking at me like I was some kind of creature that had emerged from the lake. But when I caught their eyes roaming over me much like Chris's had, it made me suddenly super aware and self-conscious of my bodysuit attire.

I coughed and stammered, "Where do you want it?" As soon

as the words left my mouth, I realised how suggestive it had sounded and mentally slapped myself.

There was a pause and a line of bemused smirks as I watched the same thought flick through their minds, before Toby broke off and headed to the pool table.

"Two shots, was it?" Toby asked.

Sean scratched his jawline and nodded. Trying not to smile.

"Just sit them down there, Tess,"

I flinched at the unexpected voice of Chris, from behind me where he stood manning the bar, his arms crossed. He was all business, no nonsense. I latched onto the clarity and put the meals quickly on the bar.

"Thanks, Tess." Sean smiled at me as he slid a meal down the bar.

I made my exit, stressed that I had at least two more meals to deliver to them without embarrassing myself. Again.

I took the shortcut through the opposite door to head towards the kitchen; I passed Ellie who was still busy with her mammoth table. When she saw me coming from the bar, she winked and gave me the thumbs up, and I couldn't help but smile and return the gesture.

I carried the meals back the same way and avoided the front bar all together. When I reached the Onslow Boys, I didn't need to ask whose meals I was holding. Toby and another boy, Stan, I think his name was, had pulled their bar stools next to Sean and a boy they'd nicknamed Ringer. I placed the meals carefully before Toby and Stan who both said, "Thanks." My heart did a little flip.

"Hey, Tess, is there any salt and pepper?" Sean asked.

"Oh … uh, I'll get some." I made a silent prayer that I wasn't blushing at such a simple question. I snuck back to the restaurant and grabbed a set. Quickstepping back into the poolroom, I passed them to Sean's outstretched hand upon my return.

He watched me intently. "What's your last name, Tess?"

Before I could answer, Toby spoke for me. "McGee," he said. He glanced up from his meal, confident about his answer and motioning for Sean to pass the salt.

He knew my name?

"Ahh, McGee, eh? Your parents own the Rose Café in Perry?

That McGee?" Sean pressed.

"Ah, yeah, Jeff and Jenny McGee."

"Best pies in town," Ringer added with a mouth full of chips. They all nodded.

"Thanks! I'll make sure I tell her the Onslow Boys approve."

Sean frowned as if what I just said confused him and Ringer, Toby and Stan looked equally confused as they eyed each other.

Sean swallowed. "The Onslow Boys?"

In that very moment I knew I had gone bright red; the Onslow Boys was Ellie's nickname for them. Not a common one everyone used.

"Oh, nothing," I stammered. "It was just something that was written on the docket, so I could find you."

Oh help!

Sean munched on a chip thoughtfully. "Let me see."

I cringed and reached for the crumpled order I had shoved in my apron from the plate. Sean took it from me.

His smile broadened. "The Onslow Boys."

"Don't forget the smiley face," added Stan, who peered over Sean's shoulder.

I felt like such a child. Sean handed the docket back to me.

"That's pretty cool. Boys, it would appear we have a new status; we now represent the entire town."

"That's a frightening thought," Chris added, as he appeared in the bar. He had a habit of appearing out of nowhere.

"Surely we could have been called the Onslow Men?" Ringer puffed his chest out.

"No, I think boys is appropriate for the likes of you lot," Chris said.

They all broke out with laughter. Stan threw a chip at Chris and the verbal onslaught continued. Chris gave me a 'back to work' look that made me scurry to action. I locked eyes briefly with Toby who seemed to be the only one not overly amused by the personal jokes being flung around.

I ducked into the alcove between the poolroom and dining room hall, stealing a moment to catch my breath. I had managed to see Toby twice in one week and he knew my name, not just my first name but my *whole* name.

He actually knew my name.

So? I thought to myself. It was a small town, everyone knew everyone's name, it was no big deal.

I couldn't help but press myself closer to the partition; I strained to overhear their voices that were mixed with laughter.

"So what do you think?" posed Ringer.

"What do I think?" said Sean.

"Yeah."

"I think she makes me want to drink Guinness," Sean said. That had them all laughing.

Guinness? I looked down in horror to see that exact word blatantly advertised across my chest.

"Easy, Tiger," Chris said.

"Whose shot is it?" added Toby, and the fray was broken with more trash talk about one another's pool skills. Mortified, I ran back to the kitchen with my head swimming in all that was the Onslow Boys and Toby Morrison, who knew my name.

By eleven o'clock, it was just Ellie and I left in the kitchen, washing all of Rosanna's pots and equipment.

"Chefs don't do dishes," Rosanna had said as she smugly made her way out of the kitchen.

We glared after her, the same thought no doubt crossing both our minds.

Chef? Pa-lease!

Rosanna had pretty much trashed the kitchen. Remnants of greasy food spattered on the work bench, spoons, pots, dishes, sodden tea towels and an overflowing rubbish bin. I could only imagine that this was a reflection of what inside her mind was like. Chaos. We were on the homeward stretch, wiping down the benches, both clearly exhausted by a long, hard night. When Chris walked in with a new set of dirty dishes he dumped in the sink, I dragged myself over to refill it with water.

"Leave it, Tess," Chris said, "you've done enough, come and have your knock-off drink."

We dragged ourselves into the main bar, pulling up the spare seats next to Rosanna who was devouring a smoke, and Melba who sipped on a vodka and tonic. Chris plonked two ice cold Cokes on the small table before us which we gratefully skulled in unison.

"Thirsty work, girls?" bellowed Sean, who appeared out of the poolroom making his way towards the gents.

I nearly choked on a bit of ice at the unexpected comment, which Melba and Rosanna thought was hilarious. They slapped their palms on the table with fits of cackling laughter.

"Don't worry love, Seany-boy has that effect on all the girls." Rosanna knocked my chair with her foot as she wriggled her pencil thin eyebrows in a 'hubba-hubba' motion.

"And he's really nice, too," added Ellie, dreamily.

"Ha! It's the nice ones you have to worry about," Melba said.

Our conversation was getting more and more bizarre in a really dysfunctional way; it was like a bonding session of sorts. And as Sean reappeared and walked back towards the poolroom, we all tipped our heads sideways, watching, in appreciation of such fineness.

Chris worked on drawing the blinds, switching off the main lights and deadbolting all the doors.

"Time for everyone to head home by the looks of it," I sighed.

"Oh, honey," Rosanna said, "they're just booting up, the night doesn't kick off till now." She butted out her cigarette.

"How so?" asked Ellie.

"They're doing a lock-in."

"What's that?"

"It's the lurks and perks of being mates with the nephew of the publican." Rosanna stood, hooking her handbag over her bony shoulder.

"Dropping me off, Melbs?"

Melba swallowed the last of her gin, slapping her hand on the table.

"Let's go. See you girls tomorrow at eleven. Don't be late."

Chris unbolted the back door and let them out. My shoulders drooped, my body unclenched. I saw Ellie do it, too. For the first time that whole night, Ellie and I collectively relaxed.

She leaned towards me. "So what do you think of Sean?"

What I wanted to say (but didn't dare – not here) was, '*what do you think of Toby?*'

"He seems nice, friendly enough." I shrugged. "I don't really know him."

"Hmm, I would like to, though," Ellie said. "I mean, seriously!" She had that glazed look in her eyes as she stared towards the poolroom.

Chris collected ashtrays and rolled up bar mats, hovering over us in a not-too-subtle gesture for us to get a move on. We skulled the last of our drinks and gathered our handbags. We were both exhausted and obviously not invited to the lock-in anyway. In order to get out the front we had to make our way directly past the poolroom, where a very merry Stan was shuffling to K.C and the Sunshine Band's 'Get Down Tonight'.

"Who put this on?" complained Ringer.

"Random," they all said at once. But the Boys sounded unconvinced, casting dubious glances at Stan who mysteriously knew all the words as he pointed to no one in particular.

Ellie and I couldn't help but laugh.

"Don't encourage him," said Chris, who couldn't contain his own smile.

"He's trying to psyche me out," Toby said as he concentrated on potting the black ball. He did, with ease.

He shook Sean's hand, who had now spotted us waiting for Chris to un-deadbolt the front door.

"So the 'Perry Girls' are off, then?"

"Perry Girls?" repeated Ellie.

He shrugged. "Seemed only fair to return the title."

She thought for a moment, and smiled. "'Perry Girls'. I like it."

Sean walked over and shook Ellie's hand, then mine.

"For services rendered in the line of duty." He smiled.

Next thing we knew, we were ushered over to Ringer who shook our hands and was fighting not to fall asleep at the bar.

"It couldn't have been an easy job, having that knucklehead order you around." He tilted his head towards Chris. "He's drunk with power, ya know?" Ringer winked.

"Watch it, Ringo, let's not forget who the gatekeeper is here," Chris said in mock seriousness.

Ringer shook his head. "See what I mean?"

And then there I was. Standing in front of Toby, who held his hand out to me. I placed my hand into his and memorised the pressure, the feel, the length of one-two-three shakes and then it was over all too soon. But he did look at my hand for a mere moment, his brow furrowed.

Oh God, was he looking at my nails? My mangy, chipped, dishpan hands?

Ellie didn't get past Stan who was still shaking her hand in a way that threatened to dislocate her shoulder.

"Come on, Chris, can we keep them?" whined Stan.

Ellie laughed and looked at Chris with the same forlorn plea in her eyes.

"I think the girls have better things to do than hang out with a bunch of derelicts like us."

The truth was, Ellie's dad would be waiting down the road to take us to our childhood bedrooms for us to curl up in our jammies in bed. It had been a long day, and I had felt exhausted, but I was suddenly wide awake, standing next to Toby.

Chris opened the front door, as if the matter was non-negotiable. This was obviously a boys-only gathering.

"Eleven am start, ladies."

With that, we were ushered outside and the door closed behind us. Standing in muted darkness, only small slithers of light streamed beyond the cracks of the window blind, the echoes of muffled laughter sounding from inside.

We started the trek down the hill towards the brake lights of Ellie's dad's car when Ellie asked, "So what do you think of Stan?"

I laughed. How things could change in an instant with Ellie.

I didn't answer. Instead, in the relative privacy of the nighttime track, I said, "That's funny, because I was just going to ask what *you* thought of Toby."

Ellie had threatened that she wanted to know all the details of this Toby crush the next day, as we couldn't exactly get into the details with Ellie's dad in the front seat. It was hysterical watching Ellie desperate to ask, but biting her lips together in front of her dad. Dads were a girl-talk-free zone.

After I had showered the sweat, grease and smoke away, I removed the remnants of my poor, melted French polish. I thought back to Toby's expression as he shook my hand. It was subtle, but obvious, that something had run through his mind.

It bothered me. I'm pretty sure my hand wasn't clammy or gross. The nails, it had to be my nails. I cringed, I didn't want to even think about it.

Before I slipped into a coma for the night, I dragged myself from my bed to my desk for my nightly ritual: to check my email.

To: tessmcgee
Toby Morrison eh?? You little Minx! Talk about must have made a good impression?

I want to know everything!!! I have a plan. Operation Toby?? (Don't stress just an idea)

ME first, which sounds better? Operation Sean? Or Operation Stan?

Decisions! Decisions!
Sender: ellieparker

To: ellieparker
Go to bed! Talk tomorrow. NO OPERATION TOBY! Do I make myself clear??

GOOD NIGHT!!

P.S Operation Stan!! I like his dance moves
Sender: tessmcgee

I was set for bed when I saw an email from Adam.

To: tessmcgee
Do you still love me???

How did you go tonight? I spoke to Chris, he said you smashed it! I take it he is not referring to a plate and assume you did well? Go you!! I knew you would do good. That is why I hand picked you, you know?

Seriously Tess, that's really great. I better go, Nan's telling me Matlock is on. Oh goody!
Sender: Adam I can jump puddles Henderson.

To: Adam I can jump puddles Henderson
How can I stay mad at you? I don't want to run the risk of

your feelings being as delicate as your bones.

And I will have you know I did totally smash it!

In the kitchen!!!

I think it's just as well you hurt yourself, because I have found my calling in life. I am the Messiah of dish pigs!

Don't cry for me though. It kills me to admit this, but I didn't totally hate it. But if you repeat that I will just deny it.

Enjoy Matlock!!

Sender: tessmcgee

Chapter Seven

The Sunday lunchtime shift was dead. It was like a graveyard shift at best.

But why wouldn't it be? Everyone was lake bound and enjoying themselves. My heart ached as I looked out through the windowpane of the poolroom, which was, incidentally, my job for the afternoon: to clean off drunken blow fish marks from Saturday night.

"I don't remember reading this in the brochure," Ellie said glumly as she sprayed Windex and cleaned fingerprints off the jukebox. Her bracelets clinked with each vigorous rub.

"Melba said we had to 'earn our keep'," I air-quoted.

Chris was nowhere to be seen. He had his own room upstairs; more 'lurks and perks' of managing the bar, on top of lock-ins, was, obviously, free board. That left Uncle Eric in charge of the day shift, something he was much more accustomed to. The place was breezy; slower and less high maintenance during daylight hours with just a handful of church-skipping tradies having a quiet cold one as opposed to the rowdy twenty-something crowd of a Saturday night.

It would be our second day into the Irish Festival and I was prepped; I wore my infamous Guinness top with a black skirt so I didn't look like a body double for that 1960s chick from the

Avengers. We had a few lunchtime walk-ins, mostly tourists all damp and sun-kissed from swimming or lying out by the lake. Seeing them put Ellie and I in a whimsical mood, so we made plans to break away to Mclean's Beach between shifts.

But until then, forced to endure everyone else enjoying their holidays, the afternoon dragged on. I couldn't stop myself from turning each time the front door opened, my heart skipping a beat in hope, but the Onslow Boys never appeared. I guessed that they had better things to do on a Sunday afternoon. I could only hope they'd venture out when the sun went down.

At shift's end, we bolted down the hill in a highly unlady-like fashion, bags bouncing on our shoulders, arms flailing, breaths laboured. Our minds focused solely on reaching McLean's Beach at the hottest part of the day. It would be crowded and overrun, no doubt, but not so much by tourists. The beauty of Maclean's Beach was that it was always crowded by locals rather than tourists, just the way we liked it. Although I would often complain about tourists, I did get it. How could I not? My parents constantly reminded me.

"No tourists, no livelihood, Tess."

Mum and Dad's cafe on the main strip of Perry – a direct line into Onslow – proved to be the perfect busy stopover. Mum was an excellent cook, taught from Gran and no doubt her Gran before her. She specialised in traditional family home-cooked recipes and Mum's homemade pies were a big hit. It had made my heart clench when the Onslow Boys gave them the tick of approval as the 'best pies in town'. I wondered if Mum would remember them coming in. I'd have to ask in a way that wouldn't make her suspicious or have me sound like a stalker.

As time ticked on towards the dinner shift, Ellie and I packed up our towels we had stretched out on for an afternoon sunbaking session and headed for the hotel. We walked past the mechanics, where I knew Toby worked. Naturally, it was closed on Sunday, but I did have the slightest hope that Toby might have been in there, anyway. He could be doing a bit of weekend catch-up. Being a sweltering summer afternoon and all, if he was in there, he'd most likely be shirtless. Hey, it was my fantasy.

My gaze skimmed the exterior of the closed building. Faded

block lettering read 'Matthew & Son' on the tangerine and blue workshop. Toby's dad, Matthew Morrison, had been the local mechanic for as long as I could remember. It was where everyone went. Since he was the only mechanic in town he could have named his price, but he was a real decent bloke and always charged reasonably. Or so my dad said. I squinted at the sign; it should have really read 'Matthew & Sons' seeing as Toby and his older brother, Michael, both worked there. That in itself was a real testament to their dad. I mean, don't get me wrong, I love my parents, but I could *never* work for them. And believe me, they had tried. One of the upsides of working at the Onslow was my parents stopped pestering me. They seemed pleased enough that I had stepped out of my comfort zone and was trying, at least. One look at my lacklustre waitressing skills, and they would probably thank their lucky stars I'd never agreed to work for them.

"Well, look at you."

Ellie gave me a side-on look.

"What?"

"Checking out Toby Morrison's workshop. It's Sunday, Tess, he'll be long gone."

I should never have told her about liking Toby. She was like a dog with a bone. Even more frightening was the scheming matchmaking side to Ellie that I knew she'd lose control of sooner or later. Probably sooner. Ugh, why had I told her?

She frowned at me. "What's stopping you? Tell me one good reason why you won't go there, Tess."

We crossed the main street, leaving Matthew & Son behind.

I half laughed at her. "One? Ha! I'll give you five!"

"Go on, then!"

I held up my thumb to begin the count.

"One! Before two days ago, I am pretty sure he didn't even know that I existed."

Although he did know my last name.

"Two! And this is a pretty big one: he's what? Twenty-two? And I'm seventeen. You do the maths."

Ellie shrugged. "Maths isn't my strong point."

It was five years too many.

"Three! He is *Toby Morrison*. Popular, gorgeous, charming …

and I am TIC TAC TESS."

Ellie sighed. "You're struggling."

"Four! He works, I'm still at school. I doubt he would be interested in coming to Deb practice."

Ellie rolled her eyes stubbornly. "I must say, I'm still unconvinced."

"And number five," I breathed out. I had a horrible suspicion. Although I hoped it might not have been true, I seriously doubted it. "Number five," I said again, "Toby has a girlfriend."

And her name was Angela Vickers.

You would have had to live on another planet to not know Angela Vickers. 5'10", blonde, hard to miss. She was School Captain when I was in Year Ten, and, oh, how all the boys mooned over her, with her perky blonde hair and perfect perky breasts. None of which would have mattered, only that even the likes of Toby Morrison was obviously not immune to her or her assets. It bewildered me that Toby was like all the other predictable males when he seemed so different from them. I had been in love with Toby ever since the first time I saw him.

At the end of Grade Six, all students from Perry Primary were taken for a one-day orientation at Onslow High School. We all gathered around like sheep staring in wonder at the 'big league' we were about to enter after our summer holidays. I was drawn to the burst of laugher that had me turning to see a boy, a boy with the most brilliant smile I had ever seen. I decided I simply had to know his name, and then, like a gift, one of the boys he was laughing with said it.

Toby Morrison.

I found out that his dad owned the mechanic shop in town, so any chance I had, I would deliberately walk past it hoping for just a glimpse or to cross paths with him. My heart was all aflutter with the sight of him, and merely the thought of him was what had me anxious to start high school, to the point I started marking down the days on my calendar.

Of course, I learned the hard way that he was in Year Twelve and had graduated by the time I started high school. So that was that. My crush on Toby faded away and life went on, even if I did always think of that smile every time I walked past his dad's shop.

For the next few years, I saw him only every now and then at the Sunday markets or more fleetingly down lakeside with his mates. It was by pure chance one time, when I was fourteen, that I walked past Matthew & Son and saw him out the front in grease-stained overalls, talking to a customer about their car. He looked older, his hair longer, hands covered in greasy remnants of a hard day's work.

He was working for his dad! And I nearly ran into a pole.

My heart had pounded just as it had that first time at orientation. My secret crush was just that, an utter secret. I told no one; I didn't even confide in Ellie or Adam. Especially not Ellie. I was always terrified about confiding in her over my secret crushes as I'd learned from experience that it usually resulted in her marching up to the boy I liked and blatantly grilling them with the most obvious question of all: "So what do you think of Tess McGee?"

So Toby had become a non-negotiable secret, for the years that followed I would obsess about him only to myself. Until one infamous day in Year Ten woodwork when the latest rumour had circulated to my table. The big news that Angela Vickers was going out with the mechanic's hot son. My heart withered at the thought, and, just for the record, bad news during woodwork is not ideal; I nearly lost a finger that day. I had to accept it: the Angela Vickers of this world would always get the boy, and I would always be Tic Tac Tess.

But then, at the Onslow Hotel I wasn't Tic Tac Tess anymore, I was just Tess or McGee. I was like anyone else. The horrors of high school would soon become nothing more than a distant memory, even if that was little comfort to me now.

"Toby has a girlfriend?" Ellie asked. "No, he doesn't. Who?"

I sighed. "Yeah, perfect Angela."

"Oh yeah, we hate her," Ellie said.

For the smallest of moments, I had forgotten. Like when he stepped out of the darkness at the party, or the way he looked at me when I brought the meals into the bar, or the feel of his hand touching mine. No doubt I had over-analysed his every movement, his every facial expression, but I'm allowed to. That's what girls do. For those fleeting moments, however, I had managed to forget all about Angela Vickers.

"So they're still together?" Ellie asked.

"I see her car parked at his place all the time," I said.

Ellie gasped. "What are you doing outside his house? You total stalker!"

"Shut up!" I said, blushing. I could feel the familiar burn in my legs as we started our climb up towards the Onslow. "It's not like that. His place just happens to be on the main road to Perry. It's kind of hard to miss."

You had to crane your neck and look really hard, of course, but I would leave that little fact out. I knew Toby had his own place, though I didn't know how I knew. It was like knowing Sean's name or Stan's name. You don't know how you know, you just know. It's what's part and parcel of living in a town with a population of less than 3000; you knew all kinds of irrelevant stuff about each and every one of them. Toby's place was a mission brown shack, set back off the main road with a long sweeping driveway hidden amongst immense bushland. Even though it was set back and private, you could always tell if he was home. His navy Ford ute parked in the drive or, worst case scenario, Angela's red Lancer parked behind it. He had lived there since he was in Year Twelve, and I thought it was so grown up that he moved out of home, unlike most eighteen-year-olds in town.

I tried to imagine what the inside of his house was like, or if he could cook and use the washing machine. I would imagine that he would be pretty good with his hands, seeing as he fixed cars for a living. All of the little quirks I had been obsessing about since I was thirteen were now back in the forefront of my mind. And admittedly, I had never felt so unhappy about it.

Chapter Eight

I walked towards the Onslow Hotel kitchen, ready to assume my station at the sink.

I thought I would save Chris the trouble of banishing me to the kitchen, and instead I used some initiative and went on my merry way. If you could call it that. But I was merry; I had taken off the remnants of last night's battered French nail polish, I was working my Guinness shirt with a non-offensive skirt instead of leggings, and I had even managed a bit of colour from the afternoon spent at McLean's Beach with Ellie. There was nothing like a healthy dose of vitamin D and the beginnings of a tan to boost your spirits. As I pushed through the swinging kitchen door, ready to greet cranky Melba and crazy Rosanna, I was met instead with a set of glaring blue eyes.

Eyes that were attached to Amy, Uncle Eric's fifteen-year-old only daughter. She was elbow deep in dishwater and stared me down with dagger eyes.

"Oh, hey," I said, "Amy, isn't it?" I smiled politely and wondered why she was there until Chris stuck his head into the kitchen.

"Tess, you're on the floor tonight."

Bewildered, I looked from Chris to Amy and back again, my surprise evident.

"Really?"

"Really," he said. "Unless you think you might suffer from separation anxiety from Melba and Rosanna?"

"NO!" I shouted, probably a bit too readily.

Chris smiled. "I didn't think so. Come on, Amy's gonna take your place."

I looked back at Amy, ready to offer her a smile, but her glare deepened and I side-stepped away. Wow. I was on the floor again. Guess I didn't do as badly last night as I thought. And this time I was determined not to stuff it up.

"What is this?" A long, immaculately manicured fingernail pointed to their plate.

I tilted my head and leaned down a little to have a closer inspection.

"Uh ... a piece of capsicum?"

"And what was it that I specifically asked *not* to be served?" She gave me a hard stare, as I fumbled through the backlog of dockets in my booklet.

"Oh, uh ..." There it was, clear as day, scrawled in block letters.

NO CAPSICUM! I fought not to cringe.

"I'm sorry, did you want me to change it for you?"

The lady rolled her eyes at her friends.

"No, I think you have done quite enough." Her voice dripped with sarcasm. I skulked away. Wow, it was amazing how a rather upbeat day can be torn down within a blink of an eye.

Ellie met me at the cutlery drawer.

"Don't worry, Tess, I have something that will make you forget all about Cruella de Vil over there."

"Capsicum spray?" I asked in hope.

Ellie frowned, confused momentarily, but she shook out of it and plastered on a big grin as she handed me a docket.

"Take care of this, would ya, babe?"

She sauntered off to wait on the next table. In my hand sat a crinkled piece of paper. A dinner order for the Onslow Boys decorated with love hearts. It was then I realised the distant pulse of the jukebox through the wall; it was nothing compared to the beat of my heart.

There was a lull in dinner service, which had me anxiously awaiting the sound of the bell to tell me the order was up. I paced within earshot; twenty minutes went by before I heard that magical ding. I slid sideways as I overshot the kitchen door in my haste. Elegance and grace, as always.

I was there before Rosanna spiked the order as done. She wiped the perspiration from her brow and curved the other at me.

"I see the Onslow Boys have made quite an impression on you girls."

I tried not to smile; even Rosanna was calling them the Onslow Boys. I plastered on my best poker face, attempting to appear cool and casual even though I had never been so eager to deliver two Chicken Parmagianas in my life.

"Just be careful, hon," Rosanna said.

"Oh, are the plates hot?" I flinched back just before my hands made contact.

Rosanna laughed. "No, but hot boys can burn you just as easily."

Oh no! Love advice from Rosanna. Now was not the time for a deep and meaningful; in fact, with Rosanna, *never* would be the time. To avoid the next cliché, I quickly grabbed the plates and legged it. I was about two seconds into my commute when I realised maybe Rosanna's words did have a double meaning; the plates were bloody hot! I bit my lip as I quickstepped through the bar, scurrying as fast as I could to the poolroom. I breathed deeply and grimaced at the pain, and when I entered the poolroom, I managed to voice the fact.

"Ahh-eee-aaah," I said, "hot stuff coming through."

I dumped the plates on the bar, shaking and blowing on my now free hands.

Oh God, did I really just announce that to the room?

"McGEE!" Sean shouted as he looked up from his pool shot that he'd just pocketed with ease. He straightened and swaggered towards me, brushing passed me as he reached for his beer on the bar. He saluted 'cheers' towards me before taking a sip.

"Murphy!" I tipped my head.

"Ah, so you've done your research? You know my name."

"I think everyone knows your name."

"Really? Why?" he mused.

I gave him an incredulous look. "'Cos of footy, of course; star ruck-man, why else?"

Stan slapped Sean on the back as he took his seat to get stuck into his meal.

"It's that, or the fact that he's such a ladies' man," Stan teased.

Sean cast Stan a hard look as he watched his friend eat. "Don't choke on that, will you?"

My eyes locked with Toby's who was across the bar, about to swig on his own beer. He was smiling at his mates' banter, and his eyes never left me as he took a long, deep drink. My burning hands were long forgotten as I felt other areas of my flesh burn up, with those eyes on me. Toby swallowed his beer and opened his mouth to speak when he was cut off by two hands covering his eyes from behind.

"Guess who?"

He smiled broadly and grabbed at the hands.

"Vanessa?"

It was then that Angela Vickers swung around to his side, hitting him with her clutch purse.

"Real funny, and who is this Vanessa, huh?" She mocked anger, but it was quickly defused as she melted with Toby's blinding, beautiful smile. She closed the distance between them, claiming his lips passionately as if it were a long-lost reunion.

Ringer groaned. "Get a room you two!"

I quickly looked away. The thought of her running her hands through his hair, pressed up against him in an embrace was just too much to bear.

I made a quick exit back to the kitchen to grab the two remaining plates that had mercifully cooled to the touch by now. I had hoped to spot Ellie en route, in the hopes that maybe she'd switch with me, but she was nowhere to be seen. At the risk of the food getting cold, I had no choice but to grin and bear it.

"Tess, can you do a glass run while you deliver those?" called Chris from the restaurant side of the bar.

Oh great, what timing. A glass run when I couldn't get out of there fast enough. I set the meals down with no witty banter from

Sean; he was too busy talking to Angela who had decided to perch herself on Toby's lap.

I slowly, methodically made my way around the edge of the poolroom, picking up empty beer glasses from the windowsills and barrels. I spotted an empty glass near Toby and Angela.

Oh great.

I shyly excused myself as I leant passed them to grab the glass. Angela, who seemed to not even be aware of my existence until then looked me over and gave me a cool, calculating assessment. She didn't like what she saw.

"Hey, bar-keep!" she shouted with a smirk.

"Her name's Tess, Ang," said Stan. For that I was totally in love with him and wanted to tell him thanks, but I didn't, as Angela had me in her sights. As she stared at me, all I could think of was *please don't call me Tic Tac, please don't call me that.*

I could see the nickname register in her cold eyes. She smiled slowly.

"Tess, would you be able to get me a glass of your house white?"

I was at first surprised by the simple question, and then I realised I would have to give her my standard answer.

"Oh … um, sorry, I'm not allowed to serve alcohol, I'm only seventeen." I blanched. Her brows rose in fake surprise. She damn well knew I couldn't serve her alcohol. She just laughed and waved me off as if to run along.

"Oh, never mind. Chriiiiisssssss," she shouted down the bar.

Her attempt to make me feel two feet tall had worked. I became embarrassed and flustered. I went to add the last glass to my stack, but it slipped through my fingers and fell. Everything happened in slow motion until it hit the floor and shattered in a loud, almighty smash.

"Taxi!" several people called out and laughed. All eyes were on me.

The entire stack wobbled in my arms but Sean jumped up and steadied them for me.

"Whoa, careful!"

I pressed my free hand to my forehead as I surveyed the damage. After carefully placing the glasses back on the bar, I bent quickly to pick up the shards, averting my eyes from all their gazes. An extra pair of hands appeared in front of me and carefully picked up some of the larger pieces. Silently, Toby had crouched beside me and my heart swelled at his kindness. His hand then grabbed my wrist as I went to lift a smaller piece.

"Don't cut yourself."

I froze, suddenly aware of him touching me, and then all too quickly he removed his hand from my skin and I looked away.

"I'll get a dustpan," I said under my breath. I also wanted to get away from them, from Angela, who I could hear laughing behind me. I was so determined to get away from the shrill sound that I nearly collided straight into Chris, who was holding a broom and dustpan.

"Thanks." I reached to take it from him, but he moved them from my reach.

"No, it's okay, I'll take care of it."

"No, it's fine, I can–"

"Why don't you go and take over from Amy for a bit?"

I did a double take. In other words: *you have made enough of a mess, Tess, get back to the kitchen where you belong.* It felt like a physical blow.

I nodded and pushed passed him. Ellie gave me a smile and a little wave from across the restaurant but I just made my way to the kitchen.

When I informed Amy I was there to take over for her, she hooted joyously and ripped off her apron with lightning speed.

With a "See ya later, losers," she pushed open the door and was gone.

"What a little shit she is," Rosanna said.

I surveyed the sink area and my new work zone. It appeared that Amy had made more mess in her attempt to clean. There was water all over the floor, and the dishes still had remnants of half-chewed food and sauces on them. I had visions of her furiously dunking them in the putrid water, fantasising it was my head as she slammed them onto the dish rack in a rage. I couldn't blame her. I was about to do the same; instead, I would be imagining someone else. I would be dunking Angela.

Chapter Nine

I stole a moment in the ladies' room, perched on a closed toilet lid for a bit of chin-trembling.

Even Rosanna and Melba must have sensed the change as, for once, they weren't taking their anger out on me. Ellie definitely knew something was wrong when I declined the end-of-shift staff drink from Chris. The Onslow Boys and Angela were still in the poolroom, and I just wanted a discreet exit out the back way. Ellie also knew me well enough not to question me about it, at least not just yet. We made our way down the sloping stretch of road where we would wait for my mum to pick us up.

"Hey, do you wanna go for a ride tomorrow?" Ellie said. "We can pick up our pays and go and blow it all at Carter's. There's this cute little skirt that would look great on you."

This was Ellie trying to cheer me up.

"Sounds good!" I faked a smile.

After I completed my nightly routine, peeling off my half-drenched, smoke-infused clothes to have a long, hot shower, I fired up my computer and found an email from Adam.

To: tessmcgee

Bad news I'm afraid! There is a Magnum P.I marathon on and guess who is front and centre?

ME! Under sufferance of course.

Although don't jump to any conclusions if I return home with a handle bar moustache.

It doesn't mean a thing.

How's things in O town? Hope you're having fun without me.

Sender: Adam I can jump puddles Henderson.

I was so emotionally exhausted even Adam's email did little to perk me up. I couldn't help but think back to Angela's arms draped over Toby, her sardonic smile as she belittled me in front of everyone. The smashing of the glass replayed in slow motion, the brush of Toby's fingers as he helped me pick up the shards.

I felt like such an idiot. I should have insisted with Chris that I'd clean it up. I could only imagine Angela's snide remarks as Chris swept up the mess.

"Ha! I wish someone would clean up after me. That's what you get for hiring twelve-year-olds", she would have said. And then everyone would have laughed with her.

I groaned and cupped my head in my hands.

To: Adam I can jump puddles Henderson
Do it! Moustaches are hot!
O Town is just peachy!
Sender: tessmcgee

To: ellieparker
All good. I am looking forward to our bike ride tomorrow. X
Sender: tessmcgee

I pumped the pedals and pressed forward over the handlebars to surge myself over McLean's Bridge. On and on it went, a never-ending mass of concrete overshadowing Lake Onslow. Up the footpath then around the curb, I peddled like a mad thing. The hot summer wind threatened to burn my skin as I boldly sailed down Macquarie Avenue, riding with no hands.

This was the freedom I had yearned for and never in my life would I have believed I would have found it on a Monday. But it was the holidays now and things had been switched up. I would meet up with Ellie after lunch as planned. In an attempt to still my overactive mind and get the most I could from the day, I had grabbed my bike and headed around the back roads of Onslow. The Mitchum bike trail had some of the best bushland scenery around. Luckily, being Australia, I didn't have to worry about mountain lions, grizzly bears or wolves ... just poisonous snakes, deadly spiders and the odd wayward wallaby that wandered down from the foothills of the Perry Ranges.

As I glided along the isolated road, I sought refuge amidst the trees that edged my way, blocking the searing sun in intervals of shade-light-shade. I had circled this area a hundred, maybe a thousand, times and each time there were new sounds, new scenes. It made me forget the mundane existence of all that troubled me. I stood straight up on the peddles, lifting my face to the sky and breathing deeply, feeling the flashes of the changing shades flicker spots under my closed eyelids. This was living. In a space that seemed like nowhere, there were no worries, nothing could touch me here. Nothing!

And that's when I heard a snap.

Remember the never-ending stretch of the McLean's Bridge? The one I just had to leave behind me? Well, that was nothing compared to the long, barren stretch of bitumen that faced me now. This seriously had no end, I was going to die here! Suddenly all the wonder and the beauty of my surroundings lost its lustre for me as I limped my bike back down the road. I stopped every few steps to survey the damage to my skinned knee that had already started scabbing over, thanks to the heat of the day.

As I stopped for the hundredth time, I was surprised and a little disappointed that there wasn't more blood flowing from my gaping wound. It stung like a bitch! I took my anger out on my bike by giving it a good kick.

"Stupid bloody chain."

It had snapped clean in half, causing it to make an infuriating clanking sound with every rotation of the wheels. I clenched my jaw and limped on.

Nature sucked. I hated nature; I hated the now seemingly blistering sun that threatened to burn my skin. I hated the trees, the lake views, the birdsong and, most of all, I hated my carelessness.

No phone, no water, no sunscreen. From now on, I would pack a survival kit that would consist of my dad's Swiss Army Knife. For what? So I could clip my toenails and open a bottle of wine?

Real smart, Tess.

My God, the heat was frying my brain, maybe I was losing too much blood? I might need a transfusion by the time I made it around the sweep of the Horseshoe Bend, my next landmark that was still nowhere in sight. After that, there was a bit of a declining slope, nothing too major and then the caravan park, owned by the Remingtons – Stan's parents. Perhaps they would let me dial triple zero by the time I stumbled through their gates. Or my mum.

Failing that, the next stop was the Onslow Hotel, where I could seek shelter and water and be nursed back to health by Melba, Rosanna and Chris.

Yeah, I think I would pass on that one.

I had a better chance of backstroking across Lake Onslow. But even though it weighed me down and I was seriously pissed with it, I wouldn't leave my bike. She was last year's Christmas present, a deep midnight purple with a tan cane basket on the front, very Jessica Lansbury circa *Murder She Wrote*. In the beginning, Adam and Ellie ribbed me about it constantly, but guess who wanted their swimming gear carted when it was too awkward to hook onto their handlebars? Oh, how they loved the Grandma basket then. Not that it served me much good now, it housed nothing more than a beach bag with my purse which held a whole $15 and my student ID.

Each time the cool breeze flowed through the trees it whipped around me, fluttering my loose peach singlet and refreshing my skin that was slick with a light sheen of perspiration. I stopped in the shade of a towering gum tree. Letting the bike rest on my hip, I pulled my hair up off my neck and closed my eyes, allowing myself to cool and rest for five.

The serenity was disturbed by the distant sound of kookaburras mocking me with their laughter. I peeked one eye open and listened closer. A sound was slowly closing in with a murmur that became louder and louder. What was that … a car? Possible salvation? Oh, *please* don't be a serial killer. I was desperate, but not desperate enough to hitchhike with a scary local who liked to play the banjo. I grabbed my bike and continued to walk, cool, calm and collected, instead of sweaty, bloody damsel in distress. I would politely decline any invitation and rough it alone, surely it wasn't much further?

The thudding of a burly vehicle and sound of music closed in behind me. The engine slowed, causing the hairs on the back of my neck to raise. The music volume lowered.

Oh no, no, no. Please keep going.

I walked faster, looking straight ahead, my bike chain rattling more insistently.

Leave me alone, it's a nice summer's day, can't a girl take her bike for a walk?

The car crawled now, it could be a creepy white van with a hooded deviant behind the wheel, I just knew it. I had watched enough late-night horror movies with Adam and Ellie to know all about stranger danger. My heart was leaping out of my chest. I know I said I would never leave my bike, but, honestly, I was getting to the point of ditching the sucker and heading for the hills screaming MURDERER.

That's when I heard my name.

Chapter Ten

"Tess?"

I stopped abruptly, before I spun to see a navy Ford crawling along beside me. I tilted my head slightly and found a mystified expression peering out at me through the open window.

"What are you doing out here?" said Toby.

Toby? Toby was behind the wheel. It wasn't a serial killer, it was *Toby*.

I inhaled a deep breath of relief. "Oh, thank God it's you! I thought you were a murderer."

His brows raised in surprise.

"Are you alright?"

No, I wanted to pout, *I am suffering from sunstroke, dehydration, starvation*. And I was all of a sudden keenly aware of how sweaty and awful I must have looked. I discreetly pushed my fingers through my hair and smiled in good humour, my eyes flicking to my bike.

"I'm afraid she has given up the ghost."

Ugh! That would be something my dad would say.

Toby pulled over and got out of his vehicle in one fluid movement. He was in his work pants and work shirt that had Tobias embroidered in yellow on his pocket. The little detail made me smile. I had only ever heard Sean call him that, and I was pretty sure it was to deliberately hit a nerve.

He gave me a coy smile as he made a direct line to crouch and examine my bike. I was mesmerised by his swiftly moving hands; he had beautiful hands. I had often wondered how they always seemed so amazingly clean, considering his job was to be covered in grease and oil all day, every day. He must have some heavy duty industrial cleaner to wash his hands with every night. This thought led me to visions of him at home, showering, getting ready for a night out with the boys at the Onslow for dinner and pool. His hair was always slightly damp, with just the slightest touch of hair product. He wouldn't do much more than that, he didn't need to; he was naturally perfect. Whenever I brushed past him in the crowded poolroom, there was always a hint of a fresh, clean, crisp aftershave. It made me want to be close to him, to bask in all that was Toby.

I snapped myself out of my daydream when he looked back up at me.

"This chain's history. Where are you headed?"

I didn't want to confess I was just goofing around on my summer holidays, giving little thought to much else. That was the beauty of it. It was meant to be a voyage to forget all my troubles, all thoughts of him and Angela last night. And then here he was straightening up in front of me, looking down at me with those questioning brown eyes.

"Oh, I should be getting home, I hadn't planned on being out so long."

Ugh! God, that sounded like I had a curfew; that I would be in trouble if I didn't scurry home to Mum and Dad. Why didn't I just say I was headed to the Onslow to pick up my pay, because I was a responsible working woman? I could have even asked if he wanted to join me for a drink? Like grownups do. Have a friendly chat.

About what exactly? Cars? School? His girlfriend?

"If you want, I can give you a lift home," he said.

I tried not to look so overjoyed, but the thought of being rescued by Toby was an even better outcome than I could have ever hoped for.

"Yes, please! I don't want to die out here, not like this."

He smirked. "Murderers, death; you have a dark mind, Tess."

And before I could hide my smile, he grabbed my bike and lifted it onto the bed of his ute. The very same one I saw parked in his drive, or occasionally at the Onslow Hotel. Deep navy, big and bulky, this was a man's vehicle. A vehicle I was about to climb into.

I fought to overcome my nerves as I opened the passenger door. I hoisted myself up inside. Toby was busy securing my bike in the back. On the passenger floor was a lunch box and thermos. I slid my feet away from the items, which wasn't difficult considering the ample room inside. There weren't individual seats but a light cream bench seat, with nothing dividing me from Toby. I leaned my arm on the open windowsill and pondered. You could fit three bodies in for a ride with ease if someone was pressed up next to the driver. I wondered who had ridden in this car with him. Sean? Stan? Angela?

Okay, let's not think about that.

Toby pulled open the driver's door, and he filled the rest of the cab's interior. He fired up the beast of an engine and pulled into gear, gloriously tearing up the bitumen. I stole a quick glance in the side view mirror and grabbed my hair that was flailing around from the open window. I held it back at the base of my neck, and my wispy fringe momentarily blinded me. I stole a sideways glance at Toby. He met my eyes briefly and smiled. I looked quickly out the window. In my peripheral vision, I watched as Toby's suntanned arm rested on top of the wheel, his other arm leaning casually on the open window. He was relaxed and confident behind the wheel. It was of little wonder; if he got his learner's at sixteen he would have been driving for six years by now. I calculated it in my mind. I would have been 11 when he started driving. I tried not to think too much about that.

An awkward silence swept over us, only to be broken by Toby's cough before he spoke.

"So, where did you go last night?"

I tried not to shift in my seat at his question. I was hoping that my sudden disappearance after the glass-breaking episode would go unnoticed. I guess not.

"Oh, you know, kitchen duties beckoned."

"Oh?" He seemed surprised.

"Yeah, whenever a crisis breaks out they shine a giant K in the sky, and I hightail it."

"So you head to the phone booth and change into your apron and rubber gloves?" Toby's mouth turned up at the corners. Just a little.

"Isn't that Superman?"

"Oh right, sorry. My bad, giant K in the sky: you're rocking it Batman style."

"Exactly. Except if I was Batman, I wouldn't be needed in the kitchen full stop. Bruce Wayne doesn't do kitchens."

"You could serve customers like the speed of a bullet."

I laughed, shaking my head. "Again, Superman. Why don't you know this stuff? What did you do as a kid, spend it outdoors or something?"

"Misspent youth, clearly. I obviously don't know my superheroes at all." He frowned as if deeply distressed. "I must look into that."

"I would if I were you, that's kind of embarrassing."

He flashed a smile my way, before turning his gaze back to the road. There was more silence, but this time it wasn't uncomfortable. I turned to peer at my bike rattling away in the back.

"So, the old girl," I tilted my head backwards, "will she ride again?"

Toby glanced at me then back to the road; that elusive upward tilt of his lips reappeared as if he was fighting not to smile.

"Let me put it this way. I thought I'd have to surround it with some sheets and bring out the 22 to put it out of its misery."

My eyebrows rose. "You carry a 22?"

"You think carrying sheets isn't weird?"

"Yeah, but sheets aren't deadly."

"You haven't been to an all-boys boarding school."

"Ew! Okay, give me a gun."

There it was, that smile. He made no effort to hide it now. It shone brightly, lighting up his entire face.

"Are we talking about guns and dirty boys' sheets?" Toby frowned.

"You started it," I said. "Sheets aside, which I really don't want to know about, did you really go to boarding school?"

"Yep, my parents shipped me off in Year 7. The longest year of my life. I ended up just mucking up until they had no choice but to bring me home."

I stared at him for the longest time. Trying to imagine Toby ever being bad, I just couldn't picture it.

"So the sheets were that bad, huh?"

He burst out laughing; it was a wonderful sound, rich and warm. It made my skin tingle.

He shook his head as he refocused on the road.

"You have no idea!"

It was a bizarre conversation, our first formed sentences alone together. Well, there was the party but that doesn't count. How would I tell Ellie about my bonding session in Toby's ute?

She would squeal and insist that I tell her everything, and she'd ask the most obvious question. "So what did you talk about?"

Umm, guns and dirty sheets?

It would probably be better to go all cryptic and tell her: 'stuff'.

We pulled into my driveway; Toby killed the engine and jumped out, rounding the back of the ute to untie my bike. While I climbed slowly from the cab, I watched as he lifted my bike like it weighed nothing, his flexed, bronzed biceps the only proof of any strain.

"Where do you want it?"

In my bedroom.

I mentally slapped myself and fought not to blush.

He waited for me to answer.

"Umm, I just keep it in the garage."

He nodded and walked it over, leaning it against the far wall.

"Just there's fine," I said, "thanks, Toby." His name sounded so strange, so intimate on my tongue. I wanted to say it again.

He looked at the bike, in deep thought.

"You'll be out of action until you get a new chain."

"Yeah, I'll go and buy one tomorrow."

Because I was now a responsible working woman who could buy things like that. I would forgo the cute little skirt from Carters and buy a bike chain.

So depressing.

"Well, if you need someone to fit it …"

"Oh, that's okay, my dad will do it."

And as soon as the words came out, I wanted to kick myself, preferably with steel-capped boots. Had he just offered to fix my bike? And I had blurted out that no, my daddy would do it?

IDIOT!!

"Cool, well, they're not that dear so you should pick one up down at Mac's store."

I started to walk him to the car, but he paused, head tilted as he looked at my leg.

"You're bleeding."

"Oh, it's nothing, just had an up-close-and-personal encounter with the bitumen," I said. "It doesn't hurt."

Like hell it doesn't!

His brows creased with concern and he crouched to examine it closer. My breath hitched in my throat as he lightly touched the skin around my knee. I fought to keep my breathing steady with the intimacy of it. He straightened, his look still serious.

"I have a first aid kit in my glove box; come on, let's clean you up."

We had a first aid kit in the house, but I wasn't blowing it a second time. I followed him to his ute.

"Jump up on the tray," he called over his shoulder as he headed to flip open the glove box and retrieve a small, blue zip-up case. I had planned to follow his advice when I noticed, due to my five-foot-nothing stature and the height of the tray, there was no way I could master it gracefully. Before I could even voice the issue, Toby had read the troubled look on my face. Without a word, he was by my side. With a small smile, he placed the first aid kit and a bottle of water on the tray.

"Here." Before I had time to think, his hands were on my waist and, as if I weighed nothing more than a feather, he boosted me up to perch on the tray. I fought not to squeal in surprise and my hands grabbed onto his shoulders for leverage.

"You okay?" he asked, his hands still on my sides, as if securing me in place.

I nodded all too quickly. He smiled at the affirmation and let me go. I could still feel the pressure of his hands, the feel and flex of his muscles as I was suddenly airborne. I could tell I was blushing profusely and hoped it might pass as sunburn.

I straightened my leg for his attention, as he rummaged through the first aid kit.

I arched a brow. "Rescue many damsels in distress?"

A crooked grin formed on his lips, but he didn't meet my eyes. "Every day! It's a tireless job."

My skin tingled from his touch as his hand clasped under my knee to hold my leg steady.

"Looks like you're the Superman then? Coming to the rescue and all."

He grabbed a bottle of water, popping the top with his teeth.

"This might sting a bit, okay, Tess? But I need to clean it."

My heart fluttered every time he said my name, I liked the sound of him saying it. I had never, in all my life of pining over Toby Morrison, heard it from his mouth before today. It had stopped me in my tracks when I had heard it through the open window earlier; I had suspected, but couldn't quite believe it to be true.

"It's okay." I smiled down at him and then he tipped a slow stream of water on my grazed knee.

SON-OF-A-BITCH!!

My entire frame locked up with the flash of pain; Toby's eyes darted upwards to watch my face.

"Sorry." He grimaced.

I tried my hardest to maintain my dignity as I clenched my jaw and forced a smile.

"It's okay."

Toby worked methodically, gently dabbing at the cut with cotton wool and Bettadine. I came to believe this was how Toby approached all things in life. Not to say just because he was ludicrously handsome that he must be a perfectionist in everyday life. It doesn't work like that. But everything he did was carefully thought out. Planned. Whether it be choosing a song on the jukebox, taking a shot at pool, or cleaning a clumsy girl's scraped knee, everything he did, it seemed, everything he touched, he did with great care.

The sting ebbed as I concentrated on the pressure of his fingers placed intimately under my knee, his butterfly touches of dabbing on the ointment. Once satisfied, he tore the package for the plaster and with intense concentration slowly placed it on my knee. Oh, he was a perfectionist alright. And he was damn good with his hands.

"Done." He stood back to eye his handiwork.

"Thanks, Doc!" I said. "Will I dance again?"

"You will dance, ride and serve meals better than ever before."

I arched my brow and examined my knee.

"Bionic leg ointment?" I teased.

I loved to make his face change, his smile was so transforming, it was the thing I loved about him the most.

I held my breath when he reached to help me down from the bed of the ute. He placed me gently onto the ground.

"Thanks," I managed to breathe. We stood there a moment. I realised I was still gripping his upper arms and quickly let go, trying not to blush deeper in the process.

'You good?" he asked.

"Yeah, thanks!"

I pushed my hands into my back pockets. Toby lifted the back tray with a thud, locking it in place, and moved towards the driver's door.

Say something, Tess, say something funny, bring back that smile, give him something to take away and make him remember you.

Instead, I said, "Thanks again."

Brilliant.

He grinned, exposing all of those perfect teeth.

"You're welcome." He fired his ute to life, leaning his arm on the open window as he checked the view behind him. He looked at me.

"When are you working next?"

I was startled by the question. I must have sported an idiotic expression because he just stared with an amused look on his face.

"Oh! Uh … Saturday! I work again on Saturday, 12 till 2 and then 6 till 9, depending on how busy we are, and then again on Sunday, same hours."

Was that too much information? It was. Shut up, Tess. It was a simple question, you babbling idiot.

He nodded thoughtfully as if trying to take it all in. I'd overloaded him, I knew it.

"Well, might see ya there?" He began to slowly edge back out of the drive.

"Unless there's a giant K shining in the sky," I threw back.

He let out that wonderful laugh again and looked at me, really looked at me, and smiled that smile.

"Well, then I'll know."

As I stood for what felt like the longest time, staring out into the distance where his car had disappeared, there were some things I knew for certain.

I really wanted to hear that laugh again, and I couldn't wait for Saturday.

Chapter Eleven

"SHUT UP!"

This was Ellie's usual reply to things that she was dumbfounded by, and my afternoon (okay, so it wasn't an entire afternoon) spent in Toby Morrison's ute was something to be dumbfounded about.

"You total slut!" Another term of endearment from Ellie.

I just smiled and stirred my iced chocolate.

"So what did you talk about?"

Milk spilt over the rim of the tall glass as I faltered at the inevitable question.

"Umm …"

Superheroes, guns and dirty sheets! Superheroes, guns and dirty sheets, my head screamed.

I shrugged. "You know … stuff."

Ellie slumped back in her seat and folded her arms. "You lucky biatch!"

Yes I was. I straightened, trying not to smile like the Cheshire Cat.

"And the girlfriend?"

And there went my smile.

I knew about the girlfriend alright, painstakingly so. Last night was my first actual exchange with her other than brushing by her in the halls of Onslow High.

I sighed. "Yeah, he's still with perfect Angela."

"We totally hate her, right?" Ellie said.

The worst thing was I didn't hate her so much as I envied her. The way she walked in and captivated a room, how she completely owned it. She ordered a glass of house wine with grace. Stood and chatted, even flirted with ease with Sean as her designer sunnies held back her sun-bleached fringe. In fitted jeans and killer heels she presented a cool, casual style all of her own. What little did it matter if she had snake eyes and a matching reptilian personality. Everybody loved her. Toby loved her.

Sensing the change in my mood, Ellie set down her own iced chocolate after a long draw.

"Spill. I want every single detail."

Ellie half choked on her drink when I mentioned the first aid incident. As I waited for her to catch her breath, she sipped more, with a frantic wave of her hand for me to continue, hanging on every word. I could see her mind ticking over frantically and knowing Ellie as well as I did, it was unnerving.

I tried not to even let myself feel giddy as I thought back on every look, every smile, every touch. He had a girlfriend. It had meant nothing more than Toby being a nice person. He'd only done what anyone else would have done, which kind of took the buzz out of the moment.

"This is huge!" Ellie said, nodding.

Oh no, no, no … just as I had come to the conclusion that it was nothing, she was going to read all sorts of stuff into it. I watched Ellie, her mind whirring as she plotted and schemed in front of me.

I needed an exit strategy. "So did you get a chance to speak to Stan on Sunday night?"

I relayed his effort of sticking up for me when Angela called me 'bar-keep'. Her scheming eyes clouded over with a dreamy, swoon-like quality as she melted in her chair before my eyes.

"He's so sweet."

Too easy.

"He is really nice, I think Operation Stan is a goer," I said, adding fuel to the fire. "So the fact that Stan is older doesn't bother you?"

Ellie straightened. "Pfft, no! Think of all the idiots I have dated that were the 'appropriate age'. They sucked."

She was right; Ellie didn't have any problems landing boys, but finding a nice, respectful one was a whole other story. Maybe she did need someone older; someone that would treat her with respect and tame her wild ways. Then I wouldn't have to worry about sitting on bonnets of cars with her latest conquest's grotesque best friend. It would be a win-win situation.

"Why? Does it worry you?" Ellie asked.

"Age difference?"

I thought of Scott, his clumsy fondling hand under my shirt, greedily grabbing at me. I never enjoyed any of his touches. I usually steered them away so as not to go too far. I wonder what he would have done if I had ever needed him, like today? I couldn't even imagine him being anything other than grouchy and put out, like he had been whenever I had my period and wouldn't let him put his hands down my pants. He was too dense to figure it out, but I had my period a *lot* when we were together.

I thought back to Toby; he was a boys' boy, sure, he could rough house and swear like the rest of them, but I could never imagine him being cruel. He never even seemed to get loud or obnoxious, not even with a few beers around his mates. Instead, he was always quiet and understated. And the guys seemed to respect him for that. But he was twenty-two. Five years my senior. That had worried me as recently as yesterday. But now … although he was older and his mere presence turned my mind to mush, I didn't feel anything other than really safe with him. How could that be bad?

"No," I decided, "no, it doesn't bother me."

The gurgling slurps of Ellie's iced chocolate were loud in the café (and embarrassing) as she finished.

"That's settled then. Operation Stan for me, and Operation …"

"*No!*" I cut her off.

"What?" she tilted her head innocently.

"Don't even think about it."

She blinked at me, like she didn't have a clue what I was

talking about.

"What I was going to say, before I was so rudely interrupted, was Operation Summer Fun!"

I didn't believe a word of it. I folded my arms and curved my brow in disbelief.

"Fine! Have it your way ... Operation Dull and Boring." She slumped back in her seat.

"Why do we need to be Operation anything?"

Ellie gasped in mock horror. "What are you saying? You mean just ... go with the flow?"

I shrugged "Why not?"

She smiled sardonically. "Could be fun?"

"With you in tow, I have no doubt."

Operation "Go with Flow" had us pick up our pays from Uncle Eric at the hotel, followed by stalking the clothes racks at Carters. I held up a pale green summery halter that I had had my eye on for weeks. I pressed it against me, tilting my head in the mirror and admiring the sheer fabric. I shouldn't buy it. I needed the new bike chain. But it was so pretty ... surely I could have both? I checked the price tag and gulped. No, no I couldn't have both. My heart plummeted as I placed the halter back onto its rack.

"What are you doing?" Ellie asked. "You have been mooning over that for weeks!" She passed me on her way to the changing room, her arms piled high with clothes.

"I don't have to have it. I can get more for my money with other things." Other less expensive things, less beautiful things.

We shopped in mind for the next weekend's shift, knowing that we didn't have to wear our Guinness tops anymore. Instead of the gorgeous halter, I bought a boat neck style top that was a bit clingy for my taste, but Ellie squealed and insisted that I *had* to wear it Saturday night. I also wanted to buy a new Lip Smacker lip balm, and some Impulse body spray. Our afternoon of blowing our wages actually perked me up for the weekend to come, and I was even surprised at the disappointment of realising it was only Monday.

I had ten bucks left over, allocated to Operation Bike Chain, though I didn't know if it was even nearly enough. What do I know about bike chains? And once my parents found out it had, in fact, taken me a mere three hours to blow my first pay, there would be no sympathy for my cause. My bike would be garage bound for another week until the next pay day. So I would be pounding the pavement as I didn't think it would be a good look to have Ellie dink me on her handlebars. We weren't thirteen anymore.

When I got home I lay all my purchases out on my bed, planning for a fashion parade. I had a thought that had me going into the lounge room and rummaging through dad's tape deck, all segmented in order. I shook my head at some of his rather disturbing choices in music but then I found what I was looking for. I padded barefoot back to my room, popping the cassette into my tape deck.

Don Henley started to blare out of the small speaker and I smiled to myself. I hung out in my room for the rest of the day, trying on different outfits, adjusting hairstyles, experimenting with make-up, all whilst dreaming the day away. I allowed myself this small luxury in the privacy of my own heart, because I knew that as soon as I stepped out into the real world, all my wants didn't count.

To: tessmcgee
Are you ready for your mind to be fully blown?
Something so big, so EPIC it will change your life forever?
Sender: Adam I can jump puddles Henderson

To: Adam I can jump puddles Henderson
You're coming Home???? :)
Sender: tessmcgee

To: tessmcgee
What if I am?
Have you fainted? Do you need to sit down??
I know how your life has been barren and lonely without me.
Sender: Adam I can jump puddles Henderson

To: Adam I can jump puddles Henderson
I cry myself to sleep every night.
WHEN????????
Sender: tessmcgee

To: tessmcgee
Soon my pretty. Soon!
Don't know the full details yet, but I think they might be releasing me for a weekend for good behaviour. It's a small mercy. But I will take whatever I can get.
Excited much?
Sender: Adam I can jump puddles Henderson

To: Adam I can jump puddles Henderson
I wait with bated breath.
Let me know! xox
Sender: tessmcgee

A strip of light streaked through the darkness of my closed eyes. I would not let the pesky sun disturb my slumber, so I rolled over, away from the offending beam. I had managed to kick off my blanket during the night and the oscillation of the fan still didn't threaten to chill me. I remembered that the irritatingly bubbly weatherman had promised a scorcher, and I had fist pumped my way to the fridge to grab a Coke, thinking *'do your worst weather dude'*. But as the sun lifted and the breeze stilled, humidity was at its sticky worst and I changed my mind and cursed the summer and all who gloried in it.

A prod to my exposed foot caused me to drag it away from the edge. A tickle and I kicked out. Scratching my nose, I rolled over to push my face into the pillow with a sleepy groan.

"Wakey, wakey," an upbeat voice sing-songed. Mum.

"Noooo, go away."

"I have a surprise for you," she coaxed as I felt the mattress dip next to me.

She had my semi-attention now. I squinted at the clock.

"But it's so early."

The bright and breezy note in my mum's voice lowered in astonishment.

"It's 11.30!"

"Wake me in half an hour." I turned over, hugging my pillow.

"I guess you don't want this, then." I heard the rustling of a bag as she got up to leave.

I sat bolt upright, blinded by my wayward hair which swept across my face at haphazard angles.

"What is it?"

"Never mind, you're too tired," Mum teased.

"Oh, be the grown-up, Mum, what is it?"

Mum became all excited as she hid an object behind her back.

"Close your eyes."

I was fully awake now. I loved surprises. Had I told her about that top I had been eyeing off? She must have noticed I came home without it yesterday. I sat on my knees, pushing my bed-tousled hair back.

Holding out my hands, I closed my eyes. Mum placed something in them, and they dipped under the unexpected weight. Okay, definitely not a top. But it was solid and cool.

"Open your eyes," Mum said, barely able to contain her excitement.

I opened them with haste as Mum ripped the plastic from the top with as much flair as a magician pulling a rabbit from a hat.

"Ta-DA!"

"Oh …" I said, "wow." That was about as much as I could muster as I took in the hot purple, marbled bike helmet in my hands with, oh Jesus, was that a lightning bolt on each side?

"Do you like it?"

"Wow. It's … wow."

Mum nodded in appreciation.

"I saw you came home with another scrape on your knee, and thought you really need to have one of these. It's the new shape, like the racing people wear, very smart."

Smart was not the word I would have used. *Helmet hair* screamed inside me. I had never been so happy that my chain snapped, rendering my bike useless.

"I know you kids don't get around with helmets, but I think once one starts wearing them, it will catch on; the next thing you know, you'll all be wearing them."

I offered my best fake smile. "Thanks, Mum."

"Try it on!" She beamed.

I humoured her by placing the egg-like dome on my head. It

slipped forward, into my face.

I gave her a double thumbs up. "Awesome."

She patted my cheek. "Looks great, you'll have to give it a test run."

I grimaced, trying not to overact my disappointment. I was a terrible actress.

"I can't until my bike's fixed; the chain, remember?"

"Oh that's right, well Dad can-"

"No rush, it's kind of nice walking – won't do me any harm."

In fact, I was pretty sure it may just save my reputation.

As Mum went to leave my room, she stopped and said, "I almost forgot." She fished out my mobile phone from her pocket that I had left charging in the kitchen.

"This thing keeps beeping at me." Mum wasn't very savvy with technology, and she handed it over as if it had a bad smell secreting from it.

I waited for her to leave before taking my helmet off with great gusto; I didn't want to hurt her feelings. I placed it on my chair giving it a horrified look.

Oh hell, no! Mum I love you, but this I cannot do.

A reminder beep went off, and I crawled back into bed to read 5 missed calls, 7 messages from Ellie. What the?

9.06 am

Oh me Gawd! Oh Me Gawd!

Ring me!!!

9.10 am

Why haven't you rung me??

9.38 am

OMG!! Check your emails woman!

And pick up your phone...I have to talk to you!!

9.44 am

OH MY GOOOOOOOD!!!! Tell your dad to switch your home phone over from the fax, I mean seriously!

9.46 am

Are you mad at me??

9.50 am

Because seriously now is not the time to be mad at me...TRUST ME!!!

10.00 am

I am coming over to kick your skinny butt!!!!!! Plus I want to see your face when I tell you!!!

I dove out of bed, tripping over my sheet that was tangled around my legs, while I attempted to dial Ellie's number and fire up the computer all at the same time.

I pressed the power button on the old computer and, as usual, it whirred, groaned and chugged to life. I swear, my parents had given me what must have been the oldest, slowest computer in the southern hemisphere. And if that didn't have my leg jiggling in impatience, I pressed the power on the modem and waited, waited and waited some more as the dialup beeped and buzzed, connecting to the internet. Thank God it was a separate line; between Dad's inability to switch the phone back over from the fax, or the fact that Mum and Dad were constantly using it for the business, I would never have got a look in. I convinced them on my sixteenth birthday that it was vital for my future study to get with the times. So they got me a secondhand computer and the internet with its own separate phone line. And I *did* use it to study. Right after I chatted to Ellie and Adam for a couple of hours each night on MSN Messenger.

Ellie wasn't answering; guess it was payback or she was riding over to kick my butt. What on earth had her knickers in such a twist? I was used to Ellie's dramatics, but this seemed different, far more intriguing, even more so than my hideous helmet.

Finally, my computer connected to the web, and I tapped into my email account. I expected to see one BILLION messages of harassment from Ellie, but there was only one from 8.04 am.

To: tessmcgee
Operation Go with Flow initiated!
Oh me Gawd! Oh me Gawd!

I hope you are sitting down, and I hope you have relieved yourself because otherwise you are seriously going to pee your pants!!!

I walked to the corner shop this morning to fetch the paper and who do I run into, in his work rig, fueling up?

That's right! Stan Remington, looking all windswept and

interesting. Seriously he is so adorable!

Anyhow we got to talking and he invited us to go out on the boat with him and the boys...THIS AFTERNOON!!!!

Hold onto your helmet honey...(Oh yeah I know about that by the way. I mean I had to help your Mum pick it out and all. So cute don't you think??)

Anyway I will call you for rendezvous.

Meet the boys at the Onslow Hotel at 1pm.

Ellie X

P.S If you're wondering...Toby will be there.

PP.S And Angela has gone to visit her grandparents and won't be home for two weeks. (Just saying)

Sender: ellieparker

Boat.
Toby.
1pm.
Shit!

Chapter Twelve

I looked at the time in a panic as I tried to dial Ellie's number.

"Come on, come on, Ellie where are you? Pick up." My leg was jigging rapidly, what had she done?

By 12.00 pm I was showered, dressed and still unable to get onto Ellie. Now it was my turn to kick her skinny butt. You couldn't just drop a bombshell on someone and then not answer. Furthermore, you do not encourage and help your best friend's mum to pick out a hideous bike helmet and expect to get away with it. I would put that in the memory bank for later. For now there was nothing else to do but grab my bag and pocket my phone.

"Mum! I'm heading to Ellie's."

Luckily, Ellie lived only three blocks over (be it three large blocks). The weatherman's words echoed in my head. *It's going to be a scorcher!*

Lesson learned! I had water, sunscreen and coconut cream lip balm that I never left home without. I had opted for a light yellow summer dress. Cool and airy.

I found Ellie in her bedroom, looking radiant as ever in her cut-off denim shorts and halter top; she looked like a catalogue model, but that wasn't new.

"I trust you got my messages?" she asked as I entered. She was sitting at her dressing table, moisturising her long legs.

"Ah, yeah, are you serious?"

"I would never joke about such a thing."

I believed that. Boys were an extra-curricular activity Ellie took *very* seriously.

"Oh-my-God! Look at the time, we gotta go!" Ellie leapt to her feet and grabbed for her beach bag, eyes searching the floor for her thongs. "We have to meet at the hotel at one."

I had to force my heart to stop racing, everything was happening too fast.

"I have to swing by my house first and grab a towel and my bathers," I said.

"No time! I've packed you everything you need. Dad is going to drop us off. I told him we had a staff meeting and then we were going to McLean's for the afternoon. I suggest you tell your mum the same." Ellie shouldered her bag and squealed with excitement. "Let's go!"

I tapped my foot and bit my nail as I stood in the Onslow Hotel ladies' room, staring at two microscopic strips of bleached white material. Ellie had chosen a bathing suit for me. I use the term 'suit' loosely, as when one usually thinks of a suit, one would think of actual body coverage like the one-piece bathers I was more accustomed to.

I should have worked out something was a bit fishy when Ellie changed with lightning speed and left me alone in the change room, dumping the bag in front of me.

"There you go! Everything you need. I'll be out in the bar waiting for the boys."

I thought she was just overeager for them to arrive. I thought little of it until I took out the rolled-up towel and peered into an empty bag. My heart clenched with fear; in Ellie's haste she had totally forgotten a bathing suit for me! But as I unraveled the towel, a white square fell out, revealing two tiny pieces encased in a sheer, barely there sarong. My suspicion was right. She had forgotten a bathing suit, because this was barely anything.

I hated her, cursed her and stood there, staring for a full ten minutes. I couldn't go on the boat with them in this. And if I did, I just wouldn't swim. Simple. I could keep my dress on and have a bit of a tanning day. That'd be alright.

I gritted my teeth and tried the bikini on. I had never felt so utterly naked, not even when I *was* naked. I crept out to adjust the foreign pieces in the mirror and *Oh my God!* There was just so much skin … and was that a hint of cleavage? Not possible.

Ever since I had been branded Tic Tac Tess, I had taken to wearing loose, flowing tops that diverted all attention away from *that* area. It was not until I was forced to wear the Guinness top that I was forced to reveal any form of shape in that department, hence why I was so uncomfortable now. Not only were they out there for the world to see, but they were barely contained by tiny strings that felt like they could be blown undone by a breeze.

I was going to kill her! Before I could dive back in to the cubicle and change into my clothes again, Ellie burst through the door. My instant reaction was to cover myself with my arms as if I was standing naked, which wasn't too far from the truth.

Ellie's eyes bugged out; even *she* thought it was too revealing.

She looked me up and down. "Tess, you look amazing!" she gaped.

"Yeah, well take a good look because this is not going anywhere."

Ellie grabbed my arm, preventing me from walking back into the cubicle to change.

"They're here and waiting in the bar."

I frowned, pulling away from her. I didn't care; this was a bad idea. I should have known from the very beginning. I guess I did know, but I should have had a plan for when it happened, when the second I confided in Ellie she would be pushing me into things I didn't want to do. Now I was literally poured into a bikini that I would never have worn even in the privacy of my own bedroom, let alone in front of the Onslow Boys.

"Tess, trust me! You *want* to wear that. If you want to grab someone's attention, this is how I'd do it."

"I'm not you!" I snapped.

"No, you're not," Ellie said. "You're Tess and you're beautiful. And believe me, when people see the real you, Tic Tac Tess will be a thing of the past. Come on, Tess, just this once?"

It was like a physical blow, saying that name to me. Adam and Ellie never *ever* uttered those words, knowing how much the nickname hurt me.

There was a knock on the door.

"Come on, you lot, you ready?" called Sean. "You're taking so long the seasons are changing."

"Coming," yelled Ellie.

She gave me an imploring look, grabbing my shoulders and turning me towards the mirror.

"Learn to see what others see," she said as we both appraised my reflection, "because, believe me, that girl in high school, the supposedly flat-as-a-board nobody ... this is not her."

"Fine." I slipped on my dress over the bikini.

We weaved through the restaurant, sighting the Onslow Boys propped on stools in the main bar.

"Don't think I've forgotten about the helmet, either," I muttered like a bad ventriloquist, plastering a fake smile on my lips.

"Geez, did you wake up on the wrong side of the bed or what?"

I thought back to my lack of sleep, and Mum's annoying awakening.

"You could say that."

Sean and Toby led the way down to the jetty. Boats of all shapes and sizes dotted the harbour, a hub of distant splashes and screams echoed from the water as people lapped up what was the beginning of the hottest part of the day. We neared an impressive boat with navy inscription scrawled along the hull.

Southern Son.

"Whose boat is this?" I asked.

"Stan's, isn't he a nice boy?" Sean mocked.

Ellie just scoffed, tipping her sunnies on as she crossed her arms and looked out to the jet skiers, churning circles on the water.

Toby jumped into the boat followed by Sean as they went to work on their safety checks.

"You okay?" I asked Ellie. I hoped that she wasn't going to be in a mood for the rest of the day. Ellie didn't take too kindly to being stood up.

She flashed a winning smile. "Sure, this is going to be fun." She pushed past me, over the edge of the jetty and held out her hand. "Sean, could you help me?"

Sean dropped his rope and scooted over to help her into the boat. Ellie squealed and clung onto his arm as she landed awkwardly on the rocking deck.

"Careful," he said, steadying her.

I rolled my eyes.

Sean motioned me over and helped me into the boat. His hands circled my waist as he lifted me down. I had never had so many hands encircled around my waist in my life as I had in the last couple of days, and every time it made my cheeks flush from the intimacy of it. The ripped cords of muscles in his arms felt foreign under my touch. Scott had always been lean and gangly, like he still had growing to do, which he mostly did, he was a teenager after all, as opposed to the Onslow Boys.

I sat on the sideboard, watching Sean and Toby work with expert precision, finishing up the safety checks.

"Sweet! Full tank. Good on you, Stan, my son," Sean said.

"I think he had a big day planned," Toby said, more to himself than anyone. And my heart did ache a little for Stan, who was now stuck helping his dad on this hot, sweltering day, when he was supposed to have been firing up the engine, which Toby did instead.

As the engine churned dark water into white froth behind us, I thought about what we were about to do. I was about to embark on a day on the lake with *Toby Morrison*. If anyone had told me last week this was how I'd be spending my summer, I would have never believed them.

"Where to?" called Toby over the hum of the motor.

"McLean's?" posed Sean.

"Too busy," Ellie yelled.

"How about over Horseshoe Bend? Pretty secluded there," I suggested.

Sean smiled wickedly as he moved to sit beside Toby. "You want somewhere private, do you, Tess? What do YOU have planned for the day?"

I blushed, horrified at what he thought I was suggesting.

"I just meant ..."

"You heard the lady, Tobias, drive her around the bend."

Chapter Thirteen

We powered along, giving a wide berth to all the other boats that were littered throughout the lake.

Once we were clear of them, Toby floored it, jerking us backward and causing Ellie and I to hang on for dear life. The thrill of the surge and the power of Stan's boat was exhilarating. It was fast; very fast. I looked at Ellie, who mirrored my own gleeful smile, as we set across the never-ending stretch of water, the wind spray of the water cooling my face.

"Faster!" Ellie yelled.

Toby leant sideways, struggling to hear. "Faster?"

"Yes, faster!" we screamed.

Toby accelerated before the words were fully out of our mouths, and we hung on with white-knuckled intensity. I dipped my head to prevent my eyes from watering. Sean and Toby were laughing as they looked back to check on us (probably to make sure we were still onboard).

All too soon, Toby lowered the throttle, slowing the boat down as we reached our destination. We were on the opposite side of town, and I could see just offshore the very place I had been limping along earlier in the week.

As if it triggered a memory in Toby, too, he turned to me. "How's the knee?"

It was now only an embarrassing pink mark and looked far less fatal. I tried to bend my knee away from his eyes.

"Oh, it's nothing."

"What's this?" Sean's ears pricked up.

"Nothing," Toby quickly changed the subject. "Help me with this, Sean." He concentrated on something complicated on the control panel.

I guessed that Toby didn't stop for an iced chocolate with Sean after dropping me home. Didn't tell him all about his afternoon and how he rescued me, fixed me up. Didn't exchange smiles and laugh at each other's jokes.

I guess that's not really a guy thing to do.

Sean obviously didn't know what Toby was referring to. It seemed his knight-in-shining-armour rescue apparently wasn't anything worth mentioning to his mates, unlike my analysed play-by-play and detailed breakdown of events with Ellie.

I knew boys were different, less analytical, less emotional than girls (I mean I had done the survey in *Cosmo*, so I was kind of an expert), but I wondered if Toby would look as disappointed as Stan did when he broke it to Ellie about not being able to make it today. And then I scoffed at the thought; why would he? He had a girlfriend, he was probably disappointed about *Angela* not being here. *Wake up, Tess!*

"Time to shine, Tess," Ellie whispered to me.

She scooted out of her denim cut-offs and peeled off her top, revealing a black bathing suit that exposed her flat stomach. Her suit was linked together by large rings along her sides, giving it the illusion of a one piece. Sean looked up from the logbook he and Toby were leaning over.

He smirked. "You girls must get the most unfortunate tan lines."

Ellie laughed as she adjusted the gold links. They really would leave unusual whites circles on her skin.

She looked at me expectantly.

"Where are the tunes you boys are so famous for?" Ellie asked. She stretched her long arms above her head, tying her hair up in a messy ponytail that always somehow managed to look good.

I took a deep breath. Here we go. I chucked my thongs off,

trying not to think too much as I crossed my arms and peeled my dress upward, over my head. Thank God for all the times Ellie and I sunbaked in our backyards, turning every couple of minutes like rotisserie chickens, and the only time I ever exposed my midsection. One thing I wasn't bashful about was my ability to tan a sweet, golden brown colour. It was the best thing about summer: my hair lightened and my skin darkened. And at this very moment, my darkened skin was exposed to two new sets of eyes that trailed over my attire – or lack thereof. I quickly glanced away, embarrassed, as Toby and Sean's eyes lingered at my chest.

Oh my God, Toby was looking at my boobs.

Toby coughed and tried to find something on the boat to occupy his attention. Sean's brows raised, and he glanced at Toby with a not-too-subtle smile. Ellie looked triumphant, smiling, twirling her hair around her finger. I only prayed she wouldn't embarrass me further by giving me a thumbs up.

I pretended not to notice when Toby's eyes betrayed him, when his gaze strayed back towards me in a long, assessing look. He wasn't wearing sunnies either, so there was no hiding it. But he wasn't smiling like Sean had been; he seemed uncomfortable with it. With me.

I wasn't sure how I felt about that. Mission accomplished: I had gained his attention, yes, but I wasn't sure it was in a good way.

Ellie was working on sunscreening her nose and cheeks, slathering it over her neck and shoulders.

"Tess, can you do my back?"

I squirted the lotion onto my hands and rubbed it vigorously into her skin like I had done a million times before.

Ellie threw the sunscreen over to the boys, landing at Sean's feet. "That sun's got a bite in it."

They looked at the bottle, then uneasily at each other.

"Sorry, mate, but I am not lathering you up," Sean said to Toby.

"Likewise." Toby frowned.

Ellie rolled her eyes. "Honestly, what big babies! Here …" Ellie snatched the bottle off the deck and squirted some lotion on her hand as she approached Sean. Oh, she was good. "Turn around," she said, in a no-nonsense way.

Sean even looked taken aback. "Yes ma'am." He pulled off his shirt and tossed it on top of his bag.

Now it was our turn to try not to stare, and judging from the smile that crept onto his lips, he totally knew it. His broad muscular shoulders were something to behold on his six-foot-three-inch frame. A chiseled six-pack, I didn't even know guys in Onslow were built like that. He cast a wicked grin at us as he turned around to expose the taut curves of his smooth back. All of a sudden I was envious of the task Ellie had before her. Even Ellie, who was no stranger to the ways of skin on skin, seemed to pause and showed a moment of fluster. I tried not to smile. Was she blushing? She shook off her moment of weakness, placing it in that locked cage of hers, and rubbed the lotion onto his shoulders.

Sean stretched his neck and leaned forward a little.

"A bloke could get used to this. So what do they recommend? Application every hour?"

"Every four," Toby corrected, as he peeled his own shirt off and walked over to stand directly in front of me. I stood frozen with sunscreen-covered hands.

He gave me a small smile and said, "Be gentle with me," before turning his back to me.

I had so enjoyed Ellie's moment of unease. Not so much fun when it was me. The only difference was, unlike Ellie, as I studied the lean bronzed lines of his shoulder blades, I didn't have the skill to tamper down my awkwardness. Ellie threw over the sunscreen, which I dropped. Twice.

Toby flinched as I touched the middle of his back with my lotioned hand. I paused momentarily, and watched him relax before starting again. I started to rub it in until the whiteness disappeared, and it blended into his deep brown skin. His back was so smooth. Whenever I applied lotion onto Ellie, I did it with a slip, slop, slap and all done! She would always ask if it was rubbed in properly, and I usually lied and told her yes, even though it never was. I hated having sunscreen on my hands and just wanted to get it over and done with.

But in this instance I wanted it to last forever. I was slowly working in the lotion, sweeping circular motions, as I became more at ease with touching him. When I glanced at Toby's profile, I saw his eyes were shut, his expression serene. By this point, Sean was smearing his face with sunscreen and rubbing it over his chest, arms and legs as Ellie looked dreamily on. All too soon every last drop had been absorbed into Toby's skin and my job was done.

I coughed, and said, "Good to go."

I held up the tube to Ellie, miming for her to do mine, but she just shrugged and cringed, showing me her hands.

"Aw, Tess, I just wiped them clean."

I glared at her. "I'm sure that ..."

"I'll do it," Sean and Toby said in unison.

Ellie smiled broadly. Her smug smile spoke for her. *'Aren't you glad you wore the bikini?'*

Sean and Toby looked at each other, surprised. Motioning to Toby, Sean swept his hand in my direction as if to say, *'After you'*, and now Toby was the one that looked out of sorts.

"You have to make sure she gets covered well, Toby; Tess burns easily," Ellie said.

It was an utter lie, which I made obvious when I glared at her. She dipped her sunnies down her nose to give me a wink before she pushed them back in place and leaned back on her towel in the sunbaking position.

With a subtle, deep breath, I turned around and Toby placed his hands gingerly on my back. I could feel his breath on my neck and my body swayed with each hypnotic caress. I fought not to let out a moan as he massaged the sunscreen into my muscles. It felt so intimate. I blinked with surprise as he dabbed sunscreen on the top of my ears.

"Oh, I forgot to do yours." I spun around.

His eyes went to my hands and a look flashed across his face, a look I had seen before, the night in the poolroom when he shook my hand.

"What?"

A crooked smile formed as he shook his head. "Nothing."

"What was that look for?" I pressed.

Toby grabbed my wrist and brought my hand up towards him, turning it from side to side in deep scrutiny.

"Your hands are tiny," he said.

"Shut up, no they're not. Thanks a bunch, I'll make sure to

sign up for the freak show next time the circus is in town, shall I?"

A crease formed on his brow; he looked annoyed.

"I didn't say it was a bad thing." He grabbed my other wrist and turned my hands over so my palms faced the sky. He smiled slowly; my skin tingled under his fingertips.

"So dainty." He looked at me now.

"Dainty?" I repeated.

"Yep." He held his hand up in front of me and motioned for me to do the same. I placed my hand against his. The tips of my fingers only touched the top crease of his, he bent the tops of them as if to prove a point. I mock-glared at him.

"Don't be fooled," I said, "they pack a mean punch."

"I'm sure they could. At the right angle, they could slip between my ribs."

"They are not that small."

"What were you saying about the circus?" he teased.

I went to hit him with my freakishly tiny hands, but he grabbed my wrist, too quick.

"Oh, you're fast," he said, fingers locked around my wrist as I tried to pull it free. He grinned. "But I'm faster."

I struggled to break free from his vice-like grip.

"Tobias, didn't your mum teach you to play nicely?" Sean said dryly as he and Ellie watched on.

It was a Mexican standoff now; Toby didn't want to let me go in case I lashed out.

"Truce?" he offered, watching me suspiciously.

I smiled sweetly. "Truce."

He slowly let me go, and I calmly placed my hands by my sides. He seemed to relax, thinking it was over. I moved to brush past him and, with his back to me, slowly picked up the sunscreen. I silently pointed and squirted a stream right across his shoulders. He froze and slowly half turned towards me. I covered my mouth trying to contain my laughter.

He gaped at me, like he couldn't believe what I had done.

"Oops!" I said. "My dainty hands slipped."

He nodded as if all was fair in love and war. He went to reach for a towel but he faked out and instead lunged for *me*. I screamed, darting over the side benches and trying to escape him. I jumped behind Sean.

"Save me, Sean!"

Sean stood firm like a fortress protecting his people, until of course I realised his people was Toby. And I learned a very valuable lesson as Sean shrugged, as if to say *What's a fella to do?'*

Toby stepped by him and grabbed me.

"How could you?" I cried at Sean in over-exaggerated horror.

Sean held up his hands. "Sorry, my sweet, brothers in arms."

Toby flipped me over his shoulder, my legs flailed and screams echoed across the ranges.

"Toby, put me down!"

"It's been nice knowing you, Tess." He walked me over to the edge of the boat.

I couldn't catch my breath for my own hysteria, it was like getting tickled to the point of madness; he eventually propped me down on the boat ledge. I was leaning precariously backwards, Toby the only thing keeping me from tumbling over the edge: his stomach pressed up against my legs, holding my upper arms.

"Don't you dare!"

His smile was wide and wicked, exposing all his bright white teeth.

He slowly pulled me towards him and leaned his head to the side. My ear tickled, his lips brushing against them as he whispered.

"Tess?" His voice was low and seductive. I was hypnotised by his proximity, his deep brown eyes. I couldn't form words, I just held my breath.

The corners of his lips lifted into a curve. "I'm sorry." And with that, he let go and I plunged backwards into the ice cold lake water.

Chapter Fourteen

I resurfaced, coughing and spluttering, completely sobered and most definitely no longer drunk on Toby.

Just as I gained my breath a huge explosion catapulted next to me, and I flinched against the force as rivulets of water and waves toppled over my head. All of a sudden, Toby appeared from the depths, flicking the excess water from his head in that famous head flick boys do when they swim. He beamed at me.

I retaliated with a splash of water to his face. "You're such a child." I glowered at him.

"Aw, don't be like that," he laughed.

Laughter rang from the boat as Ellie and Sean leaned over the rail, observing us.

"He had little choice, Tess, mutiny means walking the plank."

"Traitor!" I threw back at him.

Sean clenched his heart and looked hurt.

Toby caught my eye, and he didn't even need to say what he was thinking. We were on the same page. On the count of a silent three, we let Ellie and Sean have it. With a unified sweep of water, we saturated them with a giant splash.

Before we knew it, we were set upon by a six-foot-three-inch sized human bomb.

And it was ON!

I decided to escape the caveman display of who could outdrown the other and made a wide berth for the boat.

While Toby and Sean continued to wrestle like rolling crocodiles in the murky lake water, Ellie was waiting for me with a towel and a knowing smile as I hauled myself up the side of the boat.

Toby followed thereafter, causing the boat to dip slightly as he effortlessly hoisted himself in.

Glistening droplets fell off his shoulders and down his flat stomach. I eyed the beads with a slow, lingering look that made me want to reach out and touch them.

Sean was next. He scurried over to Ellie and captured her in a huge, soppy, saturated bear hug.

"Ugh, *don't!*" she grimaced.

"At least you didn't get thrown overboard," I said, as I threw an accusatory glare at Toby. He shrugged as if he had no idea what I was referring to.

"It can be arranged," said Sean as he grabbed for his towel.

Boys.

"Don't even think about it," Ellie threatened.

I realised we could be hoisted overboard at any time if they suddenly felt like it. Although I had secretly loved every single minute of it, there was a part of me that wanted some form of revenge, for the sisterhood. Something to wipe those smug smiles right off their smoking-hot faces. And then I had a cunning plan, it was a risk, but I thought it was my best possible chance.

"You better watch your backs, boys, or you'll be the ones hoisted overboard next."

"That's some serious trash talk, McGee, you think you and your dainty self could take us?" Sean rubbed his head, eyeing me with interest.

I shrugged. "I think I could take Toby."

This scored me some laughing and incredulous looks from them both. Even Ellie lifted her glasses onto her head, her expression suggesting that I had lost my mind.

"Is that right?" Toby asked.

I tried to play it cool. "I'm just saying if push came to shove ..."

I eyed Ellie, hoping to transport some sort of telepathic message to her, but she just stared back at me blankly.

"What do you think, Ellie?" I asked. "Do you think I could outdo Toby … say to …" I looked for a landmark and found one, "the pylon?"

The three of them followed my gaze to the concrete pylon that served as support at the base of the bridge; it looked like a little island. I had seen teenagers lounge and jump off it like a colony of seals, but today it was noticeably barren. Ellie's penny dropped; I knew it had because she gave me a winning smile, and if she was telepathically sending me a message, I could tell it was something like *'DO IT!'*

"Let me get this straight, are you challenging me?" Toby pointed to his chest, as if he could hardly believe it.

Cocky much?

I laughed. "Well, if you're too afraid …"

"Whoa, whoa, whoa … so what are you suggesting, McGee? That you could beat Toby to the pylon?" Sean said.

"Oh, I don't think, I know."

Trash talk was fun.

They both looked over my five-foot-nothing stance. I stood tall and proud, my hands on my hips. Who would have thought that a mere couple of hours before, I was hiding in the ladies' toilets at the hotel, threatening to go home? Now I stood, staring down two seriously hot boys, challenging them, in my soaking wet bikini. An element of self-consciousness came over me as I remembered just how much of my bare flesh was in front of them, a thought that ripped my focus back to the present.

A devilish smile formed on Toby's lips that silently said *'challenge accepted'.*

Ellie and I knew I wasn't outgoing or a go-getter. You wouldn't find me being the life of the party. I was more often than not a wallflower, praying not to be noticed. A creature of habit in all things school and home life, but when it came to the water, now that was where I shone. Naturally, like many a local, we were born on the doorstep of the Lake District. With a small population, there was little else to do for fun other than water activities. Whether it was swimming, water skiing, boogie boarding, fishing, canoeing, or something else – you name it. We were all water bound, one way or another.

My preference was (and always would be) swimming. No one had ever beaten me in sprints to landmarks. My mum's scrapbook was littered with first-place ribbons. I was small and 'dainty' but I was fast ... *real* fast. I looked at Toby and knew I could take him.

Boys being boys, it was clear by the way they looked at me that they underestimated me. And Ellie knew it, too.

Ellie balanced on the edge of the boat, staring out to the pylon.

Toby and I looked each other in the eyes, like two opponents about to face off in the boxing ring.

"Okay! It's simple, when Tess beats you, she'll hand your arse back to you in a hand basket, does that sound fair?" Ellie said.

Only then did Toby's eyes frown from me to Ellie.

"Why don't we make this interesting?" added Sean. "Sort of 'winner takes all'."

"Oh, this sounds good," I agreed.

Toby laughed and shook his head. "You are something else."

My heart threatened to leap out of my chest, as I stared up into his eyes. His crooked smile formed on his lips.

"What do you suggest?"

I bit my lip. Exaggerating deep thought, I clicked my fingers in a Eureka moment.

"If I win, you fix my bike." I was quite pleased with this.

"And ..." added Ellie, "until you do, you have to be her personal chauffeur and take her wherever she needs to go."

My head nearly spun off my shoulders as I threw a dirty look at Ellie, who seemed quite proud of herself.

Toby crossed his arms, uncertainty clouding his eyes.

"That's two things."

"What's wrong, Toby? You afraid?" Ellie teased.

He squared his shoulders. "Fine. Done. But if I win ..." He thought for a moment, flicking a quick look to Sean. "If I win, you have to supply me and the boys with a stash of pies from your mum's shop. Freshly baked and delivered."

Like taking candy from a baby, I thought. And then my heart did a little flip at the realisation that he must have held my mum's pies in really high esteem.

"Shall I put my order in now?" Toby said. "The apple and rhubarb is a particular favourite of mine."

I held up my hand. "Best not to build up your hopes, save the disappointment."

Toby and Sean were enjoying this. In their minds, there was no contest. True, Toby could hurl me around like a ragdoll, but once he entered the water, I was lighter, faster and younger, something I would rub in after I won.

We stood on the edge of the boat, poised for the command. My heart raced as my adrenalin spiked. We gave each other a final long, lingering 'psyche out' look. When you chose to hang with the big boys, you had to prove your metal, earn your respect.

Sean shouted, "On your marks … get set … GO!"

I smashed into the concrete pillar with such force, waves of water carried me forward, and I had to place my hands up to stop myself from slamming into it. I knew I had won. It wasn't by much, but it was enough. Ellie screamed and jumped for joy, dancing around Sean on the boat, who stood with his hands on his head.

"Dude!" he yelled.

Toby and I clutched the concreted ledge, our breaths ragged and our senses blurry as everything slowly caught up to us. He was a mere inches away, looking at me. I managed to smile and once I gulped in enough air, I spoke.

"Hello, slave!"

The boys were surprisingly good losers, and Ellie and I weren't thrown overboard. Instead, after more cruising around the lake, we headed back inland and back to the Onslow Hotel for a drink.

I felt so giddy and fresh from the day in the sun with the boys. With Toby. And he hadn't laughed at me in my barely there bikini; instead, he had looked me over with a lingering male appreciation that I was happy to get used to.

I tied the sheer, matching sarong around my hips so that the split ran along my leg. We arrived as we had left, Ellie and I trailing the boys across the grassy embankment with Sean carrying our beach bag over his shoulder.

"Aren't you glad you wore the bikini?" Ellie whispered.

I just shrugged and played it down. I didn't want to have to admit I was wrong, *again*.

"Oh come on." She shouldered me. "Did you see the look on their faces when you took off your dress? *Priceless!*"

I wanted to press further; in fact, I wanted to stop her dead in her tracks and break out in song: "Tell me more, tell me more." But her thoughts had quickly moved on.

I was interrupted by her high-pitched, ear-tingling squeal. I followed her manic gaze just as she screamed.

"Adam!"

Chapter Fifteen

Adam stood at the top of the embankment under the sweeping verandas of the Onslow Hotel.

We charged forward, running as best we could in our flip flops and wet bathers as we passed Sean and Toby. Sprinting in a direct line, we smashed into Adam, giving him a dual, fierce, bear hug.

"So I guess you're pleased to see me, then," he laughed.

It seemed like an eternity since I had seen him, but really it had only been a few weeks. We were finally all together, where it all began. Even if the circumstances had changed, it mattered little; it was the perfect ending to a pretty freakin' perfect day.

The look Adam gave me as he stood back from our hug made me glance down to check I didn't have anything hanging out that shouldn't have been.

Nope, all in place.

Adam took a subtle step back and chose to strike up a conversation with Ellie. My excitement ebbed. Was that a look of disapproval? All of a sudden I wanted to run and grab my clothes. I felt naked, exposed; Adam had made me feel stupid just by one look.

We sat down on one of the picnic tables. I was across from him and glad of the barrier it provided between us.

I had gone quiet, I couldn't help it. It wasn't like Adam to judge; it was the only way you could survive a friendship that involved Ellie. We had agreed the three of us would always be a judgment-free circle, and it had always been so … until now. He had put a damper on our reunion.

Toby and Sean brought out a tray of drinks and then remembered Adam's presence.

"Sorry, mate, did you want something?" Sean pointed to the bar.

"Ah, no thanks." Adam seemed edgy.

You know the old saying 'two's company, three's a crowd'? Well, the same applies for four's company, five is excruciatingly awkward.

If Adam hadn't turned up, the day would have probably ended with Ellie, Sean, Toby and I having drinks at the Onslow, reliving the day's events with further verbal sparring and razzing. I wouldn't feel ashamed by what I was wearing, and I most certainly wouldn't be sitting here in uncomfortable silence tracing the condensation on my pot glass, trying to stem the tide of anger at Adam that was building up inside me.

I had been so excited to see him. I had no idea he was going to be home this soon, perhaps he hadn't known either, or maybe he'd wanted it to be a surprise. Oh, it was a surprise alright, though it seemed more so for him.

I was itching to punch him in the ribs and ask, "*what was that look for?*", but while we sat with Toby and Sean, I kept quiet.

Sean glanced awkwardly between us and started up a conversation with Adam in an attempt to diffuse the tension. He asked him how things were in the big smoke and how his arm was healing. *Oh crap, his arm.* I snapped out of my daze.

"How is your arm?" I managed.

They both looked at me. Adam was about to reply when Ellie cocked her head.

"What's that scribed on your cast, some city chick's phone number?"

"Pfft, I wish." He twisted his cast so it was readable to us all. Scrawled on the inside arm of his cast in big, black, permanent texta was:

You're GROUNDED! Mum xox

"Kind of a buzz kill for the opposite sex, don't ya think?" He smiled.

I smiled to myself. Typical Adam.

Ellie shrugged. "I think casts are cute."

"Hey, there's Stan," Sean said. We all swiveled around and sure enough, there was Stan through the window at the bar, talking to Chris. Ellie sat up straight; her expression may have been one of disinterest, but her body language gave her away entirely.

"So it is," Ellie said. She pretended not to care but, oh, she cared alright.

"It was nice of him to lend us his boat for the day." I subtly kicked Ellie under the table.

Adam picked at the frayed edge of a beer coaster.

"Now there's a man who burns easily." Sean took a swig of his beer and looked pointedly at Ellie. I didn't get it. Was he saying Stan got sunburnt easily or … I don't know. Was he being metaphorical and saying Stan was a sensitive soul who got burned in love easily? Either way it was directed at Ellie, and by the look on her face, she couldn't decipher what he meant either.

Matching my silence, (in fact trumping it), Toby sat next to Adam, playing with his mobile, intently scowling at the screen.

"What's up, Tobias?" Sean said. "Trouble in paradise?"

"Hmm? Oh … yeah, something like that," Toby said, climbing to his feet. "I'll be back in a sec." He walked off without even looking up, only noticing Stan coming out with Chris as he dodged them.

"What's up with him?" Stan said with a frown.

"Woman trouble."

Stan and Chris groaned as they made themselves at home on the picnic table bench.

A spike of jealousy ran through me as I pictured Toby speaking to Angela on the phone at that exact moment. She would ask him what he had been up to, and he would shrug and say nothing, and that every waking moment without her was torture and please come home soon. Okay, so maybe it wouldn't be *exactly* like that, but my imagination was my nemesis so I zoned out in a cloud of misery.

I caught Adam staring at me, that quizzical frown back in place as he studied me. Seriously, what was his problem today?

"So!" Stan began. "Seeing as though I busted my rump today helping my old man, he agreed that we could have the shed tonight for some extra-curricular festivities." Stan addressed us all, but his lasting gaze was on Ellie, checking her reaction.

"Are you actually going to show up at this event?" she said icily.

He tipped his drink to her. "Yes, ma'am. Gonna crank up some tunes and dust off the old pool table."

"Shweeeeet!" Sean sing-songed.

"Ladies?" Stan asked.

Ellie replied enthusiastically on our behalf, but my inner conscience was thinking about what my mum and dad would think about going to a twenty-two-year-old's party until all hours. I had been out all day and the details of my whereabouts had already been sketchy at best. I hadn't mentioned the Onslow Boys to my parents; I didn't think they'd understand. To them, boys (aside from Adam) were all after one thing: to deflower daughters, get us pregnant and ruin our lives. My parents had nothing to worry about in that area. Seeing as though I was still most likely the last living virgin in Onslow and surrounding regions, I was pretty safe.

But I really wanted to go to this party.

After a while, my heart sank as I realised Toby wasn't returning to the table. I didn't want it to end on such an anti-climactic note. It had been the perfect day. I thought dreamily about the way his hands had glided over my skin, how he held my wrists with such gentle strength, or of when he placed his hand against mine, smiling at the difference. He had been so animated, so lively, more so than I had ever seen him. Maybe that was the way he was with his mates? I rarely saw him uninhibited. I doubt it was due to anything I did; sure, he gave me a look over when he saw me in my bikini, but so had Sean. They were guys and that's what they do; it didn't mean anything.

But Toby wasn't like the other boys; he seemed reserved, quiet and respectful – aside from throwing me overboard, but I liked that side of him, his playful side. And then I envisioned him throwing Angela overboard, and all of a sudden I didn't like that side to him nearly as much.

The Onslow Boys said their goodbyes and said they would see us tonight.

"Hey, Ellie," Stan said as the boys headed towards the door, "can I talk to you for a sec?"

She sighed deeply, but I knew she was secretly delighted.

This left me and Adam, who sat directly opposite me, giving me a strained smile. Oh, no you don't, I thought; there was something underneath that facade that bothered me, and I had to clear the air.

"Why do you keep looking at me like that?"

"Like what?" His eyebrows shot up, like he was genuinely surprised.

"As if there's food on my face and it turns your stomach."

"Wouldn't it be easier to say a look of disgust?"

"Is that what it is? I disgust you?" My voice rose.

"Oh God, Tess, no ... Jesus, keep your voice down," he said, glancing around. "No, that's not it at all." He looked forlorn.

"Then what is it?" I demanded.

"It's nothing, you're just paranoid."

"Don't give me that, I know you well enough to know every single one of your looks, and I have never seen that one before, so spill."

By now the coaster in Adam's hands was shredded into a million tiny pieces, and he was staring at his little pile of cardboard when he offered a low, casual, one-shouldered shrug.

"You look different, you seem different."

I was taken aback, was he serious? I straightened.

"I'm not!"

"Yeah, you're right, okay, good, I'm getting a drink."

"Whoa, whoa, whoa," I said, "back it up, buddy, don't think you can bail on this. What do you mean I've changed? We've barely spoken to each other, how can you gather that?" Had the city pollution warped his brain?

He brushed bits of coaster off his hands.

"Don't mind me, I'm just tired. I only got back this morning and I'm beat."

"So, guess you won't be going to the party, then?"

He scoffed. "Party? You're a real party goer now," he said sarcastically.

He was really starting to tick me off.

"Well, how's about you go and take a nap and wake up on the right side of the bed before you come and see me again." I got up to leave, but he followed me.

"Tess, come back, don't be mad."

I swung around to face him "Don't! God, Adam, this the first time I've seen you in ages and this is how you act?"

He stared me down. Yeah, this wasn't going anywhere.

"You know, I was actually looking forward to you coming home, but I didn't think you would make me feel ..." I broke off looking out at the lake.

"Feel what?"

God, wouldn't he take the hint and leave me alone? I cut him a dark look.

"Make me feel bad about myself."

His brows rose as if I had dished out a physical blow. *Good.*

I turned, chin held high, and strode away.

Chapter Sixteen

After the long, agonising walk home, I shuffled my flip flops across my front lawn and thought to myself how heat stroke can make you delirious.

I stood in the open doorway of the fridge, basking in the coolness that poured over my overheated, sweat-sheened skin. I greedily downed a bottle of water. It was a good thing that Mum and Dad were out as I made my way to peel off my bikini, ever grateful to be rid of it as I headed for the shower.

I let the lukewarm cascade of delicious clean water wash all the sand, sunscreen and sweat from my body. What a disappointing, frustrating end to what had been such an amazing day. Adam's distance, Toby disappearing without so much as a "catch ya later". No, he had to leap to Angela's beck and call. I was grumpy and tired; maybe there was something to Adam's claim of fatigue making him act strange towards me.

But I wasn't in the mood to make excuses for him. I was now too busy trying to think of my own excuses, if I was going to get to Stan's party tonight. I sat on the edge of my bed, the towel wrapped around me. I had darkened at least two shades today, with a slight tinge of red that I hoped was my temperature and anger and *not* sunburn. It was nearing on 6 o'clock, and Mum and Dad would be home any minute. I was pretty beat. Did I even feel like going to the party? Did I just want to crash and wallow? You bet I did. I had dressed myself in my cut-offs and spaghetti strap navy singlet when the phone rang.

"Where are you?" Ellie all but shouted down the phone like a pissed-off parent.

I yawned. "Home."

"I'm coming over." The line went dead.

I groaned and flung myself back on the bed. And so would begin an array of predictable events.

It would start with "What are you wearing? We have to get our stories straight, what's wrong with you? What do you mean you're not going? Of course you're bloody well going!" and so on until I gave in and just went to the party.

My head pounded already.

There was little time to corroborate stories before my parents got home. I felt bad about the half-truths I was feeding them of late but I needed to have some sort of fun over the holidays, it just happened to involve a twenty-something-year-old's party. A twenty-something-year-old *boy*. This wasn't going to be easy.

Mum and Dad had just pulled into the drive when Ellie rocked up in her Sunday best. She radiantly beamed a smile at my parents and chit-chatted pleasantly with them. If only they knew what happened as soon as my bedroom door was closed, and she flipped her backpack off, the contents vomiting onto my bedspread. She all but cried a war chant as she stared me down and started whispering about tonight's plan of attack.

My parents seemed happy enough that Adam was back in town and that we had plans to meet up with him. Those usual occurrences meant late nights watching DVDs at one of our houses. We didn't give the specifics, but I told them I would have my mobile on me. They just told us to have a good time. With an "I'm not sure what time the movies will finish" I was curfew free. Mum and Dad were usually in the deep stage of sleeping by the time I crept through the door. Not that I had made a habit of it. And this was the first time I felt the pang of guilt, because usually what I had just said was the truth.

I folded my make-up bag and choice of clothing in Ellie's pack; we would go via her place for the change so as not to raise any questions. Ellie's mum was a nurse and on night shift, so we could be in and out undiscovered. Ellie's dad would barely glance up at us, especially if the cricket was on. I had always thought her incredibly lucky to be given such a free rein, but now, the lack of attention they paid her made me kind of sad.

"So has Adam been filled in on our plan of deceit?" I asked rather unenthusiastically.

"He has and he is going to meet us there." Ellie looked at me side on as we walked along the street.

But I didn't offer any reaction. I half expected her to ask what was going on between us but either she didn't want to pry or she was way too distracted by Stan and his impending party to worry herself with the drama. I was betting on the latter. She talked animatedly about Stan, and how he had apologised again for not coming. Said he'd make it up to her. I'd tuned out by the time we crossed McLean's Bridge.

The plan was to rendezvous at the Onslow Hotel, before wandering off to Stan's later on. It felt surreal and a bit intimidating walking up the grassy embankment, even though we had been there only a mere hours beforehand. This time the sun had dimmed and the fairy lights lit the eaves above the picnic tables that were now occupied by a mass of people, enjoying the music from within. We had never been here when we weren't working. Never been ordinary patrons. I felt as if I didn't know what to do with my hands, as if I should be reaching and collecting empty glasses on the way in. We were stared down by a group of older girls, and were cast a wink and a smile by a guy we brushed passed; some older gents nodded "Ladies" as we weaved our way to the bar.

Chris was flat out taking money and filling pots; he looked up to see us standing before him as he pulled on the beer tap. His serious gaze didn't change.

"Two Lemon Ruskis, please, Chris," Ellie said sweetly.

"Everyone's in there, don't draw attention to yourselves." He set two glasses of coke on the bar for us, and walked away to serve the next customer. I guessed that was a no to the Ruskis, then.

Ellie slumped in bitter disappointment. "Could we look any more like teenagers?"

"We are teenagers," I said.

"Yeah, but I don't have to be reminded." She took a long draw from her straw. "I suppose people might think it's Bourbon and Coke?" she said hopefully.

"Well, don't complain too much, they were free. I doubt Chris's generous mood will last."

The poolroom was packed, a trail of gold coins lined up along the pool table's ledge indicating there was a fair wait for the next game. The forty-four-gallon barrels dotted around the room were stained by circles of drinks and ashtrays, as people sat around them on bar stools. The couch in the far corner was overcrowded to the point people were forced to sit on the coffee table or perch on the arms of the chair. The French doors were wide open letting a breeze roll off the lake and filter through the bar, which helped a little with the smoke and strong cologne all the boys caked on for the night's festivities. I was only interested in one kind of cologne and I looked around, wondering who Chris had been referring to when he directed us to the poolroom.

Then I saw him.

Toby was leaning in the alcove of the French doors, talking to someone I didn't know, a shorter guy with a buzz cut and a sock tan that clashed against his boat shoes. He leaned closer to him struggling to hear over the loud music. 'Hurts So Good' blared from the flashing jukebox. A couple of girls flipped eagerly to find some Shania Twain. Ellie spotted Stan leaning over the bar for a straw; she made her way over, sneaking up behind him, and whispered in his ear.

"Hands behind the bar, please," she said. He spun around, grinning from ear to ear.

"You're not going to tell the big guy upstairs, are you?" he teased.

"Maybe, can't make any promises."

I wanted to roll my eyes at the goofy looks they were giving each other, but an inner pang of jealousy overcame me. I envied how they could be openly flirtatious with one another. They were sending out signals to each other, and they both knew they were reciprocated. I was used to unrequited love and just as I was about to cast my usual doe-eyed longing glance across the room to the boy I knew I couldn't have, I froze to see his eyes were on me. I smiled, and he mirrored me. I made my way over, and he watched my every step as he took a deep drink from his beer then placed it on the window ledge and leaned back on the doorframe.

I looked at his beer with an arched brow.

"Can't even hold your own beer," I said. "Are your arms that sore from all the swimming today?"

"Almost as sore as my ego, but I'll live." He looked at my drink with a frown. I didn't want to have to confirm I was only drinking Coke. I wanted to pretend as Ellie had done that I was not seventeen, and that I was just hanging with a boy in a bar on a summer's night.

"I'll have the contract drawn up by my solicitor and have it to you as a matter of urgency." I felt nervous, half thinking that he would laugh at me and say, *You didn't expect me to follow through with the bet, did you? I was only joking, kiddo.* But instead he grinned; it was the teeth-exposing kind, the true grin, the unhinged Toby that made my tummy flutter.

"I suppose two out of three would be out of the question?" he mused.

"Not on your life, I couldn't handle the humiliation," I said.

"Yours or mine?" he laughed.

"Wow, were you seriously not there today when I shamed you? You were literally choking on the lake water I was kicking up in your face."

He crossed his arms, laughing. I sipped on my drink, innocently looking at him, loving every minute of our exchange, the exchange I was hoping to have this afternoon that never happened.

Toby was wearing jeans and a navy polo shirt. He smelled amazing, his cologne was fresh and sharp. I wanted to step closer to bask in it all.

Instead, I played it cool, waiting for his retort.

"Tess, if it wasn't for your manicured nails, I would have beaten you today, that's how close it was, photo finish."

"You mean I have my dainty nails, on my dainty hands, to thank?"

He picked up his beer, and then nudged me playfully with his foot.

"You know I didn't mean anything by it, right? When I said your hands were dainty. I meant it as a good thing."

"Oh yeah, sure." *Act cool, Tess.*

I knew it wasn't meant in a spiteful way. Had I gone home and looked up the meaning of dainty in my pocket Macquarie dictionary? Maybe. Did the meaning state:

Dainty: Delicately pleasing in appearance of movement?

It sure did.

And perhaps he didn't know the meaning of the word so thoroughly as I did now, but it definitely wasn't meant as a bad thing.

As we gave each other a sly smile, each almost lost in our own world, a figure walked in the open French doors and wrapped herself around Toby like an octopus.

"There you are! I wondered where you got to." Angela smiled.

And the moment was gone.

Angela completely ignored my presence, turning her back to me as she pawed at Toby who stiffened in the surprise of her appearance.

So much for being away for two weeks.

"You sure you won't come?" She pouted.

"No, you go with the girls. Have a good time." He held her upper arms, which were linked around his neck. I tried to sidestep away. I wanted to dissolve into the crowd, retreat into wallflower Tess again. I was about to back out of the French doors when I heard it, that all-too-familiar voice shout out from behind me.

"TIC TAC?"

Chapter Seventeen

There are many levels of mortification.

I turned slowly around and there he was. Scott, frozen on the footpath outside the French doors, looking at me as if he couldn't quite believe his eyes. Oh no. No. Shattering a glass had been embarrassing. Wearing the teeny tiny bikini had been humiliating. But nothing – nothing compared to the flush of mortification, the rush of horrible high school memories. I felt it in Mr Burke's Biology class when he read out that stupid note and coloured the rest of my high school experience with that stupid name. But nothing compared to the shame I felt now, in front of the Onslow Boys – in front of Toby.

Angela, Toby, the girls at the jukebox, Sean from outside and even Chris, flat out in the bar, still managed to hear over the deafening music and collective chatter. He may as well have shouted through a megaphone, it was *that* loud.

"I thought it was you, we were just on our way to Stevie's when Dusty said, 'Hey isn't that Tic Tac?'" Scott said. "I thought 'no way is it Tic Tac; Tic Tac Tess would never be hanging in a bar'."

Oh God, could he say that name any more times?

It was like someone punching me, again and again, punching a hole in my chest. And the worst thing was, he wasn't even trying to be malicious. To him, it was just my name.

But to me, it really wasn't. I couldn't breathe. I had to get out of there. I had to. Scott was polluting the air with his mouth, and I could feel Angela and Toby's eyes burning into the back of my head. I just gave a small smile and excused myself, darting through the crowd, straight to the refuge of the Ladies' toilets.

Again!

I slammed through the door and clutched the basin with a white-knuckled intensity, thankful that I was alone. I flipped on the faucet and concentrated on the water, its circular motion around the sink and down the drain as it made its way out into the great beyond. Oh, how I wished I could go where it was going. I didn't dare look at my reflection; I didn't want to see my scarlet flushed cheeks, or the tears that welled in my eyes. Why here? Why now? I had been doing so well. I had finally started to become something more than high school, more than that name. But then Scott thrust me straight back there. No, he had done worse than that, he had brought it into my new world, where I was not Tic Tac, I was simply Tess McGee.

I had become a girl that could hold her own, could verbally spar and even flirt with the best of them. But now it was all tarnished. As soon as I gathered myself, I would walk out of here and just go home. It was a good plan. Ellie wouldn't mind, she had Stan to hang with, and I would be home by a decent hour, and keep my parents happy. Win-win.

The door opened, and I knew it would be Ellie checking on me. But it wasn't. Angela sauntered in and propped her designer bag on the basin as she smoothed out a perfectly manicured eyebrow with the tip of her equally perfectly manicured fingernail.

I busied myself with washing my hands, a task I pretended to be so fascinated by, that I couldn't even tear my eyes from them. She was still; I could feel her watching me in the reflection of the mirror. I pretended not to notice. She tilted her head a little in my direction.

"It's Tess, isn't it?" she asked in a gentle voice.

"Yes," I managed to say.

She ran her fingers through her hair, fixing her already perfect reflection.

I could see her eyes dart to my chest, and I felt myself flush even further, if that was possible.

"You're not small, you know?"

Oh my God, this was not happening?

She turned fully to me, facing me directly. There was no denying it: yeah, this was really happening.

"He's probably never even touched a booby in his life." She shrugged and turned back to the mirror to reapply her lip gloss. "I would seriously doubt he is an expert on the subject." She pouted at herself in the mirror and scrunched her hair.

Was Angela Vickers going all deep and meaningful on me? And did she seriously just say booby? Who *says* that?

She cast me a fleeting smile and without a word, picked her bag up off the counter and sashayed out of the bathroom.

I stood stunned from what I could have sworn was a small act of kindness from Angela Vickers. I didn't know exactly how I felt about it.

I could do one of two things. Get Chris to sweep up my shattered ego off the poolroom floor, while I ran out the back door. Or two, I could play the 'ignorance is bliss' hand and go out and pretend that it didn't even happen, all while completely avoiding Toby for the rest of the night. I was so humiliated I couldn't even bring myself to look at him. Maybe Adam was right. I had changed, and Scott had wrenched me jarringly back down to reality. Reminded me who I was. I pulled my mobile out and began to text.

To: Adam
Fashionably late as usual? Where R U at bozo?
We're at the O Hotel.

A second later the screen lit up.

Adam
Bozo?? I'm out the front.

And with that, I gathered myself together (making sure I didn't look too pitiful) and left my refuge to hang with Adam. Instead of going with the flow, I was going to go with what I know.

And I knew Adam.

We made peace. Things seemed back to normal between us as we both obviously didn't want to bring up the conversation from earlier. Turned out Adam was only home for the weekend, so I was glad that I had this time with him. We sat on the outside picnic table, sharing a packet of crisps, when we saw Angela and four of her friends pile into a car. They were way too overdressed for Onslow. They must have been heading to Redding, the next biggest city half an hour away; it was the place to go once you turned eighteen.

Adam snared the last chip.

"So you going to Stan's later?" he asked.

"I don't know, not fussed either way."

"Who's going to look after Ellie?"

"I think she will be right. Stan's a good guy."

"Yeah. I don't think she'd know if we were there or not, the way they're making doe eyes at each other." He shuddered.

"Well, well, well, what do we have here?" My seat dipped as Sean sat down next to me. Toby was right behind him, standing at the head of the table. His cool, reserved manner was back and I mentally slapped myself for the flips my traitorous stomach made at the sight of him.

Get a grip, Tess.

"We're heading off soon, there is far too much Shania Twain pouring out of the jukebox."

"The netball girls are on a bit of a rampage tonight," added Toby.

Sean stood. "You coming?"

I made a point not to look at Toby even though I could feel his eyes on me, waiting for my reply. Instead, I looked at Adam and posed the question to my best friend.

"What do you wanna do? It's your weekend."

"Hmm. Shania Twain or a party at Stan's?" He drummed his chin thoughtfully with his finger.

"I don't know how much better it will be," Sean said. "I'm pretty sure you'll be reduced to witnessing Ellie and Stan suck face all night if their actions in the bar are anything to go by."

I cringed. I'd left her alone for five minutes, and she had

already publicly disgraced herself.

"One thing I *can* be sure of, though, there will be no chick power ballads," Sean added.

I pouted. "What? No 'I am woman, hear me roar'?"

"Definitely not!"

Either we were to stay at the Onslow with the netballers and be subjected to tabletop dancing or head to Stan's for a game of pool and semi-decent music. Deep down, okay, not even too deep down, I knew what my choice was. I knew it the second I looked up at Toby.

We walked through the night, making our way to the caravan park nearby. We gave up worrying about waiting for Stan and Ellie who were stopping every five minutes for a quick pash against a tree. I wanted to get as far away from them as possible. The rest of us walked in uncomfortable silence, and Ellie giggled and squealed followed by sucking noises behind us. Over and over again.

I felt the butterflies in the pit of my stomach. I didn't miss Scott, that was for certain, but I did miss the weight of a boy on top of me, making out for hours, and chaste stolen kisses on the walk home at night. I missed the heart palpitations and the strange stirrings I was only just beginning to understand. I missed being the object of someone's affection.

As we walked, Adam and Sean played footy with a crushed beer can, even going so far as to run some commentary for themselves. According to the commentators (Adam and Sean), Sean was the number one Champion in the World and Adam was the undefeated five-time Premiership Captain.

They were somewhat ambitious. I laughed at their deluded fantasies as they darted further in front of Toby and me.

And then I was painfully aware that I was walking in the dark with a boy. Not *a* boy, *the* boy. But I couldn't have him. I couldn't steal kisses from him. I shouldn't even look at him the way I do, the way I always have. Still, it didn't stop me from wanting to walk closer to him, just so I could listen to his breathing or his low laugh as Sean tripped over his own foot.

"And the World Champion goes down!" he mused.

"Oh no! The impact of his ego hitting the ground could tilt the world off its axis," I added.

"Tsunamis and earthquakes will ripple through the world."

"A crater will form and create a new lake system."

"Where are you heading? Oh, we're just going to Lake Sean."

We both lost it in dual fits of laughter at our own commentary.

"What's so funny?" Sean asked, but we were far too amused to answer.

We stopped at the gate to Remington's Caravan Park, thinking it only appropriate to wait for the host of the party to lead the way. Toby climbed onto the gate and sat, while I fidgeted with impatience and shuffled from one leg to the other. Finally, a figure appeared from the darkness. Ellie was walking, her eyes cast down, arms crossed against her chest as if stemming off a wayward chill that didn't exist.

"Where's Stan?" Sean asked.

She walked straight past us through the gate. "Who cares?" she said coldly.

Adam and I looked at each other with grim expressions.

Uh-oh.

"Is she alright?" Toby jumped down from the gate.

"Yeah, it's probably nothing," I said. Knowing Ellie, it was definitely something, so friend duty beckoned, and I followed her into the park.

I sat opposite Ellie on one of the logs that had been cut purposefully and arranged in a circle. So campers could sing 'Kumbaya', probably. It took everything in me not to so much as crack a smile as I stared blankly at Ellie, registering what she just told me. She was pretty upset so I had naturally thought the worst: that nice guy Stan wasn't actually a nice guy after all and tried to force Ellie into something back in the bushes. But as unlikely as it seemed, I was truly taken back when I found out why Ellie was *actually* so distraught.

"You know how I have put on a bit of weight since school stopped ..."

I didn't know or notice. Still I humoured her with patient silence, urging her to continue.

"Well, we were kissing and his hands were wandering around my back. Which distracted me and I just said to him as a joke, 'Don't touch my flabby bits' and then he said 'But I like every part of you, even your flabby bits'. Can you believe he said that?"

I cringed inwardly, not because he said what he said, but because my heart went out to the guy. What had been meant as a really nice compliment along the lines of 'I like you just the way you are' had received punishment. He had suffered one hell of a case of foot in mouth that would take Ellie some getting over.

"He said I was fat!"

I grabbed her hand and gave it a reassuring squeeze. "Oh Ellie, that's not what he meant."

"Well, that's what he said." She sniffed.

Oh God, how did I even begin to save this train wreck? I knew she wouldn't see reason. So I did what best friends do. I deflected.

"Scott called me Tic Tac in front of the entire bar, in front of Angela and Sean, Chris and Toby."

Ellie's eyes narrowed with sympathy. Yep, it was working.

"Don't worry, Tess, they don't know what it stands for."

I gave a half smile. "Angela knows what it means, so they'll know."

"Oh, fuck Angela," she snapped.

My eyes widened.

"Who cares, anyway, stuff them all, let's go find Adam and have a good time. We can make our own fun. You, me and Adam and my back fat."

I burst out laughing, and even Ellie joined me. We had managed to drag each other out of the depths of despair once again. We heard a snap of a branch to see Adam appear with a guarded look on his face.

"Everything okay?" His eyes flicked from my face to Ellie's.

We could only manage to nod.

"Do you need me to call Stan out? Kick his arse?"

This only made us laugh even harder.

"I'm serious," he straightened. "I could take him."

Ellie snorted which made Adam break into a smile and join us in our laughter. The kind where the outside world would look in on us and think we were mad. Though it had been a bit rocky this afternoon, we were back. We understood each other perfectly and no matter what, we would always be there for one another.

"Oh, my God! I gotta go pee, wait for me?" Ellie wandered off to find the toilet block. I wiped away tears that had emerged after laughing so hard. Adam straddled the log to sit next to me.

"Seeing as this seems to be some kind of circle of truth," he said, "I have a confession to make."

All of a sudden, I was very sober and my laughter died down as I looked into Adam's serious, earnest eyes.

"I did give you a funny look today." He started to pick at the bark on the log, a sign that he was uneasy.

"I just didn't recognise you; when I was standing on the porch at the hotel I saw Ellie walking up with some girl, and I was watching this girl, in this hot, white bikini, and I thought I have to know this girl, and then you came closer and I saw it was you, but it couldn't be you. This girl was so carefree, confident. I thought it was the sexiest thing I had ever seen. Then you looked up and saw me, and the look on your face was the Tess I knew. The goofy Tess McGee. I was a bit taken back. I saw the way Toby and Sean were looking at you, and I kind of went all Alpha male on you."

He smiled sadly.

I didn't dare breathe or think about asking what he meant by the way Sean or Toby looked at me. I just remained quiet.

"I was just being a jackass. I had only been away for a few weeks and I felt, I don't know, replaced. Pretty stupid, huh?"

"Yes," I said, "idiotic! As if I could replace you!" I kicked him. So he wasn't judging me – well, not in the way that I had thought.

"Adam, you're my best friend and that's not going to change, I can tell you that, so stop going all Alpha on me, okay? Unless you want to avenge my honour with a banana because you can totally do that anytime you want."

He kicked me back, and we were us again.

"So ... you thought I was sexy, huh?"

He threw his head back and groaned.

"You thought I was sexy." I grinned.

Adam rolled his eyes.

"You totally love me, you want to write me poetry, and ..."

Adam covered my mouth with his hand, which only made me laugh. "What is revealed in the circle of truth remains in the circle of truth."

"Nuh-uh, only if the circle of truth has a cone of silence and as you can see …" I lifted my hands up to the sky. "Nothing."

He gave me a bored look.

It was then a delayed thought registered. "So what you're saying is the goofy Tess you know is *not* sexy?"

"Ugh, Tess, quit it already!"

"No, no, I want to know," I said. I pointed to myself. "You wouldn't want to tap this?"

"Right now I want to choke you."

He slid over to me and grabbed me closer to him. My smile fell from my face with the unexpectedness of it. His hands cupped my face, his lips hovering above mine.

"You seriously want to know, Tess?"

He closed the space and claimed my mouth with an urgent, hot, delving kiss.

He smiled. "You are sexy, in your own goofball way, you're sweet and beautiful and smart and funny and, although you kiss to the point where I feel like I want to go back for seconds, you're my best friend, and that's why I don't want to tap that."

I was breathing heavily, he had wiped my brain blank, all thoughts, all smart-arse retaliation, everything evaporated from my mind. He thought all those things of me, but, above all, he valued our friendship. It was something I would cherish for the rest of my life.

There was a coughing sound, and I broke away from Adam with such speed I nearly toppled off the log. The Onslow Boys stood before us. Sean gave a wry smile. Toby was deadly serious, and poor Stan's worried eyes weren't focused on us; he had his own troubles. My eyes darted back to Toby, who unflinchingly stared back at me with a deep, burning gaze.

"Don't mind us." Sean propped himself on the opposite log. As usual, Toby chose to stand.

"Do you know where Ellie went?" Stan asked. "Is she still pissed?"

Adam answered for me. "A word of advice, Stan, let that one cool down for a bit."

It was Ellie's laughter that sent me in the opposite direction of the toilet blocks. I found her near the swimming pool talking to a couple of tall boys with towels draped around their necks, smiling down at Ellie.

"Tess! Come and meet Wes and Mark."

I didn't want to meet Wes and Mark. I just wanted to get to the shed, and I wanted Ellie in tow.

I offered a pleasant enough smile as I turned to Ellie. "They're waiting for us."

"Oh, right!" Ellie agreed (thank God!).

"Do you guys wanna come to a party?"

"Uh, Ellie, I don't think we're in a position to invite people," I whispered.

"Oh, it'll be fine." She waved me away, which really got my back up.

"Half of Onslow will be there, and the boys are staying at the caravan park anyway, right?"

I knew exactly what she was up to, and I did not like 'Operation Make Stan Jealous' one bit.

"Whatever! Do what you want, I know you will anyway," I snapped and walked off without so much as a backwards glance.

I loved Ellie, but she sure could infuriate me sometimes.

Chapter Eighteen

I followed the thunderous rock music that filtered through the night.

It led me towards a giant shed that housed an array of mismatched sofas, a pool table, a folded down table tennis; aside from the high tech stereo and a giant television, the rest looked like stuff that had been salvaged from hard rubbish day. It was a man's paradise!

Sure the style was stuck in the 70s, but the shed was packed with people, most I had never seen before. Seriously, *did I know anyone here?*

'Heartache Tonight' thumped out of the mounted sound system, and I tried not to scoff at how appropriate the song choice was. I spotted Toby reading the back of a CD cover near the stereo, when he looked up at me.

I wandered over. "Your choice, no doubt?"

"What makes you say that?" He looked back down at the cover.

"Oh, I don't know, seems like your kind of music. Plus you were playing The Eagles in your car."

He didn't say anything.

I picked up the cover to the album, looking over the track list. It was the same as my dad's tape I had been listening to in my room.

"I like number nine," I announced.

Toby didn't respond; instead, as the song faded out he took the CD from my hands and put it into the player, flicking it to song nine. Then he turned and sat on the couch.

Huh. Maybe he'd had a fight with Angela? I silently hoped so. I sat next to him as Timothy Schmit's voice filled the room, with 'I Can't Tell You Why'. I tilted my head down, getting in his eye line to coax him to look at me.

"Please don't make me have to use a really hideous cliché," I whined.

That had him looking at me, frowning as if he didn't speak English.

I rolled my eyes. "Fine. You asked for it: penny for your thoughts."

"Oh." That made him smile. "Yeah, that's pretty hideous."

At a loss as to what to say, I thought I would give not being a smart arse a go and see how that worked.

"Look, you don't have to fix my bike. I was just razzing you about it."

His gaze flicked up. "No, no, a deal's a deal … I don't mind."

"Just saying."

"Do you need a lift home later?" he blurted out.

I stammered at the question.

"That was a part of the second condition, wasn't it?"

"Ah, yeah, it was." I felt all uncertain and coy.

"Just checking." He leaned back on the couch, his eyes lighting with that familiar spark.

"I haven't read the contract yet, so I'm a bit fuzzy on the details."

I smiled and shook my head. "My secretary is so fired."

Toby seemed to relax. "Give her a go, she's probably out on the town with the netball girls."

"Ha! Even more reason to sack her."

"I wonder if there is any Shania Twain in here somewhere." He jumped up to paw through the CD collection again.

"Don't you dare." I grabbed his arm, pulling him backwards. His eyes darted to where my hand rested on him. I didn't move my hand, I couldn't physically bring myself to break the contact; all of a sudden there were no smiles, no jokes, just him and me and our space on the couch. I could only hear the music and be aware of the heat of his skin and the rapid rise and fall of my chest in this moment.

The only thing that snapped me out of my daze was Toby's words which seemed low and raspy.

"Is Adam your boyfriend?" His gaze flicked over my face as he waited for my answer. My mouth gaped open; I couldn't hide the fact I was dumbfounded by the question.

I blinked quickly and took my hand from his arm. I struggled to construct a legible sentence.

"Oh – um, no, we're just friends, it's not like that."

His stony expression didn't falter, didn't reveal any kind of emotion. He was so hard to read, and I wanted to read him so badly. He gave a small nod and handed me the CD cover.

"Better go and make sure these guys aren't cheating." And without another word, he got up and headed towards the pool table.

I tried to gather my thoughts. He had been intense and distant, and then we were joking and then BAM, an out-of-the-blue question, and then he was gone.

I didn't want to sit there with a perplexed look on my face all night, so I headed for the fridge for a drink, only to spot Ellie walking into the shed with the taller tourist, Wes. Oh yes, she did!

Adam wandered over and took the open can from my hand.

"She works fast."

Everyone's eyes went to Stan who was standing by the pool table, glaring at the happy new arrivals. Toby patted him on the back and handed him the pool cue, flicking Sean his own unamused look.

"What must people think of us?" I said.

"Ellie's her own person. It's got nothing to do with us."

"Yeah, but guilt by association and all that."

"I don't think you could ever be compared to Ellie, Tess, you two are chalk and cheese."

Ellie laughed obnoxiously loud at whatever Wes had said. My heart sank. Ellie's stupid games really bugged me. I just never understood the logic; you like someone, they like you, isn't it a no-brainer? My gaze rested on Toby who was lining up for his shot.

What would I know? When I wasn't making out with my best friend, I was mooning and flirting with a very-much-taken twenty-two year old. Yep! I was all about the moral high ground.

"When did things become so complicated?" I sighed.

"No idea. I must say, I'll be glad to head back to the city and watch re-runs of M*A*S*H; you girls are far too exciting for me these days."

"Oh? Must be the new Tess, that's far too cool for school. Got to make sure I don't lose myself by the time you get back next."

I elbowed Adam playfully.

"You better not."

I frowned. "I won't, dummy."

"Just saying." We turned to watch the pool game.

"Do you want some words of advice, Tess?"

I glanced at Adam's profile as he sipped.

"Don't give your heart away too easily." He turned to me. "Make him earn it."

And with that, cheers echoed throughout the shed. Toby potted the black.

I'd had enough of cryptic messages, and didn't get a chance to ask Adam who exactly he was referring to. Who had to earn my heart? And why didn't I get the chance to press him further? He was suddenly too busy glaring across the room. I followed his gaze and my eyes froze on the only thing that could possibly have evoked such a reaction in Adam, because it evoked the same in me.

Scott, Steve and Dusty walked into the shed like a bitter wind. So much for avoiding the horrors of high school.

Sean sauntered over to get another beer from the fridge beside us.

"What is he doing here?" Adam spoke, low and bitter.

I just shook my head in amazement. "It's Onslow. You can't swing a dead cat without hitting someone you know."

I wondered how Ellie could stand it? Hooking up with all these different boys and constantly running into them. But then again, nothing much really got to Ellie, I mused, as she flirted with

Wes right in front of Stan.

Sean followed Adam and my seething glares.

"What's the deal?"

"Tess's ex." Adam glowered.

Sean laughed with surprise. "Geez, Tess, how much more of a trail of broken hearts can you leave? You're a lucky man, Adam, best defend your honour."

"We're just friends!"

Adam frowned. Maybe that had come out a bit loud.

"You don't have to sound like the idea repulses you so much."

"That's my cue," Sean said, retreating back to the pool table.

Scott made his way over to us.

"Don't you move," I warned Adam.

"Hadn't planned on it."

"Tess, Hendo, what's happening?" Scott spoke like we were long-lost buddies.

"Thought you were going to Stevie's?" Go on, run away, I thought.

"Apparently this is where all the action is." He looked over at Ellie and Wes who were getting closer and closer, leaning in to each other to speak over the music, which wasn't that loud anymore.

Scott's gaze focused on me, giving me a long, lingering once over, with a smile I just wanted to wipe clean off his face.

"Looking good tonight, Tess."

"Well commit it to memory, because we're out of here." Adam grabbed my hand to leave, but Scott stepped in front of him.

"Whoa, whoa, whoa, Hendo, I was just talking to the lady."

"Lady, is it, tonight?" I said. "Not frigid, or Tic Tac or some other degrading nickname?" I spoke slowly, quietly, but I couldn't wholly contain my venom.

"Oh, come on, Tess, you know I'm just razzing."

"Step aside, Millo," Adam said sarcastically.

Scott's smile turned snide. "Wait a minute, Tess, you're not fucking Hendo, are you?" He started to laugh like the snivelling germ he really was.

"No, she's fucking me."

A deep voice floated over from behind Scott, who instantly sobered, his eyes widening as he turned to face a wall of Sean's muscular chest. Sean looked down on him with a cold, hard stare. The entire shed went deathly quiet as they watched the showdown. I squeezed Adam's hand, threatening to break his skin.

"What of it?" Sean's voice was low and filled with malice.

I heard Scott gulp as he assessed the danger he was in. His eyes darted from Sean to me as if hardly believing that such a pairing could be possible. I just smiled sweetly at Scott, quirking my brow, silently daring him.

Go on, just try it!

"Your shot, babe." Sean passed me the pool cue. Because? ... Oh yeah. I was like, totally playing pool with my fictional boyfriend.

I took the cue from Sean who stepped aside, touching me lovingly on the lower back to usher me past.

Oh, he was good.

He continued to stare down Scott who couldn't hold eye contact.

"You come near Tess again, and you and your friends will be fish bait. My old mate Tobias over there ..."

Toby gave him a two-fingered salute from his brow.

"... Well, his family is connected to the Mafia, and they don't look too kindly on little boys walking in uninvited and harassing our friends."

Toby flicked me a perplexed look, like he had no idea what Sean was talking about, and Stan's smile reappeared to the point he had to turn his back on the scene so as not to give the game away.

Steve and Dusty looked like a pair of rabbits in the headlights.

Steve croaked, "We were just leaving, weren't we, Scott?"

Scott nodded quickly and backed away, his face ashen.

None of them dared to even look my way as they quickly made their exit. As soon as they were gone, well, that's when laughter erupted.

Sean came up to me. "Sorry, Tess, no doubt we're going to be the next hot gossip in Onslow."

"I dare say all of Onslow and Perry will know by now," added Adam.

"The Mafia? Really?' Toby shook his head.

"How come you didn't give my family underworld status?" Stan asked, his expression surprisingly earnest.

"Come on, Stan. Look at Toby, all dark and broody, he could easily be linked to the mob, now if you were connected to the Irish mob, you would have been perfect."

"Maybe next time." I said. Stan seemed to have momentarily forgotten about Ellie and Wes, until she spoke.

"That was the funniest thing I have ever seen, can we hire you for all occasions?"

"Weddings and Bar Mitzvahs." Sean nodded.

Ellie came over and hugged me. "We're heading off now," she whispered in my ear. I shot her a look that begged her not to, but she just winked at me, her mind made up.

"Might see you guys later." She deliberately directed her speech away from Stan who had immediately soured again. Poor Stan.

This was one night I would not be waiting for Ellie. She made her own decisions so she could deal with the fallout. Wes took her hand and guided her out of the shed. The party atmosphere fizzled out as we all watched them leave.

Adam whispered in my ear. "So that's okay with you, is it? Making everyone believe Sean and you are together?"

"Ellie is about to wander off into the dark with a stranger and you're asking me about a mythical relationship? If it means Scott leaves me alone for the rest of my life, then Onslow is welcome to think I'm Sean's girlfriend.'

I turned from Adam to walk over to Sean. I stood on my very tippy toes and, placing my hands on his shoulders, I kissed him on the cheek.

"Over the top, but thank you."

Sean beamed a winning smile at me. "People talking about me and you? I don't mind the thought of that one bit."

The moment for appreciation was interrupted by a thunderous crack of the billiard balls as Toby broke with a shattering force.

"Sean, you're up!"

Chapter Nineteen

Great. Both Adam and Toby seemed in a mood.

Tonight was not turning out to be ideal. The rest of the night went by with a certain lack of drama. I just sat and watched the boys play pool, drank too much soft drink and tried to forget about Ellie.

They tried to coax me into playing pool, but my heart wasn't in it. Adam snapped out of his bad mood after a little while, never one to hold a grudge, but Toby seemed a little off, just like he had been when I first walked in. Maybe he was thinking about what Angela was getting up to. Maybe he was annoyed by all the teenage gatecrashing and resented Adam and I even being there. I managed to convince myself that it had something to do with me, to the point I felt utterly miserable and decided to bow out early, say my goodbyes and go home.

Adam agreed to walk with me, and then the Onslow Boys had had enough too and decided to walk with us back to the Onslow.

Stan walked us out to the gates, he had his hands in his pockets, shoulders slumped, forehead furrowed; he looked like he had seen better days. I wanted to tell him to forget Ellie, to say something that would make him feel better, but I had nothing to add. Probably just as well because now, surrounded by his mates, was not the time or place.

We navigated our way through the darkened streets, the four of us walked the long stretch back to the Onslow Hotel. I only hoped that we wouldn't bump into Ellie on the way.

Sean talked a lot, mostly just to drown out our gloomy silence.

Adam and even Toby added additional remarks on the fishing at the weir, but I zoned out midway, setting a fast pace, eager to end the night. If they thought I was quiet, no one said anything. They might have thought I was upset over the Scott incident or Ellie. I doubted they would ever suspect in a million years that it was actually because I feared that any ground I'd made today with Toby was lost. I would go home and he would go home and Angela would probably get dropped off at his place tonight. I felt sick to my stomach. And angry. How could I have been so stupid? I knew he had a girlfriend. There was no way me and Toby could end well.

It had been great of Sean to defend my honour, but in all honesty I was a little put out that it hadn't been Toby. Of course, it wouldn't have worked because everyone knew he was with Angela. Still, I wondered if he was annoyed at Sean, dragging him into it. Who knew? All I knew was every time I tried to catch his eye he would make an effort to avoid mine. He walked on the opposite side of our group, Adam and Sean between us. I didn't know what his problem was but all of a sudden I didn't care as I could see the glowing window lights of the Onslow Hotel. It wasn't quite twelve yet, so there was still time for a lock-in. It occurred to me this was probably their plan: play more pool, reclaim the jukebox and say goodbye to us pesky teenagers.

Adam was crashing the night at the Onslow. He had his pick of the rooms upstairs as most tourists stayed in the holiday parks rather than stay at a pub with its overpriced, un-refurbished rooms. So vacancies were pretty high at the Onslow, they made more money out of meals and the bar than having to worry too greatly about accommodation. Uncle Eric didn't have much flair for such things and Claire Henderson was never around. I gathered she must have been present at some stage as there were touches of her taste dotted all around the restaurant. John Waterhouse paintings lined the walls, a shiny black grand piano, plush mahogany and cream rugs with black fringed borders, antique-style furnishings and subtle lighting added for ambience. The woman was highly strung, but I couldn't fault her taste.

Sean and Toby walked in the open door heading straight for the main bar. I paused outside and Adam hovered, waiting for me as I dialed my mobile.

Ellie's phone went straight to voice message, and I sighed in irritation as I waited for the beep.

"If you received this message I can only assume you haven't been murdered and buried in a shallow grave somewhere. It's 11.40 and I'm heading home."

"How you getting home?" Adam asked.

"It's a nice night." I shrugged. "I'll walk."

"And you're worried about *Ellie* being murdered."

"I'll be fine, I've done it a million times from yours and Ellie's houses before."

"That wasn't quite so far."

"Stop being an old woman."

"I can't help it, I've been hanging with one for too long."

"Well, you are who you hang with."

"Well, in that case don't go turning into an Onslow Boy, you're too pretty for that."

"I don't need to turn into one, I'm dating one, apparently."

Adam grimaced. "Yeah, well, that's going to be around like wild fire by tomorrow. Hope no one congratulates your parents for gaining a new twenty-two-year-old son-in-law."

My smile dropped from my face. "Oh God. I didn't think of that."

Adam nodded. "Oh, I did."

I bit my lip. "Man, if Mum and Dad hear that, I'll have my arm in a plaster cast like yours with 'grounded for all eternity' marked on it."

"And Sean will be fish food."

"Or pie filling." I cringed.

"I'll walk you home."

"No, no, no … You're on a good behaviour bond, remember. Just stay here, I'll be fine. Most of the moon is up. It's light and a nice night. I'll be okay."

"I'll get Chris to run you home."

"Will you stop? Chris is busy. I. Will. Be. Fine." I kissed him on the cheek. "Goodnight."

"What, no tongue?" He smiled wickedly.

"Shut up! Or I'll get my big twenty-two-year-old footy-playing boyfriend to beat the crap out of you."

Adam imitated Scott to a T, fidgeting and gulping in a convulsive way that had me laughing until it hurt.

"Night, Bozo." I backed away, knowing that if I didn't he would talk me into letting him walk me home. He looked at me with an uncertain frown on his face.

"Text me a progress report on the way home, I want landmarks and updates until your foot is in your front door, you hear me?"

"Yeah, yeah."

Once again, I made my way down Coronary Hill, leaving the distant weekend noises of the hotel behind me. I managed one look back when I reached the bottom; Adam was a speck on the verandah silhouetted by golden light. I knew he would stay there until I was out of sight. As soon as I made my way around the bend and hit Main Street, I texted him.

To: Adam
Turned a corner happy now?

He texted back.

To: Tess
Yes! Now go on, git!

I strolled leisurely along Main Street. Onslow was relatively well lit in this part of town, but the moon hung like a beacon lighting the way in darker spots, and I never once felt afraid. I knew this town like the back of my hand, it was as much a part of me as was the smaller territory of Perry which housed nothing more than a milk bar, a post office, and Mum and Dad's cafe on the edge.

I texted Adam again as promised.

To: Adam

Brimstone Street. Still alive.

There were still a couple of cars around, mostly young joy riders, but they paid me little attention, their music up full, probably headed for McLean's Beach or up to the Point to go parking.

It took me no time to make it to the fluro lights of the 24-hour Caltex. I texted Adam the breakthrough.

To: Adam
Pit stop at the Caltex. Yay!!

I perused the shelves, but didn't find anything of interest. I went to the ladies' room where the fluro lights continued, highlighting the dark circles under my eyes from smudged eyeliner and my hair all curled with the humidity of the night. I saw very little point in making any touch-ups aside from my lip smacker. As I went to dry my hands with the towel dispenser I glanced to my right and froze midstep. There, mounted on the wall, was the condom vending machine. It brought back a memory of when Ellie and I had come in here one afternoon after being at the lake all day. We were in Year Seven and we saw this very same machine. We dared each other to put in some coinage and get one out each. We giggled while we did the unthinkable. We held the silver foiled wrappers in our hands like it was this wondrous, mysterious thing, which it was. Then Ellie said we should have a competition, see who would be the first one with a chance to use it. She was all wide eyed in excitement.

"Okay," I agreed, feeling like a daredevil, even though we both knew Ellie would win. I hadn't even kissed a boy, whereas Ellie definitely had. We giggled as we got one for Adam as a joke. We put them in our Hang Ten wallets, bought ice creams and went on our merry way. That night at dinner I couldn't take my mind off the 'thing' in my wallet. It felt like it was burning through my pocket. The very sin of it. I was so sure Mum and Dad knew what I was up to. I didn't eat much, for the fear of looking them in the eye. After tea, I went straight to my room and took the foil square out of my wallet and hid it in the shoebox with all of my other keepsakes that I hid in the back of my wardrobe. I breathed a sigh of relief, but jumped out of my skin when Mum knocked on the door.

"Tess hon, *Monkey Magic* is on." If I didn't go and watch my favourite show like I did every other night, they would definitely know something was up.

For weeks, every night before I went to bed, I peeped into my shoebox, secretly smiling at the thrill of rebellion I felt by possessing something so forbidden. I didn't know how Ellie felt, although I knew for a fact she carried it with her because she was bragging to the girls in the school toilets and showing them.

Adam, on the other hand, thought it hilarious and broke straight into it as we sat on the banks of Lake Onslow in our secret place we used to go swimming and fishing. He thought it brilliant to put over his head and blow it up so it expanded into a big white dome.

"You really are a dickhead, Adam," Ellie had laughed, which caused him to laugh and the condom went flying off his head. I picked it up with a stick, Ellie and I both looking at it with wide, horrified eyes at the sheer size of it. I gulped and we both tilted our heads in wonder.

"Surely it's stretched." Ellie looked on in distaste.

Adam was lying on his back, squinting at the wrapper.

"It says extra extra large," he sighed. "Gee, I hope it fits."

He threw a cheeky smile our way.

"It does not say that," I snatched it off him.

He just shrugged, put his hands behind his head and closed his eyes, lying in the sun. It was then that my breath hitched as I read the packet.

"What does it say?" Ellie whispered, moving closer, balancing the parachute on her stick. I swallowed hard and looked at Ellie in dismay.

"It says regular," I whispered, and we both turned to look at the limp white rubber thing on the end of the stick.

"Jesus!"

I smiled at the memory of how excited we had been over such a thing. Ellie now popped coins in it like it was a gumball machine. I even noticed Adam's flash of the infamous square foil in his wallet when he paid for things.

I knew Adam had done it when he went out with Nicky Briggs last year for eight months. They were all over each other, and he was forever catching the bus to her house after school. I was secretly jealous of Nicky taking up so much of Adam's time and when I overheard Nicky and Adam had done it, I unexpectedly felt a deep misery. I felt like I was the last standing virgin alive. Which was actually most likely true.

I put a coin in the slot and pulled the lever, then grabbed the foil packet that fell out. A different kind of thrill surged through me as I held it now. When I was in Year Seven, I often wondered who my first would be, but never really into the scary technicalities like I did now. Ellie often told me details of her being with boys, and although it embarrassed me, I was also fascinated at the same time.

"Does it hurt?"

"At first," she had said, "but then it's better and better." She smiled dreamily. "Honestly, Tess, you don't know what you're missing out on."

I placed the condom in the inner pocket of my handbag where I kept my compact. I didn't exactly want anyone to recognise that unmistakable flash of silver that I had seen in boys' wallets all over Onslow. And then I thought, what difference did it make? According to the population, as of tomorrow, I had been sleeping with Sean Murphy. My stomach did a little flip at the thought of being so intimate with the likes of Sean. I shook my head; hanging around condom vending machines was sending me crazy. That or the fluro lighting.

As the automatic doors opened, and I stepped out of the Caltex, I froze stock still. A familiar navy Ford ute was parked in front of the shop. It was unmistakable, as its owner was leaning casually against the car door, his arms folded with almost an air or amusement, as if to say, "Fancy meeting you here."

"Adam said you were walking home, nice night for a murder."

I rolled my eyes. Traitor.

"What is with you guys and murder?"

"I watch *Crime Stoppers.*"

"Yeah, well, so do I and apparently Mafia-affiliated men

driving navy pickup utes are to be avoided at all costs."

"Is that so?" he smirked. He was back.

"Afraid so." I tried not to give up my smile so easily, but it was difficult when his was so damn contagious.

He raised his brows, sighed and straightened from his casual lean to shoving his hands in his pockets, glancing back at his ute.

"Well, this is awkward."

He walked to the passenger door and opened it, waving his hand in the direction of the interior.

"Deal's a deal!"

I looked down at my feet. "Um …"

"If you're wondering about my drinking, I was drinking Coke for the last four hours. I'm good to go."

Had he really? I frowned, trying to remember the pool game at Stan's, but other things must have distracted me. Every time I looked at Toby, it wasn't to check out what he was drinking.

"You didn't not drink because of me, did you?"

That caught him off guard. He glanced at the Caltex roof, his shoes, then back at me.

"Well, a deal's a deal."

My shoulders slumped, mortified. He had sacrificed a night out with his mates to play chauffeur to me because of our stupid bet. I bit my lip; the look of dismay must have been all over my face.

"Hey, Tess, I don't mind, it's no big deal."

"I didn't want to ruin your night."

"You didn't," he said earnestly.

"I feel awful, I don't mean for you to think that –"

"Tess!"

He cut off my rambling and pointed.

"Get in the bloody car."

Chapter Twenty

I was in Toby's car. Again!

We drove around the streets of Onslow with the windows wound down, the summer breeze blowing my hair.

José Feliciano was on the radio crooning out his version of 'California Dreaming' and I thought I would die from happiness. I looked at Toby's profile as we pulled up to the only set of lights in the whole town, and he tapped his fingers on the steering wheel.

He caught me watching him. "What?" he smirked.

The breeze had been cool on my skin but now we had stopped, the warmth in the air came back to me.

I looked at him, really looked at him. The glow of the streetlights behind him ... I didn't know what to say. My gaze flicked to the bow of his lips, and I quickly glanced away.

I looked at my hands that fidgeted in my lap. "So you're not mad at me anymore?"

Before he could respond a sounding horn blasted from behind us. The lights had changed, rocking Toby into motion. As we moved our way forward and back into the present, my phone rang and Adam flashed up on the screen.

"Hello?"

"Are you a ghost speaking from the afterlife?"

Toby threw me a questioning look. I mouthed 'Adam', then

realised maybe he was still trying to decipher what I had just said to him. Something I regretted as soon as the words left my mouth, that's what. I was after affirmation, the kind only insecure teenage girls would ask for, and that was the last thing I wanted to come across as.

I rolled my eyes. "That's right! And I am going to haunt you for the rest of your days."

"You hadn't checked in so I thought I would … what's that noise?"

"I'm hitchhiking."

There was a moment's silence on the phone, and then he twigged.

"Toby found you!"

"Yes, you dibber dobber."

"Hey, don't blame me, when I said you had walked home he basically accosted me and then high-tailed it after you. I said if I knew you, you would stop at the Caltex for junk food."

"Oh, you think you know me, huh? Well, it so happens I didn't buy a thing."

Condom! Condom! Condom!

"Nothing from a certain vending machine?" His voice was teasing. I nearly dropped my mobile switching to the other ear away from Toby. Damn him! We had been friends for too long.

"No!" I said a little too high-pitched.

Adam chuckled on the end of the phone. "You so did! And you can't even blame it on Ellie this time."

"I'm hanging up now."

"Oh, hang on a minute." There were muffled voices followed by scratching and static.

"Tess?" Sean's voice came on the line. "Can you please put Toby on?"

"Oh, um, he's driving. Hang on a sec, I'll put you on loud speaker."

"Toooooobyyyyyyyyy, Toooooooobyyyyyyy," sing-songed through the phone like a nightmare.

"Can you come and pick me up? Old buddy, old mate, old pal … what do you say?"

Toby sighed and gave me a bored look.

"Do you mind?" he asked.

A destination to delay me from getting out of this car, hell no.

"Fine by me."

"Be back there in five." Toby worked to turn the car.

I was just about to hang up when Adam's voice echoed through the loud speaker.

"Tess? Okay, so where were we before we were so rudely interrupted? Oh that's right, you went and got yourself a co…" I hung up the phone with lightning speed and threw it on the dashboard.

Toby did a double take. "Everything okay?"

You mean apart from forgetting to turn off the loud speaker and nearly having my best friend reveal that I was packing heat? Apart from that, fine!

I texted Adam a very brief 'SHUT UP!' message and then placed my phone on silent. If Toby wondered what Adam was talking about, he didn't let on. Maybe I bought myself a *Cosmo* mag or something. That could work.

We pulled into the Onslow car park, which was nothing more than a big circular space of gravel out the front of the hotel. There were people everywhere, loitering, most intoxicated after a big session. We couldn't see Sean, and neither of us really wanted to get out of the car.

Near the front entrance a fight broke out; there was a lot of pushing and shoving before their mates held back the two obviously hammered guys.

We wound up the windows at this point and waited for our package to be delivered.

We both jumped as a sound thudded against Toby's window.

"Toby!" A muffled sound with a smattering of condensation as Angela pressed herself drunkenly against the glass that she then proceeded to kiss.

This could not be happening.

"I missed yooooouuu…" she crooned. Toby unwound the window, and Angela's eyes lit up now that there was nothing stopping her from getting her claws on her man. She paused as she caught sight of me, tilting her head in wonder. I gave a small smile.

"Tic Tac?" she said. I flinched. So much for our bathroom bonding, at least her predictable behavior made it easy for me to hate her. "What are you doing in here?"

Toby saved me from answering. "I'm just dropping Tess and Sean home."

"Sean?" Angela's eyes squinted into the interior thinking she might have overlooked him the first time. How anyone could overlook Sean's six-foot-three stature, I couldn't be sure.

"He's inside, do you want to grab him for me? I don't want to leave the car."

Her smile didn't quite reach her eyes. "Sure thing, babe, I know the law doesn't look too kindly on people leaving kids in cars." She looked pointedly at me and laughed at her own joke.

Before she went, she pulled Toby into a full-on kiss, her eyes on me, laying claim on her man. Finally she pushed him away and zig-zagged through the crowd.

Well, that was awkward.

At least she didn't call me out and try to claw my face off, but the night was still young. We just sat in silence. I could tell Toby was embarrassed by public displays of affection. It was always Angela pawing at him, and although he looked at her affectionately and smiled, you would never see Toby getting all gooey. I was thankful for small mercies because I didn't think I could stomach that. Sean stepped through the front door, sauntering his way across the gravel with a pot glass of beer in hand.

He came around to my passenger side to get in.

"You can't take that with you," I said.

"It's for my collection, don't tell Chris." He put a finger to his lips and climbed in, his giant frame filling the inner cabin. I scooted over to the middle, and he leaned on me, spilling a bit of beer on himself. It was at this point I realised I was pushed right up against Toby, his bare arm burning against mine. I gave him an apologetic smile, even though I was not in the least bit sorry.

Toby whispered to me, "I think we better get him home first, if he passes out we'll have no hope."

"Agreed." I muttered and tried to push Sean away from crushing me.

"Hey lookie, it's my girlfriend." Sean put his arm around me. "What's for tea, honey? Are all the house chores done?"

"One: in your dreams, and two: it's the 1990's, not the1950's, you sexist pig."

I felt the vibration of Toby's laughter through his arm as we both watched Sean's brows rise in surprise.

"Tess, will you marry me?" Toby laughed.

I blushed, not knowing what to say, when a familiar cackle sounded from across the drive. Angela had stumbled over in the garden. Her equally drunk friend tried to help her up, but she was too busy laughing.

"Wow, someone's drunker then me. Impressive." Sean threw back another mouthful of what looked like flat, warm beer.

Angela hauled herself up and spotted us again.

"Heeeeyyyyy, where are you going?"

"I'm just going to drop –"

"You can't go." Angela pouted, glanced around her and then cupped her hands around her mouth. "Chris is going to do a lock-in." She whispered in a loud, obnoxious way, as if she was privy to this amazing secret. As I looked over her dishevelled state, I knew Chris wouldn't let her stay; she was a loud, messy drunk and Chris wouldn't have that time bomb in his pub. Lock-ins were risky enough. All hush-hush as the beer continued to flow past their 12 o'clock licence. It could mean big trouble for Chris and his uncle if they were found out.

I prayed that my little cozy refuge, pressed up against Toby, wouldn't be spoiled if Angela convinced him to stay with her. But he didn't budge.

"Stay here, Ang. I'll come and get you after I drop them home."

Her eyes cut daggers at Sean and me, like he had chosen us over her. Which he kind of had.

She shrugged. "If I'm here, I'm here."

"Don't be like that, I won't be long."

She flicked her hair and walked off in a huff. What a child. I could stress and blush, and ask all the stupid naive questions in the world, and I still would look more mature than Angela Vickers every time. Toby stared after Angela with a deep scowl; he resonated such anger, I was sure he wouldn't go after her. His jaw pulsed as he tightly clenched the steering wheel.

"She'll be alright, she's got her friends. She'll be here when you get back." I tried to pacify him like the idiot I was.

She's a freakin' idiot!

"Yeah," Toby said as he started up the engine. He slung his arm over the seatback to check his back view. "I'm not coming back."

Chapter Twenty-One

Life could be worse than being wedged between the Onslow Boys in Toby's ute.

Sean suggested we go for a drive, and from the moment we had left Angela back at the Onslow, a new-found awkwardness had settled over the three of us. Toby's solemn silence was thick and heavy; I couldn't see his face, but I could feel the tension in his body where it was pressed against mine. I stole a quick sideways glance at Sean who could only respond with a helpless shrug.

Regardless of the change in mood, I was glad we were churning into the darkness; the last thing I wanted was for Toby to have a sudden hit of remorse and head back to the Onslow to pick Angela up for a make-up session ... yeah, I didn't want to think of that.

The possibility of turning around became bleaker as we drove further and further away from the hotel, veering onto McLean's Bridge en route to Perry. My heart spiked with panic; maybe Toby took going for a drive as a male bonding thing? I didn't want to go home yet! Sure I had desperately wanted to earlier, but now? Pressed next to Toby, feeling the warmth of his skin against mine; I never wanted to go home.

I listened to the rhythmic hum of wheels along the stretch of the never-ending concrete bridge that connected me to my impending doom. Home.

Be cool, Tess, be cool!

Then Toby sped past the turnoff to my street and kept driving up the winding road into the dense bushland. I tried not to smile too wide as relief flooded through me. He continued passed the Rose Café, leading deeper and deeper into the Perry Ranges, veering down the Point turnoff.

We were heading to the Point?

We climbed higher and higher. Toby laughed for the first time when he noticed that I was making a funny jaw movement to force my ears to pop.

"There's chewy in the glove box." He motioned with a head tilt.

I leaned across Sean who was like a brick wall; he lifted his arms to maneuver out of my way a bit, allowing me access to the glove box. The inside of the ute cabin was claustrophobic, pressed in between Sean and Toby – but don't get me wrong, I wasn't complaining! The glove box light momentarily highlighted a bemused smirk on Sean's face, as if he was loving every minute of me lying awkwardly across his lap. Was the chewy worth that smug look? Yeah, I decided, it kind of was, as I accidentally on purpose elbowed him in the side as I straightened back into my seat.

"Ugh! Christ, Tess." Sean clasped his side.

"Oops, sorry!" I offered sweetly, unwrapping and popping a piece of gum in my mouth. Toby took a piece from the pack.

The close proximity of the cabin wasn't the only thing that caused a swirling giddiness in my stomach. I had never been to the Point at night. Come to think of it, I had only been there a handful of times during the day.

Once was with my Uncle Bernie who loved to go bird watching (yeah, that had been a riveting afternoon), so much so that my mum promised she would never subject me to it again. The other time was for a Grade Six field trip to replant trees after a bush fire swept through the ranges.

The Point was a popular haunt for young rebellious delinquents who were looking to hang out. I knew this because I had witnessed plenty a young couples stopping off at the cafe in the early hours of the morning. Their kiss-swollen lips, dishevelled hair and creased clothing. Oh, how I secretly envied them.

Unofficially, the Point was the designated playground for the eighteen-plus crowd, mainly because, thanks to the steep incline, you could only access it via car. Adam, Ellie and I had attempted it once by bike, but the winding ranges were far too steep for our little peddling legs; it didn't take long for us to breathlessly voice, *"You know what? We can totally wait 'til we're older"*.

The shadows of bushland passed by in a blur; I tried not to imagine what my parents would think. Me, travelling to the Point with two twenty-two year olds; I quickly shook the thought from my mind. No time for guilt tonight. It took us about ten minutes to make it to the final turnoff, abandoning the bitumen and winding up the rough dirt track that seemed much steeper at night. Up and up we crawled, not seeing more than a metre or so in front of us. The canopy of trees cast an eerie blackness, and as I looked out at the dense scrubland, I thought it would be the perfect place to bury a body. Had Toby and Sean not been debating the hard-hitting topics like chickens being the greatest of all of God's creatures, I might have been a little bit nervous.

"Chickens?" Sean said in disbelief. "What about echidnas? They're so tough you could run over one in your car, and it would still be alright."

Toby chewed thoughtfully on his gum for a long moment. "Yeah, echidnas are pretty cool." He nodded.

Yep, pretty thought-provoking stuff. I stifled my smirk, and my thoughts switched momentarily to Ellie. I wondered where she was right now. A part of me knew I should have stayed with her, but if I had, I certainly wouldn't be pressed up against Toby, mere metres from the Point. Instead, I would be playing lookout for Ellie and her new fling; God only knows what kind of company I would be keeping.

The track evened out at the very top of the climb. It was so dark it felt like we could have easily driven off the edge of the earth for all we knew, but like everything with Toby, he maneuvered his way up the track with great care.

The Point was a mass clearing on top of one of the highest parts in the Perry Ranges. Sheer rock boulders sloped downwards into the abyss of darkness that ended with the distant twinkle of the town lights of Onslow. A derelict, boxy, wooden shack sat to the right of the clearing that had once been the fire observation tower. Over on the left of the clearing stood two ugly pylon towers, servicing as some beacon of technology. They were fenced off but it still didn't prevent adrenalin junkies scaling them and climbing the pylons on drunken dares. Miraculously no one had plummeted to their death, yet. At least, not that I'd heard of.

And sure enough, tonight we were not the first car to crunch up the gravel track to the Point. Three other vehicles were parked in a circle and a crowd of people perched on bonnets. As we edged closer, Toby sounded the horn and wound his window down. He pulled over to where Ringer stood, cigarette in one hand, can of Jim Beam in the other.

"Well, if it isn't the Onslow Boys. What brings you to this neck of the woods?" Ringer took a long draw of his ciggie, past his smirking lips.

"We're out of options, we have partied it and pubbed it," Sean said.

"And now your here parkin' it?" Ringer laughed.

"Not with you bunch of pervs." Toby smiled.

Ringer looked at me as if seeing me for the first time.

"McGee!! What you doing stowing away with these bums?"

"Oh, you know, enjoying the view." I looked out towards the dark smudge that would be Lake Onslow, speckled with dotted lights from the town.

Toby steered us slowly closer towards the edge where the lookout was more prominent.

"Whoa, hang on a sec," Sean said, "you two kids take a look at the pretty lights, I gotta go whizz."

Sean climbed out and stumbled into the night.

Toby smiled and placed Sean's empty pot glass in the cup holder. "Although I don't doubt his authenticity, something tells me he won't be heading back in a hurry."

I cast Toby a questioning look.

He drove forward bringing his ute closer still to the edge. He pushed it into park and killed the engine, flashing me a devilish grin.

"He's afraid of heights."

We were silent for a while as we stared at the beauty of our little town. Growing up in Onslow seemed mundane, even claustrophobic at times, but sitting above it, as we did now, it looked well ... kind of beautiful. Toby shifted and relaxed in his seat. I became all too well aware that I was still pressed right up against him, I hadn't even bothered to move across when Sean had gotten out. I was torn between scooting across, because that seemed like the appropriate thing to do, or not saying a word; act like I didn't even notice and stay right where I was.

I chose to be ignorant a little bit longer.

Toby gripped the steering wheel with one hand.

"What made you think I was angry at you?"

Damn! Memory like a freakin' elephant.

Just because I desperately wanted to forget the things that came out of my mouth didn't guarantee others would.

"Oh no ... I just thought you seemed a bit quiet tonight, that's all. I didn't think it was solely directed at me."

Yes I did.

He nodded, seemingly satisfied with my answer.

He laughed a breath through his nose.

"I think you would be the last person I could be angry with."

My head swung around to look at him but his eyes were diverted as his fingers played with a thread on his shirt.

"I'm sorry about how Ang treated you tonight," he said.

My mouth gaped. "It's not your fault," I said.

Angela had pronounced Tic Tac in front of Toby as a means to deliberately humiliate me. Fresh anger boiled to the surface. Actually, yeah, maybe he should apologise for her. It was because of boys like him thinking she was a goddess that gave her grounds to be so cocky. My silence must have made Toby uncomfortable because he pressed further.

"You know, I had a nickname in high school." My head snapped up, that had my attention.

Oh God, he knew, he heard. Of course he did.

"Oh?"

He gripped both hands on the steering wheel sighing deeply as if psyching himself up to tell me. I tucked my foot under my leg, settling in, waiting for Toby to continue.

"They used to call me Toby–Wan."

Okaaaay? I frowned, unsure as to how it compared.

He looked at me expectantly. "Toby-Wan-Kenobi," he repeated slowly, as if my first language wasn't English.

My hand flew up to my mouth to mask the smile that automatically formed on my lips.

Oh please, don't laugh.

He smirked. "You think that's funny?"

I shook my head violently, biting my lips, trying not to lose it.

"On the contrary, Star War's references are hot. Gives you street cred."

"Yeah, not quite."

"I thought you were going to say Tobias."

"That, and they used to call me Toblerone."

"Hey, I wouldn't object to being named after that."

Toby shook his head in disbelief. "Chicks. Always with the chocolate."

"Always!"

We stared at each other in silence, neither one of us looking away.

"Thanks for telling me your nickname." I smiled. "It's not quite the same, but I can appreciate it."

Toby's gaze never wavered from mine. "People will always make fun of what's different, Tess."

An uncomfortable shiver ran down my spine. Even Toby knew I was different. That I was awkward, clumsy and clueless.

I broke eye contact, untucked my leg and sat up straight. "Yeah, I'll definitely look out for that circus when it comes to town next," I said, focusing intently on the twinkling stream of car lights below.

That was Toby's cue to insist that he didn't mean it that way. I was not a freak, and he was welcome to gush about how wonderful I am.

Instead he laughed, which had me frowning his way again.

"What?"

"Well, if they set you in the kissing booth, let me know, I am always willing to donate for a worthy cause."

Was he flirting or being friendly?

Toby collected himself and shifted in his seat, his arm

brushing against mine, causing my skin to prickle with the sensation of his skin on mine. "Sorry I dragged you up here, I sort of didn't even ask if you wanted to?"

"No! No, I wanted to. I mean you really didn't have to give me a lift home, I didn't expect you to."

Moon rays filtered through the windshield, giving the cabin an otherworldly glow.

Toby's perfect teeth were illuminated when he smiled. "You know, you are the worst winner!" He shook his head. "Ever since you won the bet, you've been apologising. Just go with it, enjoy it, because I assure you, next time ..." - he leaned closer - "... you will not be the winner." He pulled back, smug.

I curved a brow. "Next time?"

He nodded. "I fully intend to redeem myself."

"Want a chance to rebuild your shattered ego, do you? I bet you're itching to fix my bike so you can be rid of me once and for all." I shouldered him gently, teasing him as I would Adam. And then I realised what I had done; I had treated him like my friends. He looked down at his shoulder, then up at me. His eyes shadowed with untold meanings that I couldn't read.

"What if I didn't want to fix your bike?" he said in all seriousness.

"Why, is my company so stimulating that you can't bear the thought of being without me?" I teased nervously.

I was aiming for light and airy, but something must have gone wrong with my delivery because Toby's face went blank. He looked out into the lights of Onslow, ran his tongue over his bottom lip and sighed.

"Bring the bike in on Monday, and I'll have a look at it."

"Oh, okay, sure." My heart sank. That was rather anticlimactic.

He tapped his fingers on the steering wheel. A silent awkwardness had swept over us.

"We better get you home. The last thing you need is for rumours to circulate tomorrow that you went parking up the Point with Toby Morrison."

A thrill shot through me at the thought of such a thing. A girl could get used to that idea.

"I can see it now, love triangle splashed across the local

news," I said, again attempting with the lame nervous humour.

Toby frowned as he started up the car. "Yeah, Ang would love that."

And there it was, how to kill a conversation. All good humour died a sudden death. We picked up Sean who was socialising with the masses and edged our way down the winding ghostly roads of the ranges. I was now definitely ready to go home.

Chapter Twenty-Two

It was 2 am when I tiptoed into my house.

I was unaccustomed to such big days and heavy nights that had me traipsing across the countryside and emotionally dragging myself backwards through a hedge. I was exhausted and managed to crash fully clothed into bed. Judging by my numb arm the next morning, I'm pretty certain I never moved, not once.

When you lie to your olds there comes a certain responsibility to follow through the next day. A shadow of paranoia followed my every move. I had some scrambled eggs and a side of guilt for breakfast, trying not to make eye contact with my chatty mum. They grilled me with a myriad of questions, like, "What did you have for tea?", "What movies did you watch?" and "What time did you get home?" I had to think on my feet with my best 'I'm not guilty' responses. My inner monologue was screaming *liar!* I tried not to choke on my breakfast juice as my conscience laid into me with steel-capped boots. My next point of call was to word up Ellie, and fast. That's if she wasn't too sleep-deprived from last night's escapades.

Ellie's phone rang out, and I was quietly pleased. I wasn't in the mood to chase her down and listen as she retold what an amazing night she'd had. I placed the receiver back on the hook and sighed with relief. Oh well, I'd see her at work. *Work, ugh.* Still suffering from my own sleep deprivation, I had to really psyche myself up for my afternoon shift. The only thing that kept pushing me through was that Sean and Toby said they would come in and annoy us for some lunch. Every time the front door of the main bar screeched open with its hundred-year-old unoiled hinges, my heart rate spiked with anticipation. Mostly it then plunged just as quickly as my searching eyes saw crusty locals, or nameless tourists, pour through the door.

I had suspected an unbearable afternoon with Ellie's voice ringing in my ears as it usually did the day after her conquests, so when I was met by her with silence that stretched on for an uncharacteristic age, well, I admit, it got the better of me.

"So how was your night last night?" I asked as she fumbled in the linen cupboard with some tablecloths.

Ellie shrugged and offered a weak smile. "It was alright."

"Just alright?" I tipped my head, trying to see her eyes.

She nodded lightly but I saw her chin quiver, and with that, friend mode kicked into gear. Lunch had not officially begun yet, so I ushered Ellie into the ladies' room. I guided her into a cane chair that was wedged in the corner next to the sink and hand dryer. This place was so handy for meltdowns and emergencies.

I sat her down, making sure she didn't bump her head on the hand dryer. "Ellie, what's the matter? Did someone hurt you?" I crouched in front of her.

Her eyes widened. "No, nothing like that, it's just ..." Her voice broke away.

I grabbed her hand to urge her to talk. "Well, what then?"

Her big, blue eyes welled with tears as she looked down at me.

"Why am I always so stupid? It's like I'm floating above my body, and I can see the things I'm doing and hear what I'm saying and I go to scream but nothing comes out."

Had Ellie had a breakthrough during the night? Guilt usually didn't follow Ellie's escapades. "What brought this on?"

The tears began to flow now, and my heart broke for her. Ellie was the rock in our relationship, so seeing her crumble ... well, it really rocked me, no pun intended.

Struggling as to what to do, I grabbed her some toilet paper.

"I saw Stan on the way to work." She took it from me and

blew her nose.

I cringed at the thought; this town was far too small. Maybe Ellie wasn't as immune to his presence as she pretended.

"Was he mean to you?"

I imagined Stan giving her the cold shoulder, a death stare, even maybe calling her on a few home truths. After last night, any of those reactions would have been warranted. I felt awful for thinking it.

"That's the thing," she sobbed, "he was really nice to me, lovely in fact. The same Stan, he treated me like nothing had happened. If anything, he stumbled over his words and apologised to me and said that he didn't mean what he said."

Well, yeah, I could have told her that. Oh Stan! Will you ever find out that your maturity in the matter had made such a breakthrough? I wondered.

"So, this Wes guy?" I pressed.

"I don't want to talk about him, I don't even want to think about him, I just want to pretend none of it even happened. Then I don't have to think about what a horrible person I am."

"You're not horrible; you're hard work, I'll admit, but you are the sweetest person I know." I shrugged. "I love you."

"You're the only one." She blew her nose again.

I knew this was coming from deeper wounds, from a family in which she felt like a third wheel to her parents' independent lifestyle.

"And Adam, and we're awesome."

She laughed through her tears. "Yeah, I guess you are pretty awesome."

"Are you sure that Wes guy didn't do anything?"

"No, he was fine. I've had worse. And after seeing Stan this morning, it just made it hit home all the more."

It was right there and then that I, Tess McGee, decided to step up to a challenge, for once. A cunning plan stirred within my brain. It was called Operation Mend Stan. I wouldn't voice my genius; Ellie was still pretty raw and needed some time. I had also seen the hurt and anger in Stan's eyes last night; he could poker face his feelings all he liked, but I knew he would still be angry inside. I would have to proceed with caution, but I knew it was the way to go.

After pacifying Ellie and managing to sneak back into the restaurant away from Melba's scrutiny, I grabbed a heap of serviettes to take into the main bar. What met me there had me grinning from ear to ear. Sean, Ringer, Stan and Toby were all lined up along the bar, throwing beer nuts into each other's mouths.

"You do realise that unwashed, dirty old man hands have been in those nut bowls," I said.

Just as Stan caught the last flying nut he broke out into a coughing fit, spluttering as my words resonated. All eyes swung around to me. But it was Toby's broad boyish smile that really caught my attention. It soon fell into a cringe as the four of them picked up their drinks and washed the beer nuts down, with repulsed shudders. Sean pushed his beer nut bowl away with distaste.

I giggled and plonked down beside them for a spell.

"Heard any good gossip lately?"

Sean straightened. "Apparently some hot footy player is dating some pretty little waitress from the Onslow Hotel. It's quite the scandal." He winked.

My eyes widened, my blood running cold. "Really?"

Sean laughed. "Actually, I have no idea. I've been working all morning." He shrugged. "I didn't get sledged for anything."

"Give it time," Ringer said. "Good gossip needs time to grow and mature, like a fine wine."

"Or a jumper that warms with age," added Toby dryly.

I heard the cool room door fly open, and I quickly hopped off my stool and got back to something that resembled work.

I headed back to the restaurant and brushed past Chris who was carrying a slab in from out back. I paused, then slipped through the partition and turned to the boys, offering some last-minute, friendly advice.

"Remember, boys, hands off your nuts."

Chris almost lost his grip on his cargo. As I slid through and stood behind the partition I could hear the uproarious laughter; Stan had nearly choked on his beer, and I could hear someone pummeling him on the back as he coughed and fought for air. I peeked through the partition, seeing Toby's shoulders vibrating from laughter.

Shaking his head, he turned to Stan. "She is something else."

Chris pushed through the swinging kitchen door, spiking a lunch order docket for the Onslow Boys, something I silently resented; it was, after all, my job. Maybe he didn't like the nut comment?

Geez, what a square.

Even though it killed me, I decided to let Ellie take the meals out to them, so she could reacquaint herself with Stan. After how she behaved last night, I didn't know how the others would respond to her. They seemed pretty loyal guys. I could only hope that if Stan was alright with her, then they'd respect his wishes and take their cue from him.

And that's exactly what they did. Ellie picked up and was back to her normal self by the end of the shift. I bet guys our age wouldn't have been as mature about it.

We were on the homeward stretch when we heard the creaking of the staircase that led down to the main reception area of the restaurant. A rather seedy, sorry-looking Adam shuffled down the stairs, hair all messy, sleep still in his eyes.

"Where am I?" he croaked.

"You're not in Kansas anymore, Toto, that's for sure." Ellie looked him over with a bemused frown.

He clasped his head in his hands. "Why are you shouting?"

"What on earth did you do last night after I left?" I asked.

"Lock-in," Adam groaned.

Ellie and I looked at each other in surprise. "You mean Chris let you stay?"

"Don't sound so surprised," he snapped at me.

But I *was* surprised. Chris wouldn't let me and Ellie in a lock-in and Adam was Chris's younger, grounded, naughtier brother. He was always extra hard on him. The whole thing made no sense.

"He got me to take over the bar for a bit." Adam gingerly pulled out a chair and pressed his forehead to the tabletop.

Now this made even less sense.

"He left you in charge?" I asked, my disbelief pouring off me.

"Yes! God, is there an echo in here, or something?"

"Why would he do that?" Ellie asked.

He looked up at us as if we were deluded, and then it was like a light bulb went off in his mind – a low, painful, groggy light bulb.

"Oh, that's right, you weren't there." He buried his face in his hands and attempted to wipe the sleep from his eyes.

"Weren't there for what?" I pressed.

He lifted his head out of his hands and a huge, cheeky smile broadened across his face.

"When Angela Vickers puked all over the bar."

Whaaaaaaat?

Gold! The stuff to tell your grandchildren. Adam relayed how Angela Vickers had been dancing drunk on top of the bar. Chris had been yelling at her to get down but she just ignored him, so when he yanked her down to kick her out, she spewed all over the bar, the floor and herself.

Awesome!

Chris ended up taking her home because everyone else had been drinking. And that's when Adam stepped up to the plate. A win-win situation for all, apart from Angela. So sad!

The boys finished their counter meals and waited around until Ellie and I knocked off. Even though I was surviving on little-to-no sleep, I had never felt so alive. I washed dishes with great enthusiasm, polished silverware like a thing possessed. I noticed the same eagerness in Ellie. We both had a core focus: get the work done and start living again (between the hours of two and six).

The only person who didn't seem to be so in love with the world was Adam. He glared at us from across the room every time we made so much as a clinking noise with the cutlery.

Every time the kitchen door was pushed open, and we brought food out, he turned a deeper shade of green until he couldn't take it anymore and quickly disappeared, clawing his way pitifully back up the stairs. We didn't see him for the rest of the shift. Some catch up.

At shift's end, Ellie and I darted behind the door where we kept our bags in the restaurant section of the bar. We didn't need to talk; there was a humming undercurrent of excitement running through each of us at hearing the jukebox in the poolroom and that familiar laughter. We took turns in fixing our hair in front of the small mirror, crudely nailed to the wall. We sprayed some Illusion

Impulse body spray to mask the eau de Windex and sweaty kitchen hands that we currently smelled like. We topped up our lips with strawberry Lip Smacker. I could tell Ellie was a bit apprehensive. Stan and the boys were being pleasant enough to her, which helped, but she was still embarrassed. This made me strangely happy. It was like this new Ellie, with a conscience. I liked it. Maybe Stan was rubbing off on her.

"Okay, I'm going in." Ellie breathed deeply. "Wish me luck."

"You don't need any luck." My words came out funny through my stretched lips as I applied the sweet lip balm.

I spun around but she was gone.

I had a sudden thought and delved my hands frantically into the pocket of my soiled apron, which I had hung behind the door. I sighed with relief as some small objects made chinking sounds as my fingers brushed them. My rings. I had almost forgotten to put them back on after dish duty. As I placed the gold circles back onto my fingers I heard the unmistakable blast and hiss of the steam from the coffee machine, followed by a crude coughing fit. I peeked around the door to see Uncle Eric brewing probably his ninth cup of coffee for the day.

"Ah, young Tess, just the person I was looking for!" He poured the frothy milk into his mug. "Would you like one?"

Had he just coughed all over the mugs and coffee machine? I decided to pass, and made a mental note to Spray and Wipe the coffee machine tonight.

"No thanks," I said.

"Well, come join me in the beer garden for a bit, I want to have a quick chat."

Uh oh.

Chapter Twenty-Three

My mind was reeling as I tried to think of all the possible reasons I needed to be pulled aside.

Was he unhappy with my work? Was it about hanging out in the bar after hours? Was I fired? I felt sick.

The beer garden was a grapevine-infested Amazonian jungle, dotted with tiki torches and picnic tables. A rather exotic refuge if I didn't readily associate it with Uncle Eric's passive chain smoking. It was his own kind of sanctuary; where he sat with his coffee, paper and cigarettes when the day allowed him to get away from the bar. A place where he and his poker buddies sat in the evening, gambling and smoking cigars.

A brick BBQ and vine-covered gazebo sat in the corner and was a nice space, even though the area needed a desperate blower-vac. Today was slow and calm with Chris covering in the bar, while Uncle Eric led me out to his refuge at an umbrella-decked table with his coffee in hand.

The day was warming up, but I wasn't sure if it was truly hot or if it was my nerves that made me flush as I took a chair opposite Uncle Eric.

"You enjoy working here, Tess?" He tapped a cigarette from his pack.

I gave it a brief thought; I guess I did, now that I thought of it.

I was both pleased and surprised by this revelation. I seemed to have found my feet now, even knew what I was doing ... kind of.

But why was he asking? I squirmed in my seat. Maybe I wasn't doing as well as I thought; maybe Chris had reported back one of my earlier calamities.

"Relax, Tess," Uncle Eric chuckled. "Don't look so worried. I hope you enjoy working here, you've been a real asset to our staff."

My shoulders slumped with relief.

"Thanks, I really do like working here. It was a bit hard in the beginning when I was trying to get my head around things, but I like to think I'm not making too many mistakes."

"You can't learn if you don't make mistakes." He flicked his ash in the ashtray. "You seem to fit in very well."

I smiled. It was nice to hear these things.

"You seem to get along well with Chris's friends."

My smile slipped a little. "Yeah, they've been really nice to me."

He took a deep drag of his cigarette. "They're good boys."

His gaze then flicked to mine. "Sean Murphy is a particular fan of yours, I hear."

My smile was all but gone, and I could feel the colour drain from my face.

Flicking another ash, he sighed. "There's not much that gets past me, Tess, there isn't much a publican isn't privy to. Though I don't tend to listen to much idle gossip, when something concerns me, I listen. I'm not going to give you a fatherly lecture, or pull the boss card on you, Tess. I just want you to be careful. I know that this is your first job and it's all new and exciting. But these boys, these young men," he corrected, "however nice they may be, well, they'll have different expectations compared to the high school boys you're accustomed to. They won't settle for hand holding for long, and I don't want you to feel pressured into anything you may regret. Not on my watch."

"You don't have to worry, Uncle Eric, we're just friends. It's not like that."

"I see the way you and Ellie look at the boys. I don't expect you all to be saints, I just don't want to see anyone hurt, or do something they'll regret. You're a good girl, Tess. I wouldn't want anyone to take advantage of that."

I'm sure in years to come I would look back at this and be grateful for his concern, but right at that very instant I was looking for the closest way to escape. He must have sensed my unease because he allowed me a reprieve.

"So I'll see you back here at six, then?"

I nodded with my best 'nothing weird just happened' smile.

"Thanks, Uncle Eric, see you later."

I shot to my feet and as I was nearly home free, he said, "Tess?"

I paused, cautiously turning at my name.

"If you need to speak about anything, me or Claire are always happy to listen."

I wanted to die.

There was a certain amount of discomfort from having your boss assume you were having sex when you weren't *actually* having sex. Now every time Uncle Eric looked at me, I knew that was somewhere in his head, and that idea freaked me out. The only thing that would get me through the evening shift was the fact that Uncle Eric retired early, otherwise it would have been Mission Avoid Uncle Eric's Knowing Eyes.

I entered the poolroom like a zombie, perching on a bar stool next to Ellie.

"What's wrong?" she asked.

"Oh, nothing. I'm just tired. I might head home, catch up on some sleep before tonight."

After all the buildup and enthusiasm for knocking off to hang with the Onslow Boys, all of a sudden I didn't want to be anywhere near them. If that was what Uncle Eric was thinking, what would others be? When Sean had defended me against Scott, I thought it was heroic, awe inspiring; to be honest, a bit of a joke. But now the news had travelled and to, of all people, my boss, it somehow didn't seem so funny anymore. I felt ill.

As a group of tourists flooded the poolroom, I took the opportunity to sneak away. I didn't even speak to Toby or the boys. Ellie said she wanted to stay a bit longer, her nervous gaze constantly flitting to Stan. I nodded, distracted, as Uncle Eric's mortifying words repeated through my mind.

Walking through the front bar as I started the evening shift, my gaze instinctively turned towards the poolroom. Surprisingly, I spotted Sean, alone at the bar. He wasn't often on his own so I jumped at the opportunity to give him the heads up on what was going around.

I hadn't anticipated how hilarious he'd find it. Sean's entire body convulsed in spasmodic fits of thigh-slapping laughter.

I glared at him.

He wiped away tears and fought to catch his breath. Chris walked through from the main bar, casting a curious gaze from Sean to me.

"What's so funny?"

"I think I'm to expect a heart to heart with your uncle soon, Chris." Sean saluted him with his beer. "I can't wait."

I rolled my eyes. "You're seriously demented, you know that, right?"

"Maybe we should get Unc to chaperone us like in the olden days, he could walk ten paces behind us while we take a turn in the garden."

He was loving every minute of this.

"Or better yet ..." I leaned closer. "My dad can escort you to a shallow grave in the Perry Ranges, because if he finds out, that is going to be a far more probable outcome."

"If who finds out what?" Stan said, as he and Toby walked through the poolroom door.

My heart leapt at the sight of them. I hadn't even heard the door open. Stan was in his usual good humour, but Toby looked between Sean and me in guarded silence.

It made me uneasy; aside from the small exchange this afternoon over the beer nuts, we hadn't spoken at all since the ranges. Now there was not so much as a hello; he didn't say it, so I didn't say it.

Since Sean had been alone in the bar, I'd figured Toby must have had better things to do tonight. But here he was, flicking his wallet out of his back pocket and ordering a beer, looking better than ever. Tonight he'd opted for jeans and a Pink Floyd T-shirt under an open black and white checked shirt; his hair was still damp from the shower and glistening from a little carefree product application. It probably took him only seconds to arrange it into its gorgeously disheveled state. It was sexy. He walked behind me to settle on a stool, and the fragrance of his aftershave made me want to press closer, but I had to control myself. Even if I did want to squeal and jump up and down clapping like a wind-up monkey with brass symbols for hands.

"Oh nothing, just some trouble in paradise." Sean winked and gave me a wicked smile.

It was nice that he found it all so amusing, but I'd been serious about my dad not being happy. I didn't even dare let on that I was spending most of my days with a group of men (though young ones). There was no way he or Mum would approve.

I shrugged and gathered the last of the empty pots and pints on my way to the kitchen.

"It's your funeral."

I gave Toby a wide berth as I headed back to the kitchen. Though I was over the moon to see him, I didn't want him to think that he was in any way obligated to take me home after work. This spur-of-the-moment bet was starting to seriously backfire, and I wished that I'd never made it, or at best that I'd let him win. I would have made him his damn pies and that would have been the end of it. Maybe now he'd be greeting me with a smile instead of this weird silence. I may not have acknowledged him, but it's not like he acknowledged me. Ha!

Geez. And I was critical of Ellie's mind games. Could it be that I was playing my own? Either way, I'd told myself on the way back up Coronary Hill this afternoon that the next time I saw Toby Morrison I would play it cool, and that was exactly what I'd done. I just didn't expect him to do it, too, and so well.

Chapter Twenty-Four

Tonight Onslow hosted its famous annual Summer Show.
There were food stalls that sold hotdogs, fairy floss, kebabs and Danish pancakes; there were craft stalls with handmade jewelry, tie-dye clothing and knitted blankets and toys that smelt like lavender and old ladies. Come midnight, fireworks filled the night sky, casting a glorious reflection over Lake Onslow.

Everyone in Onslow and the surrounding regions flocked to these events. It broke the monotony of daily life in these sleepy towns, and got everyone together. For me, it had mostly been worth going because every year I had been guaranteed to spot Toby.

This year, I'd hoped it would be different, that I wouldn't be mooning over Toby from a distance.

Ellie and I didn't even manage to break out a sweat in the evening shift, only a handful of meals for the regulars and a few touristy blow-ins for drinks. Yet with so little to do, I hadn't even noticed the bar empty out. Without even a goodbye, the Onslow Boys were gone. So much for me not caring. Chris didn't seem to care about missing out on the show. I suppose he wasn't exactly a show bag kind of guy. Still, I would have thought he would at least want to hang out with his friends.

I did my best not to openly whine about my reluctance to be

at work. I didn't want to be that girl, but being next to Ellie's increasingly enthusiastic nature (it seemed things were back on track and she'd made amends when I slipped out between shifts) tended to drag me down further. I delivered a meal to a couple enjoying the sunset on an outside table. My heart ached as I could hear the distant beat of music, laughter and screams from the show. It taunted me. I had never missed a Summer Show. Ever. Sadly, there was a first time for everything.

I had just hoped it wouldn't have been this summer. So far, my holidays had wildly exceeded all my low, low expectations, not to mention confused me more than ever. And now I was angry, angry at being stuck here, angry at Ellie's happiness, at Toby for the effect he had on me.

I would be stuck working until midnight, probably witnessing the fireworks on the front porch of the Onslow (if I was lucky), in my smoke-infused work clothes. Ellie was miffed about it, too, but was pacified by checking her mobile every possible chance behind the staff room door. She would smile and giggle and sigh with every incoming message. Stan.

Ellie would no doubt meet up with him after work, he would come and pick her up, and hopefully offer to take me home so I could go to bed and dream about the things that were a joke to think I could have.

By eleven I was wiping down the last of the kitchen benches; I wasn't able to hear the distant screams from the show, which I was happy about. I was about to throw myself in the fires of hell when I took it upon myself to grab a bucket and dust pan and clean out the open fireplace in the front bar. I moved the fireguard and was about to get on all fours when a voice startled me.

"We have a cleaner that does that."

Chris leaned against the bar, his arms crossed, gaze transfixed on the mute TV. Was he watching *Grease*?

"Well I wish you had've told me that when I was scrubbing the kitchen floor."

Chris shrugged. "She's no spring chicken, you did her a favour."

"Yeah, well, I don't think this fireplace has been cleaned out since 1974."

"You can do it if you want, I just thought you'd have preferred to head down to the show."

I froze mid-sweep, studying his emotionless face as he watched Olivia Newton John sing 'Hopelessly devoted to you'.

"Oh, um, does that mean that ..."

He sighed. "Knock off, Tess, it's dead tonight. Go and enjoy yourself."

"Ellie, too?" I all but squealed.

"Do you honestly think I could stop her? Go!"

I returned the fireguard quick smart, doubling back to the kitchen to dump the cleaning supplies. Ellie was sitting on the kitchen bench with her mobile when I burst through the door.

"Think you can get us a lift?"

My mood had lifted (as any person's would for early release on their sentence for good behaviour).

The show turnout was huge, bigger than last year. I had felt the giddiness of what it was like to go to the show, but this year it wasn't for show bags, water fights, or rides. This year I just wanted to hang out with fun people. The very people we now pulled up next to. Stan parked next to a huge convoy of utes and cars lined up along the edge of trees opposite the main strip. It looked like a Show and Shine inspection except the cars weren't anything special and just had a bunch of people hanging out, like they did every year. I remembered always looking over at the older crowd that lurked along this strip and thinking, wow! They were out of school, had jobs, drove cars and were *so cool*. Now here I was, climbing out of Stan's Hilux, about to infiltrate the gang.

"Well, look who finally made it." Sean was perched on the edge of a ute; everyone turned to witness our arrival. A sea of inquisitive eyes rested on us, but there were two sets in particular that made me wish I had been dropped off at home instead.

Toby's unreadable gaze and Angela's murderous one.

Angela was wrapped around Toby like one of those anacondas you see on the Discovery Channel. Seriously, she was going to give him a neck injury. I had to pretend like they weren't there, that I had no interest in their presence. Yeah, that would be best.

I, the third wheel, broke away from Ellie and Stan who had

managed to not unlink their hands since exiting the car. I made my way over to prop myself next to Sean on the ute tray, the only friendly face I knew.

"How was work?" He nudged me with his shoulder.

"Dull and long."

"You missed me that much?" Sean grinned.

Rolling my eyes, I said, "So what have all the cool kids been up to?"

"Oh, you know, leaning on cars trying to look cool. It's exhausting."

"I think the problem is that you're just not doing the lean right?"

He curved his brow at me. "Is that so?"

"Yeah, you have to give it more elbow action, perhaps the odd bobbing of the head to an imaginary beat."

"Like this?" He propped his elbow on the edge of the ute for the cool casual lean and then bobbed his head in an over-the-top fashion that made me giggle.

I grimaced. "You look like you have a nervous tic."

"Ha! A *cool* nervous tic." Our laughter broke off at the slamming of a car door. Toby's car door.

"Are we going to the Point?" Toby seemed impatient when he spoke. Snappy. Sean jumped off the tray and stretched, revealing a flash of muscled stomach in the dark.

"Okey dokey." Sean groaned mid-stretch.

"Did you just say okey dokey? Is that the lingo for yesterday's generation?" I teased.

"Yesterday's? Youch! So what should I be saying? 'Like, whatever dude!'" He drew it out like an American surfer boy.

"Now you just sound like a Teenage Mutant Ninja Turtle." I shook my head, my legs swinging from the tray. The engine to Toby's ute roared to life as he revved the accelerator an impatient two, three times.

"Any day now, Murph." Toby adjusted his mirror in agitation. Angela was busying herself by looking in the reflection of her side mirror, pouting and fixing her lip balm.

Sean turned to me, offering me a hand off the edge of the tray. "We're all heading up to the Point to watch the fireworks, you wanna come?"

Stan broke away from nuzzling Ellie's neck. "Best seats in the house."

"Okay, cool."

We all piled into Stan's car, Sean in the front passenger seat, Ellie and I in the back. Half a dozen other cars followed as we left the Show behind and made our way out of Onslow, over McLean's Bridge and up into the Perry Ranges. Toby's car was directly behind ours and the last in the long line weaving up the hills. Our windows wound down, the hot summer night whipped through our hair. Stan navigated the turns like a rally driver, and I tried not to think of the increasing drop on my left as we climbed higher and higher. Instead, I kept turning to see if Toby's headlights were visible; his car was close enough behind us for me to see their silhouettes but not close enough to make out faces. No doubt Angela was burning a hole in the back of my head.

It was then I saw the flicker of Toby's indicator. He turned into a side track, marked by a sign I couldn't make out.

"Oooh, looks like someone has their own fireworks in mind," laughed Sean, looking in his side mirror.

"Where are they going? Should we wait?"

Stan peered into the review mirror. "They're heading to the Falls."

My stomach plummeted. Everyone knew about the Falls. There was only one reason anyone went to the Falls of a night time, and it wasn't to see the impressive waterfall that flowed into a series of natural pools. It was a parking hot spot. If you wanted to socialise, make out, watch fireworks, you went to the Point. If you wanted privacy, you went to the Falls.

"I doubt they will be gracing us with their presence this evening," Sean half laughed.

"No wonder Toby seemed so toey," added Stan.

I stopped looking back; instead, I focused on the back of Sean's seat.

That was that, then. I convinced myself that it should be a relief. I didn't have to waste my time with romantic fantasies, by analysing every look Toby gave me, every touch. That was that. The last nail in the coffin. Absolute closure.

Ellie reached for my hand in the darkness and gave it a squeeze of silent support. It was then I felt the ache in my heart, the churning of my stomach. I breathed deeply to control the emotion that threatened to well. If this was a good thing, then why did it hurt so bad?

Chapter Twenty-Five

The fireworks were spectacular, something to truly behold and remember for all of our lives.

Or that's what I guessed, since I hadn't paid any attention or cared in the slightest. The rest of the evening went by in a blur of self-pity. I should have gotten Stan to take me home straight after work, but no, that would have delayed the inevitable, no matter how much it hurt. I guess I needed to see it. See Toby's indicator flash through the darkness and his ute peel away.

After the fireworks display, and what felt like an agonisingly long time of forced socialising, me, Ellie and Stan mercifully wound back down the hill again. Sean decided to stay on at the Point because apparently the night was young. He had tried to convince me to stay but all I wanted to do was take my sorry self home and fall into a coma for the rest of the summer. Stan's phone had beeped with a message while he drove but he couldn't look because it was in his back pocket. We pulled up at my house, and I said my goodbyes and dragged myself up the garden path. I was at the front door when Stan yelled out to me.

"Tess, wait!" He was frowning at his mobile screen. I was about to shush him when he held his phone out to me and said, "This is for you, it's from Toby."

I dropped my bag and practically tripped over my own feet as

I quickstepped back to the car, suddenly not giving a damn if Stan woke the entire neighborhood. I grasped the car windowsill and tried not to look desperate, but I wasn't pulling it off too well.

"What does it say?" I asked, trying to keep my breathing even.

Stan passed the message to Ellie; he squinted, struggling to read it. Ellie held it up to the overhead light. She winced and her sad eyes turned up to me, her smile pained.

"He wants you to bring your bike into the shop tomorrow, so he can fix it."

I snatched the phone from her hand. It did say that, but Ellie had left out the last detail.

So I can get it out of the way.

You know how I said that the turnoff to the Falls was a last nail in the coffin? I was wrong. Fixing my bike was it. He would fulfill his end of the bargain and get me and my bike out of his way. I had been half tempted to get Stan to text back, 'whatever, never mind', but then I thought, No! I would take the moral high ground.

To prove even further that I had no-hard-feelings-let's-be-friends, I chucked in my own deal. I spent the portion of the next morning at the Rose Café making pies. Much to my mum and dad's surprise, I negotiated some hours helping them out at the shop if I could make up some pies. Mum and Dad kept casting me wary looks as if there was some alien creature in their kitchen. I suppose there was.

"So what are you going to do with the pies?" Mum asked.

"My bike is getting fixed today; it's a kind of payment, a little thank you."

"How very Dr Quinn Medicine Woman of you; sure they don't want to trade for eggs and chickens?" Dad laughed.

I just glared at him as I rolled the pastry with pin.

"And they're okay with that?" Mum frowned.

"Yes, it's all sorted. Apparently your pies are quite the hit among many."

Mum straightened with pride.

'Well, I have a new recipe. We should try it."

I held up my hand. "No, Mum, it has to be made by me, and I'm doing the Summer Berry pie deal."

I had watched my mum make these pies a hundred, maybe a

thousand times, so I was confident in being able to replicate the same crisp, sweet, sugary flavour. I made four large ones in total.

Three were Summer Berry marked with a pastry 'O' for Onslow Boys, and one was baked with a 'T' for Apple and Rhubarb pie. Toby's favourite. I didn't want to take so much pleasure in making something for Toby. I wanted to slap myself for lovingly painting the egg wash on the T with a smile. Until reality flashed back in the form of that flicking indicator that changed everything.

Dad had offered to give me and the bike a lift into town, but it was not an overly hot day. The walk was so calm and peaceful until I made it to the main strip and that peace turned into sweaty-palmed anxiety as I approached Matthew & Son. Hopefully Toby was out and I could just handball my bike to his dad and then hightail it out of there.

No such luck. The radio was blaring with the Eagles and the shop was empty aside from a pair of unmistakable legs that lay under an old, metallic blue Kingswood, one foot tapping to the beat. A muffled voice sang and whistled from under the car. I coughed and rang my bike bell and the voice froze. In one fluid motion Toby wheeled himself out from under the car, casting a winning smile that flashed brilliantly white against his grease stained face. It was the smile that caught me off guard, the one I certainly didn't expect to see greeting me. Talk about four seasons in one day; one minute he would be all smiles and joking, the next I couldn't even get a hello.

I tilted my head to the music. "What, no Glen Campbell?"

It was a universally known fact that if you passed by Matthew & Son, you would always hear Glen Campbell from the stereo.

His smile broadened. "Not on my watch." He maneuvered his way to his feet and wiped the excess grease off his hands onto a cloth.

"Well, you knew I was coming, so I guess I'll never truly know."

He crooked his finger and motioned me to follow him. I leaned my bike on the steel pole in the middle of the room and went with Toby into the office. It was a small, paper-infested space with a map-filled cork board and empty boxes piled in the corner from incoming parts orders.

Bills were spiked and clipboards with scrawled details were racked. Toby opened a filing cabinet stacked with cassettes. He grabbed one and held it out to me. I smiled. Glen Campbell's *Greatest Hits.*

"I knew it."

"Right." He took it from me and placed it back in its slot, and picking up its case, he showed me the inscription on the side. 'Matthew Morrison' was written in thick black texta.

"Dad's stash." He placed it down, picking up the next box. "Mike's God-awful stash." Sure enough, 'Michael Morrison' was inscribed on the side. He then picked up the last box, raising his brows. "My stash."

I eyed him warily as I checked out the spines of the tapes. The Beatles, The Eagles, Credence; sure enough, no Campbell.

"Still quite the mature-aged selection," I mused.

"I like to think of myself as an old soul."

I picked up a cassette I wasn't familiar with. "Sam Cooke?"

Toby's face lit up as he took it from me. "Ah, now he is an absolute favourite, you've probably heard this in my car." He looked at me expectantly.

I bit my lip in deep thought.

Toby shook his head. "You don't know who Sam Cooke is?"

I grimaced. "Maybe if I heard him …"

Toby ejected the Eagles cassette, popped in Sam Cooke and pressed play. A melodious tune oozed out of the speakers and I instantly recognised it as the song that had played when Toby had driven me home from Horseshoe Bend.

The wind flapping around the cabin, Toby's bicep flexed with tension at the wheel. The awkward side-smiles at one another in our first real encounter together. The first time we were alone.

Sam Cooke was singing through the stereo about a cupid casting its bow, and I was lost with the wonder of his beautiful voice.

Our trance was broken by an incoming whistle to the tune, and Toby's dad entered the office, pausing in surprise at the sight of me.

"Oh, hello."

"Ah, Dad, this is Tess."

"Hi, Tess." He shook my hand with vigour; I could feel the roughened calluses from years of labour.

"So what are you kids up to?"

Toby squirmed uncomfortably, it seemed no matter how old you got, there was a universal trend: parents were put on this earth to embarrass. But I didn't think Toby's dad was embarrassing, he was friendly, and charming. He had laugh lines in all the right places with dark blond hair and tanned skin. You wouldn't have automatically thought them father and son but then Matthew Morrison smiled and suddenly there was no mistaking the link.

"We were just discussing Toby's love for Glen Campbell." I smiled sweetly. Toby laser beamed his gaze into mine, silently imploring me to be quiet.

Matthew's brows raised in surprise. "Really?"

"Mm hmm." I nodded.

"He is the best!" Matthew added excitedly. "Guess all those years with Glen Campbell playing at home finally paid off. I knew you'd come around, son." He patted Toby on the shoulder. Toby looked pained.

"Why, on his sixth birthday we bought him a cowboy suit and he used to ride around the yard on his stick pony."

"Right." Toby snatched the cassette cover out of my hand. "Time to go." He ushered me towards the office door.

I had to laugh. "Nice to meet you, Mr Morrison."

"Please call me Matthew." He tilted his head and smiled.

I grabbed the edge of the door, buying some time as Toby pushed me forward.

"Well, Matthew, I would really love to learn the rest of that story someday."

Matthew rubbed his lightly whiskered chin. "I dare say I can even drag out some old photos." He winked.

"Oh, now that I would love to see."

"Out!" Toby grabbed my hand from the doorframe.

Back in the garage, I grabbed my bike and brought it forward for inspection, but I was more keen to unveil my prized pies.

I wheeled the bike over. "I brought you a present."

Toby looked over the bike, looking not in the least bit excited.

I rolled my eyes. "In the basket."

This only resulted in a curved brow of skeptical interest as he lifted up the blanket over the basket as if he were expecting a striking cobra to rear up.

"No you didn't …" He ripped the white and red check cloth from the top.

"Freshly made this morning by yours truly." I beamed.

He cocked his head as he noticed the pastry initials.

"Oh, um, these are the Summer Berries. 'O' is for Onslow Boys." I blushed. "And 'T' is for … well, it's your favourite Rhubarb and Apple."

He looked into the basket with a deep affection as if it housed a litter of fluffy kittens. He looked up at me.

"You didn't have to do that, you know."

I shrugged. "I know."

We looked at one another for a long moment, and then all of a sudden the speaker dipped and stopped and Sam Cooke was playing again, crooning out 'You send me'. Toby's gaze quickly darted down, with what I thought was a blush.

I mentally slapped myself for getting carried away. I was here so he could fix my bike, and the deal would be finished and there would be no more obligations to one another; he now had pie so all was fair. It was then I noticed Toby had looked back at me.

"What?"

He frowned, making me feel uneasy. He stepped closer looking at the side of my face.

"Keep still."

I froze "What?!"

"Don't panic, you just have a little something." He reached out and wiped his finger down my cheek.

"There."

The penny dropped as I saw his face break into a cheesy grin. I walked to peer into the side mirror of the nearest car to find a long, black streak down my cheek and Toby trying not to drop my bike as he laughed, waving his dirty hand at me.

"Oldest trick in the book."

I rubbed my cheek. "Almost as old as your taste in music."

"Right, that's it." Toby leaned the bike next to the car and held out his greasy hands to grab me.

I ran, squealing. "Toby, don't!"

I reached the safety of the street outside and Toby paused in the archway.

I wiped my cheek vigorously. "Is it gone?"

Toby shrugged with a devious smirk on his face. "Guess you'll never know, just like the Onslow Boys are never going to know about those pies."

I gasped. "I am so going to tell them."

He shook his head. "I have your bike for ransom now."

"You're a cold-hearted man, Toby Morrison."

Toby leaned against the doorframe, arms crossed as he looked me squarely in the eye. It was unnerving, as if he was peering all the way deep inside me, into my soul. All of a sudden he wasn't smiling anymore; his whole demeanour had sobered.

"So I have been told," he said in all seriousness, and with that he straightened, uncrossed his arms and turned and walked back inside, leaving me in the street, breathless and confused.

Chapter Twenty-Six

To keep my mind busy, and to the utter shock of my parents, I offered my services to the Rose Café' from Mondays to Thursdays.

I know, right? I just couldn't take lying on my bed being in my head all day. Or worse, hanging with the Onslow Boys. With Toby and Angela.

Once over their own shock, Mum and Dad had agreed wholeheartedly and even insisted I was paid properly and everything. Looks like that top I had been eyeing off wasn't so far away, after all. It was good to be there, we all liked it. Over summer, the peak tourist season, I usually rarely got to see my parents at all.

And it's not like I had anything better to do. Ellie started spending her every waking moment with Stan. Adam had headed back to his nan's in the City.

It wasn't until Thursday afternoon at the café that I saw a familiar six-foot-three figure at the counter, peering into the glass cabinet. He was wearing his navy work shirt and pants and an impressively fluorescent orange safety vest, with reflective trimming.

I walked up slowly. "I'm sorry, sir, but I'm afraid your attire is in a serious colour clash with our décor."

He turned abruptly with a surprised smile. "McGee!"

"Murphy!"

"What are you doing here?"

"I work here Monday to Thursdays."

"Two jobs? You put us all to shame."

"No I think that fluro vest ensemble puts you to shame."

I walked around the counter to grab an order docket. "So I have to ask. Did you happen to receive a pie this week?"

Sean looked at me blankly.

"A Summer Berry pie?"

Still nothing. I shook my head. "Unbelievable, you wait 'til I see that Toby Morrison."

A spark of recognition flickered in his grey-blue eyes.

"If you are referring to a parcel I received at work containing a crust of a pie with a note saying, 'Tess made us pie. It was delicious', then, yes, I received a secondhand portion of pie."

My jaw fell open. "That is so mean. The pies were meant to be for all of you."

"Pies? Plural?"

I told him about the pies I had lovingly made from scratch and instead of being mad, Sean laughed, scratching his chin.

"Right! Well, I guess this means war."

"Uh oh!"

"It's been a long-standing Murphy-Morrison tradition, war has," he said. "It was his turn for payback. Now it's my turn. I'm going to have to have a think about the next one. However long it takes."

"Riiight, okay," I said, "well, I'm not getting involved. I don't want my bike mailed back to me in pieces."

"Fair enough." Sean went back to studying the contents of the glass cabinet. I watched him as he chose. His cheek dimpled for a second and was gone again. It was an unexpected delight each time he smiled, but he wasn't really a smiler, more like a wicked grinner. He looked older than twenty-two, but maybe that was because he was so filled out, so muscular, that it made it hard not to ogle him. His short-cropped hair made it hard to decipher what colour it was, probably brown. He wasn't beautiful like Toby, but he was handsome.

"Why don't you have a girlfriend, Sean?"

Had I said that out loud?

He leaned on the counter studying me like a bug under a microscope.

I blushed, flustered. "Sorry, that's rude, it's just I don't understand why you wouldn't."

He nodded. "Because of my dynamic personality and my freakishly handsome good looks?"

"Never a serious answer with you, is there?"

His mouth curved at the corners, and he adjusted the serviette dispenser on the counter. "I don't know, why don't you have a boyfriend?"

It was my turn to fidget under scrutiny. "Guess I just haven't found the right one yet."

A moment passed between us of mutual understanding. It was nice. It felt like I was connecting with Sean for the first –

Mum sidled up alongside me and pretended to look at something on the cash register. Typical Mum move. She stared at the register with a look of fierce concentration, a scowl that didn't lift when she rose her gaze to Sean and held it there. Oh my God … what had she heard?

Then I remembered that I wasn't at the Onslow. Any fun, harmless bantering (if not borderline flirting) with an older boy wouldn't be looked on kindly by my bosses here.

How much had she seen?

"Tess, honey, why don't you jump on the coffee machine and fix table five some cappuccinos for me, please. I'll serve this young man."

Mum handed me a docket from her apron pocket. In other words, get away from my daughter. Yeah she'd been listening alright.

Sean's Adam's apple bobbed as he swallowed.

I would prepare myself for twenty questions later.

I made my way towards the opposite counter and started work on table five's cappucinos. Funny, considering my early fear of this apparatus, I now fancied myself quite the barista extraordinaire. I even went so far as to make quaint little shapes with a shake of the cocoa powder dust. No wonder my parents looked at me suspiciously. What had I become?

After serving Sean, Mum came over all smiles, an enigma of easy going. I knew she wasn't feeling easy going, and I knew what was coming next.

"So who was that?" This was just the beginning of my interrogation. I supplied the details she could handle, but failed to mention that Sean and his friends were a big part of my extra-curricular activities. I also failed to mention that Ellie was dating Stan Remington, or that Toby Morrison himself was fixing my bike. I knew if I gave my mother too much information she would piece it all together and draw her own conclusion.

Men-drinking-taking-advantage-teenage-pregnancy-*game-over*! My parents were prone to jumping to this conclusion. I think they were overrating my effect on the opposite sex.

So I played it down and soon she was partially satisfied, got bored and gave up, leaving me with a sceptical, wary 'I'm-not-thoroughly-convinced' look on her face as she put table seven's croissant in the toaster.

As November merged into December, Christmas-party season was well underway and the Rose Café had been booked for the local doctor's surgery shindig on Friday. Mum and Dad had pleaded for me to help and said they would make it financially worth my while so I couldn't exactly say no. Besides, I knew how busy it was and rushed off their feet they were. It's not like I wasn't going to get anything out of it: it was money and, not to mention, sure to score me some brownie points with the olds.

And it was just one night; what's one night in the grand scheme of things? I mentally chided myself any time my heart ached about not seeing Toby. I had to stop myself from thinking that way. He didn't belong to me; he was well and truly Angela's.

Although I could have sworn there were times when something passed between us – looks, touches, even the gaps in conversation.

When we sat in his car at the Point that night, I thought that maybe, just maybe, for the smallest of moments that he felt what I felt.

Argh! I was thinking about Toby again! Maybe a night away from the Onslow social scene would do me some good. Let them converge on the hotel without me.

I knew Ellie would be there because when she called me she whinged and whined incessantly about the fact I had to work.

"But it's Friday." The horrified words travelled through the phone receiver.

"I know, but I promised."

I then used my skills of deflection and switched the subject to Stan. Worked like a charm. Apparently, they were going to the hotel to hang out, and then the group would head up to the Point. Relief washed over me, because witnessing Angela and Toby together was definitely not my idea of a good time.

"Come on, Tess, at least come to the Point with us after, you'll be finished by then, surely."

No. *No.* I would take a stand. One night off. Surely I could manage that.

Chapter Twenty-Seven

Ellie wouldn't exactly miss me in the company of Stan; no one else really existed in their sickeningly loved-up little world.

I was tired of seeing their constant displays of public affection, the kissing and cuddling and hand holding. Tired and envious of it. There were no emails from Ellie with updates of Friday night shenanigans when I checked on Saturday morning; no text messages, either. Yep, Ellie was off the radar alright. She had a boyfriend. It wasn't official as such, yet, but I knew the pattern: when Ellie was unreachable, she was happily lost in Boyfriend Land. Someone who I knew was definitely not in Girlfriend Land (more so Nana Land), was Adam. He was proving to be an excellent pen pal.

To: tessmcgee
Kill me now! Seriously!
I am set to go on a shopping expedition to Central Plaza tomorrow with Nan and Aunty Claire. You know what that means? Hours spent at Millers, Lincraft, Spotlight, oohing and aahing over the feel of fabric. And gossiping over gluten free cake, over how Mum should be more independent and how she's getting too skinny on her latest Weight Watchers obsession. And then I'll be

forced to have a haircut that I don't need at one of those 'Just Cuts' sweat shops. I am predicting at least 8 hours of hell. But I don't need to complain. How is working for the parentals? I must say I'm not sure how I feel about all this work caper.

OMG Tess. Are you changing?? Remember you have to let me know.
Sender: Adam I can jump puddles Henderson

To: Adam I can jump puddles Henderson
I have changed! I am rolling in the $$ now, so I can go to large shopping complexes and ooh and ahh over the feel of fabrics.

Do you want to come? Ohh that's right…you're 'busy'.

Shame you can't come home this weekend. There is a Cricket Club disco in the beer garden tonight. (So I have been told via a blunt voice message from your brother) Which means Chris and Uncle Eric will be running around stressed and snappy as they try and set things up. Oh yay!

I saw your mum the other day, she hasn't lost too much weight she looks fantastic! Do I sense a bit of the green eyed monster in Aunty Claire? (Don't repeat that)
Sender: tessmcgee

To: tessmcgee
I am so going to repeat that.
Sender: Adam I can jump puddles Henderson

I smiled to myself, shook my head and logged off. I was not relishing the thought of this afternoon's shift back at the Onslow. I predicted chaos. Chris would be in a foul mood, snapping at everyone, and I'd be exposed to plumber's crack from Uncle Eric as, ciggie hanging from his mouth, he tried to connect extension cords. Melba would be muttering under her breath and Rosanna wigging out over bookings. It would be like Irish weekend, but worse.

On the plus side, I had never felt so rich. Mum and Dad had given me a rather healthy pay packet which I'd sat on my bed and counted over and over again. After finding out about the disco, I thought, what better way to treat the hard-working woman in me than with a shopping spree.

I hitched a ride into town with Mum, and I couldn't help but stare at Matthew & Son as we drove by. The lights were off and the garage doors were pulled down. I didn't have much time before I had to get ready for work, but managed to stock up on moisturiser, lip balm, some make-up and Impulse spray. I made a quick dash to Carter's to finally buy that top I'd been mooning over all summer. The top I had tried on a hundred times. The top I loved, the top that was GONE.

I frantically flicked through the racks; maybe someone moved it? No-no-no. I asked the peroxided, bubblegum-chewing shop assistant if there was another one in stock. She shrugged. "Sorry hon. What's there is there, must have sold it."

I trudged slowly out of the shop. *I would not cry over a top.*

I would, however, be severely depressed and moody for the rest of the day. My heart wasn't into shopping anymore and I slumped myself back to the car for Mum to take me home. Ellie had texted me to say that she was going to be late and not to wait for her. She was no doubt just crawling out of bed after a late night rendezvous with Stan.

Whatever.

When Mum dropped me at work, it was exactly as I'd expected: chaos. But it was good chaos. I walked through the beer garden entrance expecting to find nothing good. Instead, I was amazed. The dance floor was prepped, the DJ station in place and a man was working on the lighting. There was no shouting, or bum crack, it all looked rather under control.

I swooped down on some dirty dishes (probably from Uncle Eric's breakfast) and made my way to the kitchen.

Amy was sitting on the bench swinging her legs, seemingly in a good mood. Until she saw me. Her smile vanished, and she glared at me in her usual death stare I'd grown accustomed to. Talk about holding a grudge. Beside her, Melba peeled carrots and Chris leaned casually against the bench, his hip cocked and arms crossed. Rosanna was flailing around the kitchen in her usual flurry of insanity.

"I mean it, Chris, this kitchen is getting shut down at nine pm sharp! My kid's sitter charges like an asshole a minute after that, and I will not be taking a single order after nine."

I wasn't completely sure what an asshole charged, but it made me smile. I did find Rosannaisms quite funny when they weren't directed at me.

I took the initiative of filling the sink up and making a start on the mess from breakfast. Plus, I didn't mind making Amy look bad; that was a small part of it.

"Don't stress, Rosanna, I've got it. Nine sharp," Chris repeated.

"Anyway, I think it's only fair, we want to go to the disco, too, you know," Amy piped up.

Chris raised his eyebrows and turned to Melba. "Is that right, Melba? You hanging to bust a move on the dance floor tonight, too?"

Melba just scoffed and brushed away his words. "Oh, you."

"How about this? Kitchen shutdown at nine sharp and as long as things are shipshape here, the rest of you can knock off at ten."

I spun around. "Serious? Ten?"

Chris turned as if noticing me for the first time. "Just this once."

"Hells, yeah!" Amy screamed and swung her legs more rapidly.

"But this kitchen has to be spotless," Chris added before leaving.

"Looks like you will be busting a move after all tonight, Melbs," Rosanna teased. "Where's my drink, chook? I'm thirsty like a son of a bitch."

Amy passed Rosanna a pot of soda water which she drained in three giant gulps.

"Now, spill! Right from the start, this is some good shit." Rosanna leaned forward, her full attention directed at Amy, kitchen work forgotten now that she had negotiated her nine pm knock off. She seemed more relaxed, for now. Was that just soda water?

"What have I told you two about gossiping?" Melba said with exasperation.

Rosannna waved her off. "Oh, shush. You love it, go on, chook."

Chook's (or rather, Amy's) beady eyes swept around the kitchen, as if she was some kind of P.I, before settling into the gossip she was about to unload. Such an attention seeker, I thought, as I dipped the wok into the sink to soak.

"Okay, so I wasn't allowed to stay out to watch the fireworks (which was so unfair) and my friends were having a party at McLean's Beach, and I couldn't go because my dad's a dick and he thinks I'm, like, going to get pregnant and drink and shit."

I raised my brows as I set into scrubbing a pot. It sounded familiar, but, wow, she had a mouth on her. Either this was how fifteen-year-olds talked now, or Amy had been hanging out with Rosanna for too long.

"Anyway, I had to wait for Dad to go to sleep which took *forever*, because he never really settles until he knows everything is locked down. So, no worries, I knew the party wouldn't be cranking up 'til later, anyway. So it was real late when I climbed out onto the fire escape for my grand exit."

"I don't know if I should be hearing this." Melba frowned.

"Anyway … that's when I heard the voices under the stairs. I was like, shit!, and ducked like a ninja. And that's when I saw movement. Two shadows talking under the stairs. I thought, ooh, gross, slobbery drunks pashing in the beer garden. So I had to get a better look, right?"

"Of course." Rosanna nodded vigorously, hanging on every word. And then I noticed – so was I. I had been working on the same plate for the last five minutes.

"But they weren't pashing, they were sitting on the bottom steps, and one of them – the girl – was crying … like *really* crying, while the boy rubbed her back and then she looked up at him and was like, why? Why would he do that? And I was like, holy shit, I know who that is."

"Who?" Rosanna, Melba and I all asked at once.

And before Amy could deliver her climactic line, Ellie burst into the kitchen.

"Toby broke up with Angela!"

The plate slipped out of my hands and smashed into a million pieces. Ellie had solely addressed this to me with an elated spark in her eyes.

Everyone looked at me. At the china shards at my feet. At Ellie, then back to me, as if the information should have meant something to me.

Which it did.

Oh my God, it did.

Amy gave Ellie a pissy look. "You ruined my story."

"Sorry."

"So it was Angela?" Rosanna asked. "Under the stairs?"

"Yeah, and Chris," Amy continued. Apparently, the reason why Toby was moody and fidgety on the night of the Summer Show was not because he was taking Angela up to the Falls for some canoodling. He was taking her to the Falls to break up with her.

Angela had then relayed it all to Chris in between sobs in the wee hours of the morning. She had begged Chris, asking if he had known about it and why Toby would have wanted to break up with her.

"What did Chris say?" Melba was hooked like the rest of us.

Amy shrugged. "Some big speech about people growing apart and things happening for a reason. Deep shit. He was real careful not to be specific and break the bro code."

"The bro code?" I asked.

"Yeah. He would have totally known why Toby dumped Angela. Guys *do* talk. At least those ones do. Not to mention Chris is like David Bowie in that Labyrinth movie. That guy is all seeing, all knowing. Has a crystal ball or something. What he doesn't know doesn't exist. Lurks and perks of the profession I guess."

"Well, no wonder he was Angela's first point of call then," Rosanna mused.

"Your turn. What do you know?" Amy snapped at Ellie.

"Stan told me. It was an accident. I asked him who was coming to the disco tonight, and when I name dropped Toby and Angela, he had this funny look on his face; it was enough to tell me something was up. So I made him spill."

Amy gasped. "You broke the bro code?"

Ellie straightened with pride. "Guess I did."

With each placing of individual cutlery on the table, it triggered the same thing over and over in my mind.

Toby broke up with Angela – Toby broke up with Angela.

Those headlights I had watched with great interest through

the back window of Stan's car, the indication to the Falls that all but broke my heart and changed everything. The text message to Stan about bringing in my bike the next day. God, he sent that after he'd broken up with Angela.

My head spun. Toby had been single when I went to the shop, when we teased each other about song choices, when he wiped grease on my cheek. He did seem more relaxed than the night before. But I would never have guessed why.

Ellie found out from Stan that the Onslow Boys, including Toby, would be in attendance tonight, but Angela had gone away for a girls'/healing weekend.

Ellie clicked her fingers in front of my face, snapping me out of my own frazzled thoughts.

She giggled. "I know what you're thinking about," she sing-songed.

I was speechless, absolutely at a loss, as I fumbled my way through the silverware.

"You know, breaking the bro code is really quite simple." She leaned forward and whispered, "You just threaten to hold off on the goods!"

"Ew! Ellie, too much information, thanks."

"I'm telling you, works like a charm." She winked. "I'll get some dirt before tonight, just giving you the heads up."

Ellie was loving this, but I was uneasy.

Obviously, the entire saga was intended to be hush-hush. And I didn't want Ellie to be too inquisitive in case Stan became suspicious.

So, Toby was a free man; that didn't change things. Maybe he wanted to be single? To be free of women, to hang with the boys.

No, it didn't change anything. I would still just be Tess. The same dorky girl getting her bike fixed.

Then why was it that during the break before the dinner shift I checked my messages every two seconds in case Ellie had an update? And I got ready three hours before my shift began, paying particular attention to every detail, ensuring everything was perfect.

I was in the shower, exfoliating, shaving, conditioning up a storm when I heard my bedroom door open.

"I'm just going to the cafe, hon; have fun at work and don't break a leg on the dance floor," my mum yelled out.

My mouth was full of toothpaste as I paused brushing.

"Bwye Murm." I heard my bedroom door close.

In a burst of steam, like a magician entering the stage, I exited the bathroom. Hair in a turbanesque twist on my head, towel wrapped around me, I froze in the doorway thinking perhaps I was seeing a mirage, that my mind was heat affected from the shower, because hooked on my mirror was the light mint top I had dreamed about for all eternity, the one that had been sold. I walked over to it, touching the soft, silky fabric to ensure it wasn't a dream. A note was clipped to the hanger.

To our hard-working daughter.

We are so proud of you.

Thanks for all your wonderful help and for being an utter joy.

Lots of Love Mum and Dad. x

P.S. Ellie helped us pick this out.

My chin trembled as I picked up the top, the top I would definitely be wearing tonight.

Hours later there was a knock at the front door. I knew it would be Ellie trying to catch me out undressed, unprepared. She loved fussing over me before any big event, to do my hair and dress me up like a life-sized Barbie doll. No luck this time. I was ready, dressed and primed to go when I opened the door.

"Tess!"

"I know, amazing, right? I'm actually ready." I circled with pride.

She beamed at me. "You look beautiful."

I grabbed her in a bear hug. "Thanks to you I do."

Ellie laughed. "You could wear a hessian bag and you would still be gorgeous."

"Well, you're my best friend, you're supposed to say things like that."

Ellie walked in, a smile stretched across her face.

"Firstly – no, I don't have to say things like that, and secondly – I'm not the only one who thinks you're beautiful." She wiggled her brows at me.

"W…what?"

Her smile broadened, barely containing her excitement. "I

know something you don't know," she sing-songed tauntingly.

"Tell me."

"Sorry, I have to honour the girlfriend code."

"The girlfriend code?"

"Let's just say, Stan confided in me something that I vowed I would never repeat."

"That's really touching." I moved from the front door into the cool of the lounge, trying my best to disguise my rapid breathing as my heart hammered against my chest in anticipation.

If I didn't take the bait Ellie would get bored.

She followed me into the lounge. "Yep, something *very* interesting."

"You're right, don't tell me. You don't want to break that girlfriend code, now." I straightened the pillows on the couch. My heart pounded like crazy.

I could see Ellie's excitement dipping. "It's something about you." She stood with her hands on her hips.

I cast a fake grin. "That's nice."

Oh God! Tess, just breathe, don't freak out.

Ellie's mood darkened. "It's about someone thinking you're pretty. Goddamnit, Tess, don't you want to know what it is?"

"But the code."

"Oh, screw the code, come on, sit here." She slapped the couch cushion next to her, and I obeyed.

I squeezed my hands together in my lap, in an attempt to disguise the slight tremor of anticipation. "Ellie," I paused, "I know this might sound strange, but do you mind if you don't tell me? I kind of just want to go along with things and just enjoy the summer. Go with the flow, remember?"

What the … what was I doing? What had I just done? I could hear the words coming out of my mouth, but I seemed powerless to stop the utter stupidity I was speaking.

Ellie looked at me as if I was some wacko. "Are you serious right now?"

Was I? What was wrong with me? Any normal, red-blooded teenage girl would have thrown themselves at Ellie's feet and begged for details, had her repeat them several times, asked for the tone of voice it was said in, facial expressions, time and setting of conversation. All the usual over-the-top analytical questions. What was I afraid of? That something that I'd wanted for so long might be possible? That what I'd felt with Toby wasn't imagined? After so long of having an unrequited crush ... I didn't know how to digest the possibility.

I nodded adamantly, the tension ebbing from my veins. "I am. I don't want to know."

Ellie watched me for a long time as if half expecting me to change my mind. I met her look unwaveringly.

The corner of her mouth tilted. "You are unbelievable."

"Why, thank you."

"Okay, so I won't break the code, but all that aside, can I give you some friendly advice?"

"Okay ..."

"When you knock off work tonight, go looking for Toby, because, trust me, he will be looking for you."

Chapter Twenty-Eight

I was stalling; I knew I was. Delaying leaving the sanctuary of the toilets.

The door burst open with the sound of laughter and I snapped out of my daze. A couple of girls stumbled in, swaying their way into a line in front of the mirror, though one headed straight to the empty cubicle. I dodged the incoming traffic with a polite smile.

"Pass me a tampon, ho face," the girl from the cubicle yelled out.

Charming. I left them to their affectionate name calling.

The evening's older clientele huddled around the main bar inside. Not really into the disco scene, their entertainment for the evening was Uncle Eric behind the bar. Chris was, no doubt, manning the beer garden bar, cutting off (and trying really hard not to strangle) the drunken just-turned-eighteen crowd.

I weaved my way around tables through the closed, dark restaurant to the sliding door out to the beer garden.

Looking through the thick glass, it was actually quite pretty now the sun had gone down. The entire garden was enclosed by overgrown ivy, which Eric or somebody had woven with fairy lights. It made the space feel intimate and cast a romantic glow throughout. Huge glass vases filled with lit candles dotted each picnic table and speakers were strategically placed around the perimeter for everyone to enjoy.

Shame about the choice of music, though. I could hear 'Kung Fu Fighting' muffled through the glass door, no doubt ten times louder out in the garden.

I took a deep breath and opened the sliding door. It opened directly onto the dance floor, where a sea of drunk girls flailed their arms around in what I could only assume was their attempt at dancing. It was what I imagined walking into a snake pit would be like.

The poor choice in music only seemed to encourage the drunken horde of screaming, laughing girls. There was a mixture of muffin tops protruding from tight-fitting jeans, short skirts and boob tubes. Bare arms struck *Karate Kid* poses, karate chopping each other to the song.

As I stepped out into the garden, sliding the door closed again behind me, I was blinded by the flashing, spinning globe above the dance floor that was the disco ball, before I took a deep breath and zig-zagged through the mass of writhing bodies, intent on avoiding the smoke machine as it belched out wads of nastiness that would no doubt induce asthma attacks and coughing fits in the boozed-up girls on the dance floor.

I actually would have quite liked to see that.

Stan was perched on a picnic table, Ellie in front of him, his legs straddling her hips and her arms snaked around his neck. Ringer sat at the same table with his girlfriend, Amanda, whispering sweet nothings into her ear. I looked around the shadowy garden and the dance floor and all of a sudden felt very alone; no Toby, no Sean in sight. Looked like my only option was to sit with the happy couples and become the dreaded fifth wheel.

I plonked myself on the bench seat with a sigh, only to notice I didn't have a drink. Damn.

I had nothing to occupy my hands with. It wasn't because I was thirsty; I looked around the packed beer garden and seriously doubted all these people were all so parched at this one particular moment. It wasn't about thirst, it was about keeping your hands busy. It was a social thing. If you didn't have a drink you could smoke, or text someone. I had nothing to occupy my hands with so

I awkwardly folded them in my lap. I tried to be cool, tried not to look around too much in search of Toby. I tried not to interrupt the canoodling couples.

I gave off an air of nonchalance, when really I wanted to stand on a picnic table with binoculars and search for him. I felt a dip in the seat and then the press of heat next to me as Sean sat and slid along the wooden plank to bump into me.

I quirked a brow at him.

"You're going to get a splinter in a very unfortunate place if you keep sliding along like that."

Sean held a jug of beer and with a steady hand he topped up his pot glass, a smile on his face.

He nodded in the direction of Ellie and Stan. "I think the only ones in danger of getting a splinter in unfortunate places are those two."

They sat in front of me, kissing and pawing at one another, completely oblivious to everyone around them. Honestly, couldn't they get a room or something?

"You want to give it a go?"

My head snapped around towards Sean.

He tipped his head back and gave a deep belly laugh.

"The look on your face is classic. You don't have to look so frightened, Tess, I was referring to a beer."

He held out a freshly poured pot towards me with a knowing twinkle in his eye. He wasn't just referring to the drink. We both knew it.

I straightened my back and lifted my chin. I didn't want the drink, but I took it, had a sip and nursed it like an old familiar friend. Sean watched me with an amused smirk. Damn him.

"Of course," he said, "if you had something else in mind, I would be open to suggestions." He took a deep swig of his glass.

"What? Dry humping on picnic tables?" I posed innocently.

Sean coughed, spluttered, and beer shot out his nose. He thumped himself on the chest, his eyes watering.

Ha! One-all! I proudly took a sip of my beer.

Urgh, it was awful.

I gagged and squinted, after far too big a mouthful.

"How do you drink this stuff?"

Sean fought to speak past his spluttering. "Even worse, try swallowing it down the wrong way." We must have looked a funny pair, coughing, wincing and spluttering.

I was hyper-aware of every movement as I scanned the beer garden. My heart fluttered, pulse thumping in my ears. Beads of sweat dribbled down my back and I started to feel nauseated. Maybe it was the heat? I took another swig of my pot in the hope it would cool me down. Urgh! Maybe it was the beer? My stomach churned, and I fought not to cringe afterwards, because that's not what cool people did.

I caught Ringer giving me a long, side-on look.

"What?"

"Better not let Chris catch you with that."

Oh, right. I'd forgotten that I was downing alcohol in a public place. So weird, society's rules. Sure, people could dry hump and make out, that was acceptable, but underage drinking was seriously frowned upon.

I wanted the ground to open up and swallow me whole from the embarrassment. I hated being reminded of how young I was. I pushed the beer away and wiped the cold condensation from the pot glass on my thighs. I straightened defiantly before getting up, walking a direct line to the bar where Chris was pouring a line of shots.

I needed something to wash down the aftertaste. Something legal.

Chris glanced up at me as he reached the last shot glass. "The usual?"

I nodded. "Straight up on the rocks."

"Coming up!" He smiled, flipping a glass into his hand and scooting ice into it with smooth precision.

Chris handed me my Coke, and then looked directly at me. "Hey, Tess?"

"Yeah?"

Oh God, did he see me with the beer?

He leaned forward so we could hear one another.

"Do you think you could go and request some decent music? I don't think I can handle more crap like this."

My shoulders sagged with relief. That I could do.

As I carried my drink carefully over to the DJ, I dodged a few flailing limbs as they struck their best Saturday Night Fever poses.

Dear God.

The DJ was housed in a little protective alcove with black velvet drop sheets behind him, which advertised in tacky, glittered block letters 'DJ Rosso'. Doesn't everyone secretly dream that their name would be up on velvet someday?

The disco ball glinted off the thick gold chain around Rosso's neck and he kept re-tucking the cigarette behind his ear so the ladies got a good look of his arms in his muscle top. He probably didn't even smoke, just thought it made him look cool.

My eyes watered as I leant towards DJ Rosso; his cologne took my breath away, and not in a good way. I asked if it was possible to play something a bit more modern; he shrugged and pointed me to behind the velvet curtain where I found a thick, yellowing, well-used book full of songs. Thumbing through the selections, I took my time in the privacy of the little alcove. I took my job seriously; I had to save the party from cheesy hits of the '80s.

I leaned against the table, sliding the book towards the disco lights that didn't quite reach behind the curtain, only in dim flashes from the disco ball. A trail of fairy lights twinkled above me, but they weren't exactly bright enough to read by.

The song ended and another started up. I noticed the difference straight away as 'Funky Town' died out and a slow melodic guitar swept into the space. A pleased patron let out a 'woop' somewhere on the other side of the curtain as Live's 'Lightning Crashes' filled the speakers. A smile curved my lips. I loved this song.

I held the book closer to my face, squinting at the song list.

"You'll hurt your eyes doing that."

I squealed and spun around, knocking my knee on the table. The book fell out of my hands but Toby caught it in a juggling motion as he tried not to spill his Corona.

Toby.

"Sorry, I didn't mean to scare you," he said, grinning that gorgeous grin. My heart hammered against my ribs like an excited butterfly. I fought to catch my breath.

"You chose this song?"

"Guilty." Toby took a long swig of his beer, but his eyes never left me. He leaned forward, placing the book back on the table next to me.

"You don't need that, haven't I taught you enough about good music?"

I tilted my head to look up at him, he seemed different, more relaxed than I had ever seen him. I wondered what number Corona that was in his hand.

"I like this song." I smiled, my gaze darting downward. If this was a staring contest, he would outdo me every time.

I didn't know if it was the Corona, or the song, or the secluded atmosphere. This new, electric swirl of tension between us drew my gaze back to his, into those eyes. His tall silhouette glowed with the backdrop of fairy lights, his beautiful face lit by the blue, green, red strobes through the fabric.

"So, what's it gonna be, McGee?"

He shifted his weight from foot to foot and inched closer to me. He was so incredibly close I could feel the heat of his skin, feel his breath. I struggled to answer; it felt like my brain had completely shut down.

His gaze flicked to the song book with an amused smile. "What song have you chosen?"

"Oh," I said, blinking, "right … um …" I burned red, thankful for the dim light. I turned but his hand stilled me; he clasped my elbow and drew me around to face him.

I was drowning. I was drowning in him. My heart raced, and I couldn't think of a thing to say, all song choices, all reason, all ability to construct coherent sentences was lost. So I just said the first thing that came into my head.

"Is your name really Tobias?"

What …?Why had I …? Why was I such a freak?

Amazingly, he didn't seem taken aback by my random question. Instead, the edge of his mouth curved up, and he handed me his beer as he reached into his back pocket and flicked out his wallet. He frowned, holding it high to find some good lighting. He caught the edge of a wayward fairy light and dragged it down towards us.

I had to step closer to him in order to see the licence. As he held it over us, the fairy light lit my face; it wouldn't hide any blushes. On the plastic card, I saw the line of a serious face, a frowning younger image of Toby, which made me smile. I then saw, right there in block letters, sure enough it read: Tobias E Morrison.

"Satisfied?" he asked.

I curved a brow. "What's the 'E' stand for?"

Toby laughed and tucked his wallet back into his pocket.

"Not a chance." He took the beer from my hand, his fingers brushing mine. Goosebumps prickled on my heated skin.

I crossed my arms. "Come on, *Tobias*, don't be shy."

He finished off the last of his drink and placed it on the table beside him. Without a word he grabbed my hand and elevated my arm, leading me into a twirl as Live's lead singer (and a whole bunch of party goers) hummed on the other side of the curtain. I went with the twirl, and he pulled me back towards him, closer still.

He was trying to distract me. He was pretty good at it.

I tried to remember to breathe as he held me close.

"Nice distraction technique," I said.

He snickered, pleased. "Pretty good, isn't it?"

"I didn't think you were a dancer."

His hand squeezed mine and a flicker of some new emotion spread across his face. He leaned so close to me I could feel the press of his lips against my ear.

"Who said anything about dancing?"

He pulled back slowly keeping his face near mine. I was dumbstruck, the way his heated gaze rested on me with a knowing smile, his words … was this really happening? He stilled, watching me. I swallowed hard. Toby Morrison slowly closed the distance between us, his eyes closing. This was really happening. This was really –

The alcove was flooded with light.

"Where's the song book? I don't see it?" A beehived, sequined girl flung the curtain out of the way and stumbled into the alcove. "Roooooosssooooo, I can't see it," she whined, hands on her hips, ignoring us completely.

Toby let go of me, grabbing the book to hand over to her. She accepted it with a hiccup instead of a thank you and stamped her way back to the DJ. The curtain snagged on the edge of the DJ booth, leaving us exposed.

Toby picked up his empty beer and waved it with a shy smile. The moment was gone.

"Better fill 'er up." He went to step through the curtain and then paused and turned back.

My eyes lit up hopefully.

"Did you want a drink?"

Oh. I glanced at my Coke on the table, now watered down from the melted ice.

I offered him a weak smile. "No thanks."

He turned to go, and my shoulders drooped. I looked at my feet with a sigh. When the curtain didn't lower again as Toby left, I looked back up. He was still there. And he was staring at me. I couldn't read his face; I didn't know what he was thinking. What was he doing?

Just when I thought he would turn to leave, he stepped forward, back into the alcove, placed his empty bottle on the table and in one fluid moment, without taking his eyes from me, Toby yanked the fabric back into place, enveloping us in darkness. My heartbeat spiked at the unexpectedness of it. Toby strode towards me, his hands cupped my face and his lips claimed mine. My surprise soon melted into his touch, my hands entwined around his neck as I kissed him back. Toby's hands were in my hair, his soft lips brushed against mine, gentle at first and then more intently as the pressure of his kisses coaxed me to open my mouth, his tongue delving gently to taste my own. I followed his rhythm and pushed more eagerly against him, my hands moved to divide the thick, silken folds of his hair. I had dreamed of those lips, but never had I imagined they would be so soft, so utterly mind shattering. A small noise escaped me in pleasure; I could feel Toby smile against my mouth as he slowly edged me back against the table, the weight of his body pressed against mine; it felt like a dream, like I should wake at any moment, but no, this was real, this was definitely real!

My hand slid up under the back of his shirt to feel the long, lean flex of his muscles. Toby shuddered as my finger lightly traced his spine downwards, he kissed me so passionately as his hand slid towards my hip, down along my thigh, bending my leg to curve around his waist. I thought I might die of happiness then and there at such an intimate gesture. The edge of the table dug into me through the thin fabric of my skirt, but I didn't care. All I knew was Toby, the feel of him moving against me, the sensation of his tongue in my mouth, of his hands circling gently on my skin. As if breaking the trance, he let my leg slowly fall to the ground and eased his body off me a little, but his lips still hovered over mine. Our breath laboured, he reached out and tucked a wayward strand of hair gently behind my ear and his thumb slowly ran down my cheek. His eyes flicking momentarily to the motion of my tongue sweeping along my bottom lip, Toby pulled away slowly, a knowing tilt to his luscious mouth. He backed away and with one last lingering look he grabbed his empty bottle, peeled back the curtain and was gone.

Chapter Twenty-Nine

I wasn't overly surprised that as I lay in bed after the disco, sleep eluded me that night. I stared up at my bedroom ceiling replaying the evening's events over and over in my mind.

I had kissed Toby Morrison. I had fucking kissed Toby Morrison!

Or more to the point, *he* had kissed *me*, and I had most certainly kissed him back, oh yes I had.

When Toby kissed me it was like I burned from the inside; I had never felt more alive, more wanted. The edges of any doubts I'd had, had melted into him. It had been fast, hot and completely unexpected, and then like that he was gone, leaving me in the darkened alcove, my hands shaking as I had touched my kiss-swollen lips.

When I had finally ventured out from behind the curtain, I had watched Toby's every move. He had mingled at the disco, his eyes darting towards me every now and then with an amused glint. And what did I do? I sat at the picnic table in a catatonic state of shock. As midnight struck, I lost Toby in the crowd as everyone poured out of the beer garden and lingered on the footpath under the bug-infested lights. I wandered around, trying to seek him out, but his truck was gone. It was a bittersweet feeling; he was gone but the memory of his kiss replayed in my mind.

The sun eventually crept into my room, and if I dozed at all, it had been briefly and with a wicked smile on my face.

It wasn't a dream.

As I skipped into the kitchen, already showered and ready for work, Mum and Dad both did a double take. Dad peered at the time on the microwave and cast a confused look back at Mum.

"Good morning!" I said, giving him a kiss on the top of his head.

"Who are you and what have you done with our daughter?"

I rolled my eyes and opened the fridge. I was absolutely ravenous.

"Going somewhere?" Mum looked alarmed; my early rising had deeply unsettled their routine.

I shrugged grabbing the milk. "Work."

"Honey, it's 7am, you don't have work for another five hours."

Yes, five long, hideous hours. I couldn't wait to see Ellie to tell her what had happened last night. I had thought of messaging or emailing her, but I wanted to see her reaction in person.

Five long hours away also meant hours without seeing Toby.

"What's wrong with being organised?" I threw back.

"Nothing, it's just …" She floundered to think of something. Poor souls, I thought, first a summertime job, then helping them at the shop and now rising with the sun; it was all too much.

"What time did you get home?" Dad asked over his paper.

Uh-oh. If I told them, it wouldn't take them long to calculate just how little sleep I'd had and then they'd get all kinds of suspicions as to what had made their daughter so chipper this morning.

"Oh, not too late, you know how I love my beauty sleep."

He nodded and turned back to his paper, accepting it.

Boom! That's how it's done. Bullet dodged … for now.

Ellie sat opposite me in the restaurant, before we officially started our shift. She had just listened intently to my play by play of the night's events: from the encounter behind the DJ station, to *the kiss*, to Toby's disappearance. I retold it beautifully, played it out to full dramatic effect.

Not once did she interrupt me or look shocked or even happy

for me. Instead, she listened with a pained expression on her face and an uncharacteristic silence.

Quite frankly, it wasn't the reaction I had expected.

I fidgeted in my seat. "What? What is it?"

"Nothing." She couldn't even bring herself to look at me as she smoothed out invisible creases in her black apron.

I frowned. I didn't get it. Last night, she had been my own personal cheer squad, told me to seek out Toby because she had inside information that went in my favour. What had changed?

"Nothing?" I repeated. "Well, THAT'S crap!"

Ellie sighed and finally spoke. "I just don't …" She broke off as if picking her words carefully.

"You just don't what?" My patience was wearing thin. "Out with it."

She gave me a sad smile. "I just don't … I don't want you to do what I do."

I crossed my arms defensively. "And what's that exactly?"

Ellie shifted in her chair. "I don't want you to jump in the deep end with him. Hold back a little."

"That's not what you were chanting last night."

"I know, but take it from someone who knows."

"Knows what?" I said. "Has Stan said something?"

"No! No I don't even think he knows anything. We haven't even talked about last night."

Didn't surprise me, I seriously doubted they could speak much with their tongues in each other's mouths all the time.

Ellie grabbed for my hand and gave it a squeeze. "Just don't let yourself be the rebound girl."

"The rebound girl?"

"Tess," she continued carefully, "he only just broke up with Angela after dating for *over a year.*"

I took a deep, calming breath. I didn't want to hear this.

"Just don't expect too much, okay? Just take a step back."

I pulled my hand away and pushed my seat back. It gave an ear-piercing scrape against the polished floorboards.

"Noted," I said, "thanks for the pep talk." I got up to walk towards the kitchen. If I didn't move now, I would say something I would regret.

"Tess, wait." Ellie caught my arm, jolting me to a stop. "I'm sorry, that's great, I mean really great. I'm excited for you. I just don't want you to get hurt, that's all."

"You mean you just don't want me to have a life," I bit out.

Hurt flashed across Ellie's face. "That's not true."

"Isn't it? Well, maybe if you'd thought outside your little world for one moment, you could have saved me from making such a huge mistake."

I spun back around towards the kitchen, tears threatening to overflow from my eyes. She wasn't allowed to see them, she wasn't. This time she let me go; she didn't call out. This time she didn't say a word.

I had wanted Ellie to squeal and hug me and help me with my next outfit to dazzle Toby in, to keep me filled in on the Onslow Boys' next social event. But as we worked together in silence for the whole shift, I knew it wouldn't happen. As much as I fought against it, Ellie's words rang in my ears and fed into my paranoia. Why did he kiss me and then just leave? Maybe he wasn't into it. No, no he was definitely into it. A myriad of thoughts crowded my overworked mind; it was a full-time job pushing my doubts aside. As if that wasn't bad enough, my heart all but stopped when I heard the front door screech open and familiar laughter filled the front bar. I found an excuse to go to my bag behind the door so I could peer inside at the boys as they pulled up their bar stools.

Sean, Stan and Ringer looked over the menu.

No Toby.

I loitered a little longer and eavesdropped on their conversation.

"Where's young Tobias?" Chris asked, handing over their drinks.

I pressed myself against the wall, hanging onto every word, and peeked through the crack in the restaurant divider.

"I dare say he is probably facedown in a world of pain right about now," Sean said with an evil smile.

"He was pretty wasted," Chris laughed.

"'Coronas are the devil's brew', I believe he said?" added Ringer.

They all shuddered and laughed. "I doubt we'll even see him

today. Serves him right."

Their conversation shifted to lunch, and I made my way back to the restaurant before Chris saw me. He hadn't seemed that drunk to me, but what did I know? 'Devil's brew' and 'wasted' ran through my head as I pictured Toby at home, feeling sick and sorry for himself and the stupid things he'd done the night before. Like kissing the rebound girl.

I felt sick. I told Ellie as I passed her that the boys were in the bar and made my way, once again, to the refuge of the ladies' toilets.

I managed to hold it together. I tried not to think too deeply about all my fears about kissing Toby and the way he'd up and left like that, with no warning. I felt exhausted. I just wanted to go home and crash into oblivion before the stress and agony of the dinner shift. I wanted to avoid Ellie's eyes that would no doubt reflect a silent 'I told you so'.

When I finally made it home between shifts, scuffing my feet as I trudged towards the driveway, I froze. My bike was propped up under the carport, sparkling, shiny and fixed. I wondered if my lack of sleep was making me hallucinate.

My heart threatened to beat out of my chest; I ran up the drive and clasped the handles. Yep, it was real. I dashed inside but the house was empty.

"Damn it!"

I frantically dialed the shop number and heard my mum's usual spiel after the second ring.

"Good afternoon, Rose Café, Jenny speaking."

"Mum!"

"Oh, hi honey, how was work?"

"Just awesome, hey listen, my bike?"

"Oh yes, sorry, I meant to put it in the garage but I was running late."

"When did it get dropped off?"

"Not long after you left for work, just five minutes later, and you could have ridden it there. You could have finally used your new helmet."

I cringed away from the receiver.

"Who dropped it off?" My voice seemed smaller now.

"Matthew Morrison, himself, did. I was late for work because of it, got caught up chatting to him. He's such a lovely man, isn't he? And a real fan of my pies, so he's definitely in the will."

A coldness settled over me. Toby's dad dropped it off? Toby had gotten his dad to return my bike instead of him. That clinched it. He was avoiding me. The bike was fixed, so that was that. He didn't need to see me anymore. Hot tears welled in my eyes. I was so *stupid*.

I tried not to sound too different on the phone; Mum could sniff out unhappiness like a bloodhound.

"Cool, thanks, Mum. I better go."

"You can ride your bike to work tonight," Mum said, sounding excited.

"Yeah." I tried to match her enthusiasm. "Yay!"

The phone clicked as she hung up, and I listened to the silence of the empty house. The realisation swept over me.

I was the rebound girl.

Chapter Thirty

I was so tempted to call in sick, to avoid the rest of the weekend and everyone in it altogether.

But Chris could have eyed the beer in my hand last night, combined it with my silence during lunch service, and it wouldn't take him long to conclude that I wasn't sick, I was hungover. He'd give me the sack for that, I just knew it. It was a tempting thought, to be honest. Maybe if I broke my arm, I would be sent away to my nan's house in the city for the rest of the summer. Not that I had a nan in the city, but still. I needed Adam. He could have cheered me up, especially in lieu of Ellie's and my heated debate at lunch.

After a catnap, I showered and had a quick bite to eat. Although I felt human again, I didn't feel much better until I started getting ready for work. In the process, my self-pity morphed into determined resilience as I stared hard into the mirror.

I opted for a cute little top and skirt. If I was going to face an audience, I was at least going to do so looking hot.

As I walked into the bar that afternoon, I had on my best happy-go-lucky face and flashed the customers a winning smile and false confidence that had everyone fooled. Mostly everyone knew me by now, and I was always greeted with either a 'Tess!' or 'McGee!'.

Days of Tic Tac Tess were light years away. I couldn't believe that used to be my biggest problem: a stupid nickname by an immature boy.

I hung my bag up behind the door. Ellie's bag was already there. I was still mad at her, but it would take far more energy to keep up the silent treatment than to be civil. She couldn't rain on my parade anymore, because I simply wouldn't confide in her about my love life. I knew that would hurt far more than the silent treatment, even though, in its own way, it was kind of the same thing.

Ellie was still on edge around me as if she wasn't wholly buying the act, and I knew that if anyone could see through it, it would be her.

Rosanna, Amy and Melba seemed to suspect something was amiss though I chatted animatedly to them about all sorts of things. Maybe too animatedly. I was over-the-top bubbly with the customers, and I even caught Chris giving me a confused frown. After a few hours, my face ached from all the smiling, and I was exhausted. How could Ellie stand this all the time? Being a wallflower conserved so much more energy. I let my smile slip for a breather as I gathered some cutlery for a table. Beside me, Ellie reached for some silverware for her table.

"Toby's here," she whispered.

And when I met her eyes, she smiled a small smile and then whisked herself away.

Oh shit.

I had no intentions of running to the poolroom, or even crossing his path at all if I could help it. Even though I had completely resented Ellie's advice, I knew there was something to it. I already felt like a big enough idiot.

When Chris asked me to deliver a meal into the poolroom, I paused so long he thought I hadn't heard. I had heard alright. Even though the order of a single bowl of chips didn't have 'Onslow Boys' written on it, it didn't have to; to me, the poolroom was a no-go zone. Enemy territory. I had to woman up. The last thing I would do was get Ellie to run the meal for me, so instead I ran fingers through my hair, straightened my clothes, took a deep breath and grabbed the meal.

It felt like every step I took was in slow motion. The achy

melody of Portishead echoed from the poolroom as I dodged traffic in the front bar on my way. All of a sudden, I wasn't paranoid about dropping the plate or spilling the contents, I was just hoping that Toby might have been in the men's room when I delivered the meal.

No such luck; I spotted him through the alcove, laughing at some bad shot that passed from his opposition. He leaned casually against the windowsill, pool cue in one hand, beer in the other. He didn't look hungover to me, I thought. As I paused, watching on just beyond the doorway, his eyes flicked up and met mine just as he was about to take a shot.

My breath hitched at the acknowledgement; the first time since last night. The contact was broken when Sean heckled him to hurry up and take his shot. He did, making the white ball rebound on the cushion and pot the wrong ball.

"Oooooh, two shots, son!"

The poolroom filled with cheers and exclamations of shock at the rare occasion Toby made a mistake on the pool table. The boys pounded him with back slaps and ruffled his hair. He shook them off with a smile. My face felt on fire; he'd lost concentration because of me.

I hurried into the poolroom, trying not to draw attention to myself while they were all preoccupied.

It was then that I looked at the order. 'Bowl of chips' with an angry face next to it, in Ellie's handwriting. Then I realised why, as a group of Angela Vickers' friends sat around a barrel on stools, pursing their lips in disdain as they sat in the corner feeling superior.

Awesome, I thought. Icing on the cake of a brilliant day.

"Bowl of chips," I said in the friendliest way I could.

Three sets of cold, angry eyes met me, all casting me a death stare.

They begrudgingly moved their drinks aside for me to place the bowl down. I offered them another friendly smile and escaped while the going was good.

Only to be stopped by a shrill voice.

"Hey, bar-keep!"

I turned, dread swept over me; the snarky comment had

drawn the whole room's attention.

My brow quirked in question as I met her gaze. Just try it, I thought. I was in no mood for her.

The girl's manicured claw pointed to the chips.

"We said chips and gravy."

The docket didn't read with gravy, but the customer was always right, no matter how evil they were.

"I'll grab you some," I replied sweetly.

The blonde with her eyes a little too close together feasted distastefully on a chip.

"And we said chicken salt, not ordinary salt."

"God, who would have thought you would actually need a brain to waitress," Pencil Eyebrows scoffed.

I bit the side of my jaw, ready to grab the bowl from the barrel and pelt them with chips when I heard a voice next to me.

"Lay off, Jules." Toby lingered near the French door, chalking his pool cue.

Pencil Eyebrows had a name, and now her death stare was focused on Toby.

"Oh, I forgot that jail bait here was you guys' little pet. I guess you can't handle a real woman with a brain."

"Which instantly rules any of you out," Toby added coolly as he blew the excess chalk off his cue and gave them a knowing smirk. Laughter and catcalls sounded in stereo as the Onslow Boys overheard the exchange.

"Go fuck yourself, Toby."

Jules stood up, chucking a handful of chips at him and stormed out, earning me three bumps in the shoulder. But that did little to upset me when I met Toby's gaze, and he gave me a wink.

Sean slung an arm around my shoulder. "Never mind them, Jail Bait, they can't help it. They were born with chronic evil."

I smiled at Toby. "You okay? You're lucky a wayward chip didn't take out an eye."

He laughed then, the warm familiar one I loved to hear.

"Could have been worse, there could have been gravy."

I sighed, my attention moving towards the mess that had been dumped on the floor.

I retreated for a dustpan and headed back in, ice broken by, of all things, a bowl of chips.

Chapter Thirty-One

"Seriously, what is the point of going to the Point?" Stan whinged.

"Well, do you have a better idea, lover boy?" Sean smashed the billiard balls with a satisfying crack.

Stan shrugged. "I don't know, just thought we could try something different, that's all."

"McLean's Beach?" someone chucked in.

Sean faked snoring.

"How about the Falls?" added Toby, as he flicked through the jukebox's song selection.

"What? Hang out with all the deviants?" Stan scoffed.

"I don't know, Stan, sounds like your kind of scene."

He flipped Toby the finger.

Toby grinned wickedly before turning back to his task with a shrug. "There's good swimming there, that's all, it's hot enough, it's just an idea."

"Swimming at the Falls, eh?" Sean rubbed his soft stubble in deep thought. "Why not?"

"Whatever, can we wait for Ellie to knock off work first?"

"Aw, don't worry Romeo, we won't leave without Juliet." Sean grabbed Stan and made kissy noises. Stan pushed him over.

I couldn't help but smile at their banter as I gathered the last of the chips from the floor; my smile slowly faded when I caught Toby staring at me.

He was leaning back against the glass display of the jukebox, his arms folded. "So, you in?"

Play it cool, play it cool.

I shrugged. "I guess."

Whoops and cheers echoed down the dirt path as the boys raced each other towards the secluded swimming hole down the bottom of a rocky incline. I could hear the distant thundering of the waterfall clearly, even though it was still a fair distance off.

Ellie and I lagged behind as we climbed out of Ringer's car, shaking our heads as we secretly wondered who were the teenagers among us.

"Are we okay?" Ellie asked as we shut the boot and carried our borrowed towels.

I bumped her shoulder. "Of course."

I could make out her brilliant white smile in the moonlight.

As we neared the path, our attention turned toward the slamming of a car door, where Toby stood leaning against his ute.

"You not swimming?" Ellie asked.

"Nah, I'm just the ideas man."

"Cool, well, I better go make sure these fools don't kill themselves." Ellie flashed me another smile and ran after the boys.

Toby pushed off from the door, hitched himself up onto the back of his tray and made a place on one of the rugs. He casually patted the space next to him, and I attempted not to smile too broadly at the relief of such a small gesture.

"Unless you wanted to swim?"

Before he could even finish his sentence, I chucked the towel into the tray and climbed up and over to sit next to him.

"I guess that's a no then?"

"It was a terrible idea, I can't believe they're all down there." I laughed.

Toby lay back, linking his hands behind his head and closed his eyes.

"A terrible idea, or a brilliant idea?" He peeked an eye open before closing it again with a smile.

I was suddenly very aware of how alone we were. The distant yells and cascading water were a million miles away, or so it felt.

I picked at the frayed edge of the rug. "Thanks for fixing my bike."

"Oh," he smirked, "that."

"Yeah. I'm back on the road again."

"Yeah, I was kind of pissed at my dad," he said, his eyes still closed.

"Why?"

"He didn't ask me. He just thought he'd do me a favour and deliver it for me."

"Well, that was nice of him."

"I guess. It's just ... I wanted to deliver it myself."

Relief flooded me. In a moment of panic, I had feared the worst, that he was avoiding me. But he wasn't.

"Well, it was a good effort to fix it while you were hungover."

Toby's eyes opened as he frowned at my words; he straightened.

"The boys said you were hungover today."

He still looked confused. "Oh! I didn't fix the bike today."

Now it was me who looked confused.

Toby fiddled with the frayed edge of the rug, his hand close to mine as he spoke, not looking at me. "I fixed the bike the day you gave it to me, Tess."

My frowned deepened. "Why didn't you tell me? You know ... give it back?"

He looked at me now. "Remember I said, 'what if I didn't want to fix your bike?'"

I remembered. "Yes ..."

"I didn't want to fix it, because I liked driving you places."

I stared at him, unable to believe it was true.

"Not that I was the most reliable taxi service." He rested his elbows on his bent knees.

"Oh, I don't know," I said, "you were there when it counted. Saved me from perishing on the Horseshoe Bend. Took me on my first drive to the Point to watch the fireworks, it was only last night ..."

His eyes flicked up to mine as I broke off at the last two

words. Last night.

"Yeah, last night," he repeated.

"Guess you won't be drinking Coronas again anytime soon."

The corner of his mouth curved up. "Not if I can help it, no."

He regretted drinking the Coronas; I wondered if he regretted anything else as well.

I shifted to sit next to him and leaned against the cabin rear window.

Don't jump in the deep end, Tess, play it cool.

Pulling back and taking it slow was good advice. That's what I decided to do.

"Am I just the rebound girl?" I asked. That didn't last long.

Toby stiffened, his scowl deep and so penetrating I had to look away from it.

"What makes you say that?"

Now I was uneasy. Me and my big mouth.

"Because we are sitting in probably the same place you sat a week ago when you broke up with your girlfriend."

I regretted it as soon as the words left my mouth. I could feel Toby's anger pouring off him in waves. Suddenly going for a swim seemed like a great idea.

"I see," was his cold response.

I cleared my throat, finding myself utterly fascinated with the edge of the rug I fiddled with. I couldn't take my eyes off it, couldn't look at him.

"I'm just saying that you don't have to worry about me expecting anything more. I know last night was just a bit of fun, and that if you had any regrets today, to not worry about it. It is what it is, and I'm cool about it."

Stupid words. Stupid words coming out of my stupid mouth.

I expected his shoulders to slump in relief or his icy exterior to thaw, but it didn't. He seemed more agitated as he ran a hand aggressively through his hair.

"Is that what you think?" he said. "That I regretted last night?"

I looked at him then, trying to hide the hurt in my expression. "Don't you?"

He sat up straight and grabbed my hand to stop it from

fraying the edge of the rug.

"I may have been buzzed last night, but I remember everything. I can't promise you that I won't want to drive you home, or kiss you like crazy again. Because I will. I do." His eyes shifted towards my mouth and then back to meet my eyes.

"I like you, Tess."

I was supposed to act cool and indifferent and hold back from falling in too deep right now.

Take it slow, Tess. It's good advice – take it slow!

I kissed Toby for the second time. I pushed him to sit back against the window as I straddled his lap, feeding the hunger, living for the moment. We weren't coy and polite this time; Toby's hand slipped under my shirt, his fingers skimming my bare belly, his mouth catching my exhales as I cupped his face and tilted his head to the side for better access to his lush mouth.

Toby nipped playfully along my neck, which made me giggle. He grasped the curve of my knees and drew me closer. I felt the unmistakable evidence of his desire pressed between my legs as his hands slid up my bare ribs and pushed under my bra to touch my breasts. I rocked slowly on his lap pressing into his touch, never feeling more alive than with the new sensations that tingled in foreign places. Never before had I wanted Scott or any other boy to touch me as I wanted Toby touching me now. I relished in the brush of his work-roughened fingers gliding over my skin and the way he moved under me. His hands suddenly bunched my skirt up in his fists as his tongue filled my mouth to duel my own.

I braced myself for the hand that was sliding along my thigh, daring to delve between my legs to explore me like no other had. But just as his finger pulled the elastic of material he froze and panic shot through me at the thought that all of a sudden he had come to his senses, that he thought it – us – was a bad idea. I breathed hard, tried to catch my breath as his head tilted to the side, listening for something. That's when we heard it, the incoming laughter and voices of an approaching stampede of swimmers.

I slid off Toby's lap and worked at adjusting my skirt and fixing my hair. Toby had a far worse problem as he pulled on his shirt to hang over the large tent in his shorts. We sat apart and cast knowing smiles to one another as we both tried to gather our breaths and look casual, like we were just hanging out, not dry humping in the back of his ute.

Toby looked around and feigned surprise at the disheveled, soaking figures that approached.

"Back already?"

"Tobias! That was the *worst* idea you have *ever* had." Sean shivered.

"I take it you didn't have fun, then?"

"Ffffucking ffffreezing," he stuttered.

Toby flashed a grin towards me. "I guess we had a better time?"

I blushed and glanced away.

A better time? Oh yeah we did.

Chapter Thirty-Two

**Mum and Dad gave me Monday and Tuesday off to make up
for my work-filled weekend.**

They said I couldn't work seven days a week, even though
they did and they still wanted me to have *some* fun this summer
because I was working so hard. It made me feel a bit guilty
considering I was telling them so many white lies lately about
where I was and who I was with. The last thing I wanted was to
smash the illusion of being the perfect daughter, especially given
my extracurricular activities with a certain gorgeous twenty-two
year old who could kiss like no one else.

Ellie's ongoing advice played on my mind even though I was
convinced that I wasn't Toby's rebound girl seeing as he obviously
had some feelings for me.

He said he liked me, and he had fixed my bike ages ago and
that was when he was still with Angela. Ellie thought that was a
major development.

I thought the mere fact I had kissed Toby twice was an *epic*
development.

But Ellie still wanted me to take a step back, which meant no
accidentally going past his work and 'bumping' into him and no
joint daytime trips mid-week with the Onslow Boys, (which I
thought ludicrous and unfair).

"Trust me, Tess! Haven't you heard the old saying treat 'em mean to keep 'em keen? The more unavailable you seem, the more he'll want you."

"That sounds like playing games to me."

"You'll thank me when he's pawing over you at the weekend, begging for your time."

Talk about confusing advice. If not a tad hypocritical.

Apparently the boys had gone water skiing mid-week and McLean's Beach Friday night, and with the view of 'playing it cool', I didn't go to either and now Saturday lunch and well into Saturday night, Toby was a no show. Great plan, Ellie.

I gave her my best 'not happy' look.

"Don't worry, they'll be here," Ellie reassured me.

And the Onslow Boys did rock up. At least Stan and Sean did. No Toby, though. Ellie gave me a worried look, and I went back to the kitchen. Obviously, 'absence makes the heart grow fonder' was more like, 'out of sight, out of mind'. As I dumped dirty dishes in the sink, I vowed never to take Ellie's advice again.

"What's your problem?" Amy glared as dirty dishwater splashed her in my dumping fury. I stormed out the back to kick a milk crate across the cement and slumped on to the back step to take a few breaths. I was angry at the world, at Toby, but mostly at myself.

Maybe I *was* the rebound girl.

At Sunday dinner service, when Toby was a no show again, doubt rose in me. Apparently the Onslow Boys had gone fishing, which was just Jim-dandy, but a whole week had gone by and the buzz from last weekend was quickly wearing off.

"You stress too much, I haven't exactly seen a heap of Stan this weekend either," Ellie said.

"You mean aside from your mid-week catch ups and yesterday and today? That's not classified as 'a heap'?"

"Not for our standards."

I really didn't give a crap about what their standards were, I was too busy feeling sorry for myself as I sipped on my Sunday night after-work staff drink. I hit the heavy stuff tonight. Double shot raspberry lemonade; yeah, I was depressed.

"You may not think it now, but in time you'll thank me for

this."

I just grunted into my syrupy lemonade. The weekend was over. I felt like a little lap dog waiting for the door to open, waiting for the boys to come waltzing in. Ellie had tried to find out more info from Stan about their whereabouts and if they were coming in, but they must have been out of range. We couldn't even grill Chris, who was absent from his usual weekend shift. He wasn't out bonding with the boys; instead, he had taken a break to go to the city and stay with his nan and Adam.

Adam. I wished Adam were here. Ellie was sapping my energy with an entire summer devoted to her. I needed a buffer.

I nearly knocked my drink over at the sound of the door; I whipped my head around so fast it threatened to snap off my neck. A lone figure walked through. Stan. My shoulders slumped as Ellie brightened.

"Hey, you!" She beamed, swiveling in his direction.

His smile was warm and authentic, his eyes lit up when he saw her and there was no doubt how he felt about Ellie. There was no guarded, unreadable, broody expression on Stan's face. He was an open book; they both were.

Ellie flung her arms around his neck and kissed him. He held her, causing Ellie's feet to hover off the ground.

Stan winced. "Ah, Ellie watch my sunburn."

He was noticeably flushed, and Ellie pulled back his collar with a gasp.

"Stanley Remington, you deserve a right arse kicking."

I shook my head. "Boys and their inability to rub sun screen on each other."

"Believe me, it's not worth the hassle." He cringed as he sat down.

"I can see that." I eyed him skeptically.

"So where is everyone?" Ellie asked innocently.

"Home, I guess, big day."

Stan looked beat. A combination of drinking and sunstroke was nasty indeed. I wondered if Toby had suffered the same fate? He wouldn't burn like Stan because of his beautiful olive complexion, but I was appeased by the fact that they had had a big day and that was the reason they didn't come in tonight. But still.

Stan had; he would have walked on fire to get to Ellie. My heart spiked with jealousy at how their relationship had developed.

Stan and Ellie dropped me off at home, early even for a Sunday night, on what had to have been the most anti-climactic weekend of the summer. With no Onslow Boys and no Chris to hold a lock-in, the bar had closed an hour early and so there I was, sitting in my room all before midnight. My dad had even stirred to get a drink and seemed utterly amazed I was home already. At least that would make me look good, I thought.

I checked my emails knowing there would be nothing from Ellie. Her emails became less and less frequent these days. Plus, she was no doubt in Stan's bungalow right now sponging him down with aloe vera cream.

Old faithful Adam, however, sat in my inbox, which made me smile no matter what my mood.

To: tessmcgee
Guess who can finger knit? Jealous much? Yeah you should be!

Hey I will finger knit you a scarf, I think if I start now it should be ready for winter in about 4 years' time…. Watch this space!

So what's happening McGee?? Chris is here but he won't dish the dirt, he is such a killjoy. I wonder when Mum and Dad are going to tell him he's adopted?

Maybe this Christmas?? Hand over his Bruce Springsteen's Greatest hits CD with a P.S…You're adopted!

Live to hope.
Sender: Adam I can jump puddles Henderson

To: Adam I can jump puddles Henderson
Sorry dude! There is no mistaking your family resemblance. Brothers to the bone! If anything, I suspect you were cloned from the same petri dish, aside from the whole serious broody thing (Don't tell him I said that).

If you can't manage the adopted angle how about dropped on his head as a baby? That might explain a few things. But then again you might have been dropped on your head as a baby too? Which in any case would also explain a few things.

Like ah Finger knitting??? What the?

Sender: tessmcgee

To: tessmcgee

People are afraid of what they don't understand Tess. Finger knitters everywhere have been suffering from the prejudice for centuries. I have to say I am a little disappointed in you.

Considering I fell off a billiard table recently I think I will avoid the whole dropped on head topic, it might back fire.

What are you doing home from work?

Sender: Adam I can jump puddles Henderson

I hit reply. I wanted to tell him about my horrid weekend, about Ellie's boy theory which I was seriously starting to doubt. I wanted to tell him each scenario and every painstaking analysis I had all week. But in order to do that, first I would have to tell him about the boy. Something I had been avoiding and something I couldn't do via email.

Screw it, I thought, and picked up the phone.

My fingers threaded nervously through the curve of the phone cord as it rang. Then he answered. Much like Ellie, there was surprised silence after I told him a (sugarcoated) version of events. He didn't need to know about the dry humping. But if he was about to echo the same spiel as Ellie, for one, I didn't think I could stand it and two, maybe they couldn't be all wrong?

Adam blew out a breath. "You've been busy."

"Oh, you know, just the typical summer drama." I winced.

"Tess. I have been finger knitting. A typical summer is not in my existence."

"I guess you'll have to live vicariously through us, then."

"I'll say. Toby Morrison, huh?" He sounded as if he needed it to sink in, as the phone line fell into more silence.

"So do you think I'm the rebound girl?" I asked, afraid of the answer.

"Possibly. But aren't we all on the rebound from someone? I mean, no matter how much time goes by, the next person will always be the rebound person. Was Stan the rebound guy for the tourist sleaze bag? Or was the tourist sleaze the rebound from Stan?"

I sat up straighter now. "I guess."

"Do you want some advice?"

I nodded, which in hindsight was pretty dumb on the phone but he continued anyway.

"Don't over-think it. Trust me, blokes aren't complicated creatures."

"So do you think I should hold back?"

"What for? If you like him – I can't believe I am having such a chick conversation with you – but if you like him, let him know. Not in a stalkerish 'I want to have your babies' way, but if you wanna hang with him, do it. If he's keen, he'll appreciate your honesty more than playing stupid games with him. Good God, woman, you're taking boy advice from Ellie? Seriously?"

"You weren't around, Adam! Besides, it's not exactly like I talk to you about this stuff."

"Yeah, well, this is the one and only time I like not having a vagina."

"Gross."

"Like I said," Adam continued, "the male species isn't as complicated as you think, so just go with it and do your own thing."

I felt a wave of relief pass over me at Adam's no-nonsense, honest words. Maybe it was because it was what I wanted to hear, but it was also good to get a guy's point of view. Adam was my last point of call before I picked up my mum's copy of *Men are from Mars, Woman are from Venus.*

"Thanks, Adam."

"No sweat. I better go, this scarf won't knit itself, you know."

"You sure you don't have a vagina?"

"Whatever, Toby lover!"

"Don't say anything to Chris, okay? It's not exactly common knowledge."

"Ha! That's what you think."

I froze. "What's that supposed to mean?

"Here's another helpful insight into guys, Tess: opposed to what girls think, mates talk. We are mostly apes with our brains in our pants, but don't underestimate the power of the bro code."

"The bloody bro code."

"It is a strong, unbreakable bond."

"Ellie broke it," I laughed.

"I bet she freakin' did." He laughed, too.

"Any last words of advice, oh wise master?"

"If you take up finger knitting, make sure you use talcum powder so the wool doesn't rub on your fingers."

"Got it. Anything else?"

"Stop playing games and go get him."

As I hung up the phone, that was exactly what I decided to do.

Chapter Thirty-Three

I had looked down this drive maybe a thousand times before, but none of those numerous times held as much weight as it did now.

I lowered my foot to balance my bike as I came to a stop. A singular porch light shone like a beacon down the long curving driveway, casting a shadow across Toby's car.

Light on. Car in drive.

He was home. I supposed anyone would be at 2am on a Monday morning. I was in two minds, I was ready to turn around and head for home; I paused, a murmur of music inside had my heart thumping in a matching rhythm. He was definitely home, he was awake and before nerves demanded I leave, I walked my bike down the drive, towards the light, towards the music.

I propped it near the wall of the cabin, moving through the darkness of the carport, skimming myself sideways so as not to scratch Toby's car. I placed a hand against the bonnet. Cold, Toby must have been home all night. I realised how creepy that was so quickly pulled my hand away.

Stop being such a stalker, Tess!

Before I could put too much thought into where I was and what I was doing, I followed the ever-increasing thud of music that led me around the back. Then I had a thought. *What if he wasn't alone?* I faltered for a second, then pushed forward. If I chickened out now I would never get any peace. I wanted – needed – to do this so before any more self-doubt forced itself into my mind, I turned the corner.

A dim single bulb lit the back deck that housed a couch … in which Toby sat. And he was alone! Surprise lit his face as he saw me. He paused mid-sip of his beer, and went to speak then thought better of it.

As he sat there, all relaxed, nursing his stubby, my heart leapt into my throat. He was so incredibly sexy in low-rise jeans and a black Bonds singlet, he was barefoot with bed-tousled hair and he was here, at his home, sitting and staring at me.

All of a sudden I felt weird and out of place.

An amused crease tilted his brow. "What are you doing here?"

What was I doing here?

When I didn't answer, Toby melted further into his couch, swigging on his beer, only momentarily taking his eyes from me.

"You want one?" He held up the stubby.

"Sure."

He stood, towering over me. Skimming past as he walked towards a bar fridge on the back deck, I quickly concentrated on trees that lay beyond Toby's backyard, silhouetted in the moonlight. Crossing my arms and staring into the nothing, it took every ounce of my strength not to watch Toby bend to the bar fridge, clinking the bottles as he rearranged the shelves. I didn't really want a beer, but I thought it would make me seem less awkward, have more of a purpose, because that's what friends do, right? They hang out on back decks listening to music and downing a few beers.

As I tried to justify my presence, something blisteringly cold pressed against the back of my neck. I gasped and stepped away, spinning around. Toby grinned wickedly as he held out a beer.

"Cold enough?"

I rubbed the back of my neck and threw him my best death stare. That only seemed to amuse him more. His gaze dipped to my shoulders, then back up to my face again. He stepped forward, all amusement suddenly sobering into that serious gaze I'd seen so often.

"You caught a bit of sun today." He ran the back of his

knuckles gently along my upper arm. His hands were both full of our beers but that didn't stop him from touching me. I didn't know if it was the shock of the ice-cold beer on my neck or Toby's touch that caused gooseflesh to form on such a warm night.

The song ended, and Toby's attention was drawn away from me, snapping me out of my own daze as he placed my beer into my hand.

He disappeared through the sliding glass door; I could barely make him out in the dim interior. He restarted his tape, the same melodious symphony I'd heard from the driveway.

I took a swig of beer and fought not to choke on the vile taste of it. Seriously, how did people drink this stuff?

Toby increased the music's volume this time, and I was plunged into blackness as the back porch light switched off. Toby skimmed through the sliding glass door and moved towards the couch again.

I had an idea of what the darkness meant; it was a 'do not disturb' sign. I swallowed deeply. I could just make out Toby as a light from the kitchen window shrouded the couch in a light orange glow through the mottled glass.

"Do you like this song?" I asked.

It's his tape, he put it on, of COURSE he likes this song.

"It's my absolute favourite," he said in a low, dreamy voice. He sat back down on the couch and slowly patted the space next to him.

Why is it that people take a long swig of alcohol before they do something they need courage for? One sip could hardly give me enough to conquer my nerves and fears, so I took two big ones and sat next to Toby.

"What's it called?" I asked, trying not to cringe at the disgusting taste, to keep the conversation flowing casually.

Toby's arm lay carelessly across the back of the couch, my neck pressed against it. The couch seemed a lot smaller than it looked. It was cosy; I relaxed into the dip in the middle so that I leaned in to Toby. He ran his fingers through my hair in a slow, comforting motion. I closed my eyes and rested my head on his shoulder.

"It's called, 'A Change is Gonna Come'," he whispered into

my temple.

Toby leaned forward and rested his beer on the floor with a delicate thud; my eyes opened, breaking my dream-like state as he took the beer out of my hand and placed it on the floor next to his. All of a sudden finding a place for my hands didn't matter as Toby closed the distance between us. My tummy tingled with the gentle, lingering touch of his lips to mine. I reached up, my fingers entangled through his thick, dark hair as our bodies pressed closer, melting into each other as the music played and the darkness hid our roaming hands. Toby broke away first, leaving me breathless and fearful that he had decided to stop, but his eyes met mine in a silent question, and I gripped his singlet and pressed my forehead to his.

Toby's breath drew in a long shudder. "Are you sure?"

I answered only in trailing light kisses along his jaw leading to his mouth. I could feel Toby's Adam's apple swallow hard, his breath laboured as I playfully hovered over his lips, deliberately looking into his eyes as if memorising the moment. I captured his beautiful mouth with a sweet, teasing caress, and that was all the invitation he needed.

The couch creaked with each movement as the weight of Toby's body pressed down on me, and we desperately maneuvered into place. I could taste the remnants of beer on Toby's tongue, but it was strangely intoxicating on him: I liked it, as opposed to when drinking it myself. His hands moved, skimming up my thighs, bunching my skirt to my waist. Each movement was slow and deliberate at first, as if with each bold unraveling he expected me to stop, push him away, but every touch only caused my stomach to twist in excitement. A heated look of understanding flashed in Toby's eyes as he knelt back and looked down at me. I sat up, peeling my top over my head, and we lay down again. The heat of our bodies melted together, his strong assured hands grabbed at the elastic of my knickers and dumped me out of them. Panic jolted through me in the swift movement as Toby's dark form hovered over me, blocking out the moon. It was then I heard the confident fumble and flick of his jean button and then the zip.

This is really happening, this is really happening.

Toby lowered my bra strap, then paused. "You're shaking."

Was I?

I fought to keep my breath steady. "I don't mean to, I just ..."

Toby's voice was low, soft near my cheek.

"We don't have to ..."

"I want to!"

If he stopped looking down at me and just kissed me that was all I would need. Instead, he kept his concerned gaze focused on me, his beautiful face highlighted by the tinted, mottled glass from the kitchen. It shone a warm glow across us.

Toby's lips tilted, forming a coy, lopsided smile. His fingers traced lazy, comforting circles against my skin.

"It's only me, Tess," he whispered.

It was all I needed to hear. I pushed myself up to sit before him and gathered the fabric of Toby's singlet, slowly peeling it over his head.

I knew this face.

I knew this boy.

My fingers traced a line over his smooth, bronzed skin, from his shoulder, across his collarbone; they trailed a long, teasing line down to his jeans. His breath hitched as my fingers rested on the parted buttons of his Levis, and I couldn't help but smile.

Did I know what I was doing? Did I have any idea of what I was getting myself into?

He snaked his arm behind my back and lowered me onto the couch again. In that very moment, there was only one thing I knew for certain: I wanted Toby to block out the moon.

Chapter Thirty-Four

We lay on the couch in silence for the longest time.

The music had long since stopped and a warm, gentle breeze swept over the deck, cool against my dampened skin as I lay in Toby's arms.

A deep chuckle vibrated against my cheek.

I tilted my head up. "What?"

"Nothing. I just thought I was in for a quiet night, and then you showed up at my door."

I leaned on my side and looked down at his flushed face. "Do you wish I hadn't?"

He ran his fingers through my hair. "No, I'm glad you did." He smiled. "You lunatic."

I frowned and went to hit him but he caught my wrist, dragged me down into a heated kiss, and I crumbled into him. Toby pulled down the rug draped over the back of the couch and arranged it over us. We lay in a twisted cocoon until the first rays of light pierced the sky. I managed to doze in short bursts, but even though I was sore and exhausted I couldn't still my mind.

Wow. So that was sex.

I lay on my side and watched Toby's peaceful, sleeping profile; the rise and fall of his chest; his arm curved over his forehead, and his perfect bow shaped lips slightly swollen from our kisses. He looked so young, and I smiled as I pushed a wayward strand of hair off his brow. He rolled toward me, blindly moved my wrist away from his face, snaking an arm around me.

"Get some sleep, McGee," he mumbled.

I giggled. "I can't."

He peeked one eye open. "You're going to kill me, go to sleep."

"Oh that's right. I'm much younger than you, I keep forgetting," I teased.

He poked me in the ribs, and I squirmed with laughter. His eyes were still closed but a broad smile spread across his face.

"Get some sleep, Tess."

I nestled into Toby's warmth and closed my eyes, but sleep did not follow easily.

Hours must have passed as the sounds of bird calls in the surrounding bushland greeted the morning. Toby stirred next to me, and I knew what he wanted. I wanted it, too. This time it was easier. His movements were slower, his mouth captured my gasps and moans. He pushed me to new points of madness, a blinding intense place, a place I never knew I could belong, but Toby took me there.

I was still sore, but I was able to immerse myself in his warmth. There was nothing else in that moment except Toby and me as he gathered me against his chest, both breathless; his thumb stroked my bottom lip as he tilted my head up, to look into my eyes.

"You're shaking," I whispered.

He kissed the top of my hair, and I listened to the frantic beat of his heart; I smiled, revelling in the fact that I was the one responsible for it.

Sleep must have found me eventually, as I jolted awake when the blanket shifted. Toby sat up stretching, his bones clicking and popping as he stifled a yawn. I smiled, shifting towards him, squinting; I shielded my eyes against the morning sun's rays. As Toby shuffled his jeans on, I watched the muscles contort in his back. He glanced back down at me with a coy smirk.

He leaned back on his elbow, his eyes studying mine and we watched each other openly, comfortably. Toby's hand rested on my stomach and as he began to sit up he froze as his gaze dropped towards my crumpled skirt pushed high above my waist.

He sat upright, swearing under his breath.

"Jesus, Tess!" Frantic, apologetic eyes met mine.

I sat up to see dried blood smeared against my thighs.

"Shit, I'm sorry. I didn't know, I just thought that … oh, Christ, did I hurt you?"

I shifted the skirt downwards as I sat up and gave him a reassuring smile.

"Only a little." I grabbed his hand, but he flinched away which hurt more than anything that happened last night.

"I'm so sorry, Tess. I thought, if I had known …"

Suddenly all the wonder and beauty of the languid, lazy affection we had shared moments before was gone, overcome by shame and guilt. As I searched for my shirt and undies, wanting to quickly cover myself, I hardly noticed that Toby had moved away from me. The sliding door was shoved open, and Toby appeared with a washcloth. He knelt down and wiped at my legs, his gaze intense, focused, as if erasing the blood would erase what happened last night.

I stilled his hand and took the cloth from him.

"Thanks."

Comprehension dawned on his face, and he left to let me clean myself up. I stood up and wiped my legs clean, then redressed. I found the empty condom wrapper at my feet, which I discreetly tucked into my shoe. I flamed crimson, in the heat of the moment I hadn't even thought about it, hadn't even realised Toby had used a condom. I was silently thankful that he had.

Toby came back outside, this time in a clean T-shirt and holding a glass of juice.

I held the cloth awkwardly, my cheeks burning with embarrassment. He handed me the juice and took the cloth from me.

"It's okay," he said, "I'll sort it." He ducked back inside and quickly disposed of it before returning with his own glass of juice. I wanted to die.

I gulped on my pineapple juice in an effort to distract myself from the awkward silence that loomed over us.

After a moment, Toby took my glass and set it aside. He lifted my chin to meet his eyes.

"You okay?"

I tried to smile and nodded, but it wasn't very convincing.

"You're a bloody lunatic, you know that?" he said, lips tilting into a lopsided smile as he shook his head.

I relaxed slightly as his fingers brushed against my cheek to tuck a sleep-tousled strand of hair behind my ear.

"So I've been told."

He bent down and kissed my forehead, and then my lips, but they didn't linger.

"I better get home," I said, "I don't want anyone to file a missing person's report."

He walked me round the front, his hands plunged into his pockets, neither one of us looking at each other.

I grabbed my bike and we stopped at the end of the drive, in silence.

What do you say in times like this? "Thanks for last night"? "You were great"? "We should really do this again sometime"? "Thanks for taking my virginity"?

Not that one.

Instead, I settled for, "Okay, well … see ya."

I didn't look back as I started wheeling my bike down the street, knowing I couldn't hide my cringing face, knowing the dull ache between my thighs.

"Tess?"

I paused, my heart stopping at the sound of my name. He watched me thoughtfully, blinked, and it was once again broken by a smile.

"See you on the weekend?"

I wanted to cry with relief at such a minor semblance of normality. I smiled back.

"Sure," I nodded.

Once I walked around the corner, I straddled my bike with a deep breath against the pain and rode home with the sun in my eyes, a thousand memories swimming through my mind and a dumb, dreamy smile on my face.

Chapter Thirty-Five

I did it … twice! No, I had done it *twice* with Toby Morrison.

I stood in front of my bedroom mirror with a towel wrapped around me, wondering if anything had changed; if I were to walk down the street, would people look at me differently? Could they tell? I towel dried my hair in the same daze I had been walking around in all morning.

I crept into the laundry to put my stained and rumpled clothes in the wash myself. Mum and Dad didn't need to see this. I checked my pockets as my mum always did, in case of coinage and wayward chapsticks. I had lost far too many to the washing machine; it wasn't funny. And when my Cherry Bliss chapstick had worked its way through Dad's work whites, well the parentals were not happy.

I praised small mercies as I reached into my skirt pocket and fumbled against not a lip smacker, but the crinkling of a foil packet. I quickly pulled it out and revealed the torn, empty condom wrapper. In my haste this morning, as I had kicked off my shoes, the foil packet had stuck to my foot. I'd scooped it up and shoved it in my pocket in a desperate attempt to hide all evidence.

Now, I held it, in my home. Thank God I'd decided to wash my *own* clothes. I had a horrific flash of my mum emptying my pockets and finding it.

I dumped my clothes in the washer, piled in ample detergent and high-tailed it to my room, only to be stopped by Mum in the hall.

"Are you doing your washing?" She looked at me with surprise.

"You don't have to look so horrified." I clenched my fist tighter, holding onto its contents. Panic prickled down my spine.

Mum shook her head. "You never cease to amaze me, Tess."

I was certain of it. I was sure Mum would have been amazed that I'd snuck out last night and back in this morning undetected, and she'd sure be amazed at what I held in my sweaty palm right in front of her. Here she was thinking I was her little angel, when I had never felt more like the devil as her loving eyes looked over me.

She pecked me on the cheek. "You've been such a help this summer, thanks sweetie." I breathed a sigh of relief as I quickstepped to my room, the foil wrapper burning a hole in my hand.

"Tess?"

"Yes?" I flinched, all too guilty as I turned back around.

"Why don't you ask Ellie over tonight? You haven't had anyone over these holidays. You can have a girls' night. Your dad and I won't be home 'til late."

"Okay, thanks Mum."

As I closed my door, I pressed my back against it and exhaled in relief. Losing my V plates last night with the boy of my dreams, and tonight a slumber party with my BFF. How unpredictable was my life? I dragged the shoe box from my wardrobe and placed the empty wrapper beside the expired foil packet from when I was thirteen. I couldn't help but shut the lid with a goofy smile.

That night, Ellie sat at the breakfast bar, watching me suspiciously as I covered a pizza base with cheese, humming joyously over such a mundane task.

"What's with the Mary Poppins thing?" Ellie asked. "Why are you so happy?"

"What? God, just because I do my laundry and make dinner without a scowl, what's weird about that?"

"You did your own laundry?"

"Uh, yeah, my arms aren't painted on, you know."

Such a dad saying, I thought.

"You're working two jobs and doing your own laundry? Please tell me it is under sufferance from your parents. Like you're being punished or something."

"Nope!"

"Tess, you had to be begged to get *one* part-time job these holidays, what's happened to you?"

Toby, I thought. He made me want to be a better person, a more mature person, responsible as he was and had been even when he was my age. It would sound dumb if I said it, though.

Toby and I parted on such good terms that I had been humming and smiling all day, but as the light dimmed and the sun set, so did my doubt. I thought back to the look on his face when he realised I had been a virgin, the way he had stammered 'had I known'. Had I known, what? Would he have not touched me? Would he have backed off completely? I tried to block out the negatives, my embarrassment, his anger at himself, his regret. Instead, I wanted to think about the moments of pleasure, the feeling of his breath on my neck, his mouth on me, how he held me after and folded his fingers through my hair the way he seemed to like to do.

I sighed, wiped my hands on the tea towel and glanced at Ellie. I had debated if I should tell her, and how to do it. I knew I would regret it, knowing she wouldn't approve.

But of course I was going to tell her. How could I not? Before she had arrived, I'd prepped the cassette player in the kitchen. As she watched me suspiciously, I walked over and pressed play. I looked Ellie dead in the eye, watching her expression as Madonna's 'Like a virgin' blared out of the speakers.

"I made it through the wilderness," Madonna sang and Ellie frowned with confusion as it slowly registered. Her gaze flicked to the stereo, then to me and widened in shock.

"No way!"

"Way." I waited and watched as an array of emotions played on her face.

Confusion, doubt, disbelief, horror and then a grin.

"Toby?"

I lashed out with a flick of my tea towel. "Of COURSE, Toby.

Who else? Jeez, Ellie."

"Oh my God, Tess." She rounded the counter and gave me a huge hug, leaning back to slap me across the arm.

"Hey!"

"What did I tell you about playing it cool?"

"That hurt." I rubbed my arm in a scowl.

"I bet that's not all that hurts." She curved her brow, giggled and slapped me on the behind, sauntering back to sit at the breakfast bar.

"I must say, that was rather dramatic. I've never had news broken to me via song before, thanks, Tess."

I placed the pizza in the oven.

"So? When did this happen?"

"Last night," I said, "at his place."

Ellie drew in a breath. "Tell me more, tell me more." She leaned forward.

"What else is there to tell?"

"Ooooh, no you don't! Tessa Ellen McGee, I have told you every dirty little detail over the years, you're not getting out of this."

Yeah, every dirty detail, except for important things like blood and awkwardness afterwards. I knew I shouldn't have told her, now she wants to know EVERYTHING.

"It's private," I said. "I'm not you, okay?"

"Come on, tell me."

"I don't want to, Ellie."

"But I tell you everything."

"No."

"Please? Come on, so how big –"

"I said NO, Ellie!"

Ellie closed her mouth, shocked. A newfound silence set over us; she looked hurt but quickly swiped it away.

"Whatever. I better get going." She slapped her palms on the counter for leverage as she got up to leave.

"What?" I said, confused. "I thought we were going to watch a movie, have a slumber party. Pizza won't be long."

"Yeah, well, I forgot I have my own slumber party to attend to with Stan." Ellie sidestepped to the door.

"On a Monday night?" I crossed my arms sceptically.

"Not so different from your escapades last night, now is it?" And she was gone.

Ellie left without a smile or a backward glance. I had offended her. My worries had been founded. With or without Madonna's aid, telling Ellie had been a mistake.

I didn't know exactly what to expect from Ellie when next I saw her; I knew she was mad and just like every other time she was mad, the silent treatment ensued until she got over it.

But as for Toby, as each day passed at the Rose Café, I half expected him to wander through the door with a smile. Not that he had ever done so before, but now I hoped, I don't know, that something had changed. He had made no promises, no declarations of love but as each day went by that I didn't hear from him I felt more miserable than ever. Come Saturday night, when Toby was a no show at the hotel, I'd had enough of lying in my bed, night after night, every detail of *that* night on repeat in my mind.

I didn't know for sure, but it was in the air. It felt like everyone knew. Any time Toby's name was mentioned, Ringer smiled at me and Chris frowned in disapproval … but maybe I was just paranoid.

"You're being paranoid!" Ellie said (yeah, she was talking to me again).

"So you haven't said anything to Stan?"

Ellie rolled her eyes. "Not everything's about you, Tess.'

For the first time in … well, forever, Chris let Ellie and I stay for a lock-in. The outside lights were switched off and the hotel was cast into darkness. The blinds were drawn and the inner lights dimmed. All but the selected few patrons were booted out and with the doors locked, Chris jumped the bar to join in with his mates.

From what I had gathered in bits of conversation and from Ellie, Toby had gone to the city to pick up a car with his dad and wouldn't be back 'til late. Then he and the boys had an early fishing adventure on the lake.

All was of little comfort to me. By midnight I'd had enough; without Toby, the lock-in was kind of boring as Ellie and Stan canoodled by the jukebox, Ringer nodded off to sleep in the corner and Sean and Chris argued over pool table rules.

So they wouldn't make a big deal of it, I snuck out the back and into the night. The gravel crunched under my feet, and they pounded a steady pace towards a destination I wasn't so sure I should be going.

If he had wanted to see me he would have been there, no matter what kind of day he'd had. I felt sick with the thought that everything that went on between us would change. In a bad way. That he thought it such a huge mistake he would avoid me for the rest of the summer. I wanted to know, I *needed* to know that we were okay. I needed to tell him that that night had been great and not to regret it because I certainly didn't. Above all, I wanted to tell him I was glad he was my first and that I wouldn't change a thing. And if I was brave enough, I would tell him I would really like to do it again.

My mind flashed to the new foil package that was in my back pocket, from my own packet from the Caltex. I thought it rather presumptuous of myself but better to be prepared.

Little did I know that protection would be the least of my problems.

As I rounded onto the main road, closing onto Toby's street, I had already rehearsed what I would say a thousand times. I was in danger of seeming like a stalker, winding up at his place uninvited *again*. But I needed to put my mind at ease, get all of these emotions off my chest. By the time I turned into Toby's driveway, I had worked myself into such a determined state that I had no time for fear or doubt, I just had to march on in there and face Toby. As I marched up Toby's driveway, I spotted something and stopped. I froze, stock still, all my bravado, all my hope plummeted with a heartbreaking thud. Toby's back light was in 'do not disturb' mode and Angela Vickers' car was in the drive.

Chapter Thirty-Six

I didn't go in. I couldn't. Instead, I walked around Onslow through the night with no purpose, no clear direction.

Toby and Angela Vickers. I was numb. The numbness was so debilitating, all I could sense were my rapid, shallow breaths. Had I been walking for minutes, hours? I couldn't be sure. All I knew was I had backed out of Toby's drive and walked and walked, as far away as I could. I didn't allow myself to think, to feel anything. I put up a wall to everything except my breathing, the rhythmic sound that drove me away, as far as I could go.

Random strobes of lights pierced the darkness as Saturday-night joy riders passed me on the main strip. It was only when a flick of a high beam from behind and a frantic sounding of a car horn caused me to pause and shield my eyes.

A window rolled down, and it took a moment for my eyes to adjust, for my mind to clear as I peered into the car to see Ringer's girlfriend, Amanda, behind the wheel, Sean beside her. He leaned across her, peering out at me.

"There you are. You went AWOL. What are you doing roaming around on your own?"

"N-nothing," I croaked out.

"We're heading to the Point, wanna come?" Amanda asked.

Before I could decline, I heard the click of a car door.

Sean was out of the car, holding the front passenger door open for me. "Hop in the front, Tess, I won't subject you to the torture of sitting with these goons."

His gaze dipped to the back seat. Amanda's brother, Ben, and Ringer sat there, exchanging insulted glances. I hadn't even noticed they were there.

"I would hop in if I were you, it's not every day Sean gives up a front seat for someone."

Before I could object, Ben passed a West Coast Cooler through the window.

"Here, hope you like wine."

I eyed the bottle, grateful it wasn't beer. "What's with you and the girly drinks?"

He shrugged. "They're Amanda's."

"Oh, whatever, Ben. Don't hide your love for chick drinks behind me." Amanda cast a dark look in the rearview mirror.

I unscrewed the top and skulled half the bottle in one go. I wanted to feel a different kind of numb. When I finally dipped my bottle, four sets of eyes rested on me with a mixture of surprise and respect.

Sean frowned at me. "You alright, Tess?"

I took another swig and snapped my lips in a gasp of appreciation.

"Yep! Let's go!"

By the time we reached the Point, I had downed two West Coast Coolers and was handed my third with a lecture to slow down from Sean. He half laughed about it, but I could tell he was serious.

But I didn't care. I just needed to forget. Forget Angela's car in the driveway and most certainly forget Monday night ever happened.

I felt sick.

The Point had filled out to a respectably sized gathering. Someone pushed an old metal drum out the back of their ute and they filled it with twigs, newspaper and a dash of lighter fluid, and it wasn't long before a circle of people stood and sat around it.

"A bonfire in this heat?" I mused.

Sean shrugged. "Feels pretty stupid standing around in a circle without one."

"What, like fire creates ambiance?" I scoffed.

"Amongst other things. You don't think it does?"

By now I was a little buzzed, the alcohol chilling me out somewhat. This was what I was after, but it wasn't enough, so I followed Ben and Ringer as they towed the esky toward the fireside. A chilly breeze blew in over the tops of trees and penetrated the Point, dropping the temperature within minutes. I guess the drum wasn't as ridiculous as I first thought. I went to crack the lid of the esky when it slammed back into place. Sean sat his arse down on the cooler.

"Do you mind?" I said.

"Oh sorry, did you want a drink?" He batted his eyes at me innocently. Like hell.

"Yes, Grandpa," I said, "move."

Sean nodded gracefully and lifted so he could delve his hand into the icy recess, only to pull out a can of Coke, which he slapped into my palm. I snatched it out of his hand and threw it over the cliff towards the flickering lights of Onslow. I stared at Sean in my best death stare.

"Geez," he said, "I hope that doesn't break a window." Sean curved his brow.

I held out my hand again with a 'don't mess with me' look on my face. Sean handed me a Cooler, his face unreadable.

Sure, he probably thought I was crazy, but what did I care? Judge away. The opinion of the Onslow Boys meant bugger all to me at this point, and all I cared about was working on my alcoholically fuelled buzz.

I squeezed onto the esky next to Sean. As I took a deep swig, I could feel his eyes burning into the side of me.

"*What?*" I snapped, glaring at him, challenging him. The light of the fire accentuated the twinkle in his eye as he fought not to smile.

"Your lips are swallon," he said. "Looks like pash rash."

There was no danger of that, I thought. Lips hadn't touched mine in six whole days, and those particular lips never would again. I thought about Toby's lips on Angela's and wanted to throw my drink. I wanted to start walking again, away from here, away from these people, away from everything. I was so angry I couldn't bear it. The wine fueled my fire instead of numbing it.

Not-too-distant laughter broke me out of my thoughts. I noticed two snickering idiots, Carla and Peter, two of Scott's friends from school. How did they get up here? Was no place sacred? They had always taken great delight in making me miserable. They walked by, and Carla elbowed Peter and laughed behind her hand at me.

"Friends of yours?" Sean asked.

I looked down at my drink and started picking the label off. "Doesn't matter where you go in this town, you always run into someone you don't want to."

My voice was lower, calmer. I was weary. It seemed like I'd rolled through anger; I could only guess I was spiraling into self-pity as I let the judgmental snickers affect me.

Sean leaned in and spoke quietly into my ear.

"Do you want to go for a walk?" His brows were furrowed in concern. I looked around the people at the Point, including Carla and Peter, and I decided that it was exactly what I wanted to do.

"Grab me another drink, okay?"

Sean sighed. "Yes, ma'am."

We trudged through the darkness and navigated the rocky terrain far enough away that the sounds of laughter and music from a car stereo grew faint. A cylinder of light and sparks shone into the sky from the fire. We walked in the opposite direction at the base of sloping rocks behind the shack of the fire lookout. The moon was full and high enough in the sky for me to make out Sean's broad back as I carefully followed him.

Sean effortlessly wove down the path in a fast stride, my drink dangling from his fingers. I stopped and leaned against a boulder to catch my breath.

"Wait," I huffed, "slow down."

Sean paused, turning back.

"One of your steps is equal to, like, six of mine." I could make out the brilliant white of his teeth. He tilted and looked at my legs.

"Sorry, I forgot."

I reached out for my drink. He held it towards me but just as I was about to take it he lifted it out of my reach.

"Don't be a dick." I jumped but he held it up and away.

With hands on my hips, I glared at him and hoped there was enough moonlight to show my murderous look. Sean lowered the bottle and just as I reached for it, he lifted it again with a laugh.

"You're such a fucking child!"

"Am not times infinity, no returns."

I tried not to laugh but couldn't help it and leaned against the rock, arms crossed, refusing to play the game. Sean handed me my drink and joined me against the rock as I twisted the top off. The metallic snap and hiss of bubbles from his can as he opened it pierced the silence.

We both took a swig.

"Can I ask you a personal question?" Sean flicked the ring of his can away into the darkness.

I followed suit and threw my bottle top. "I guess." I suddenly felt uneasy.

"What's going on with you and Toby?"

Any momentary light mood Sean had put me in was overshadowed by a searing pain as my mind flashed back to Angela's red Lancer behind Toby's ute. I turned away, hoping he hadn't noticed my reaction.

"Nothing, why?"

"Just wondered."

I looked back at him. "Yeah, well, there's absolutely *nothing* going on."

Sean's eyes narrowed in thought, looking at me as if he was weighing something up in his mind, his expression unreadable as he took in my answer.

"Fair enough." We were quiet for a moment. "Can I ask another personal question?"

I sighed and tilted my head at him in annoyance. It made him smile.

"Can I kiss you?"

Wait … what? All thoughts, good and bad, evaporated from my mind. Sean gazed up at the stars, as if he hadn't said a word, hadn't asked me that bonkers question. An outrageous question, a question that had me thinking, and then moving and him looking down at me. And then the next thing I knew I was kissing Sean

Murphy.

Chapter Thirty-Seven

Maybe it was the buzz of the alcohol?

Or the secluded darkness and the attraction I had always had for Sean, but as he lifted me and pressed me against the rock I knew that it was all in an effort to forget. I kissed Sean so fiercely it had taken him back initially, his brows raising in surprise as my hands wrapped around his neck, my tongue slipping inside his mouth. Sean broke away breathless, holding my wrists and looking down at me like I was a stranger. Then, as if reading my pleading gaze, silently telling him that this was what I wanted, what I needed, he pinned me against the rock and met my urgent, forceful kisses. As our mouths feasted on one another, I knew it was exactly what I needed. My mind was clearing, erasing every touch, every memory, every moment with Toby Morrison. And as Sean lifted my leg to bend around his waist, I wanted to hurt Toby, hurt him like he hurt me. A new excitement ran through me, a new urge as I moved and moaned against Sean's muscular frame, his arms pinning me in like a cage, lifting me as if I weighed nothing. I wrapped my other leg around his waist and gasped at the new pleasure I felt as he pressed in between the junction of my thighs. Now all thoughts of anyone else were gone as I was blinded by the thrill that threatened to surge as Sean's hips rocked into me. We were fully clothed but with heated, passionate kisses and touches I was on the edge, and as his hand slipped from my breast to between my legs and his friction intensified, the pleasure so intense, so unexpected, I screamed into his shoulder and went limp in his arms. Sean's groans ebbed as my own died and he slumped, his weight on me pinned me to the cold slab that stung through my shirt and, what I suspected, grazed my back now I could feel the sting.

Hot breaths heated my neck, and then Sean's gravelly voice half laughed in my ear.

"Christ! I haven't come that hard since high school." He chuckled and kissed my neck.

I let the aftershock of my climax ride over me; I felt the wet patch and the bulge pressing against me from Sean's jeans. I pressed my face into the alcove of Sean's neck, and sobbed. I sobbed so hard and so violently my body shook. All my hurt, anger, confusion and shame flooded through me.

"Hey, hey, hey … what's wrong?" He cupped my face, forcing me to look into his worried eyes.

"What's wrong, did I hurt you?"

I laughed through the tears. "Hurt me? No." God, if only he knew what he just did to me. "I'm sorry." I broke away, straightened my clothes and fixed my hair. I tried to wipe my face.

"This was a mistake. I shouldn't have come here with you."

Sean rubbed my arm. "Do you want to go home?"

I hiccupped and nodded. "I'm sorry," I whispered.

He smiled. "Hey, don't be, come on."

We walked back to the group, moving slower this time and together. Sean kept glancing at me as he stepped over rocks and steadied me as I went along. As we walked back into the clearing of the Point, Sean pulled his shirt over his crotch and I straightened my skirt and top. We rounded the corner of the old fire shack and walked right into the path of Carla and Peter. Their stunned gazes roamed over our dishevelled states, my bloodshot eyes, our kiss-swollen lips. They exchanged knowing smirks and walked off without a word, whispering and snickering to each other.

I couldn't take any more. I had never felt so ashamed; I had used Sean and behaved in a way … who was that girl out in the bush with him? She didn't seem like Tess, that's for sure.

I squinted one sleepy eye open as my phone chimed. A text message.

Breakfast at the Diner you dirty stop out. From: Ellie.

I had disappeared on her last night without a word, something we promised not to do to one another, so I figured I owed her. Plus, I had to tell her that my Toby phase was well and truly over and that I didn't want to talk about him, ever again. My summer was to enter a new phase and this one didn't involve the Onslow Boys – any of them. It was the only way I could see surviving with my reputation intact, not to mention my sanity.

I was exhausted, my hair still damp from my hot shower – a useless attempt to get rid of my hangover. Stupid West Coast Coolers. It really was the devil's brew.

A block away from the Caltex diner my phone chimed a message from Ellie:

Toby's here :)

A cold shiver ran down my spine. She thought she was passing on good news. I paused and contemplated going home again, but then squared my shoulders, held my head up high and kept walking.

Sure enough, a long line of cars parked out the front, and right in the middle of the car park was Toby's navy Ford ute. I recalled the vague mutterings of the Onslow Boys' fishing trip. Was that today? All of a sudden, I felt grateful for stopping by his house; it would prevent me from mooning over him and making an even bigger fool of myself than I had already. Even though my head tried to convince myself, my heart wasn't buying it for a second.

I pushed through the door. The Caltex booths that lined the front windows were packed and, as usual, the place was a hub of activity. Sunday mornings were always chaotic at the Caltex, a regular meeting point before people set out on their lake-bound adventures. More importantly, you could fuel up on greasy eggs and bacon after a boozy Saturday night. My stomach churned; I couldn't think of anything worse. A sea of inquisitive eyes rested on me, including Toby's. A boyish smile lit his face when he looked up from his menu; I never hated him more because my traitorous heart still skipped a beat at the very sight of him. I exchanged niceties and said hello to everyone and no one in particular, making a point of not looking at him. The Onslow Boys and company occupied two booths; there was only one space left and mercifully it wasn't in Toby's booth.

Everyone slid sideways and bunched up a little closer to allow me space; Sean moved his things and shifted without a beat even though he was in deep debate with Stan who sat opposite with Ellie. I didn't even mind the fact I was wedged in next to Sean. When he dropped me home last night, we had agreed our tryst in the bush would be our secret. Even now, the fact he didn't offer me a reassuring smile made me grateful and relax a little. Unfortunately, the line of our U shaped booth had me sitting directly back to back with Toby. He was so agonisingly close, I could feel the seat dip and shift every time he moved.

Ellie beamed at me and raised her brows as if I was sitting in the best seat in the house. It seemed to take all her effort not to give me a double thumbs up, and I was definitely grateful that she didn't. Sean slid me a menu.

"Something to reline the stomach?"

"Coffee to reignite my shattered soul."

He laughed. "With a dash of fruit-flavored wine?"

"Sean, I swear if you don't stop talking, I will claw your face off."

Sean cat-called and laughed a deep, happy laugh in typical Sean fashion. I smiled back. Even though we had overstepped a massive line last night, nothing had changed. That was something, at least. I tried to swallow the nauseous feeling that swelled in the pit of my stomach; being so close to Toby was killing me. When it came to him, no matter what beautiful, friendly and totally oblivious smile he threw my direction, I knew nothing would be okay with us. I tried not to let my heart spike each time I heard his voice from behind me, I felt the clamminess of my hands trying to keep my breaths even. Being so close to him, to Sean, I couldn't take it. I had to get out of there.

"Where did you get to last night, anyhow?" Ellie tried for mad, but she was more curious then anything.

Sean didn't flinch, but I must have shifted uneasily, and the booth behind me shifted with movement, and I watched Toby pass and walk towards the counter. He was back with Angela. I meant nothing to him. My misery spiral was interrupted by the sound of skin sliding against vinyl.

"Hey, did any of you hear about last night?" Amanda's elbows appeared over from the other booth and rested on the back of our seat between Sean's head and mine.

I gripped the salt shaker.

"No doubt we're about to," mused Stan.

Amanda looked around like she was some A-grade spy before she continued.

"Guess who's back in town?" Her eyes lit with excitement.

She had all our attentions now.

"Angela Vickers," she whispered, perhaps a bit too loudly, as she flicked a glance towards the counter.

The salt shaker flew out of my hand and rolled across the table. Sean grabbed it and gave me a weird look as he placed it back in the holder.

"So?" Sean snapped as he moved his head away to avoid Amanda's elbow.

"*So*, apparently she went round to Toby's last night."

Ellie's eyes widened, her gaze darted to me, and I was all but ready to get up and leave. The last thing I needed was details.

"Apparently, she rocked up at some ungodly hour, drunk off her head and started roof rocking his house."

A snort escaped Stan and Sean broke out in laughter.

"It's not funny," Amanda continued.

"He had to call her parents to come get her. She was smashing the place apart, broke all his lights with rocks, broke a window ..."

My eyes darted towards Toby who was in a conversation with a local by the counter. Oh no.

"Then what happened?" Ellie pressed.

"Her mum and dad came and got her and, boy, were they pissed. Her mum went right off at Toby, saying he broke their precious daughter's heart, she even slapped him across the face."

"How do you know all this?" I said.

Amanda smiled. "I know everything." With a wink, she looked pointedly from me to Sean and flopped back down in her seat again as Toby returned.

What had I done?

Ellie missed nothing. She looked from Sean to me with a troubled expression.

My throat closed up, my heart beating rapidly. The diner started feeling too small; way too small. I needed air. I needed to get out.

"I have to go." I jumped out of my seat.

He wasn't with her, he wasn't with her.

As I strode across the car park, the door slid open again behind me.

"Tess, wait up." Ellie followed me. "What's going on?"

"Nothing, I'm just hungover."

"Bullshit. What's wrong with you?"

How could I summarise the week's events in a Caltex parking lot, within a stone's throw of the Onslow Boys?

"What's up with you and Sean?"

"Nothing," I said too quickly

She rolled her eyes at me, her jaw set. "I saw the look you two gave each other after Amanda said that stuff, why don't you tell me anything anymore? I thought we were best friends."

"We are."

"No, best friends tell each other things. They're not all secretive and leave in the middle of a lock-in without telling me. It's like … who are you, Tess? I don't even know you these days."

My stomach soured. "Sorry to be so inconvenient, Ellie. For once, I have a life and you can't stand it. What do you want me to do, wait on the bonnet of cars for you for the rest of our lives?"

"What are you talking about?"

"You know what I'm talking about. If you think I've changed, then you're right. Maybe I have. It's called not living in your shadow anymore, so get used to it."

Ellie watched me for a moment then stepped closer, her look grave. "Tess, I just don't want you to whore around."

"What, like you?" I regretted it the moment it left my mouth, I regretted the look of hurt it caused to flash across her face and I regretted hearing her response.

"Go to hell, Tess."

Ellie walked off just as Stan approached, hearing the final outburst. In a way I wished she had just hit me; I deserved it.

The door slid open again and Stan and Ellie passed Sean, Ringer and Toby on their way back. Oh God. I would have completely crumbled, except Sean handed me a coffee in a polystyrene cup.

"You forgot this."

"Thanks."

Sean and Ringer walked on towards the car, readying themselves for the epic fishing adventure, leaving Toby who stood next to me, the two of us alone for the first time since ... well ... just since.

If he asked me if I was okay, I might have screamed, but in typical Toby fashion, he didn't pry.

"I didn't know you liked coffee." He slid a pair of Ray Bans on, shielding him from the bright morning glare.

I tried to smile but I knew I didn't pull it off. I blinked away the tears that threatened to come and wished I had my own pair of Ray Bans to hide my eyes.

How was all this possible? How had I managed to do so many stupid things in such a short span of time?

Toby sensed my mood and struggled to find words of ease.

"Well, if I don't get sunstroke, I'll see you tonight?"

"Sure."

Sean and Ringer cat-called for Toby to hurry up, and he gave me a shy smile as he walked away.

"Toby!" I called after him.

He turned, peeling off his shades so his eyes met mine. It was like a silent exchange before he broke into a brilliant smile, and I knew instantly he wasn't trying to avoid me. If anything, my guilt over last night's train wreck had me wanting to avoid him and his beaming smile. A smile that still showed even after last night and his showdown with Angela, he was still here smiling at *me*. He winked at me, a secret between just the two of us, replaced his shades and jogged towards the ute and his boys, without a care in the world.

What had I done?

Chapter Thirty-Eight

I know I said Ellie usually got over things, but this time was different.

The afternoon shift was tense and awkward as my attempts at small talk with her, let alone apologise, were met with stony silence. Any time our paths crossed in the restaurant, Ellie made a not-too-subtle attempt to avoid me all together. In the evening, when I made my way into the kitchen, I felt sick at the thought of enduring more of the same cold treatment.

I deserved it, I knew that, but it didn't mean I had to like it.

Laughter echoed out from the kitchen as I pushed my way through the swinging kitchen door. Ellie, Rosanna and Amy stood around the prep area. I was met with a casual 'hello' from Rosanna and Amy. Ellie's laughter dried up and her smile dropped at the sight of me. She pushed her shoulders back and with a casual flick of her pony tail, gathered her apron and left the kitchen without a word.

"What's going on between you two?" Amy frowned.

"Long story." I sighed. It wasn't really that long; I just didn't want to talk about it with the likes of Amy and Rosanna. Amy shrugged and continued her conversation with Rosanna. I pulled my rings off and dropped them into my apron pockets, glancing wearily at the kitchen clock – 5:55pm; it was going to be a long,

long shift.

At least my fallout with Ellie took my mind off other things, the things that really troubled me. It was the only positive point I could take from the drama. I looked blankly at the docket whose table number I had forgotten to write down; Christ, I couldn't even remember who I'd served. This mistake wasn't an isolated incident tonight. As soon as I thought I was getting my shit together at work, I was back to making stupid mistakes, like the good old days. I walked from the restaurant into the bar trying to jog my memory. Was the salmon for that old guy with the comb over? How about this Lamb Rogan Josh; had that lady in the leopard print ordered it? Had I served her? I had no idea. Shit! I didn't fancy being yelled at by Rosanna, not tonight. I moved towards the poolroom and frowned at the docket, hoping if I stared at it hard enough, it would jolt my memory.

But it didn't. Instead, my body was jolted as I slammed into what felt like a brick wall. Knocking me off balance, I juggled the plates precariously.

Oh no, oh no, don't drop them, oh no …

A pair of hands reached out to steady me.

"Whoa, look out!" Toby held me still for a moment until I seemed to have my balance again.

I didn't drop them, thank God I didn't drop them.

He grinned down at me. "You okay?"

I had been so distracted I hadn't even heard the front bar door open, or seen the Onslow Boys walk in, until I had collided with one. Sean and Stan were behind Toby, trying not to laugh. My face flushed.

"Sorry, I was in the zone." I stepped from his grasp, the small space in front of the door seemed claustrophobic all of a sudden; Toby's hands dropped but his touch had burned into my skin.

"Stop manhandling the staff, Tobias," Sean muttered into Toby's ear as he pushed passed Toby who still blocked the front door. Stan followed but didn't contribute. I guess Ellie must have told him what we were fighting about. What I'd said.

"Rough night?" Toby asked.

"Yeah, I just wish it would be over already."

"So I guess the last thing you want to do is go for a drive after work?"

"What?" I said, in perhaps a too high-pitched voice.

"Did you want to go for drive," he repeated, "with me?"

I tried not to smile too widely. "Um, yeah sure."

He nodded, a lopsided tilt to his mouth. "Well, you know where to find me."

He weaved his way through the poolroom, his skin darkened by his day fishing in the sun. He must have gone home and changed – now he wore a navy T with khaki cargos and boat shoes. He didn't smell like fish, but the Cool Water aftershave I had eyed in his console, it was my favourite smell in the whole world now, much more appealing than cooking oil and garlic bread which infused into my clothes each night. Seeing Toby (or rather, *colliding* with Toby) had lifted my spirits, and the thought of leaving here with him after work made my stomach flip in excitement. It was an unexpected delight in what I had thought would be a night from hell. Now the night couldn't end early enough, but for a whole other reason. And just as I pushed my way back into the kitchen it came to me!

"Table number 29!"

As Ellie and I filled out our time cards in silence, Chris poked his head into the restaurant bar, twirling the hotel keys around his finger. "You girls staying for lock-in?"

Ellie waited for me to answer first.

"No, I'm going to head out."

Ellie said, "Then I'll stay." Another not-too-subtle jab; Chris shrugged and headed out back.

I went to get my things.

"What, you're not going to stay to cross Chris off your list?" Ellie said. They were the first words she'd uttered to me all night.

"Ellie, look, I …"

"Or is it Ringer's turn tonight?"

"Ellie, I'm sorry I said that."

"Yeah, well in future, it's best not to say anything at all. Shouldn't be too hard, you seem really good at it now."

Ellie filled out the last of her hours and spiked them near the till, without so much as a backwards glance. I sighed and leaned on the restaurant bar, cupping my forehead in my hands. A dull ache had slowly formed in my head over the last few hours, and I wished it would just stop so I could think straight. As soon as I got home to lie in the darkness, staring at the shadows on my ceiling, I knew I would think of a million clever things to say, an amazing, award winner of a speech that would have won Ellie over and made us best friends again. But right now, I had nothing.

"Are you meditating?"

I jumped and spotted Toby standing over my shoulder. Chris must have flicked the main switch off because the restaurant was dark. With my eyes closed, I hadn't even noticed, which added to my shock when I opened my eyes to see the shady figure next to me.

I clutched at my heart. "You're like creeping Jesus."

He laughed. "Sorry."

I spiked my time card with a sigh. "Can we get out of here?"

"Your chariot awaits."

"In the form of a blue Ford ute?" I curved my brow.

"But of course," he said in an over-the-top French accent.

"Sacre blur, bad accent alert!"

"Wow," he said, "Le rude?"

"Le sorry?"

"Le hurt." Toby clutched his heart.

"What can I do to soothe your shattered ego?"

Toby drummed his chin thoughtfully, pacing around me. He stopped just near enough to whisper in my ear.

"Le kiss?" He circled his arms around my waist, and I couldn't help but giggle. The feeling of being hidden in the dark with Toby, as if nothing had changed, made my heart swell with joy, until a flash of last night with Sean came to mind and I felt the waves of guilt wipe the smile from my face.

"How's about le hurry up, so I can le lock up, Peppi Le Piu."

We both flinched at the sound of Chris's voice right by us.

He flicked on the light with a sigh. "I trust you two love birds will be making a back exit?"

Toby scratched the back of his neck and smirked; Chris attempted a serious expression, but he couldn't pull it off. He unlocked the beer garden door, and we made a quick escape.

"Speaking French, Tobias?" Chris said. "Must be love?" He

groaned out the last word as Toby sucker punched him playfully in the ribs as he passed, the way it seemed even grown boys do.

As Toby and I weaved our way carefully around the tables and patio heaters in the unlit beer garden, he clasped my hand from behind and tugged me into him. I giggled giddily as he pulled me into an even darker, secluded alcove. I was so close against him, I could feel the warmth of his breath on my face.

"What do you know? This is where it all began," he said.

"Began?"

"This is exactly where I was when I wanted to kiss you," he whispered, his lips brushing along my neck causing me to melt under his touch. "So bad."

I breathed deeply trying to blink my way out of my daze when I realised we were standing where the DJ, fairy lights and black velvet curtain had been the night of the disco.

"Except this time there's no drunk netballer squawking at us," I teased.

"I wouldn't care if the seven horseman of the Apocalypse charged through the garden right now, nothing's gonna stop me from doing this." He leaned down and captured my lips with tenderness, a completely perfect kiss, like it always was. I lifted myself on the tips of my toes to meet him. His hands fisted into my hair, making no apologies as his kisses intensified, became more forceful. He wasn't back with Angela. I'd been so wrong. He still wanted me. It wasn't a mistake; he didn't regret *that* night at all. Toby Morrison wanted me.

Chapter Thirty-Nine

We drove to McLean's Beach and parked off in a leafy, secluded section just off the sand.

It wasn't the prettiest part of the beach, nor the biggest. It couldn't cater for more than a few at a time, which was what made it so perfect. The ute's headlights lit up abandoned sticks fishermen had wedged into the muddy embankment to stand their rods in. Apart from that, the beach was untouched. There were no other signs of civilisation. We were well and truly alone. As soon as Toby had put his car into park, I was already straddling his lap, kissing him deeply. It mattered little that the steering wheel jutted uncomfortably into my back; being in Toby's arms was all that I cared about.

I suppose we should have had the 'talk'; gone over where we were both at and where things stood between us. Even though all we did was make out and roam each other's bodies with our hands, neither of us wanted to break the moment. Not until there was a distant boom and burst of colour in the sky.

"Look at that." Toby nodded over my shoulder.

Fireworks lit the sky in a cascade of sparks and colour, it felt like they were swirling and exploding just for us. This part of the world at McLean's Beach was not only a secluded haven, but it was also the best position from which to watch fireworks I had ever been to, even better than the Point. They were far, yet seemed so close, like our own personal show. I rolled off him and sank onto the bench beside Toby, and we watched the sky in wonder. Toby wrapped his arm around me as I lay my head against his shoulder. When I wasn't transfixed with the beauty of the fireworks, I splayed my hand against his, linking our fingers together. Toby's other fingers folded through my hair in lazy strokes that made me smile with happiness.

"Don't fall in love with me, Tess."

I blinked rapidly, shocked back into the moment. It was like a record being scratched, or the slamming of a finger in a car door. I looked at him quickly, but his eyes were fixed on the fireworks.

Where had that come from?

Suddenly all the beauty, the intimacy of our entwined fingers, our closeness, felt cold.

"Don't flatter yourself," I said and sat up straight, breaking the connection.

Toby sighed. "I just don't think I'm the right guy for you."

Here we go, I thought. I wanted to physically brace my hand against the dash. Seemed he wanted the 'talk' after all.

"Let me save you some time," I said. "I'm seventeen, you're twenty-two, 'you're a nice kid and all, but let's face it' and blah, blah blah. Spare me the speech, okay?"

Toby grasped the steering wheel, I could see his jaw clench. "That's one way of looking at it," he said, "but I was thinking it's more to do with, 'what does someone like you see in someone like me?'"

My mouth fell open, and I quickly closed it. Was he serious? He couldn't be …

Toby rolled his eyes in frustration as if I was an idiot for not getting it.

"Tess, you're smart, beautiful … you're young! You have your whole life in front of you. I don't want to be a complication in that."

I could hardly believe what he was saying. I wanted to laugh, I wanted to cry, I wanted to beat the crap out of him for being so ridiculous.

I took a deep breath, then another one, thinking about what I wanted to say. "You know, before I started my job at the Onslow I guess my life was pretty uncomplicated. You know why? Because I was nothing. I just had Ellie and Adam. I couldn't talk to anyone else, really. Hell, I couldn't even make a bloody cappuccino without blushing. I was scared of everything; I wanted to just stay under my rock. Do you know how debilitating it is to live like that? Being terrified of everything, everyone? Being afraid of saying the wrong thing, wearing the wrong clothes, putting the wrong song on the jukebox? I have to think and analyse *every* step of my existence with this terror that I am going to fuck it up."

Toby listened, watching me; he didn't break contact, didn't even blink, as if he was peering deep into my soul. I guess after saying that, he pretty much was.

I broke from his gaze and looked down at my hands in my lap. "Then I met you and the Onslow Boys and everything changed. I can't even try and put into words how liberating it is. For the first time in my life I feel free. You did that. So if I was to choose? Then I choose complicated," I said, with a nod of finality. I met his eyes again in a silent challenge. "I choose you."

Toby looked at me for the longest time. It was hard not to break eye contact, but I simply refused to. Soon, a small smile tugged at the corner of his mouth. I swear, I didn't even realise I'd been holding my breath 'til that moment.

Toby shifted his gaze out the windscreen, into the darkness over the water. The fireworks were over; I hadn't even noticed.

"Remember the first night we spoke?" he asked after a while.

"You mean when you told me to get off your car?"

Toby threw his head back and laughed in a way I had rarely seen.

"You should have seen your face."

"You nearly made me cry, you know," I said with a wry smile.

Toby fought to contain his laughter. "You know most girls would have told me where to go, or flipped me off." He shook his head. "But not you."

"Yeah, I know, rabbit in the headlights, such a good look."

"That's the thing. I've never met anyone like you, Tess. You think you're a no one? You're so wrong. *So* wrong. You stand in a room with all the Angelas, even the Ellies. None of them can compare to you. I remember when you started working at the Onslow, I couldn't keep my eyes off you. You were so terrified. You weren't full of yourself like other girls. Every time you walked into the bar, you were like a breath of fresh air. Even when Angela was a bitch to you, you rose above it. You made me see the difference in people. You're not a nobody, Tess, you're a somebody."

I let his words run over me as I tried to fight the tears that prickled at my eyes. I didn't need to ask about last night with Angela – I should never have doubted him. I was a somebody. My chest swelled with such intense emotion I didn't think I could bear it.

"Tess, the other night when we …"

I closed my eyes, a single tear rolling down my check.

"Don't. Please, Toby. Don't spoil it."

Toby took my hand into his.

"Why didn't you tell me?"

I buried my face in my hands, afraid to meet his eyes, embarrassed about my coming confession.

"I'd liked you for so long, I was afraid that if I told you, you might have not wanted to … continue."

Toby laughed.

"Tess, there isn't a drunken, screaming netballer in the world that would have made me not want to … continue. I just may have gone about it a little differently."

He squeezed my hand gently, and I leaned into him once more, resting my head on his shoulder.

"So, you liked me for a long time, huh?"

"The longest."

"How long?" I could tell he was smiling.

I cringed. "For a stalkerishly long time."

"And how long is that exactly?"

"I saw you from across a crowded school yard."

"What? School?"

"I was doing my Year Seven orientation, and you were in Year Twelve standing with a bunch of boys."

"Wow," Toby said, "you little perv."

I giggled and the tension ebbed away. We fell into a

comfortable silence for a while, but Toby broke it with a sigh.

"What are we doing?"

I moved then, climbing into his lap. I linked my arms around his neck. That was enough deep conversation. I pressed light kisses against his mouth, gently biting his bottom lip, and he dug his fingers into my back with approval.

"Well, whatever we're doing, can it be done at your place?" I whispered against his mouth.

He tilted his head back and cocked an eyebrow.

"Are you trying to seduce me, Miss McGee?"

"Is it working?"

Before I could kiss him again, in one fluid motion he slid me off his lap and turned the key in the ignition. I giggled at the unexpectedness of it and straightened beside him as he pulled into gear.

"You betcha."

Chapter Forty

I sent Ellie what seemed like my hundredth email, begging for forgiveness.

The long, drawn-out silence of our fallout had reached a new level, a level we had never been to and I was scared our friendship might not recover from.

I was startled out of my gloomy thoughts when Mum tapped lightly on my door.

"Tess, hon, Ellie's here to see you."

I all but knocked over my desk chair when I stood up. I was afraid to hope that she'd come on good terms.

Relief flooded through me the moment she coyly stepped passed Mum, into my room, and offered me a friendly smile. Everything was going to be alright.

As soon as Mum closed the door, I body-slammed her with a bear hug.

"Jesus, Tess, it's not like I just returned from war or anything."

Tears squirted out of my eyes and there was nothing I could do to stop them. I was just so relieved. I could hardly stop myself as I sniffled and sobbed and headed into blubbering-mess territory.

Ellie rubbed at my shoulders, "Don't cry, please don't cry, Tess, its okay."

She sat me down on the bed, squeezed my hand and waited out my mini breakdown.

"I'm so sorry, Ellie, I'm so sorry for what I said and for what I didn't say," I blubbered. "You're right, best friends should tell each other everything. You're always so open with me and I should be with you, because you really are my best friend in the whole wide world." I knew I was babbling, but everything spilled out in such a rush Ellie had to clench my arm and tell me it was enough.

She grabbed me a tissue and waited for me to catch my breath.

"It's me who should be sorry, Tess." Her eyes began to well, too.

"You have nothing to be sorry about." I sniffed.

Ellie's chin trembled. "I always just expected you to be there, waiting around for me. You were right, I didn't want you to have a life. I was a selfish idiot."

"Well, we're even then. We can call it a draw in the 'being idiots' category." I squeezed her hand reassuringly.

Ellie just shook her head. "It's not even."

I looked into Ellie's red-rimmed eyes and a coldness swept over me as I tried to read the level of dread in Ellie's expression. I let go of her hand.

"What did you do, Ellie?"

"That's just it, I haven't done anything. Me and Stan, we haven't you know … done it."

I paused, surprised. "Really?"

"Yeah."

I slumped on my bed in relief. "Ellie, that's a good thing," I assured her. "It just means that you really like him, that when it comes time it'll be really special because you care about each other." I swelled all over with such affection for Ellie, my best friend, so proud of the new leaf she had turned over this summer.

My words, however, did not seem to console her. Ellie couldn't even look at me; instead, she shredded a tissue in her shaky hands.

I scooted closer. "Ellie?"

"I'm so scared, Tess. I'm so frightened of doing it with Stan."

This vulnerability in her was new, and I was so happy to see it. I smiled. "Because you like him so much?"

It was then that Ellie's tear-brimmed eyes met mine. "Because I'm a virgin."

I stood at the kitchen sink, slowly downing a glass of water with a shaky hand. I was grateful I was home alone, as any attempt at coherent conversation would have been lost on me. My mind was mush and had been ever since Ellie left.

Ellie was a virgin.

Could I believe anything anymore? Once I had picked myself up off the floor where I'd fallen off the bed and got over the sting of the carpet burn on my elbow, what followed was an epic confession from a blubbering Ellie that left me shocked, stunned and shocked all over again.

Ellie confessed that the reason why the boys were so mean to her was because she refused to put out, but she agreed to let people believe she had. Little did she know that those lies would end up being the only reason boys wanted to be with her.

I couldn't believe it. What about her confidence? Her knowledge? Her sage advice?

Probably stupid *Cosmo* magazine.

Ellie said she had adopted the certain image, the reputation she had so fully, that she didn't know who the real Ellie was anymore.

And then she met Stan.

He didn't want her for sex; he was with her because he liked her: the real Ellie.

The clincher in the surrealness of her confession was when Ellie turned to me and asked:

"So, what's it like? You know … sex."

I had blinked frantically, and my mind had gone blank. I just couldn't process that question, not from *Ellie*.

I had been with Toby a mere hours before, and I still struggled to form an answer to that question.

I had given as much detail as I was comfortable with. But as I stood at the kitchen window in the comfort of my own company, I remembered every detail from last night. It had been amazing, but my body had tensed momentarily as it remembered what it had done with Sean only a night ago.

Chapter Forty-One

To: tessmcgee
Cc: ellieparker
Lock up your daughters, Onslow!
I'm coming home!
Sender: Adam I can jump puddles Henderson

Adam's grand homecoming coincided with another disco in the beer garden. Okay, so maybe Ellie and I had begged and pleaded with Uncle Eric and Chris to hold one that weekend. Hell, we wanted to celebrate.

The best thing about having inside connections was that we managed to get the disco organised for the Friday night, a non-work night! I even suggested to Chris he could promote Amy from dish pig to fill-in waitress. He begrudgingly agreed to give her a go and that resulted in Amy becoming President, Vice President and Secretary of the Tess McGee Fan Club. No more dirty looks for me!

Amy skidded through the back sliding door to the beer garden where I sat with Ellie in a shady spot where only a small slither of sunlight reached.

"Tess, I heard your phone go off." Amy handed over my bag.

"Ta."

She smiled brightly and ran back to the restaurant to get stuck into her waitressing chores.

"She is the most enthusiastic waitress I've ever seen," Ellie said with a laugh.

My screen was lit up with the words '1 new message'.

Toby.

A smile broke out across my face.

"One guess." Ellie playfully kicked at my chair.

Life was easier now, better. I didn't have to snoop around corners for secondhand information or rely on Ellie to give me the update on when the Onslow Boys would be coming in. Instead, Toby and I texted. We had each other's numbers now. It was officially on, but we were still keeping quiet about it, keeping it on the down low for a while. We hadn't seen each other since that night at McLean's Beach and then his house; he was either at the garage or I was at the café.

So I couldn't help but beam when I read the message.

See you at 8

Toby.

"Is he sending you love poetry or something?" Ellie peeked over her shades, shades she didn't really need now that the sun had shifted.

I sighed. "Not exactly, but it's good enough for me."

I went home to change, the thought of arriving at the disco all fresh and clean, instead of stinking of kitchen fumes, my hair shiny instead of limp from steam over the stove and sink was a nice change. A brilliant change. I glammed up some fitted jeans with some fancy heels and a baby blue halter that contrasted nicely against the tan of my skin.

Ellie had arrived early to meet Stan for dinner so I knew I would be making a solo entrance. I made a point of arriving later than eight. I aimed for cool and casual, which I probably wasn't pulling off very well as I weaved through the crowd, ducking and stretching to see a familiar face.

So much for a grand entrance – I didn't know any of these people. Had I gatecrashed a private function? It was then that a pair of hands covered my eyes, and I heard the unmistakable taunt of a familiar voice.

"Look out, lady! I have use of both my arms now."

I spun around and flung myself into the two fully functioning arms of Adam.

"Hey, you!"

Adam crushed me in his grip, but I gave as good as I got.

"I missed you," I said.

Adam smiled. "Tess, stop flirting with me, please. Speaking of, where's Pretty Parker?"

I whacked him in the upper arm. "Don't start."

Adam screamed so loud, people stopped mid dance to glare at us with disapproving stares.

"*Stop* it, Tess! I have delicate bones."

I went to retort but Adam was body slammed as a squealing Ellie appeared from nowhere and threw herself onto him in a hug.

"Why aren't I a chick magnet like this with all the girls?" His voice was muffled as he tried to blow Ellie's hair from his mouth.

"Because you belong to us!" Ellie declared.

Adam threw a look behind him to Stan, who watched on in amusement.

Adam shook his head. "Chicks! They're just so needy. On the email, the phone constantly. It's exhausting."

"This coming from someone who fingerknitted us friendship bracelets and mailed them to us?" I added.

"Oh wow! Would you look at that?" Adam pretended he saw someone in the distance and waved to a girl. She looked confused and glanced behind her to see who Adam was waving to.

"I'll be right back, better circulate. People get really funny if you don't say hi." He was quickly swallowed up by the crowd.

There was a downshift in lighting and the music slowed as The Cranberries song, 'Linger', filled the night for the lovers in the garden. Ellie and Stan took to the dance floor, to not do the Robot or the Sprinkler but just to hold each other and sway. I smiled, Ellie finally got her Prince Charming.

As my gaze drifted, I saw Toby at the entrance, eyes locked on me. He broke into a broad smile as he weaved his way through the crowd, not taking his gaze from me. Not once.

I folded my arms. "You're late."

"You're beautiful." He smiled wickedly. "Especially when

you're mad."

Ringer squeezed past, guiding Amanda through.

"Why don't you ever speak to me like that?"

Toby punched Ringer in the arm.

Ringer turned shrugging his shoulders.

"Incidentally," Sean's voice jolted me. I had forgotten that we stood in a very public beer garden. "Ringer does speak to Amanda like that, when he's drunk. It's not pretty." In true Sean fashion, he was happy and carefree.

Luckily, though, we hadn't talked any more about it or anything. It seemed we were cool. Nothing had changed between us since that night at the Point. Ringer flipped Sean the bird and took Amanda to the dance floor. Toby, Sean and I stood on the edge, watching the couples hold each other close and sway. Guilt spiked through me any time I was with them together. I forced it down, fearful it would seep into my time with Toby. I had to tell him about Sean. I knew I did. But not now. Toby gently rubbed a lazy circle with his thumb on my palm.

A collective scream whooped out of the dance floor and the unmistakable guitar strums flowed through the speakers, as 'Wonderwall' sounded. This song was everywhere and everyone – even, tragically, my dad – seemed to know all the words. Ellie and Stan stumbled over, pulling the three of us onto the dance floor where there was an explosion of smashed bodies pushed together in the cramped space. Nobody cared, as the DJ lights flashed to the beat and everyone swayed and belted out the chorus. Toby held my hands, anchoring me to him in a rare, unnoticed moment in which everyone was lost in the music. We broke eye contact as Adam appeared and slung his arms around our shoulders, forcing us into some bad side-shuffling dance moves. Ringer and Amanda slow danced to our left, Ellie and Stan sang joyfully into their mimed microphones, jokingly serenading each other while Sean played air guitar like no one else. We drowned out the music as the whole disco sang at the top of their lungs. We linked into a chain of slung arms and twisted limbs. A group of friends enjoying a moment.

'Wonderwall' faded out and was replaced by 'Bow River', a real Aussie anthem by Cold Chisel. Non-dancer Toby quickly took his exit from the dance floor and mimed to Sean asking if he wanted a drink. Toby leaned into me, he was warm and smelled incredible.

"You want a drink?"

I shook my head, and he winked and squeezed my hand as he vacated the dance floor, sidestepping a flailing girl. Sean took my hand and started to Rock 'n' Roll dance with me in very uncoordinated moves that eventually just led him into flinging me around the dance floor like a rag doll. He flung me towards him too fast, and so quick that I slammed into him and stopped hard, my nose smashed against his chest. I probably would have been in pain if I hadn't been so winded.

"Sorry 'bout that." He tried to not laugh through his breaths, but it was evident we were both beyond it.

I rubbed my forehead. "That's going to hurt tomorrow." Sean had stopped laughing, instead he seemed distracted by something near the bar. I tried to follow his gaze but my view was blocked by the crisscross of the dancing crowd.

"What's wrong?"

I wasn't sure he had heard me until he flicked an agitated look my way.

"Nothing, just wait here, okay?"

Okay, Mr Cryptic.

Whatever. I continued to dance by myself, lost in the feel of the music. Suddenly Adam and Ellie flanked me, and my stomach fizzed with excitement. I thought we were about to tear up the dance floor school-social style. Ellie dug her fingers painfully into my arm; I went to shake her off until I followed her horrified gaze and then the music died.

Chapter Forty-Two

Everyone stood frozen on the dance floor.

At first we were confused, but it didn't take long to work out what was happening. My heart clenched.

Toby and Sean were facing off by the bar, and before I could even wonder what had happened, they had each other by the scruff of their necks, hands fisted in each other's shirts. Glasses shattered as Toby threw Sean against the bar.

"FIGHT!"

"Tess, don't!" Ellie tried to hold me back, but I broke away and pushed through the stunned crowd towards them.

"Toby, Sean, stop it!" I screamed, trying to get their attention. I slapped at their arms, trying to break their hold on each other, but it was of no use. Their eyes were locked on each other, murderous.

An arm snaked around my waist and pulled me back.

"Adam, let me go!"

Chris grabbed Toby, and Stan and Ringer worked to edge Sean away. They grunted and swore as Toby and Sean struggled away from them and towards each other.

"Stop it!" I screamed, tears threatening to spill over.

"Get him out of here," Chris yelled at Stan and Ringer, but Toby broke free and in a silent rage was the first to leave.

Adam let go of me. My heels clicked frantically on the

concrete as I chased after Toby. Sean's hand reached out and grabbed my upper arm, preventing me.

"Tess, don't." His tone was fierce, his expression grave.

"What is wrong with you? Let go of me!"

"He knows! Alright, Tess? He knows."

My head swam. How? How did this happen? It all became perfectly clear when I saw, further down the bar, Carla sipping on her drink, all innocence and sweetness. I caught a sideways glance at a smug-looking Peter.

She turned to face me. "Oops." She shrugged. "I guess he didn't know."

I broke away from Sean. He didn't try to stop me.

I ran as far as I could before ditching my heels, and then pounded the pavement with such force it wasn't long before I could faintly see the long stride of Toby's silhouette up ahead.

"Toby, wait!"

He stopped, as if flinching at the sound of my voice. I ran up short, trying to catch my breath.

It was then I cringed against a new sound, a series of running steps behind me. Ellie, Adam, and the Onslow Boys coming up short, their breaths laboured.

I made sure I got in first.

But before I could speak, Toby spun around, his gaze searing into me as he walked towards me.

"Deny it," he said, "tell me nothing happened."

My mouth gaped open, and I stumbled to form words, which just made him angrier.

"It's not what you think." My voice quivered.

"Did he touch you?"

Oh God, please don't do this.

"It happened the night Angela was at your house. I saw her car in the driveway, what was I supposed to think?"

Hurt and disbelief flashed across Toby's face.

"You think that little of me?"

"It's not what you think, Toby." Sean's voice came in from behind me. "We're just friends."

I stepped closer, reaching out, but he flinched away.

"*Don't.*"

I could feel myself falling apart in a blind panic. "Toby, please don't do this."

He refused to look at me. A long moment stretched between us, his jaw clenched in anger. Just as I was certain he was going to walk away, and I'd never see him again, Sean stepped forward.

"If you're going to take the high moral ground, Toby, then why don't you start by being honest with Tess?"

Honest? What?

Toby glared at Sean, a silent warning that made goosebumps form on my flesh.

"I swear to God, Sean," Toby bit out.

I looked from Toby to Sean and back again. "What's he talking about?"

"Go on, Toby, tell her. Tell her of the job offer you accepted in the West."

Sean turned to me. "Toby's moving. He's leaving Onslow." He turned back to Toby. "I bet you didn't tell her that."

"Toby?" I said. "*Toby.*"

A raw emotion flickered briefly in Toby's eyes, but he shut it down. He looked at me, unflinching. "Yeah, well, there's nothing keeping me here now."

And just like that, he walked away.

Chapter Forty-Three

If there is one thing worse than self-pity, it was other people's pity.

They all looked at me with solemn, knowing gazes and sad smiles, and worst of all, they kept asking, "Are you okay?"

No, I was not okay.

It was as if someone had punched a hole in my chest and every rational slice of my brain refused to function. Ten days had passed since the disco without a word, not even a glimpse of him. I stopped checking my phone every few minutes after the seventh day. He hadn't come to the hotel all week.

I sat in a booth at the Caltex with Sean on a Tuesday afternoon, the one person who didn't offer sad smiles or patronising words of comfort. He was just as lost as I was.

"Have you seen him?" I asked.

"Yeah," Sean said, "and he's pretending nothing happened. Every time I go to talk to him about it, he refuses to."

Like I never existed.

"God knows what Carla said to him." I sighed.

Sean scoffed. "I knew as soon as I saw him over at the bar. Carla was whispering in his ear. Then he turned around and looked at me dancing with you, and I knew. In one look, I knew." His eyes focused on his fingers as he rubbed condensation off his glass.

I felt for him; he was at as big a loss as what I was.

"At least he'll talk to you."

Sean shrugged. "To be honest, I don't know what would be better. He's not the same with me, things probably won't ever be the same again. You don't betray a mate like that. You just don't."

He'd lost his best friend, and it was all because of me.

"How were you supposed to know? We hadn't told anyone. And now you guys are fighting … Sean, I'm so sorry."

Sean grabbed my hand. "Hey! Don't you dare say you're sorry, it wasn't your fault."

"But it was," I said.

"You'd have to be blind not to know Toby liked you. It was me, I shouldn't have crossed the line."

I sighed. "Well, it hardly matters what his feelings *were*, anymore. It's pretty clear what they are now."

"He'll come around," Sean said, but he didn't sound convinced.

"Before or after he moves away?"

"In his defense, he took the job way before you came around."

"Is that why he broke up with Angela? Because he was moving away?"

Sean watched me for a long time, as if gauging whether or not I was serious.

I was deadly serious.

He stood, tossing a couple of ten dollar notes by our bill.

Was he going to answer?

After a second, Sean sighed. "It was you, Tess. He broke up with Ang because he was falling for you." He patted my head and walked out the door.

Toby had broken up with Angela to be with me. I felt worse than ever.

Two weeks. Nothing.

It was over. It was really over. I had surpassed the tears, the anxiety attacks and churned it into resignation. Though it had felt like so much more at the time, I had had my first summer fling. Toby would go to his new job, I would go back to school and normal life would start all over again.

I searched desperately for a silver lining; if Toby moved away I wouldn't be forced to see him with someone else, and if he wasn't around, I would find it easier to get over him.

Ellie even offered her own words of wisdom: "I think the fact that he took it so badly is a real testament to how much he liked you."

I curved a sceptical brow. "Grasping at straws much?"

I dragged my raggedy soul through Christmas, offering forced, half-hearted smiles and false cheer over the festive season. Work at the café and hotel was extra difficult. I was forced to be pleasant as I served the never-ending mass of customers. I'd sucked it up as much as I could, though, because I could sense Mum and Dad catching on to my despair.

I'd almost convinced myself that I would be okay as long as I could fake it. But then Ellie and Adam's parents came over for a BBQ; the forceful smiles and laughter was exhausting.

Adam perched himself on the island bench while I washed dishes in the kitchen.

There was a sense of great unease between us. It was all me. I couldn't let my guard down; I was afraid of letting down that barrier, of exposing my soft underbelly I fought so hard to keep hidden. I was tired, so tired of the way my insides ached.

I felt Ellie press beside me as she took the plate and washcloth from me.

"I don't think you can get that any cleaner, you know. You've been washing it for the past ten minutes." She smiled at me with that sad, sympathetic smile.

I flicked a bashful gaze at Adam who was looking at me as if waiting for me to crumble at any moment.

Ellie took over the dishes. She seemed nervous. Maybe it was me; things were strained between the three of us lately, and I knew it was my fault.

Adam sighed. "Just tell her, Ellie."

My head shot around to face her, suddenly alert.

"What? Tell me what?" I said, my eyes darting from Adam to Ellie and back again. "What are you talking about?"

Ellie placed the dish in the drainer and faced me as she dried her hands.

"They're having a farewell party for Toby tomorrow night."

She swallowed deeply, her eyes flicked nervously to Adam. "It's at Stan's shed, so you don't have to worry about running into him at the hotel …" She broke off.

"But we're not going, right, Ellie?" Adam added.

Ellie shook her head violently. "Of course not."

My sweet, foolish friends. I smiled sadly out through the kitchen window. It was blindingly bright outside, a beautiful, sunny day. The blue sky blurred in my vision. I shifted and anchored myself to clasp the sink and avoid my friends' pity. My tear-filled gaze rested on the towering Ghost gum near our driveway, where it cast a shadow over our sunburnt lawn.

I remembered the day we stood on the front lawn, the same kind of sunny afternoon when Toby gave me a lift home from Horseshoe Bend. So many times I wanted to step over that line, not thinking how it could change everything, alter our newly formed friendship; if only I hadn't made that stupid bet, what would have happened then? Toby and I would be speaking, Sean and Toby would still be best mates. I would probably be going to Stan's tomorrow night to say goodbye to him, to wish him a happy life. Knowing what I did now, would I have changed a thing? Would I have taken back the feel of his hands on my skin? The linger of his soft lips on mine, the way he could bring me undone in ways I had never known I could feel?

No. I wouldn't change a thing. I couldn't regret what we had, our days in the sun, our nights in each other's arms, I could never regret or give those memories up. And that was what they were now – just memories.

It was truly the end. As if the knowledge slammed into me, my guard shattered and I cupped my face into my hands, sobbing with such force my entire body shook. I felt the circling of a pair of arms and then another, stroking my hair, my back. Adam and Ellie were there when I fell, like always. Ellie rubbed my back and cried with me, Adam pressed his lips to my temple and hushed me with words of comfort.

It was over; with a bone-jarring certainty, I finally accepted it was over.

The next day was a Friday night, the night of the party for Toby, and Adam and Ellie took me out for dinner. Though they didn't say as much, I knew it was to cheer me up. I could, of course, think of other places to eat than the Onslow, but Adam was keen to play pool and listen to some tunes, so who was I to rain on his parade? After my breakdown yesterday, I wanted to redeem myself by ending the awkwardness that existed between me, Ellie and Adam. The summer hadn't exactly gone as planned, so tonight was more about recapturing the essence of our friendships, and less about my misery.

Just make it through one more night of faking it, I told myself. It would get easier, surely?

I asked Mum to drop me off right out the front of the Onslow.

What did I care if my parents gave me a lift? My days of making grand entrances and tracking up that bloody hill were over. A lot of things were over.

Adam was sitting at the picnic table out the front when we pulled up, watching Ellie pace back and forth in front of him. As I neared, my movement caught their attention. I flashed them my best smile. I could do this. It would be fine. My smile slowly evaporated as I took in their anxious eyes that darted to each other, then both at me.

"Ah, Tess," Ellie said, "you're here." She stopped pacing, but still wrung her hands anxiously. "How about we go get some Chinese at the Golden Dragon?" She walked briskly towards me. Adam stood, nodding his head as if it was the greatest idea in the world.

"Chinese? But what about playing pool?" I turned to Adam.

"Yeah, well, you know, with my history I should probably steer clear of pool tables." Adam linked his arm with mine and led me towards Coronary Hill, Ellie scurrying along behind. Was I being frog marched down the hill?

"What's wrong with ..." I stopped dead in my tracks, and Ellie slammed into me from my sudden stop.

Toby's ute was in the car park, along with Ringer's, Amanda's ... everyone was here. How had I not seen them?

"I thought you said Toby's farewell party was at Stan's

tonight."

"Yes, well, it seems tradition dictates that they have a few here, before heading to the party." Ellie grimaced.

Of course it did.

"I'm sorry, Tess, we honestly didn't think they'd be here." Adam touched my shoulder. "Come on, let's go."

"No!" I said. "I'm not leaving. I came here to have dinner and play pool, why should I leave just because of him?"

From the looks on their faces, Ellie and Adam thought I was out of my mind; they probably thought I was on the brink of another hysterical breakdown like last night. I cringed at the memory.

"Tess, do you really think that's such a good idea?" Ellie asked.

I rolled my eyes. "They don't own the place. Besides, we're all mature adults. We can be in the same building."

"But the same room?" Ellie said, biting her bottom lip.

"You sure?" Adam asked, like he wasn't buying my bravado for one second.

"I'm sure!" I spun around and stomped back towards the Onslow. As I closed the distance, as coming face to face with Toby again became an impending reality, I lost all my nerve. I was so completely and utterly unsure. My heart raced so fast I could feel the deepening thrums pulsing in my ears. What the hell was I doing? Was I crazy?

I took a deep, shaky breath as my hand splayed against the front door, ready to press it open with that familiar screech. I paused outside, staring at the timber, the only thing that separated me from the inside – from Toby.

"Tess?" Adam's voice pressed against my right ear, I could feel his hand on my shoulder. "We don't have to ..." And before Adam finished his sentence, I pushed the door open, flooding the main bar with sunlight.

Chapter Forty-Four

Distant laughter filtered through the thin walls of the poolroom into the restaurant.

The bass beat of the jukebox thumped loudly, disturbing the calming musical stylings of Enya that played from the speakers where we sat in the dining room.

Adam quirked a brow over his menu. "Enya? Seriously? Oh, Uncle Eric, I'm appalled."

I shrugged. "Blame your Aunty Claire."

Adam raised a sceptical brow. "Aunty Claire is never here."

All our gazes turned from our menus towards the bar where Uncle Eric stood whistling animatedly while he brewed a coffee. Adam shook his head. "And here I thought Uncle Eric was more of an AC/DC fan, but Enya?"

We cast knowing smiles at one another as our eyes flicked back to our menus. An old familiarity settled over us. The same effortless, friendly banter flowed like it did before the summer had begun, before Adam was sent away, before everything turned to shit. Well, mostly everything.

"So are you going to see Stan tonight?" I asked Ellie as I poured a glass of water from the carafe.

The simple enough question seemed to unease Ellie. "Ah, no, not tonight. Tonight is *our* night."

It was meant to be a touching sentiment, but I could tell there was no conviction behind the statement. Though she tried to disguise it, she was disappointed she wouldn't be seeing Stan, which was stupid because he was only a room away in the poolroom. All through dinner, I tried not to think about the fact that Toby was in there, so agonisingly close. When we'd walked through the front door, none of us glanced over there. I didn't even know if Toby knew I was in the building. We had simply veered sharply right and headed for the restaurant.

I looked at my two best friends: Ellie desperate to see Stan and Adam pining every time he heard the crack of the cue against the billiard balls. Instead of me faking it tonight, they were faking it, as well. They were putting on brave faces to cheer me up, to make it all about me, courtesy of my Toby-fuelled mini breakdown. They were such good friends. The best.

Enough was enough. I was a good friend, too. If I couldn't suck it up for one night, perhaps the last night I would ever be in the same room with Toby again, then I was just a coward and a shitty friend, too.

I pushed my chair back and stood up. "Let's go."

Adam frowned. "Where to?"

"I'm going to kick your arse on the pool table."

A wicked grin formed across Adam's face as he turned to eye Ellie. She straightened in her seat.

Adam nodded his approval. "That a girl."

We left our table and rounded the corner to the poolroom. *Okay, no biggie, I could do this. They didn't own the place and besides, they were probably gone, on their way to the party at Stan's by now and the poolroom would be ours for the taking.*

Oh fuck.

The Onslow Boys were very much in the poolroom, ever present. Sean, Stan and Ringer stood around the pool table, cues in their hands. Toby stood alone, flipping through the song selections at the jukebox.

He looked good.

It had been two whole weeks, yet my traitorous heart still skipped a beat. The very sight of him turned my thoughts into mush, and my body into a heightened state of long-suffering desire.

I tried to remind myself that what I now suffered was what I had always known – unrequited love from afar. But it was just that much harder, having had it and lost.

When Toby saw me, there was no surprise, no emotion at all. It was as if he saw straight through me.

This was a bad idea.

The other Onslow Boys were their usual jovial, easygoing selves. Stan's eyes lit up as soon as he spotted Ellie; ditching his pool cue, he made his way over, pulling her into a big bear hug. Ringer shook Adam's hand, and they started up their own conversation. But I was distracted as one song ended and a new one began: Marvin Gaye's, 'Heard it Through the Grapevine'.

Smart arse.

I watched as Toby turned back around to the jukebox and flicked through to select another song.

The atmosphere in the room was tense. Usually Sean would make fun of someone, we'd all have a laugh and it would be over. But not tonight. Sean raised his eyebrows in my direction when the song started up, but aside from that tiny gesture, he focused on his conversation with Ringer and Adam on pool tactics. Sean restricted himself to banter with his mates rather than be too openly friendly to me like he would have in the past. Much like the summer holidays, everything I had known with the Onslow Boys was drawing to an end; in a few weeks, I would be back at school and my part-time work at the Onslow would be over.

The sudden realisation hit me; this was it. This would be the last time I saw Toby, this would be the last time we'd all be together like this at the Onslow.

And we were going to let it end like this?

The tension between Sean and Toby, too, was obvious as they cast each other wary glances. I wanted more than anything for things to be the way they were again. I was just a girl. I seriously wasn't worth ending their friendship; they had to know that, right?

All I knew was I had nothing to lose, because I had already lost him.

I strode across the poolroom, past the boys, straight to Toby. Beyond my better judgment and all the courage I had mustered up, I stood before him and stared him straight in the eye. There was a flicker of surprise and a new tension swept over us.

"So this is how it's going to be?" he asked. "A showdown, here in front of everyone?"

My shoulders involuntarily slumped at his question. "Is that what you think I'd do? Humiliate you, like some screaming banshee?"

He looked at me pointedly, and then I remembered Angela Vickers, the worst screaming banshee of them all.

To be honest, that kind of pissed me off. Not the screaming banshee type of pissed, but to lump me in with Angela? I was the pretty fucking *insulted* type of pissed.

I sighed heavily. "I just wanted to say goodbye, that's all. And ..." *oh God, this was so hard,* "and good luck!"

The tension in Toby's shoulders melted, his eyes darting across my face suspiciously, warily, like he was waiting for the vindictive punchline. I met his gaze full on, and a familiar song filled the speakers. Live's 'Lightning Crashes'. It was the very same song that played the night of the first disco behind the velvet curtain. What was he playing at?

I swallowed hard. "I haven't had the chance to talk to you ..."
Okay, Tess, keep it together.

"... And I just wanted to say thank you."

His frown deepened. "Thank you?"

Oh God, I was lame ...

I glanced around, embarrassed, I edged to the corner of the room for some semblance of privacy; Toby moved with me.

It took all my strength to meet his eyes. "For a brief moment, you made me believe that I was a somebody, that, above all, I wasn't like the other girls. And I'm not." I stepped forward, so he could hear me over the music. "I know it really doesn't seem that way. And it kills me that I let you down, that I did something so stupid because I jumped to the wrong conclusion. I don't want you thinking I am anything other than who I am, who you got to know this summer."

Toby was so still, so unmoving, if it wasn't for the flex of his jaw muscles I would swear he had turned to stone.

"But you have to know, I'm really sorry. I'm sorry that I didn't tell you about Sean, but there would be days of not even seeing you, of not knowing if what was happening with us was serious. I had no idea of knowing. When I saw her car in your driveway, I thought that you and her ..." I bit my lip, the memory of that horrible, regret-filled night flooded back to me. "If you don't understand how sorry I am that I hurt you, that I never would have done it intentionally, if you don't get that, then you don't get me."

I couldn't look at him anymore; I knew my eyes were a window straight into my heartbroken soul. But he was so silent, I thought maybe he hadn't heard what I'd said at all. I couldn't say it again. I couldn't ...

And then he spoke. His voice was low and raspy. "I get you."

I looked up at him in surprise.

"The thing is, Tess, if you think I would be with you one night, and then go back to Angela ..." He shook his head. "Then *you* don't get *me*."

We stared at one another for the longest time. I guess we didn't really know each other. I finally broke away, knowing it would be the last time I would see Toby. My heart threatened to break at the thought.

"Well, it doesn't matter anymore, does it?"

"I guess not." Toby said coldly. It was as if a knife was twisting in the pit of my stomach.

"Bye, Toby." Before I realised it, I'd held out my hand. I cursed myself as it hung between us. I had never felt like such a loser than in that moment.

A handshake, Tess? Seriously? Just walk away, you idiot! Walk away!

Before I could inwardly scream at myself any more, Toby took my hand, squeezing it in a firm but gentle shake. His eyes rested on my hand. It was reminiscent of the first time we shook hands in this very room; aside from the party, it was our first real interaction, our first real hello, and now it was our very real end.

"Bye, Tess."

I slid my hand from his lingering clasp and, without meeting his gaze, walked through the crowd to Ellie.

I swallowed down the tears enough to hold it together. "Can we go now?" I said in a quiet, trembling voice.

"Of course, let's go."

Chapter Forty-Five

I rounded the corner of the locker room, trying to get my head around the new Year Twelve layout and fall back into the routine of school.

On the first day back, I knew I was out of sorts because, of all things, I was happy to be back at school. So wrong, I know.

With a sigh, I opened my new locker and gathered my bag. Irritating laughter bounced off the metal lockers and echoed around the room. A few lockers up from me, Carla unlocked her locker and cast me a smug smile.

"How was your summer, Tess?"

I narrowed my eyes. Before I could reply, another voice interrupted me.

"Shut up, Carla!" Scott opened his locker on the other side of her.

Carla's gaze flew to him in utter surprise.

He stared her down. "Leave Tess alone."

At a loss for anything intelligent to say or do, Carla just scoffed. "Whatever." She slammed her door with a bang and made sure she cast me a murderous look on the way out.

Scott gave me an awkward smile as he gathered his books and walked away.

Had he actually called me Tess?

Adam and Ellie walked around the corner and spotted me.

"There you are? You ready?" Ellie smiled.

We made our way out through the gates and under the 'Onslow High' arch. The grounds were swarming with everyone's excitement of surviving their first day back.

"Chris is picking me up, you ladies need a lift?" asked Adam.

"No, I'm right," Ellie said. "Stan should be here somewhere." She eagerly looked out over the road at the long line of parked cars, biting her lip in anticipation. Her eyes searched down the road when she suddenly froze.

"Tess."

Adam and I were equally confused until we followed her gaze, and that's when I saw him.

Toby leaned against the driver's door of his ute, arms crossed, his gaze unreadable, and fixed on me.

"Tess, are you okay? Do want us to wait?"

Ellie and Adam were just as rigid with shock as I was. It took me a moment to offer any kind of acknowledgment.

"It's okay." I took a deep breath. "I'm sure this won't take long."

Adam grabbed my bag. "We'll wait."

"Okay," I said, but I doubt it was even audible. I willed my legs to move, and after a moment, they carried me across the road, my hands fisted at my sides to disguise the tremor.

Just breathe, Tess. Just. Breathe.

As I stopped in front of him, he straightened, pushing his hands deep into his jean pockets.

What was I supposed to say? Hey? How's it going? Instead, we just stood there. God, this was horrible. What did he want me to say? Oh God, what if he wasn't here for me? What if –

"You didn't come to my farewell party at Stan's?"

Was he for real? I had said my goodbyes.

Toby shifted, but his seriousness remained. "Shame. It was a good party."

He was bummed I'd missed a good party a couple of weeks ago? I didn't understand. Everything about our exchange was so wooden, so unnatural. It hurt.

I hadn't seen him in weeks, and yet as I spotted him across

the school, my heart spiked its betrayal like it always did. I would never get over this boy; saying goodbye was the hardest thing I had done. I'd known he was still in town until today and, for some reason, knowing he was still in Onslow had appeased me, because he was still near. But now with his departure looming over me, over us, of him really leaving, of him standing in front of me, he was killing me all over again.

His head tilted slightly, his lips twitched. "Don't make me say it."

I paused. "Say what?"

"Penny for your thoughts."

"Oh." I smiled weakly.

Awkward silence wedged its ugly way between us.

"So, you're leaving?"

His fleeting moment of humour sobered as he nodded.

I was drowning inside. I dug my nails into my palms. I had faked being okay for so long, that now I needed to be stronger than ever, and I could feel my façade crumbling.

I was about to say, "Good luck" and scurry away when he stepped forward. "I head off in about twelve months' time."

"*What?*"

What did he just say?

A smile broke out on his lips.

"I *am* going, Tess, just not today."

Was he taunting me? Was he trying to punish me by giving me false hope, only to rip it from underneath me? He could have been, but I didn't believe it, because I *did* know him, and he wouldn't do that.

"I don't care about what happened with Sean ..." He took in a deep breath. "Okay, I do care. But not enough. Not enough to walk away."

"But your job ..."

"It can wait."

I could feel myself falling, the walls were crumbling with a fear to hope, to believe.

"So you're not leaving?" I whispered.

Toby reached for me, took my hands, squeezing them. "How can I? Ya see, there's this girl, and I'm kind of crazy about her."

My heart pounded against my chest.

"I've done a lot of thinking; all I know is I should have told you that ages ago." He pushed a wayward strand of hair from my brow.

I glanced around. "Did you want to talk about this somewhere else?" I asked.

"Oh, I think right here is perfect for what I need to do."

Toby smiled his perfect, wicked smile, the very one that melted me. I thought my heart might stop as he edged closer, tilting my chin up with his hand.

"What do you need to do?" I whispered.

"This." He captured my lips in a long, lingering kiss. My walls came crumbling down as I melted against him, his arms encircled me, and I was lost to the feel, the memory, of all that was Toby.

Lost in the happiness as I folded my arms around Toby's neck, we both flinched at the blast of a horn as a car pulled up beside us. Chris, Sean and Adam looked on from their seats with big, goofy grins.

Chris shook his head. "Settle down you two, there are children present."

Adam held up his hands. "Seriously, why look at me when you say that?"

Sean ignored the brotherly sparring as he grinned at us, bobbing his head in approval. "'Bout bloody time."

A second horn sounded from behind; Stan waved his arm out the window. "Come on, people, move along, nothing to see here."

Ellie sucker punched him from her passenger seat.

"Where we headed?" asked Toby, taking my hand in his.

"Well, nowhere too extravagant, it is a school night," Sean teased.

Toby flipped him the finger and everyone laughed.

"Follow us," Chris said.

Toby and I slipped into the ute, and he started the engine.

I slid over to the middle to belt in and lean against his side.

"We're going to do this? For real?"

Toby frowned. "What, follow Chris? Well …"

"No, I mean us, you and me?"

A smile lit up his face. "Yes, ma'am!"

My heart swelled at the way his warm eyes rested on me for the longest moment before he turned the wheel to fall in line behind Stan.

"Then there's one thing I need to know," I said, in all seriousness. And there was. One thing I had wondered about above all others.

Toby frowned with uncertainty, his eyes flicking to me and back to the road.

"What's that?"

I leaned into him, smiling through my words as I whispered, "What does the 'E' stand for?"

Toby broke out in a fit of deep, rich laughter. Shaking his head, he said, "Ernest ... My middle name is Ernest."

Ernest. It made me love him all the more.

Epilogue

6 months later

The place was deserted.

And why wouldn't it be? Toby and I sat in the main bar of the Onslow Hotel on a Tuesday night.

Toby grimaced. "I'm sorry this isn't much of a way to spend your birthday."

I clasped my necklace for probably the hundredth time, admiring the beautiful chain and gold disc pendant that had an italic 'T' engraved on it.

A 'T' for Tess, a 'T' for Toby.

"It's perfect!" I leaned over to show him how perfect.

"Keep it PG guys, I'm still here." Chris looked on in distaste, as he had a tendency to do whenever we were around.

"What are you doing hanging in a bar midweek, anyway?" Chris posed.

I straightened on my stool. "Hey, I'm eighteen now! I'm completely legal, so rack 'em up, bar-keep." I slammed my hand on the bar way too hard.

Chris looked on with a 'kill me now' expression; he poured a glass of the house white and placed it in front of me.

"On the house, Birthday Girl."

"Thanks." I smiled.

Even though I was secretly miffed that I had to remind Chris that it was my birthday (I mean, I had reminded everyone I had ever met for the past month that I was turning eighteen), it wasn't just Chris that disappointed me. My own parents, my flesh and blood, had sung me a rather quick, halfhearted version of 'Happy Birthday' before they ducked to work, with promises that come the weekend they would make it up to me. I had received a rather animated text from Ellie saying 'Happy Birthday' and 'call you later'. At least Adam had come over, even if he hadn't stayed long.

I had been on the verge of cracking open a tub of ice cream out of depression until Toby picked me up. I had been spilling out all my troubles when he asked me to pass him something from his glove box. I was so engulfed in self-pity I passed the white box with the pretty red bow to him without even taking a breath. I only paused when he pulled over and looked at me with an incredulous smile.

I touched my necklace again at the memory. Every time I did, Toby broke into a smile, pleased.

He picked up his beer, and held it up towards me.

"A toast to the Birthday Girl."

I grabbed my ever so grown-up house white and clinked our glasses together.

I was finally an adult!

I took a deep, confident gulp, only to gag when it went down the wrong way. My eyes watered as I tried to draw breath. Toby thumped me on my back as I coughed and spluttered all over the bar.

Yep! I may be eighteen, but the stuff was still vile.

Toby tried to salvage my dignity. "Chris, can you grab us a glass of water and some menus, mate?"

Chris managed the water. "Sorry to be a killjoy guys, but I'll have to call last drinks. I'm shutting up soon."

Toby did a double take. "What, no dinner?"

Chris shrugged. "Sorry mate, it's what happens mid-week."

I looked at the wall clock, it was only 8.30pm, and I was starving. I saw the disappointment in Toby's face so I didn't press the issue. Yeah, this was turning into some birthday.

I didn't even manage to finish my glass of water as Chris stalked up and down the bar, collecting beer mats, and wiping down.

Okay, okay, we're going, geez …

I grabbed my bag and went to walk out the front when Toby grabbed my hand.

"This way." He pulled me in the opposite direction with a devilish smile.

"But the car's out front."

He dragged me along until we were engulfed by the darkness of the restaurant, where he paused and kissed me into silence.

"I thought you might want to do some reminiscing in the beer garden." He nuzzled into my neck. I giggled as his breath tickled me.

My eyes darted. "What about Chris?"

Toby kissed me again, and all of a sudden I didn't care anymore. This was the best birthday ever.

Just as I was relaxing, getting lost in his kisses, he broke away.

"Come on." He tugged me into action; my mind was still drunk from his kisses.

I followed his long, confident stride through the dark restaurant, and he guided me to the sliding door that led out to the beer garden.

Now was as good a time as any, I thought.

I stopped him, just as he was about to open the door.

"Toby, there's something. Well, there's something I've been wanting to say."

And just as I was about to form my next sentence, the sliding door flew open and lights flooded the garden.

"SURPRISE!!" roared the crowd, followed by a rather hideous and ill-matched version of 'Happy Birthday'.

I shielded my eyes as they adjusted to the brightness, my other hand clutching at my racing heart.

They were all here. Mum, Dad, Adam, Ellie. To my right, Uncle Eric, Claire, Amy. Melba and Rosanna clapping in front. And a line of beaming Onslow Boys.

My eyes welled.

They hadn't forgotten.

After the initial shock I turned to Toby. "You!" I went to whack his arm but he caught my wrist and pulled me into a hug. "Happy Birthday, Tess," he whispered into my temple.

"Alright, alright, that's enough of that, you two." My dad broke in and took my hand. He flicked Toby his regular '*the jury is still out on you*' glance. It always mortified me. It had been six months, and Dad still hadn't fully accepted Toby. Toby still suffered through uncomfortable family dinners/interrogations. Mum, on the other hand, loved Toby and came over to link her arm through his with an apologetic smile.

Dad walked me over to a huge table fully set with gold embossed china and sparkling crystal wine glasses, and draped in crisp white linen. Tea candles and vases of white Iceberg flowers ran down the centre. My chin trembled; it was so beautiful, and it was all for me.

"Melba and I set it out this afternoon," Amy blurted out.

"It's beautiful." I touched one of the intricately folded napkins.

I sat at the head of the table, Toby to my left and Mum and Dad to my right. My eyes trailed down to the long line of friends before me.

Ellie was explaining to Adam the order of cutlery to eat with, Sean debating Aussie rules with Stan, Claire Henderson fussing over Uncle Eric's tie.

Whoa. Uncle Eric was wearing a tie?

My heart swelled with a deep, immense love for them all. Even for Melba and Rosanna who ushered behind Amy with platters of food. Food that Rosanna constantly reminded me that she had spent *all* day in the kitchen cooking.

Toby leaned into me. "What was it you had to tell me?"

I blushed at the memory. "Oh, I'll tell you later."

Toby's frown was broken by the clinking of a fork on a wine glass.

Ellie stood up, her eyes already shiny with emotion.

"Adam and I flipped a coin over who would do the best friend speech. Even though Adam lost, he said he would be pacified with the knowledge that Tess secretly held a flame for him."

Laughter was amplified by Chris punching Adam in the arm.

"What? It's true; sorry, Toby."

"Anyway, I'll make this quick. To Tess …" She held up her glass. "… the most amazing person I know. My life will always be brighter because you're the one that shines next to me."

"To Tess!" Glasses clinked all down the table, and Ellie wiped her eyes.

I fanned my face to stop the tears from overflowing. Toby winked at me and squeezed my knee.

A long line of embarrassing speeches followed. About my hopeless bar skills from Chris, my cappuccino fear from Melba, the girl in the white bikini from Sean that made me blush crimson.

"What bikini?" my dad asked, before the subject was swiftly changed. The only person that didn't speak was Toby, who sat silently by my side.

After the cake and embarrassing childhood stories and what seemed like hours and hours of laughter, the party wound down and guests left. It was time to clear the table and blow out the tea lights. I instinctively went to grab the empty glasses.

"Leave it, honey, it will all be there tomorrow." Claire Henderson smiled as she and Uncle Eric retired for the night.

They were the last to leave; now only Toby and I remained.

"They better hope it's all there in the morning. What's the going rate for fine china on the black market these days?" Toby said, as he looked over the messy table.

I sidled up to him, wrapping my arms around his neck. His attention quickly snapped from the table to me.

"I have a bone to pick with you, Toby Morrison."

"I have been keeping this party a secret for three weeks! My life would not have been worth living if I slipped up."

I laughed. "Not that! I do believe you promised me some beer garden reminiscing?"

A wicked smile broke out on his lips. "That's right, before we were so rudely interrupted."

A stillness swept over Toby. His smile changed into a serious intensity as he swallowed hard. "I love you, Tess McGee. I don't do big funny or heartfelt speeches in front of people at birthday parties, but I'm excellent in private alcoves in beer gardens." He paused. "Okay, that sounded really bad, what I mean is …"

I kissed him into silence. I pressed my forehead against his with a sigh. "I love you, too, Toby. In fact, that's what I was going to tell you before we walked into the beer garden. Right before the really bad singing started."

Toby chuckled. He let out a sigh of relief. "Ready to reminisce?"

I whispered my final word before he closed the distance.

"*Always.*"

Can't wait to read more about the
Onslow Boys?

Be sure to catch the next book in
C.J Duggan's Summer Series…

An Endless Summer

By C.J Duggan.

2013

It's Summer time 4 years on.
And EVERYONE'S coming home.

Acknowledgements

This is a twofold acknowledgment, first is to my husband and the second for everyone else.

To Mick, for bringing me drinks and food on the days I am locked away in my office with my head stuck in imaginary worlds. For supporting and believing in everything I do with your unwavering love and understanding. We have had 10 wonderful years together; I can't wait for the rest of our lives. No matter what happens, "It's you and me."

To my amazing team: it truly takes a village to raise a novel. A deep heartfelt thanks to the following villagers.

Ednah Walters, you introduced me to this inspiring world and told me *"To own what I do."* My life from that moment on was never the same. I'm afraid there are no words big enough.

Sascha Craig, you were the driving force behind me. You pushed me on the days I wanted to kill off all my characters in a freak mudslide accident. I will never forget our endless hours of late night phone edits, but most of all for believing in me when I didn't believe in myself.

To my fabulous editor, Sarah Billington: you have a true talent for making words shine. Your guidance and attention to detail lit a fire within me. You pushed me to think outside the box, and I adore your for that.

To my dear friend and incredibly talented Cover Designer, Keary Taylor: my world is so much more beautiful because you are in it. I cherish our friendship and look forward to many more future projects with you.

To my delightful Copy Editor, Anita Saunders: you are the icing on this cake. Your support and enthusiasm through your emails always make me smile.

To the brilliant Heather Adkins, my proofreading and formatting wing woman. You have such an incredible eye for detail; you are the glue that holds everything together. I would be lost without you.

To my beautiful mum for sharing her love of books with me, and the hours and hours of re-reading the same story and unwaveringly encouraging me to believe in myself.

To my crazy dad for taking me on a holiday of a lifetime and never forgetting to ring me up everyday and asking me, "How's that book going?"

To my family and friends for their love and enthusiasm in respecting and supporting my dream (especially in my moody, reclusive moments.) I am so blessed to have you all by my side.

And to all the passionate book lovers out there, you make what I do an absolute joy, never stop day dreaming about the make believe.

About the Author

C.J Duggan is an Australian author who lives with her husband in a rural border town of New South Wales, Australia.

The Boys of Summer is Book One in her Mature Young Adult Romance Series.

For more on C.J and 'The Summer Series', visit
www.cjdugganbooks.com

CPSIA information can be obtained at www.ICGtesting.com
Printed in the USA
LVOW06s1020110514

385295LV00001B/127/P